MATTSON ACADEMY

A Novel by Jay O'Keefe

BSC
Publishing
Group

New Philadelphia, Ohio 44663

This book is a work of fiction. Any references to historical events, real people, or real places are used fictitiously. Names, characters, and places are products of the author's imagination, and any resemblance to actual events or places or persons, living or dead, is entirely coincidental.

Copyright © 2023 by Jay O'Keefe

All rights reserved, including the right to reproduce this book or portions thereof in any form whatsoever. For information on Subsidiary Rights, email bsc@bscpublishinggroup.com.

First edition eBook publication September 2023.

For information about special discounts for bulk purchases or author appearances at your online and live events, email bsc@bscpublishinggroup.com.

Front cover image © 2023 by S.M. Cook
Book design by Bre Stephens

Published in the United States of America.
ISBN: 979-8-9886089-2-9

www.bscpublishinggroup.com

To my wife and son, one patient, one inspirational.

Contents

Chapter 1 5
Chapter 2 24
Chapter 3 39
Chapter 4 55
Chapter 5 69
Chapter 6 82
Chapter 7 99
Chapter 8 118
Chapter 9 135
Chapter 10 148
Chapter 11 160
Chapter 12 172
Chapter 13 184
Chapter 14 198
Chapter 15 208
Chapter 16 217
Chapter 17 230
Chapter 18 242
Chapter 19 251
Chapter 20 265
Chapter 21 278
Chapter 22 290
Chapter 23 305
Chapter 24 324
Chapter 25 339
Chapter 26 354
Chapter 27 365
Chapter 28 380
Chapter 29 394
Chapter 30 411
Epilogue 421

Chapter 1

Magic 101 - Essence
Essence is the foundational building block of the universe. Throughout history, those who were aware of it have sought new and wondrous ways to manipulate it. They have gone by many names and traditions, but today they are known as Magi.

Connor watched the cityscape of Philadelphia blur into suburbs, and eventually, open into fields. His mom's classic rock station blared while the increasingly dull scenery battered against his simmering excitement. Hay bale. Hay bale. Cow. Two cows. Bale of Hay. The end of summer air warmed his face, even as he wrinkled his nose against the myriad of pungent smells the farmlands brought. He squirmed in his seat and resisted the urge to ask if they were there yet for the hundredth time. Instead, he opted for something specific.

"Where exactly is this school?"

"In a forest in the middle of nowhere, obviously," his mom replied. She pointed to a looming expanse of green on the horizon. "Not long now."

They reached the outskirts of the forest and entered through an archway formed by two thick-boled trees. The leaves showed the golds and reds of autumn, yet the forest looked lush, as though no leaf had yet fallen, and none planned on it. The archway extended deep into the forest, a winding, natural tunnel. The trees' perfect symmetry belied their magical nature. Connor peered deep into the endless woods with wide eyes, not wanting to miss a thing. Outdoorsy stuff rarely appealed to him, but magic outdoorsy stuff? He could get behind that. His mom chuckled at her son's sudden silence.

"These woods are magic, you know. Enchantments on the forest are the school's first line of defense. Anyone who goes in not knowing what they're looking for has a way of getting themselves turned around. It's very old magic."

Old, new, in between, Connor didn't care. He was ready to learn all the magic there was.

After several minutes in the verdant tunnel, they emerged into an open expanse surrounding a rounded hill, and Connor got his first look at his new school. A tall, gray, cement block, peppered with windows, stood at the center of a sprawling assortment of similarly dull structures, each attached to the main building in odd, unappealing angles, like afterthoughts. An open-air amphitheater, closer to the size of a professional football stadium than a school facility, rested at the bottom of the hill next to the school. The school didn't *look* magical, but Connor didn't care. He was there. He was going to learn magic. Besides, he only cared about the dueling stadium; school was a means to that end.

They pulled into a line of cars waiting in front of the main entrance, each a bustle of activity between families unloading their things and saying goodbyes, and the teachers and older students helping register kids and move bags. Connor's heart fluttered at the realization that each of those kids knew about the existence of magic, just as he did. Each of them grew up holding onto the same burning secret he had, unable to share it with their friends and neighbors. Magic was real, and he didn't have to keep it a secret anymore. The car pulled up in front of the school and he leaped out. He made it halfway to the school entrance before his mom cleared her throat and he stopped dead in his tracks. She opened up the back seat and gestured to all the luggage he'd already forgotten.

An older orc girl left one of the departing cars and jogged in their direction. She wore gym shorts and a loose shirt, and sweat glistened on her gray skin. She offered a lopsided smile with a single, stubby tusk sticking out from her lower lip and asked for his name.

"Connor McTaggart? You're in room 107. I'll send your stuff in, but you should head to your room to double check before orientation, okay?" She looked perky despite being out of breath. She rolled her shoulders and stretched out her arms, placed her hands on Connor's trunk and her muscles tensed up; Connor's luggage glowed softly, then started to fade. It lost substance and looked foggy, before turning completely transparent, and finally disappearing with a soft "pop." The girl gave Connor a friendly punch on the shoulder and was off to the next car.

"Let's not make a big deal out of this, Connor," his mom said, mussing his already messy brown hair. "I doubt you want a long goodbye, and I don't want to cry in front of all the other parents," she added with a wink.

"I know you'll do great. Listen to your teachers, study hard, and have fun." She brushed her dark brown curls out of her eyes and gazed up at the great blocky edifice with fondness. Then she frowned and firmly gripped Connor's shoulder. "But not too much fun. And not too much trouble, you hear?" She noticed the line of cars growing long behind them. Her eyes glistened and her voice wavered. "Your father and I are only a phone call away if you need anything. *Anything*. We love you." She pulled him into a hug that quickly turned into an iron grasp.

"I love you, too," he grunted back. "I'll be fine, let me go. I don't wanna be late."

Connor broke free of his mom and walked toward the school he had waited all his fourteen years of life to attend, stopping to spare one look back at his mom as she drove away. She pulled out of the circle, tears running down her cheeks, and drove back to the ring of trees around the school. For a few seconds he thought he could still hear traces of her music. Realization that he'd never been away from his parents for so long struck him. He rubbed his eyes and forced down tears of his own, and when he looked up again, she was out of sight.

Connor merged with the loose gaggle of other students his own age, including more of the Folk than he had ever seen in one place. Orcs, Elves, Dwarves, Pixies, and others he didn't recognize rubbed shoulders with the human kids. He wanted to talk to them about spells, about dueling—about anything, but he also needed to find his friend Garrett.

Connor first met Garrett Clarke while doing his school shopping at the Undermarket, a secret location where the magical community met to exchange goods and services. While Connor grew up knowing of the existence of magic, Garrett was a fluke, the first in generations to show signs of power. He and his family proved out of their depth amongst the Folk, and only Connor's mother intervening in nasty misunderstanding with a minotaur got them out unscathed. Everyday stuff for the McTaggarts, not so much for the Clarkes. Connor suspected if he didn't find his new friend, and fast, Garrett might land in similarly hot water.

Through the main doors, a long hallway stretched before him, bustling with kids. Rows of dull blue lockers, dented and scuffed from years of use, were covered with colorful fliers advertising clubs and activities. A rush of air was Connor's only warning to duck as a student literally flew over his head. The blur of denim and feathers was there and gone in a flash.

No way, he thought.

Tall elves strolled by with their backpacks floating a pace behind them. A gaggle of short, green goblins hurried past him, chattering in their high-pitched native tongue. He smelled singed hair and saw two orcs wrestling with each other, one of them slightly on fire, before a teacher appeared to lift and separate them with a simple gesture and a stern glare.

The school's main hallway branched off into dozens of side-passages in every conceivable direction, and down each one Connor noted a flash of light, a strange face, or a rancid smell he desperately wanted to explore. Only a nagging in the back of his mind that he needed find his friend pulled him toward the broad double doors labeled "DORMITORY."

Through those doors, anything resembling a normal school disappeared, and he stepped into a perfectly landscaped, indoor park. Connor gasped; a sentiment echoed by several of his peers. Paved paths navigated through dewy grass and over rolling hills.

Brilliant flower beds framed clusters of benches, and fragrant fruit-bearing trees provided patches of shade. Sparkling, sapphire ponds, placid but for the occasional leaping fish, rested in the gentle dips between flowery knolls. Connor stood on his toes, trying to see where it ended, until the growing crowd shoved him forward.

    A wall of dorm rooms lined the entrance side of the park. Freshman rooms made up the first floor, with sophomores and juniors on the second and third. Above the seniors' fourth floor, a clear skylight poured rays of sun into the atrium. Connor followed the wall skirting the boundary of the park. He reached the end only to find a stairwell in the corner and another row of rooms extending out into the distance.

    "This place is huge," he murmured.

    He continued down the new row and peeked into the open doors as he passed. He saw kids unpacking, dozing, practicing spells—he lingered longest in those doorways—but no signs of Garrett. After what felt like a great deal of walking, he found room 107 with the door ajar.

    Connor entered his room to find a squat orc, with a protruding lower jaw and a tangle of black hair, unloading crisply folded clothes onto a bed made with military neatness. He wore a nice, white shirt and a gray bowtie. Connor took a quick look down at his own wrinkled t-shirt and shorts and briefly considered changing.

    "I guess you're my roommate?" Connor asked, holding out his hand. "I'm Connor."

    The boy returned the gesture with a fierce grip. "Greetings. I am Marck, son of Murk."

    Connor tried to say more, but Marck pulled his hand back and resumed unpacking. Connor haphazardly stuffed his clothes in drawers. Marck folded and sorted his before delicately putting them away. Connor slapped a few dueling posters on the wall over his bed. Marck set a framed family photo on his nightstand. Connor dumped the rest of his things onto his desk. Marck gave the pile a sidelong look, straightening a pencil on his own desk as if to make a point.

On top of the pile on Connor's desk was a beat-up, leather glove with a scuffed, red gemstone set on the back. It was his fourteenth birthday present—one he'd been unable to use until he got to school.

Mom said I should wait until I had some lessons under my belt, but what could go wrong?

Connor slipped the glove over his left hand and his vision exploded into a nauseating world of colors. Grays and blues and greens and browns swirled like a kaleidoscope. He couldn't make sense of the rainbow assault on his senses and spun in circles until he collapsed to the ground, ready to hurl. Lying on his back, the colors danced above him. He reached his hand up, and a wisp of gray twined between his fingers. He tried to grasp it, but it only slipped away. The ethereal streamer prickled against his skin, and he tried to touch it again, but it writhed out of his grasp. The glove allowed him to see the raw essence, the literal magic, around him. He'd never expected so much, so close, just waiting to be used. The twisting colors shifted, and his stomach shifted with them. Connor groaned as the bile rose in the back of his throat.

Marck approached with slow, tentative steps, like he would a wounded animal, but stopped a wary distance away.

"Are you okay, McTaggart? Should I call for the school nurse, perhaps?"

Connor grunted something close enough to "Fine," and Marck returned to his deck, but he continued to watch Connor out of the corner of his eye. Connor laid on the ground and stared up at the ceiling, taking careful, shallow breaths. So long as he didn't move the dizzying colors almost made sense, but his stomach continued to churn. He peeled the glove off and felt a pang of disappointment when the wild colors faded from view, leaving him with only the drab, cinderblock-gray walls of his dorm room. The world looked dull and uninteresting. He held the glove up to his face and stared at the simple object. Despite the severe nausea, he considered putting it back on. Instead, he used his bed for support to drag himself back up. He sat on the bed, watching Marck organize his desk. When his stomach settled, he stood up, keeping a hand on the bed post for balance.

"I'm going to go find my friend before orientation. You wanna come?"

Marck barely grunted a, "No," before Connor dashed out the door. He went back to the atrium, hoping to see Garrett's giant, round glasses. Groups of students sat in the shade of the trees, while others popped in and out of each other's rooms, exploring their home for the next year. The sounds of more conversations drew his eyes upwards to the older kids' dorms on the balconies above, but he knew Garrett wouldn't be up there. He climbed a hill near the center of the park to secure a better view. Eventually, he spied Garrett leaning against the wall by a dorm and staring wide-eyed into the open atrium. His skin was a sickly green and his breathing was ragged. Connor ran down the hill, waving and calling out. Garrett jolted at his name and clutched books to his chest like a shield, then sighed in relief when he recognized Connor. He scurried to meet him.

"This place is so... big, and," he lowered his voice, "there are so many... you know..."

"Folk? You'll get used to them in no time," Connor said, squeezing his friend's shoulder. In truth, Connor's own experience with the Folk was limited to the few excursions to the Undermarket with his mother. But at least he knew they existed; a few weeks ago, Garrett couldn't even say that much, having referred to a minotaur as "Mr. Cow."

"Did you just get here?" Garrett murmured, trembling lips almost smiling. "I waited for you. I don't want a repeat of the other day."

"Yeah, just a few minutes ago. When did your parents drop you off?"

"A few hours ago."

"Jeez, what time did you get up? Why did they..." Connor trailed off. "Oh."

Garrett averted his eyes and squeezed his books tighter. "My older brother had a piano recital. I think that's still more their speed," Garrett said.

Connor didn't have the words to help. He moved in for an awkward hug, but Garrett flinched away. The best he could offer was a distraction.

"Well, let's hurry or we'll miss orientation."

He took off at a run in the direction of the main building, but when he turned to be sure Garrett was following, he collided with something solid and bounced off, falling hard on his butt. The resultant grunt let him know it was not something, but someone. He looked up to see a girl. A tall girl. *Really* tall, and glowering at him.

"I'm so sorry," he said, dusting himself off. He held out his hand to her. She didn't offer to help.

"Uh-huh."

Connor looked up at her. She had dark blue eyes resting above a broad nose. Her hair was so dark he couldn't tell if it was black or blue, and it hung straight like a curtain around her head. She stood almost a full foot taller than him, and her muscles were sleek and toned. She wore baggy shorts, a loose tank top, and heavy-looking, black boots. She adjusted a bright blue scarf around her neck, taking care to ensure it remained securely in place, then flexed her muscles and huffed. Connor hoisted himself up.

"Did you need something else?" Her teeth were sharp and pointy, and did nothing to lessen her intimidating figure.

"Oh, what? No. Sorry, I just…" Connor said. He swiveled around, looking for Garrett or anyone else to help him escape her gaze.

"Connor!" Garrett cried, catching up. "Do we really need to run?" He paused, noticing the girl and took a reflexive step backward. "Who's this?"

"This is, um…" Connor said, gesturing to the girl.

She glared at them both. "Ninette."

"Nice to meet you, Ninette," Garrett said with a forced smile. "Are you a freshman, too? We were just heading to orientation."

Ninette's eyes darted from Garrett to Connor and back. Her mouth moved, but no words came out. Garrett offered his hand to shake and Ninette flinched away. Finally, she snorted and stomped away toward one of the ponds in the atrium.

"What was up with her?" Garrett asked, eyes fixed on the retreating figure.

"I dunno," Connor said, rubbing his sore butt. "I bumped into her pretty hard, but I think I got the worst of it. Come on, we need to hurry!"

Connor pulled Garrett down the main hall and skidded to a stop when they found the auditorium. It wasn't full—only freshmen were required to attend first-day festivities—so they had no trouble finding a pair of seats together.

A woman appeared from behind heavy, royal blue curtains and stepped to the podium at the center of the stage. Her face showed few signs of age, despite her snow-white hair, and ash gray eyes peered out at the class. Her gaze was intensified by the long, slim scar that ran from her left eye all the way down to her jaw.

"Good morning. I am Headmistress Leorra Mine. Welcome to Mattson Academy. I am pleased to introduce your instructors for the year."

A roaring wind blew through the auditorium. It kicked up the curtains and howled loud enough to shake the walls. When it settled, an orc stood at center stage. His gray skin was pale as snow and he wore loose, tattered clothes that fluttered in the remnants of the breeze. A bandana covered his eyes, but he swiveled his head to take in the assembled students, all the while wearing a cocky, self-satisfied grin. In a burst of flame, a musclebound dwarf woman, barely half the orc's height, appeared next to him. The two fist-bumped without looking at each other.

The rest of the teachers appeared in a similar fashion. Bolts of lightning, splashes of water, and even swelling shadows each deposited a new instructor to the stage. Most were human, though two were elves, and one was a faerie, even smaller than the dwarf and fluttering above the others with butterfly-like wings.

Each dramatic arrival was accompanied by an angry flinch from the headmistress. She surveyed her staff, waiting for further theatrics before fiercely rubbing her temples.

"Yes, thank you for… that." She turned to address the students. "As freshman, you will spend much of your time on introductory Will and Elemental

Magic. Your Will instructor will be Seer Brokk, son of Mokk." She gestured to the shabbily dressed orc.

Seer Brokk walked directly to the podium. He adjusted the microphone and grinned.

"I will mold your minds into finely crafted tools. Under my tutelage, you will find the limits of your abilities, then surpass them."

He nodded once and returned to the others. Garrett gulped and pressed further back into his seat, but Connor leaned forward, eager.

"Sure," the headmistress said. "Next is Professor Skreed. He will be leading your Elemental Magic classes."

A wiry old elf approached the podium, grinning. He leaned on a cane with a heavy stoop, and he was alarmingly thin. He wore long sleeves and a sweater vest despite the summer weather. While most elves' eyes were solid black, his were faded to a cloudy gray and his face was a map of wrinkles, unusual to see on the long-lived yet eternally youthful elven race.

He must be insanely old, Connor thought.

"Hello there," he said in a creaky rasp. He adjusted his spectacles. "I look forward to teaching you about the basic components of the world, and how to manipulate them in new and destructive ways." He chuckled. "I will consider it a great personal failure if one of you doesn't utterly destroy my classroom at least once."

Leorra glared at him, but he didn't react as he bowed and left the podium.

"And finally," the headmistress continued, "Lady Ariel Marqs, our enchanting instructor and the resident advisor for the freshman class. You can go to her with any of your dorm-related issues."

The burly dwarf woman walked past the tall podium, too high for her anyway, and sat on the edge of the stage. Her low voice boomed through the auditorium.

"I've no desire to hunt any of you down for fun or sport, but break my rules or run afoul of my sensibilities and you will find yourself in detention. I have plenty of uses for the free labor, none of them pleasant. Curfew is at ten. Midnight on the weekends. Were-students are to be in their rooms no later than five on the night of the full moon. Be quiet and orderly, and you'll be okay."

"Thank you, Ariel," the headmistress said taking her spot once more. "As today is orientation, the teachers and older students will be around to answer questions and lead demonstrations on the many areas you might choose to study. The cafeteria is open for breakfast, lunch, and dinner. Today is yours. Class begins in earnest tomorrow. Oh, and please note there is a dance this Friday night. Attendance is highly encouraged to meet your new classmates. Dismissed."

Connor tugged at Garrett's sleeve. "Let's go and watch the teachers. Maybe someone will do a dueling demonstration."

Back in the halls, television screens listed room numbers for each demonstration. Groups of kids crowded around the screens before scattering down the labyrinthine school halls to seek out their subjects of choice. Connor checked the list twice for dueling, but the closest thing was Professor Skreed's Elemental Magic demo. He dragged Garrett through the crowded halls as fast as he could without bumping anyone too roughly—he shuddered at the thought of Ninette's steely glare. They skidded to a stop outside Professor Skreed's classroom and joined the long line to enter.

Windows lined the far wall of the classroom and warm sunlight pooled on the floor. Rows of desks were arranged into semi-circles all facing a larger, dark wooden desk at the head of the classroom. Dozens of students filled the seats, and more lined the walls and the back of the classroom. The buzz of excited conversation was deafening. The professor idly flipped through a comic book, feet up on his desk and humming to himself. When the classroom could fit no more, he waved to two older students standing behind him. The first, a thin black kid with his hair in braids and crisp clothing, and the second, a petite girl with wavy, strawberry blonde hair and luxurious feathers running up and down the length of her arms. They stepped forward and positioned themselves at either side of the professor's desk.

The spindly elf sat up straight in his chair and leaned forward to address the room. "Mr. Anderson and Ms. Codie will be instructing you on the basics of Elemental Magic. They may only be sophomores, but I assure you, they know what they're doing. In this regard at least," he smirked and returned to his comic.

"Elemental Magic uses natural forces as the basis for your spells," said Anderson. "The more of an element there is around, the easier it is to use." He reached out his hand to a clay pot, and a sunflower sprouted from the top and grew to its full height.

"It's not that simple," Codie replied. "Not everyone can work equally with every element." She lifted both hands and a blob of water floated out of a nearby bowl. It dispersed into a fluffy white cloud, then dumped its contents back into the bowl. "Water and wind are easy for me, but I could never do what Anderson did."

"You could, Codie," Professor Skreed said without looking up. "It would be harder, but you could. Your point is well taken though. Most people are comfortable with two or three elements while the rest are a struggle. That is what we will seek to explore in your first semester—what works for you, and what does not. By the end you will have a better grasp of your innate abilities. Now, begone with the lot of you," he said, shooing the students away. "Go find something interesting to observe. There is no more for you here. Oh, and be sure to tell Codie and Anderson what a phenomenal job they did."

"I wonder what I'll be good at," Garrett wondered. He held his hands in front of his face. In just a few short days he'd seen so much he never believed possible before. Much of it seemed destructive, frightening even. He couldn't imagine himself hurling fireballs, but growing flowers seemed okay.

"I want it all," Connor said. He grinned at his own hands and flexed them open and shut. All his life he'd watched professional duelists shake the earth and stir the skies. He'd seen his mother manipulate every item in the house with a flick of the wrist and heard stories of her healing fatal injuries as if they'd never happened. Endless possibilities lay before him.

"He just said most people can only do a few." Garrett noticed Connor's dreamy stare and tugged gently on his arm. "Connor? Only a few. Right?"

Connor put down his, decidedly unmagical, hands. "Well, yeah, but *most* means some people must be able to use them all, right?" His fingers twitched and he decided to try again. No luck.

"I guess so," Garrett said.

The rest of the day was a whirlwind of magical demonstrations ending in the gymnasium. Chalkboards had been wheeled in to face one row of bleachers. Master Borodin, the summoning instructor, stood in the center of the gym with his arms folded across his chest and his head held high. He wore flowing purple robes with a shiny, golden pattern along the hem. He stroked his red and gray goatee and tapped his foot, eyeing the door for stragglers.

"This looks like a good enough crowd," the teacher announced. "I am Master Gregor Borodin, summoner extraordinaire. In my classroom you will learn the art of summoning, and it is indeed an art. Each line and rune must be drawn in exact detail or the creatures you summon may be warped into horrors straight from your nightmares—if they appear at all. I have gathered a volunteer to show you the first three levels of summoning."

One student, an elf, rose to face the rest. His hair was dyed blue and spiked at odd angles, and he had rings through his ears, nose, and lower lip. He drew a single chalk circle containing a handful of runes on the gym floor. He knelt beside it and placed his palm flat in the center; the circle glowed a pale purple, becoming a big, gray rat. It chittered and looked around before its eyes flashed purple, after which it became unnaturally still.

"You'll find most level one summons docile," Master Borodin lectured. "Level two usually isn't too bad either. Observe."

The elf knelt again and drew two concentric circles; they glowed the same pale purple. The lights merged into a gigantic Great Dane. The dog's tongue lolled out, and it tackled him, drenching him with wet kisses. After a moment its eyes turned purple as well and it sat obediently.

"Size and temperament should always be taken into account when summoning," Borodin continued. "A dog will usually succumb to the magic of the circle on its own, but some creatures may require a show of force. We proceed to level three."

The elf smirked and drew an array of three circles. The circles lit up a much darker hue. A spider, twice as big as either student or teacher, warped into being. A shiny, armored carapace covered its segmented body, and eight spiny legs tentatively prodded the hardwood floor. It had no eyes, but two sets of spiked mandibles filled its face and dripped with viscous orange goo. It cocked its head to the side, feeling in front of it with its forelegs before crying out in a shrill whine.

"A Deep Spider? Confound you, Farrun Wallus!" Master Borodin shouted over the noise. "We agreed on a Greatstone Tortoise, did we not?" He blasted the creature with a funnel of flame, and it screeched, curling in on itself and filling the room with an overpowering sweet stench. "A Deep Spider, of all things. You're lucky it didn't suck the blood right out of you."

He turned to address the gathered freshman, smoothing his beard and straightening his robes as he did so. "Well, yes. There you have it. Summoning in a nutshell. An ounce of caution and all that."

"My ears are still ringing," Garrett complained once they left the gym.

"Yeah, but wasn't that cool?" Connor pointed eagerly to the still smoldering spot where the monster had once been.

"I didn't think so, but I'm glad you liked it." Garrett put on a weak smile. "He said it drank blood." He wrapped his arms around himself. "I think I'm glad I picked enchanting. It seems a lot safer."

"Seems like a lot of studying."

"Is the rest of magic not?" Garrett asked. "Just the runes are a whole new language. There's all the Folk history, potion recipes, the monsters. How are you supposed to learn all that on top of like, normal school stuff?"

"I dunno."

He had never really thought about it before. The little magic Connor knew he picked up by instinct or by watching his mom. Studying never occurred to him because she never let him do it. Magic had to remain a secret. *Well, not here.* He laughed.

"Hopefully not by studying though."

Connor collapsed into his bed, exhausted and giddy with excitement, yet within minutes he was sound asleep.

He woke up in total blackness.

The ground beneath him was rough and cold and not his bed. He rubbed his eyes, confused as to why he couldn't see anything. Connor stood slowly, turning to look for something, anything. Eventually his eyes adjusted—it didn't help. Soot-black leaves adorned pitch-colored twigs that stuck out at all angles from midnight trunks. He stood on soil black as asphalt, weighed down by a starless sky. He took a cautious step. The ground was solid and the air dry, but he felt like he was underwater. Pressure behind his eyes throbbed and his chest tightened.

"Hello?" he called out. "This is a dream, right? Ready to wake up."

"ANOTHER COMES TO US FREELY," a deep voice echoed from everywhere and nowhere at once.

The words pounded in time with the pain in Connor's head and made his skin crawl. His heart nearly stopped.

"Hey, uh, hi. I don't know how I got here. I don't think *here* is a place. I'm going to go."

He backed into something that grasped at him and he broke into a mad dash. Sharp leaves and jagged branches left searing lines of pain on his face and arms, but he didn't stop. All the while the voice followed right on his heels.

"YOU DESIRE TO BE HERE. WE CAN HELP YOU. WE KNOW SECRETS YOU CAN ONLY DREAM OF. DON'T YOU WANT TO BE STRONGER?"

Connor stopped running. He almost turned around. The promise in the voice pulled at him, warring with his instinct to get as far away as he could. Unbidden, thoughts of dueling filled his head, images of him on the pitch like the stars he watched on TV.

"Stronger? Maybe? Yes?"

Before he finished the sentence, he jolted awake, rolling out of bed into a tangle on the floor. His clock blinked 4:30. He scrambled back into bed, desperate to catch his breath and hoping he didn't wake up Marck. The soft snoring from the other side of the room said he was in the clear.

He laid back down, trying to shake off the bad dream, but his pillowcase felt damp and clung to his cheek. He sat up and squinted in the darkness. A splotch of red marred his pillow where his face had been. He raised his fingers to his cheek and flinched when he found the scratch.

Chapter 2

A History of The Folk - Introduction
As mankind rose to dominance, non-humans disappeared into myth and legend. Some, such as elves, dwarves, and orcs, pass for humans with minimal disguise. Others, such as merfolk and faeries, must remain hidden. As a group, they are known as the Folk.

Connor bolted out of bed, threw on yesterday's wrinkled jeans and a new, yet wrinkled t-shirt, and fussed with his hair just enough to get it out of his eyes. Then he grabbed his backpack and went out the door. The desire to forget his dream from the night before, and his eagerness to learn magic, spurred him on. He wouldn't let something like a bad dream keep him from the thing he'd waited his whole life for, scratch or no scratch.

Magic school, magic nightmares. No big deal, he thought to himself.

Garrett awaited him in the hall outside the dorm park. "You're late! I've been waiting here for half an hour," Garrett complained. "I half expected you to be pounding on my door when the sun came up." Garrett adjusted his backpack, noticeably fuller than Connor's, and sighed. "We won't have time to get food, will we?"

Connor grabbed him by the hand. "Who needs to eat? Come on!"

He thought about telling Garrett about the dream. He felt like he should tell someone, but the last thing he wanted was to spend the day talking about something he barely understood and certainly didn't want to remember.

He glanced at Garrett out of the corner of his eye. The smaller boy stumbled trying to keep up while processing the wild faces and wilder magic filling the chaotic hallway. Gray and green-skinned orcs traded earth-shaking fist bumps while a dark-eyed elf girl conjured wind and water to restyle her hair as she gazed into a mirror in her locker. Troops of dwarves, none more than four feet tall, charged down the hall, clearing a path through the taller crowds. Even smaller pixies fluttered overhead leaving trails of sparkly glitter in their wake—much to the dismay of any students forced to brush the rainbow residue off their clothes. Each new sight seemed enough to send Garrett into shock.

I'm sure it was nothing, Connor repeated to himself. *No need to scare Garrett any more than he already is.*

They hurried to Seer Brokk's classroom and managed to secure seats in the front row. Four rows of desks in expanding semi-circles stretched back from a lectern at the front, while the teacher's own desk rested in a warm beam of sunlight underneath a window. More students arrived and looked for seats close to the teacher—for many of them, it would be their first chance to learn about magic and no one wanted to miss a thing.

A few of the Folk kids made sure to sit near each other in small groups. Last to arrive was Ninette, the brutish girl Connor had run into the previous day. She stomped into the room just as the bell rang and stared daggers at anyone who made eye contact. She jerked at the ends of her scarf and grabbed a seat in the back corner.

Seer Brokk coughed to get the class's attention. He wore a loose-fitting shirt and trousers, and he still wore the bandana over his eyes. His lower jaw protruded outward, small canines stuck out over his lip.

He prowled across the room to stand directly in front of Garrett and leaned in close.

"Your name, boy?"

"G-G-Garrett Clarke," he answered quietly. He pulled out his tablet, pencil, and paper, and sat up as straight as he could, desperate to avoid displeasing the imposing instructor.

"Bah, technology. You will see it in other classes, but not here," the orc rumbled. He waved dismissively. "I have been blind since birth. I did not have your screens, but my mind is sharper for it. I am Seer Brokk, son of Mokk. What was good enough for me shall be good enough for you."

The students murmured to each other, but one in particular caught the teacher's ear.

"Yes? Something to say? Girl, two rows back on my left."

"Gemma, sir. Gemma Perriwinkle," she stammered. She shriveled inside her poofy turtleneck and blinked her big, brown eyes. "If we're not going to use the materials, how are we supposed to learn?"

"Here we learn by doing." Brokk grinned, further exposing his tusks. He sauntered back to his desk, grabbed a cup of pens and pencils, and tossed them out on the floor. "Pick them up using telekinesis."

"But you haven't taught us how," Gemma protested.

"And yet I have set you a task."

Gemma bit her lip. A vein in her forehead pulsed and she scrunched her nose. After a few seconds, one of the pencils wobbled into the air and floated in her direction.

"Not bad!" the orc said. "Anyone else?"

Connor reached his hand out to the pile on the floor, trying to feel something inside him stretch toward the assorted objects. A pencil whizzed past him to someone in the back, and another to his left. He focused harder and a pen bounced around on the floor before flipping end over end to land on his desk. Connor raised his hand, and the pen mirrored the movement. He turned his hand palm up, and the pen rotated as well.

More pencils and pens rose from the ground to hover in the air before floating toward the students eagerly summoning them. After a few more minutes, one twitched and rattled on the tile floor, then jumped a foot into the air and hung suspended. It floated across the room. Twice it dipped as if about to drop, but eventually, it settled into Garrett's outstretched hand. Just as he closed his hand around it, a pen launched like a missile, screaming through the air, and lodged itself in the wall beside Ninette. She glanced sideways at it and swallowed nervously.

"Excellent!" Brokk exclaimed. "If you failed, do not despair. An honest classmate will admit the difficulty. It will not be so for long. Your essence, your ability to do magic, is a muscle many of you have never used. I will stretch it, strengthen it, train it. You will crawl before you walk, but when I am done with you, you will fly.

"This is Will Magic," Brokk rapped his fist against the top of his head. "So called because you are expending your essence to inflict your will upon the world. I cannot teach you to want something. You must learn to harness your own desires. This specific skill is telekinesis, moving objects with your mind. It is the foundation upon which we build."

Brokk sat on the ground and crossed his legs then bid the class to do the same. Most mimicked him but a few skeptics, Ninette among them, remained in their chairs. Brokk lit a strong, smoky incense and waved his hand; a soft gust of wind carried the scent throughout the room. He inhaled slowly, counting five seconds on his fingers, then exhaled and did the same. He gestured for the students to follow suit. This went on for ten minutes without a single word. Then, with a casual flick of his wrist, he retrieved all the pens and pencils and stacked them neatly in the front of the classroom.

"Again!"

Connor succeeded almost immediately, after which he entertained himself by directing the pen with the tip of his finger. The writing implement mirrored his movements, zipping and zooming in dizzying circles over his head. Garrett found himself with pen in hand much quicker the second time. His eyes lit up and he scrambled to take notes. Over half the class succeeded before the bell rang. Ninette lodged more pens, pencils, and even a pair of scissors in the wall around her. Her surrounding classmates scooted their desks further and further away from her.

Connor and Garrett left the class with pens levitating before them. Connor guided his with sharp, precise movements while Garrett's meandered over his hand with an uncertain and ponderous drift. Connor didn't see how telekinesis would help him in a duel, but it was just the beginning, and it wasn't a bad beginning as far as he was concerned. The two approached an intersection of hallways and Connor playfully shoved Garrett. Garrett's focus faltered and his pen clattered to the ground.

"Well, good luck in enchanting," Connor said. He turned down the other hall and broke into a trot.

"Thanks," Garrett called after him. "I'll find you at lunch, okay?"

Connor was too far away to hear. Students crammed shoulder to shoulder in the halls, all of them using magic. Backpacks and books floated in and out of lockers, paper airplanes whizzed by leaving streams of smoke and fire in their wake, friends harassed each other with snowballs and electric shocks. Connor's hair blew into his face when one student ran by in a blur. Other students floated overhead, avoiding the traffic by levitating to their next classes. It was everything he'd ever wanted.

Dr. Beatrix Greens taught his next class: Alchemy. The round, little woman wore circular, tinted goggles, and her wild hair stood out at all ends. Her black lab coat fluttered behind her as she scurried around preparing for class. Her lab was neat and orderly, the shelves stocked with ingredients and reagents, and the cabinets full of beakers, bottles, flasks, and more. A sharp, burning scent hung in the air. A low, flat table sat atop a raised stage in the center of the room, a perfect replica of the workstations in the students' area.

Connor searched for a familiar face, but the few people he recognized had already paired up—all except Ninette. She sat alone at a workstation wearing a deep frown. Connor quietly took the seat next to her, hoping she ignored him.

"Welcome to Potions and Alchemy!" Dr. Greens cackled. "The marriage of science and magic! I am your humble instructor. We begin! Lesson number one! Does anyone know the difference between a potion and an elixir?"

Connor's hand shot up, and the doctor pointed to him.

"Yes, excited boy."

"A potion is a mixture of magical and non-magical ingredients. An elixir requires essence in addition to the base components."

"He is quite correct. Anyone can make a potion if they can get the right ingredients, challenging though that may be, but an elixir can only be made by a Magi."

Connor's chest swelled and he beamed at the teacher.

"We'll be starting with potions. Your assignment is to brew a potion of liquid flame. The final ingredient must be added with care as, once prepared, any exposure to oxygen will ignite the mixture."

She fished a tablet out from inside her lab coat, and her gloved fingers danced across its surface; a screen at the head of the classroom snapped on to display a formula and instructions.

"You'll find all the ingredients on the shelves. Good luck!"

Connor squinted at the recipe. It looked easy enough:

> Mix equal parts water and slug slime, bring to a simmer, add a pinch of volcanic ash, then wait for it to turn orange. Once orange, add a small dragon scale, then stopper IMMEDIATELY.

In no time at all, his potion was a nice traffic cone orange.

"Ugh, why did mine turn green?" Ninette groaned.

Connor glanced over. Sure enough, her potion was viscous and a disgusting pea color.

"Can I take a look?" Thrilled by his own success, he reached to snatch her bottle but jerked his hand back when he remembered who he was dealing with.

Ninette glared at him. Her potion belched a noxious scent. She wrinkled her nose and threw her hands up.

"Sure, why not?"

Connor surveyed her ingredients. "You grabbed snail slime instead of slug slime."

"Is there a difference?"

Connor presented his flask and its perfectly orange contents with a hand flourish and a smarmy grin, then set it down next to hers for emphasis.

"Fair enough."

Connor helped her dispose of the faulty brew and find the right ingredients. While her mixture heated, explosions—no less than five—erupted throughout the class. Dr. Greens aided one student in extinguishing his shirt.

"'IMMEDIATELY' does not mean 'at a leisurely pace,' Julian! I put it in ALL CAPS! For EMPHASIS!"

Ninette's new potion was the right color, and she looked at the smoky remnants of the desks behind her, then to Connor.

"Like this," he said. He held the dragon scale tight to the bottle stopper in the same hand, adding it and sealing the bottle in one smooth motion. Ninette followed suit, and after a moment they compared their incandescent concoctions. Licks of red swirled in the bubbles of the fiery orange liquid.

"Lovely," Dr. Greens cooed. She held up Ninette's potion to the class. "This is what you were aiming for. Empty this out and you'd have a roaring blaze for hours, even on the rainiest night."

Ninette mouthed a silent "Thanks" to Connor.

By the end of the day, Connor walked into Professor Skreed's room feeling pretty great. He had telekinesis down and aced his first potions lesson. Everything was going perfectly. He and Garrett grabbed seats by Garrett's roommate, Julian—the same boy Dr. Greens had to extinguish—and a slim elf with black hair down to his waist named Vern. While they waited for class to begin, the boys each got out a pen to practice with. Connor had barely moved his hand before his pen sprang into the air.

"Your mastery is impressive," Vern said in a flat tone. It was hard to tell what he was looking at with his solid black eyes, but his head bobbed in time with Connor's pen. "Most of the humans aren't as far along."

"You say that like we're at a disadvantage," Julian said. He grimaced at his own, unmoving pen.

Vern opened his mouth, but Professor Skreed swept into the room and answered for him.

"Only because Mr. Strong grew up in a secluded village. Rotwood, if I'm not mistaken. They're a bit more open about magic than your average human community, but I suspect his parents did not let him get away with much more than yours."

Skreed winked. Vern merely shrugged.

As soon as the bell rang, the professor began his lecture.

"When you use Will-based magic, you are relying solely on your personal essence stores. In Elemental Magic, you are manipulating the essence of the elements. Magic within versus magic without."

The professor waved his hand in an arc, and, out of thin air, baseball-sized globs of clay landed on the students' desks with a hefty *splat*.

"I give you earth. I challenge you to truly feel its essence, and then, mixing your own essence with it, assert control to shape it into a sphere. Earth is solid, reliable. No tricks needed. Feel the merging of your essence with the earth and picture what you want it to be. Command it. It will succumb to a resolute will."

Connor opened his mind and tried to feel the clay in front of him. He stared at it until his eyes teared up. He clenched his fists, bit his lip, and thought *Sphere!* over and over. The red-brown lump trembled and morphed, but a sharp beeping sound broke his concentration, and he lost the connection. He pushed it from his mind and tried again, but as soon as the clay showed signs of movement the beeping returned, and his focus failed once more. He slammed his hands on the desk and got up to look for the source. He identified it as a girl in the back row, her clay not just a sphere but a spinning replica of a globe.

Her pale purple dress accented her slight build, and her copious gold jewelry sparkled. Her skin was smooth and brown, and her eyes were hazel. Her pierced nose was buried in her phone—the culprit.

"Could you maybe set that on vibrate?" Connor asked.

She ignored him.

He cleared his throat loudly in her direction. No reaction.

Professor Skreed approached the girl and placed his bony hand on her shoulder. "Ms. Crowton, your showboating, while impressive, is not appreciated. Your time could be better spent helping your classmates. Barring that, you will not be a distraction."

The girl held her phone up, set it to silent, waved it at the professor, and rolled her eyes. She then returned to perusing it without a word.

Crowton. Connor knew the name but couldn't place it. He didn't have to wonder long. Excited whispers arose from around the classroom.

"Sheena Crowton is in our class?"

"Like *the* Crowtons?"

"I heard they're loaded!"

"A-HEM," Professor Skreed blurted. "I believe the rest of you have an assignment."

Connor sat and placed his hands around his lump of clay. He tried to tune out the voices. A surprise celebrity, even one from the magical community, wasn't as exciting as getting to do real magic himself.

Next to him, Julian's lump trembled, burbled, then exploded all over him, splattering Connor and Vern in the process. The professor waved him a new one, but Julian recoiled and leaned back from the unassuming dirt. By the time the bell rang, Connor had molded his clay into an oblong ball. He looked behind him at Sheena's globe and noticed Ninette wrestling with a mound of earth three times the original size.

An announcement over the school PA erased everything else from Connor's mind: "All students interested in the school dueling team, please report to the stadium."

"Did you hear that?" Connor said, grabbing Garrett. "The dueling team! Let's go."

"I'm not interested in the dueling team," Garrett said, pulling his arm back.

"You're not even going to come watch?"

"I don't think so," Garrett said, rubbing at his arm. "I want to study. You might not have been allowed to do magic, but at least you knew it existed." He adjusted his bag on his shoulder. "I'm still playing catch up on all this, remember? Maybe next time."

Connor stepped out onto the perfectly manicured field. The green grass waved in the late summer breeze. High, concrete walls circled the field, with tunnels on either side leading to the locker rooms, and above that, the stadium seating with alternating rows of Mattson gold and blue towered around him. He closed his eyes and pictured the stands full of his friends, his classmates, his family. He could hear them chanting his name.

Won't be long.

Connor woke from his daydream and joined the handful of students huddled together near the team gates. He recognized Carrie Kung, a short, chubby girl from his classes, and a few others including Codie and Anderson from Professor Skreed's orientation. Ninette, once again, arrived last.

A moment later, two teachers walked out to join them. The first was a middle-aged man with more pepper than salt in his ponytail and beard. The second was a younger woman with jet-black hair curled in tight ringlets and green eyes that sparkled in the afternoon sun. Both wore sneakers, gym shorts, and athletic t-shirts.

"How do you like your first look at the Mattson Dueling Arena?" the man said. "I'm Coach Darren Kalett. This is Ms. Margery Poole, school nurse and assistant coach."

"Nice to meet you all."

"Let's get the hard part out of the way," Coach Kalett said. He eyed the assembled kids and settled on Connor. "Freshmen are not allowed to try out for the team until their second semester." He waited for the groans and complaints to settle before continuing. "I can't imagine any of you would make it anyway. No offense. The truth is that clever thinking and a grasp of the basics might be enough in a few months, but for now, it would be irresponsible to let you try. You'd just get hurt."

Connor's heart dropped into his shoes. The world went fuzzy, and he couldn't hear anything but an echo of the coach's words. He'd waited so long only to have to wait even longer.

"We know you're eager," Nurse Poole said, "so we want to help you prepare. High school dueling is a little different than what you might have seen on TV."

"Let's say it's more closely monitored," Coach Kalett smirked. "You're kids after all. There's a lower tolerance for unsportsmanlike conduct."

"You mean we don't get to pummel each other unconscious?" Ninette asked. "Where's the fun in that?"

"There's plenty of fun in outthinking your opponent." Nurse Poole's eyes twinkled.

A shimmering snowflake as big as Coach's head appeared out of nowhere. While everyone, including the coach, watched it, a stone floated behind him and bonked him in the back of the head.

"Clever indeed," Coach laughed. He rubbed his head and winced. "You may have noticed I'm still standing. Your bodies are smart, and they'll react defensively, instinctively, to protect you. It's tiring, though, and you're not invincible." He changed to a more serious tone. "Things can get rough, but you're not out there to kill each other. Stay in control or you may end up forfeiting."

Ninette rolled her eyes and huffed.

Nurse Poole gave a small sigh. "You can win with a knockout. A safe, clean knockout," she stressed.

"Fast thinking goes a long way," Coach Kalett said. "So be thinking about your strengths and weaknesses. Sophomores, we'll see you later this week for tryouts. Freshmen, I hope to see you in the winter. Feel free to stop by a practice or check out the matches."

After the final remarks, Connor trudged back up the path to the school with his eyes on the ground and his hands in his pockets. He fell behind most of his classmates but couldn't bring himself to care. Ninette stomped up behind him. She didn't look quite as scary with her shoulders sagging and her lips pursed in thought.

She made awkward eye contact with Connor. "Thanks again. For class." She glanced away and played with the ends of her scarf. "So, uh, you wanted to duel, too?"

"Yeah. I've watched matches on TV since I was a kid. It was the most exposure to magic I got growing up. I know I probably don't have much of a shot yet, but I at least wanted to try. Maybe we could practice sometime? Improve our chances next semester?"

Ninette stared at him. "You and me?" She let out a dark laugh.

Connor frowned. "Why not?"

"You don't want to hang around me."

Connor stopped in the middle of the path. "Why not?" He repeated.

Ninette brushed her bangs aside, then just as quickly shook her head until they fell back into place.

"Look, let's get this out of the way. I'm a mermaid. Half, anyway."

She untied her scarf, revealing a set of gills on either side of her neck. Connor's eyes widened. Suddenly the rest made sense. The sharp teeth, being built like a brick house. Mermaids were legendarily strong, and he'd heard it wasn't that long ago they were sinking ships and eating the crews. That's why some people still avoided them, but Connor was just excited to meet one.

"I mean, you're not going to eat me, right?" He eyed her with mock suspicion.

She glared back and he put up his hands in a calming gesture and stepped back.

"Look, if you don't want to practice with me, that's fine. I didn't mean to push. I'll leave you alone."

Ninette's glare softened, and her mouth hung open, revealing the very teeth Connor had a new appreciation for.

"No, I just... I'm not used to people, really. I grew up with my dad under the, well, you know. I didn't know many human kids growing up, and the ones I did were awful. Even when they didn't know. I tend to stand out. The merfolk kids were worse." She rubbed at her face, coming up with a crooked smile. "Wow, sorry, we've gotten off to a weird start. If you still want to practice, I'd like that."

She held out her hand. Connor shook it.

"Deal."

Chapter 3

Enchanting for Beginners
An enchantment is a spell placed upon an otherwise mundane object to create a magical effect usable by anyone, Magi or not. These effects are typically temporary, but there are exceptions. Such items, like the famed sword Excalibur, are called Artifacts.

"Essence is another muscle," Seer Brokk barked at the class. He leaned over his desk, challenging someone to disagree with him. "Use it to strengthen it. Use it often to build endurance. The best Magi find ways to use their essence daily."

Connor raised his hand. "I thought we had a set amount of essence, and it couldn't be changed. Are you saying we can get more?"

"Do your muscles not grow? You can improve, but there are natural limits." He flexed his biceps to demonstrate. "Mr. Clarke could spend years in the gymnasium. Will he ever challenge me in wrestling?"

The orc laughed, but Garrett paled and scooched his chair back several inches.

"You are stretching and working a new muscle. You will see rapid growth at first. Later it will settle out."

Brokk made good on his word with relentless instruction. On the second day of class, he made sure everyone could move a pen. On the third, he set up targets at the front of the class and gave every student a dart. Connor lifted his dart with ease. He guided it toward the target with deliberate slowness. The dart pierced the bullseye, and Connor looked to the teacher for approval. Instead, Seer Brokk sneered.

"So slow! You must not want it very badly. Control with your mind, not your hands! If you want the bullseye, make it so. Will it to be!"

Two days later, when Connor figured out how to lift three things at once, the orcish teacher threw a stapler at Connor's head. Connor flinched and closed his eyes. When he opened them, the stapler floated in place along with everything else.

"Why would you do that?" Connor shouted. His cheeks turned bright pink as the rest of the class giggled and snickered at him.

"To see if you could succeed," Brokk said. "Think fast!" Brokk swiped a tablet off Gemma's desk and hurled it at Sheena. Sheena caught it with ease and added it to the contents of her purse, which she spun over her head in a lazy circle, at no point looking up from her phone.

"Are you sure you're blind?" she mumbled under her breath.

"Are you sure you can see?" Brokk replied, grinning.

Other than the surprise projectiles, Connor found the control classes enjoyable. As Brokk promised, he felt his skills sharpen by the day. Having someone as talented as Sheena in his class gave him a goal to strive for. But not every day was a control day. On Friday, the classroom was littered with tires, cinderblocks, bricks, and stones. Seer Brokk sat atop his desk wearing a tank top and doing bicep curls with a dumbbell bigger than Connor's head. Friday was a power day.

"But, sir," grunted Gemma, "isn't this dangerous?"

Her knees shook as she struggled to keep a cinderblock in the air. Others in the class had already given up, collapsed in their chairs or lying on the floor to catch their breath before the tireless teacher turned his attention their way once more.

"Nonsense," said Brokk. "Hard work is good for the body. This is good for essence."

Connor levitated two blocks stacked on top of one another. With a final gasp, they wavered in the air then crashed to the ground, Connor not far behind them. Garrett had dropped his two already. Ninette, on the other hand, showed no signs of quitting. Brokk's desk hovered in front of her with four blocks on top of it. Sweat poured down her forehead, but her broad smile was triumphant.

"Incredible, Ms. Reefwalker," Seer Brokk told her.

In one swift movement, he jumped on top of the desk. Ninette yelped and fell to one knee, but kept the desk and everything on it a few inches off the ground. The bell rang and she let it drop. Seer Brokk stepped down casually and shook her by the shoulder with a mighty guffaw.

Garrett gushed over Ninette. "No one in class can do more than three, and you're making a desk-load look easy."

Ninette responded by falling over backward with an exhausted grunt.

"Take the compliment," Connor teased. He reached down and helped her to her feet.

A commotion out in the hall caught his attention. Connor abandoned his friends to rush outside. A full week of school had done little to dampen his enthusiasm for each new, magical surprise. He ducked under a gaggle of flying students and dodged aside from an elf girl with hair literally on fire—all normal occurrences at Mattson—and tried to see what all the noise was about. Students cleared the way for something. Squeals and sighs broke out from the crowd.

"What's that all about?" Ninette asked. She stood on her toes to see.

The sea of students parted, and Connor got his first good look. The boy was tall and handsome with black hair cut short and neat. He wore wireframe glasses and a letterman jacket in the Mattson blue and gold. He walked down the hall with a liquid grace, as if completely oblivious to the bubble he generated. Everyone he passed received a smile or a wave, including Connor. Connor waved back, and his mouth opened to say hi, but no words came out, only inarticulate babble.

Ninette elbowed Connor's ribs. "Drool much?"

"Shut up," Connor said. "He must be on the dueling team. We want to be on the team, right? It couldn't hurt to try and talk to him."

"Uh-huh."

Connor ignored her. He watched the young man go with a roiling mixture of envy and admiration bubbling up inside him. *He's so popular. He must be good. I wonder if he'd give me some advice. Why not? He seems like a nice guy.* Connor took a half-step after him before willing himself to stop. *Don't be dumb,* he chided himself.

But it was hard not to stare.

Garrett waved goodbye to the others and worked his way through the crowded halls to enchanting. He was the first one there, as usual, and took his seat at the front. Lady Ariel's classroom was bigger than most. Each student had their own sturdy, wooden workbench instead of the smaller desks, with plenty of space in between. Stone furnaces occupied the room's four corners, with a larger one front and center behind Lady Ariel's station—burning bright and warming the entire room. Her bench, low enough for her to reach, was a disorganized disaster.

"Early again, Mr. Clarke," Lady Ariel noted. "Punctuality is a solid trait."

"Thank you, ma'am," he said. He pulled out his chair and set his tablet and notebook on the table. "I don't want to fall behind."

"I've little worry of that," she said.

She rushed to tidy her workspace while waiting for the rest of the class to arrive. Garrett used the time to organize his notebooks and reread the previous day's lesson and notes. His tidy handwriting reassured him. He'd always been a pretty good student, always took notes and paid attention. He hadn't particularly excelled at magic, but he wasn't falling behind either. His teachers seemed to approve of his efforts and that's what really mattered. As soon as the last student entered the workshop, Lady Ariel began.

"Today, we'll be working on a rune to produce light."

A student in the back groaned. Ariel slammed her fist on the table to silence him.

"Is there a problem?"

"No," the boy grumbled. He was a dwarf with a round face that appeared young even though he had the beginnings of a beard already growing along his jaw.

"I was going to let you empower them today," Ariel said with a smirk.

The boy continued to grumble and this time he was not alone. Enchanting had so far proved more theoretical than the other classes. While Brokk had them moving just about everything they could with their minds, and Professor Skreed let them manipulate elements to their heart's content, Lady Ariel demanded perfection before she allowed them to progress. That meant a lot of notetaking and not much magic. Not that Garrett minded.

He glanced down at his detailed notes and smiled. The other classes made him nervous. He still wasn't one hundred percent sure what he was doing or exactly how he was doing it. Lady Ariel expecting them to fully understand the runes and their effects before using them seemed like a good thing to him. Though, he might have been alone in that regard.

Ariel rolled her eyes at the protests.

"Speak up. Let's hear it."

"It'll just make a little light, right?" the surly dwarf said. He scratched at his meager stubble and yawned. "It's not very exciting."

"Have you mastered Photomancy?" Lady Ariel placed her hand over her breast and her mouth hung open in mock surprise. "The teachers are informed when a student enrolls in one of the capstone elemental courses, but it must have slipped the Headmistress's mind. Light is her specialty, after all."

The boy's face turned a deep red while the rest of the class snickered. Ariel shushed them.

"This is a beginner-level class, but I assure you I am not filling your head with useless scribbles. Light Magic is complicated. Of the thirty of you, I'd expect no more than four to have any degree of proficiency with it."

"What about fire? That's much simpler, and it makes just as much light," Gemma said.

"Aye, but you will not always have something to light and cannot hold a flame forever. Not to mention the inherent danger of unintentional ignition." Lady Ariel returned to the head of the class and surveyed her students once more for more signs of disruption. "Once drawn and empowered, this rune will provide ample light for longer than you could or would want to maintain a fire or a light spell."

"We can use runes for spells we don't know?" Garrett asked.

"Indeed. Runes are incredibly versatile. More powerful spells will require greater, more complicated runes and more durable mediums. They are not always practical, for they usually require advanced preparation, but once they have been created, they can be used by anyone with the power to do so."

She sketched on her tablet, and the screen behind her projected the image of a small spiral whose tail ended in a pointed spoke.

"Practice drawing this. If I deem it sufficient, I can allow you to try creating your first runestone."

The class began scribbling like mad. A few kids sought Lady Ariel's approval after their first attempts, and she chastised them loud enough for the rest of the class to get the message. Garrett methodically traced the image. His hand shook and his lines were too wobbly. He tried again, but something about the spoke looked off. Then the spiral felt too ovular. After his fourth attempt, he raised his hand to flag down Lady Ariel.

"This will work." Lady Ariel pulled a smooth, flat stone from a pouch on her belt and placed it on his desk. "Can anyone tell me why we use stones and not paper for our runes?"

"Because you don't want your dog eating your runes?" someone joked.

"Save the jokes for when you've progressed as far as Mr. Clarke. The item the runes are inscribed on must withstand the force of magic. For a simple spell, a stone is typically enough. For more powerful spells, you might use metals or even gemstones."

Much of the first week of enchanting had been spent learning to use the chemical etching pens required for inscribing runes. The idea of a pen full of acid still made Garrett's hands tremble, but the desire to impress his teacher got him through. A few minutes later, Garrett finished with his stone. He cleared his mind and felt his essence inside of him, as Brokk had taught him. He held the stone and tried to picture the energy moving through his body and down his arm into it. A brief glimmer twinkled at the center of the spiral, gradually filling it, and by the time it reached the outer spoke the entire stone lit up like a light bulb. A firm hand gripped his shoulder.

"Good. Class, please see Mr. Clarke's example. I expect you all to bring working stones to me by Monday."

Garrett held his stone tight, his smile as bright as the glow emanating from his hands.

The first week of school ended with the dance. It took some cajoling, but Connor and Garrett eventually convinced Ninette to go with them. They half led, half dragged her out of her dorm room and down the halls toward the gym. The massive crowd migrating in the same direction provided them with some much-needed momentum to manage their resistant friend.

Once inside, they were greeted by giant disco balls reflecting prismatic light while tissue paper streamers danced up and down of their own accord. The dark gymnasium thumped to the beat of cheesy music while students of all ages danced in clumps—plenty more awkwardly occupied space along the gym walls, casting nervous glances at their shaking and grooving peers.

"The whole school is crammed in here," Garrett said.

He edged closer to Ninette as the crowd around them thickened. She started to pull away, but after seeing the uncomfortable way he eyed the large crowds—and knowing she felt the same—she accepted the closeness and awkwardly pat him on the back.

"No one would miss us if we bailed," Ninette groused.

"Come on," Connor said. "It'll be fun. You like me. You like Garrett. I bet you'd like more people if you gave them a chance. We don't have to stay long."

"I'm only here because the cafeteria is closed. All the food is here," Ninette said. She eyed the buffet, and her hand unconsciously went to her stomach.

The entire student body filled the gym wall to wall. Most of the teachers were floating around as well. Some literally. Up in the air, Speck, the faerie teacher, danced around the disco balls. The light reflected off her gossamer wings and scattered to the floor below. Lady Ariel and Master Borodin huddled together in animated conversation. The dwarven teacher was standing on her toes, waving her finger under the summoning instructor's nose, and her face was bright red. Out on the dance floor, Connor caught a glimpse of a Hawaiian shirt—a sure sign the painfully awkward Mr. Masters was near. The dark-skinned teacher was tall and lanky, and he danced amidst a crowd of students with his elbows jutting out and a goofy grin on his face. Connor didn't have him for any classes, but he'd heard stories. Heck, even the other teachers laughed at him behind his back.

"Come on. Let's eat and get out of here." Ninette grabbed Connor and Garrett by the wrists and pulled them toward the food.

Navigating the mass of dancing students took several minutes and more than a few apologies to jostled classmates. Despite being the driving force behind going to the dance, neither Connor nor Garrett held any more intention of dancing than Ninette did, so they were content to follow her single-minded quest for food.

They had just reached the buffet when an older student shouldered into Ninette and roughly knocked her aside. He tossed a cocky look over his shoulder in her direction. He said something too quiet for the trio to hear, but two of his friends burst into raucous laughter.

"Excuse me?" she shouted after him.

He turned around and studied Ninette more closely, eyeing her teeth in particular. "I thought I smelled fish. What about you guys?" he sneered.

His friends sniggered, but stopped when Ninette punched him in the face and sent him skidding across the wood floor.

"Wanna say that again?" she growled.

"You heard me," he said, rubbing his jaw. "Your kind don't belong up here."

Ninette screeched and pounced on him. His friends joined the fray and the four became a pile of swinging punches and wild kicks. Ninette's Merfolk strength kept her on even footing for a minute, but the difference in numbers threatened to overwhelm her.

"We have to help," Connor said. He tried to jump into the pile, but Garrett grabbed his arm.

"We what?" Garrett squeaked.

Connor tried to peel one guy off, but the other cast an earth spell. A boulder appeared in the air and hurtled at Connor. It hit him in the stomach, and he went flying into the buffet table. He crashed through it and landed against the gym wall, drenched in punch and covered with food. The older boy conjured a fireball, hate and blazing light shining in his eyes, but it evaporated as both he and Ninette were tossed up and suspended upside down in midair.

"Enough!" Ariel shouted. Her face flushed beet red as she stomped across a silent gym. "Both of you, explain!"

Ninette grumbled and the other boy donned a slimy, innocent smile, but neither provided a cohesive answer.

"Fine. Detention for both of you." She didn't set either of them down, instead hauling them kicking and struggling in the air behind her.

"What was that about?" Garrett asked Connor. He watched the little teacher drag his friend away.

"One of them said something nasty about Merfolk," Connor answered, trying to clean himself off. "She didn't take it too well."

"Just because she's Folk?" Garrett frowned. "I haven't heard anyone say anything to the elves or dwarves or anyone."

"There's more of them around. Ninette's the only Merfolk here; the bad blood is more recent. Orcs, elves, and most others formed a coalition with the human Magi centuries ago. Merfolk didn't." Connor pulled Garrett closer and lowered his voice to a conspiratorial whisper. "Merfolk were still sinking ships and eating people in the early 1900s. They stopped, but I guess not everyone's over it. Hopefully, that guy and everyone else will think twice about saying something like that again." Connor wiped futilely at his shirt. "I'm going to change. Wait for me?"

"Sure. I hope Ninette's okay," Garrett said.

Connor did, too. He left the gym and walked back toward the dorms, the only sound was his echoing footsteps and the steady drip of punch from his clothes. He'd expected to hear Ninette grumbling and struggling against Lady Ariel's restraints, or maybe a couple slipping out of the dance for some alone time, or even a prankster messing with people's lockers. But there was no one. He was alone. Only the emergency lights and the TV screens provided light. The empty hallways chilled Connor through his wet clothes.

"I didn't realize how creepy this place could be," he whispered.

He walked faster, almost jogging. His footsteps sounded louder, too loud. The loud thuds had to be coming from more than one person.

That's fine, he thought to himself. *It's a big school. I'm probably not the only person heading back.* Probably.

The echoes got louder. They sounded as if they were right on top of him. He turned his head to check and see if he was being followed, only to slam right into someone. The two of them toppled over together into a jumbled mess on the cold floor.

"I am so, so sorry," he apologized and scrambled off the other person. "I wasn't looking."

"Obviously not," Sheena snapped. She pushed him away and glanced down at her dress to find it stained and damp. "Ugh, you're a mess!"

"I got knocked into the buffet table," Connor said, looking down at his clothes. "Wait, why aren't you at the gym?"

"None of your business, now get out of here. I'm busy." She glanced around the corner of the hall.

"Are you spying on someone? What's down there?" Connor tried to look as well.

Sheena thrust out her arm to keep him back. "I said *leave*," she hissed.

She flailed her arm to keep him behind it. She peered around the corner again. Despite her efforts, Connor looked too, and both recoiled as an explosion of dark purple light filled the hall and washed over them. Sheena ran toward the light. Connor chased after her, in time to hear the thud of a third set of footsteps and catch a glimpse of a shoe disappearing at the other end of the hall.

"I knew it!" Sheena cried triumphantly.

She ignored the runner and bent down to inspect bizarre scribblings and patterns left behind. They were large circles, a shade of dark crimson, and still wet.

Inside each was a maze of runes. Sheena traced her fingers along one of them.

"I knew it," she repeated in a hushed whisper.

"Knew what?" Connor decided not to give chase and turned back to Sheena. "Those look kind of like summoning circles."

The wet glisten of them and a coppery scent turned his stomach.

"Oh, do you think so?" She spat. "Of course they're summoning circles you, you…" But she never finished.

Headmistress Mine stepped briskly around the corner, followed by Dr. Greens, Master Borodin, and Mr. Masters. The teachers flooded the hall, ignoring the dumbfounded Connor and irate Sheena.

"You were right, Gregor," Headmistress Mine said to the summoning teacher. Her voice was hard with an edge of concern. "Someone has been summoning. Fifth level circles, and three of them."

Master Borodin scanned the circles on the floor and walls; his eyes glowed a wicked green in the gloomy hall. He ran a hand through his dark red hair and shook his head.

"I have maybe twenty students capable of a fifth-level summoning," he said. "But three at once?"

"I can't even do two at once. Can you, Gregor?" Mr. Masters whispered.

"Obviously I can," Borodin snapped.

"And a portal," Sheena said. She proudly stepped to the ring of teachers and thrust her chin in the air.

"Excuse me?" the headmistress asked, finally noticing Connor and Sheena.

"Three circles were executed, and then someone made a medium-sized portal," Sheena said. She traced a line in the air with her finger and settled on an invisible point in the center of the hall. "Right there."

"She's right," Gregor said, following her finger to an invisible point in the air. "Probably only open for a few seconds. Explains why nothing is here." He looked back at Sheena. "Ah, yes. Ms. Crowton."

She snorted. "Clearly, I sensed the circles being prepared before you."

"Then your poor judgment shows," the headmistress said. "You should have alerted a teacher. You had no idea what you would find. Return to your rooms. I'll ask you not to spread rumors of this."

"Whatever," Sheena said. She stalked straight-backed toward the dorms, surrounded by a cloud of haughty silence.

"Mr. McTaggart?"

Connor snapped back with a start.

"Yes, Headmistress. Sorry, Headmistress."

He bolted after Sheena and stayed a step behind her. A flurry of questions threatened to pour out, but he was too nervous to speak up. With blood on the ground and the teachers rattled, she'd put herself at the center of the conversation—and she'd been right. She saw something they hadn't. Despite the sinking feeling that something bad happened, he had to admit what she did was pretty cool.

Finally, he piped up. "You know a lot about portals and circles? That's advanced stuff."

"Do you not know who my family is?"

Connor's throat dried. He knew they were famous, but not why.

"Crowton Industries specializes in rapid transit and cheap labor," she recited.

The words had a practiced feel of something long memorized.

"Portals and summoning are what. We. *Do*. My dad could do something like this in his sleep. Probably."

"Cool, cool. What's a fifth-level circle for?"

Sheena groaned. "Take Master Borodin's class next semester. It's not my job to explain it. Or find whoever did it. I would have seen them if you hadn't interfered."

She increased her pace, but Connor kept up.

"I said I was sorry. Come on, what's a fifth-level circle? They looked like they were drawn in blood."

Sheena stopped dead in her tracks. "Blood. But that would mean…" she trailed off into mumbles.

"I've never heard of circles of blood. Why would someone—?"

"Oh. My. God. Why are you still here? Why were you here to begin with? Fine. A fifth-level circle is either a magic-capable creature or something resistant to magic. Probably something strong enough to kill a senior or even a teacher." She got inches away from his face, practically screeching. "Summoning with blood is a way to enhance your power and ensure strict obedience. Are you happy? Aren't you glad you know?" She rolled her eyes and left a stunned Connor alone in a dark hallway as an announcement rang over the PA.

"Attention students. The dance will be ending early. Curfew is in effect immediately. Please return to your dormitories."

Chapter 4

Elemental Magicks - Water
As a magical element, water is known for its flexibility and abundance. A Magi with a little awareness and creativity can find it anywhere and use it for almost anything. A talented Magi has an ocean of possibilities at their disposal.

Connor tossed and turned all night. Visions of monsters—and of monster hunting—filled him with restlessness. He knew he should be scared, but a part of him couldn't deny the excitement. Real monsters. Powerful ones. And he could be the one to find them.

As soon as he awoke, he rushed out, still in his PJs, and pounded on Garrett's and Ninette's doors. Garrett answered groggily, and Ninette swung open the door with bared teeth and her fist raised. He managed to placate both of them and promised to explain.

Minutes later, they huddled on a bench under an apple tree, Connor with a book open in his lap. The

Creature Compendium had been one of his favorites as a child, a tenuous link to the magical world he knew existed but rarely saw. Drawings and details of monsters ranging from the mundane to the terrifying filled its pages, but at that moment he saw its information in a new light.

"There are monsters loose in the school?" Garrett whispered. His nervous shaking rattled the bench. "Like what?"

"I don't know," Connor said as he flipped through the pages. "The book doesn't talk about summoning, just the monsters themselves, so it's hard to guess. What I don't get is why. Why bring monsters into the school and then immediately hide them?"

"They must be a big deal. You should have seen Lady Ariel's face," Ninette said. "I don't even know how she heard about the monsters, but she must've because her eyes bulged out and she dropped both of us on the spot. She yelled at us to go to our rooms. Then she just… ran."

"That reminds me, I saw someone running away," Connor said.

"Are you sure it wasn't someone who happened to walk into a hall full of monsters?" Garrett suggested. "I wouldn't stick around either."

"Maybe," Connor said, unconvinced. "But they didn't scream or shout or call for help or anything. Just ran. It doesn't feel right."

Connor and Garrett pored over the pages of The Creature Compendium; the warm sun and floral air made for a perfect reading environment. While they read, Ninette sat on the edge of the bench and stared at the blue waters of a nearby pond. Occasionally, Connor or Garrett would point to a monster in the book and try to get her attention, but she only responded with noncommittal grunts. It wasn't long before she stood up with a yawn.

"I'll be at the gym," she announced. "Gotta squeeze it in before detention. If you find a real monster, not a picture of one, give me a shout."

She walked away briskly and disappeared over a hill.

Connor closed the book and rubbed his eyes. "I have no idea what we're looking for."

"Don't look at me," Garrett said. "I didn't know monsters were a thing until a week ago."

"We need a different book."

Garrett frowned. "My tablet only has the files for the classes I'm enrolled in. What about you?"

"Same."

"What about the library?" Garrett asked. He was halfway to his feet before Connor could respond. "They'd have to have something about summoning."

The school library resembled an old gothic cathedral. Broad double doors bordered by spiked columns lead into an expansive room with a high vaulted ceiling. Towering shelves filled every wall and much of the space in between to form a maze of knowledge. The musty smell of old leather and aged paper permeated the air. A handful of tables dotted the floor; at the center sat a circular desk, and inside stood the school librarian.

Karronus Naegus was an imposing man of exaggerated features: his hands too large, his nose too broad, his smile too wide. His silver hair shined unnaturally bright and hung loose around his shoulders. His eyes smoldered like molten gold.

"Good morning, young ones," he said, and his smile blossomed even wider. His voice dripped honey. "How can I help you this fine morning?"

"We were wondering if there were any books about summoning we could look at," Connor said. He locked eyes with the librarian and couldn't turn away.

Mr. Naegus held his gaze for a long time before breaking it. He stepped around the desk and towered over the boys.

"Ah, an interest in Master Borodin's class next semester, perhaps? The art of summoning is rather complicated," he said. "I will help you find something but heed my advice. These magics are too advanced for amateur dalliance. Do not attempt them until you have received Gregor's express permission." His serious tone was at odds with the delighted smile he wore.

"We wouldn't," Connor blurted. "We just want to learn more about it." He returned the librarian's smile with an uneasy one of his own.

Naegus led the boys through the library to a far corner, climbed up a ladder, and, without even looking, pulled a tome off the shelf.

"The Summoner's Art. This is the textbook for Master Gregor's introductory class. I expect you can't get into too much trouble with this, but I advise caution nonetheless." He secured a second copy of the book, then grasped the boys firmly by the shoulders. "Do call if you need anything. Anything at all."

An hour later, Connor leaned back in his chair and stretched. "From what I can tell it only goes up to a seventh-level circle, so five still sounds pretty bad."

"No, look," Garrett said. He directed Connor to one of the last pages. "This chapter mentions an eighth-level, but you need seven people for it."

"I'm pretty sure there was just one person last night." Connor flipped back to the fifth-level chapter. "Listen to this 'A fifth-level summon should only be attempted by a Magi with significant combat experience. Do not attempt alone.'"

"So, not one, but three *somethings?* Things *no one* should deal with alone. That's what's loose in the school?" Garrett said. His eyes darted around the library nervously.

"It's fine. The teachers haven't said anything since last night. They probably have it under control," Connor said.

He pulled out the Creature Compendium again and flipped through the pages. With each turn of the page, the pictures of wild beasts seemed to dance before him.

"Real magical creatures in the school. It would be cool to see one."

"I don't know about that," Garrett said, hunching in on himself.

"I'm not saying we should try and catch them," Connor said, though his impish grin indicated just that. "But maybe we could help find them. Maybe even see one up close?"

"I don't want to see them at all," Garrett whimpered.

"Mr. Clarke is correct," Headmistress Mine said. She appeared silently, looming over them. The harsh overhead lighting glinted in her thick-rimmed glasses.

"You don't want to see them. Mr. McTaggart, a word?"

Connor looked to Garrett for help, but Garrett was already shelving the books in a rigid attempt at nonchalance. The headmistress cleared her throat, and Connor gave up, grumbling as he followed her to her office on the second floor, wondering all the while why he was in trouble.

Leorra Mine's office was cozy, about the size of Connor's dorm room, with a simple wooden desk in the center, a large swivel chair on her side, and a smaller chair on his. A broad bookshelf occupied one wall, and behind the desk, an expansive window overlooked a courtyard behind the school. Connor sat and waited as Leorra walked past her shelf, took a moment to brush away some dust on a trophy, then stopped at the window and gazed. She let out an extended, quiet breath and sat opposite Connor, clenching her jaw and watching him through narrowed eyes.

"I understand the youthful impulse to go seek trouble. After last night, I had a feeling I'd catch you digging. You seem the type," she said flatly. "I assure you the staff are more than capable of dealing with the… incident… from last night."

"Yes, Headmistress," Connor said, head bowed.

"I know exactly what 'Yes, Headmistress' means." She removed her glasses and massaged her eyes. "I'm serious. Abandon this foolishness and focus on your studies."

"But, Headmistress, I saw another student last night. They were running away."

"We suspected as much. Likely an irresponsible prank. Someone showing off for their friends." A hint of a smile reached the corners of her eyes. "You may go. I hope this is our last conversation about this."

Connor slunk out of the office and back downstairs. If she was keeping this close an eye on him, he probably wouldn't get anywhere near a monster anytime soon. He didn't want to get into more trouble and certainly didn't want Garrett or Ninette to be blamed because of him.

Someone painted circles in blood. That's not a prank. Whatever this is, it's serious. I know it is.

Connor's heart raced, and he couldn't stop the smile from spreading across his face.

Ninette arrived for detention and grabbed a seat at the front of Lady Ariel's class. The cold furnaces in the corners gave the spacious workshop an abandoned feeling. She waited for a few minutes, propping her feet up on the table in front of her, but no one else showed. She was picking at her teeth when Lady Ariel rushed into the room, out of breath and fifteen minutes late.

"Apologies, Ms. Reefwalker," she said, dumping an armload of papers and a thermos onto her desk. "Got a late start today, and I needed to see your dance partner to his detention duties."

"He's not going to be here?" She'd hoped to land a sucker punch or two while the teacher's back was turned.

"Thought it best to keep you separate today." The dwarven teacher took a swig from her thermos and almost choked. "Anyhow, you see my forge there?"

She gestured to the dark brick dome at the head of the class, larger than the others and reeking of coal and ash.

"Uh-huh."

"You can leave once it's clean."

Ariel tossed her a rag and a steel wool pad.

Ninette buried her head inside the cold structure. It was caked in black soot, and in no time, so was she. The harder she scrubbed, the more coal dust she kicked up. She hacked and coughed and spit, but nothing got the gritty sensation out of her mouth or lungs. Her eyes itched, but she knew rubbing them would only worsen it.

"This is getting me nowhere," she said between coughing fits. "How long do I have to do this?"

Ariel didn't bother looking up from grading papers. "Until it's clean."

Ninette scrubbed and Ariel graded. The only sounds were the scrape of Ninette's brush and the scritch of Ariel's pen on paper.

"Did what's-his-face tell you what he said to me?" Ninette called out.

Ariel's pen paused mid-stroke. "He did not, though I have my suspicions. Why?"

"Because I shouldn't be here. I didn't do anything wrong."

"I've encountered my share of that nonsense. However justified, punching someone in the face will only cause more trouble."

"You only say that because you can't reach their faces," Ninette grumbled under her breath.

"I've kicked my fair number of shins," Ariel said, taking another swig from her thermos. "And I've learned better responses with age, some more responsible, others more satisfying." She said that last bit with a slight giggle. "No more chatter. Back to your cleaning. Use up some of that energy you have too much of. I'll check on you in another hour. Maybe."

An hour later, Ariel was snoring with her face buried in the stack of assignments, and Ninette was no closer to a clean forge.

"This is so stupid. Make me waste my Saturday, sure." She scrubbed harder. "Set me up with busywork, fine." She scrubbed harder. "But give me something both pointless *and* impossible, and then fall asleep?"

Ninette screamed and punched the forge as hard as she could. The rough pain in her knuckles infuriated her and she slammed her fist into it again, but this time the impact came with a loud explosion of light and fire. Dancing red flame engulfed her arm halfway to the elbow, but it didn't hurt. In fact, her hand felt better.

"Whoa." She held out her other hand and squeezed tight, trying to recall what she'd done, and it blazed to life as well. "Double whoa."

"What's going on," Lady Ariel slurred. "No magic in detention." She bolted upright and slapped herself awake. "I thought that would be obvious. Wait. Skreed hasn't taught you fire yet."

"I was really pissed, and it just happened," Ninette explained. "I, uh, I don't know how to put them out."

She extended her burning hands to the diminutive teacher. Ariel laughed.

"Skreed is going to have his hands full with you." She took Ninette's hands in her small, rough ones. "Doesn't that hurt?"

"I'd be a poor smith if I couldn't stand a little heat. Inhale, hold, hold, exhale. Shake them out a bit."

Ninette did as instructed, and the fire flickered out.

"There you go. I suspect that's enough for today. I'd watch your temper, though. If you punch someone while you're on fire, I'll be keeping you longer."

On Monday in Professor Skreed's class, Connor arrived to find a large glass, filled to the brim with water, sitting on his desk.

"Don't drink that," Skreed said. "Today we leave earth behind and move on to water." He pointed to an image on his screen. "If you'll indulge a bit of a remedial lesson, water can be either liquid, solid, or vapor. It's fairly ubiquitous, and also one of the easier elements to work with since it is so flexible. But it takes a flexible Magi to get the most from it.

"The key to Water Magic is being able to change it from its three forms with ease. I want you to practice changing it from liquid to gas and back. Then liquid to ice. Any questions?"

Ninette tentatively raised her hand.

"Uh, how?"

Sheena snorted in the back row, and Ninette hurled a fat, pink rubber eraser at her. Skreed caught it telekinetically and gently floated it back to Ninette.

"Settle down, both of you," he said. "It is a legitimate question, Ms. Crowton. Not everyone had your years of private tutelage. Where Will Magic is the imposing of your desires on the world through the use of your personal essence, Elemental Magic is the commingling of your essence with natural sources. Cooperation as opposed to dominance. Each element responds differently. Earth simply is, it awaits a firm, shaping hand. Water seeks freedom but is easily contained by clear purpose.

"Next week we will learn wind, elusive to many. It slips through your fingers and plays with your hair. It can be a whispered breath or a howling tornado. The master of wind is not forceful or controlling. They must be a free spirit willing to go along for the ride. They must provide not commands but subtle suggestions.

"I'm getting ahead of myself." Skreed chuckled, positioned his own glass of water before him, and placed his hands over it. He raised them up, and the water in the glass flowed upward, evaporating into a perfect little cloud. He lowered them, and it rained back into the cup. "Water day. Be flexible but know what you want. Give shape to your desires. Splish splash!"

Connor held the cup of water, though others stared or pointed at theirs.

"I want to make this into vapor," he said.

He tried to be aware of the breath in his lungs; how light and full they were when he inhaled. When he exhaled, the water in his glass evaporated.

"I did it! I did it!" He shouted.

"Throw yourself a parade," Sheena said.

A child-sized snowman sat on her desk. Before Connor got over his shock, it threw a snowball in his face.

"Ms. Crowton, my patience wears thin," Professor Skreed said. His usual jovial tone was replaced with one of flat displeasure. "You will see me after class."

"Worth it," she said.

The snowman waved, and Sheena returned her attention to her phone.

Connor stomped over to Sheena with painfully cold snow melting down his face.

"What's your problem?"

"Well, you let that summoner get away, that's one thing. Also, you're an easy target because you're trying so hard, and yet, I'm still so much better." She stuck out her tongue. "Get used to it and get gone."

Connor gaped, dumbstruck. Any hope of a response utterly failed in the face of her outright hostility.

Sheena looked up from her phone, her glare more toxic than her words. "I didn't mean later. Scram."

Connor crept back to his desk, brushed off the snow, and continued to work with his water. In just a few minutes, he could go from one form to another just by thinking it.

"I got gas," Garrett announced.

An undulating vapor hovered in the air over his water glass. More than a few classmates laughed, and even the professor hid a smile.

"That's not, I mean, come on guys," Garrett mumbled. He blushed, and his cloud turned to a light rain splattering on his desk.

The shatter of glass drew everyone's attention away from poor Garrett and onto Ninette. She leaned as far back as she could from a giant block of ice that took up most of her desk.

"Where did I get more water from?" she complained.

"Some from the air, but you probably made more on your own," the Professor said while stroking his chin and tilting his head to inspect her work. "You did the same with earth, as I recall. Good time for a lesson." He rubbed his hands together excitedly. "Last week I created earth from thin air. That's a bit of a trick, but an easier one is increasing the amount of an existing element.

"When you mix your essence with nature, you create a link. Done right, it becomes hard to see the line between them. It's easy to exchange your essence into the element, creating more of it. Many of you have done so unintentionally, Ms. Reefwalker loudly so. You can also see Ms. Crowton's example, which is why she's staying late today."

Sheena gave a regal wave.

"A sure-fire sign you've found an elemental match is when you can amplify it subconsciously as these two have. We'll work on this more as the semester progresses. Don't worry if you don't have the knack of it yet."

But Connor did worry. He spent the rest of the week trying to create more water. He could make gas, liquid, ice, slush, snow, clouds, anything, but never in greater amounts than he started with. Sheena tormented him with increasingly huge and complex creations of ice and snow. For the first time in his life, Connor applied himself to his studies. He did the reading, and he practiced whenever he could. He even dragged Ninette out into the gardens after class to help.

"I don't get it," Connor said. "I know what I'm doing. I have total control, but I can't make more."

"I have the opposite problem," Ninette laughed. "Look."

She dumped out a water bottle and caught the contents in a sphere. Without warning, it ballooned to twice its original size.

"See? I didn't want to do that, I just wanted to hold it."

"That doesn't help," Connor pouted.

"Maybe this will. Catch!" Ninette said, hurling the water at him.

Connor did, holding the water at bay and reshaping it into a stream to hose her down.

"Hey! Cut it out!" she cried between spurts. "How did you do that?"

"I told you I know what I'm doing," Connor admitted with a half-smile. "It serves you right."

By Friday, Connor caved and asked Professor Skreed for help. He stayed after class, not wanting to draw more mockery from Sheena. He remained in his seat and manipulated his glass of water into various shapes and forms until the last of his classmates had departed. Professor Skreed must have noticed the dejected look on his face because he closed the door and strolled over to sit at the desk next to Connor. He smiled warmly, crinkling the edges of his eyes.

"What's on your mind, Connor?"

"It doesn't work, no matter what I try," he said. "I can't make more. Ninette can do it without trying. Sheena knows how to do it. What am I doing wrong?"

"Other than not being patient? Because I recall saying we'd get there," the professor said with only a hint of gentle mockery. "It may be you and water aren't a match, but it may be you aren't suited to creation but manipulation. You're talented. You picked up earth and water on day one, so I'm expecting exciting things from you, even if you don't seem to be."

"But how? If I can't create what isn't there, what am I supposed to do?"

"Always plenty of earth and air around. Water, too, usually." Skreed reached out and squeezed Connor's hand. It was meant to be reassuring.

It wasn't.

Chapter 5

> Elemental Magicks – Wind (Air)
> Air magic can be used in small drafts to mimic telekinesis or in massive gales to manipulate atmospheric pressure and control the weather. It rewards a quick mind and can produce rather quick feet.

Professor Skreed wore a thick, wool sweater when he entered the classroom. "Might get chilly in here today. Calling for sharp gusts."

He turned on the screen at the head of his classroom to a video of a young woman dancing in a field of waist-high grass. The yellow field whished one way, then abruptly another, always in time with the woman's movements. The camera panned away and up to reveal the wind blowing in multiple directions at once to create a beautiful pattern in the field.

"I hope you're not telling us we have to dance," Ninette grumped.

"No dancing required," Skreed replied. "But perhaps loosening up. Brute force and stubbornness will not avail you today. This is about going with the flow. The airflow." The professor took a mock bow to the groans of his students. "I expect this classroom will have a different feel today." He eyed Sheena, but she wasn't looking. "No objective, just see what you can do. I'll be about to assist as needed."

At first, no one in the class knew what to do. Professor Skreed's lessons usually had something approaching an objective, if not always as rigorous and well-defined as some of the other teachers. He also usually provided the elements they'd be working with. Most of the kids recognized this wasn't necessary—the air was all around them, after all—but their quizzical stares up, down, and all around provided no answers.

Ninette, uncomfortable in the growing silence and determined to act, swished her arms back and forth vigorously. She tried making broad fanning motions with her hands. She took a deep breath and blew it out as hard as possible. If she did anything magical, Connor didn't see it. He leaned back in his chair and smirked at her.

"I don't see you doing any better," she grunted. "You're not even going to try?"

Connor let his chair fall back into place with a heavy thud. "I dunno. What's the point? I'll just move what's already here. I can't make more. Would you like some more of the air conditioning?"

Connor twirled his finger overhead and lazily pointed it at Ninette. A quiet hiss passed through the classroom. It rustled papers and fluttered loose clothing before rudely blowing Ninette's hair out of place.

"Jerk. You didn't tell me you already knew how to do this."

"Yeah, can you show me?" Garrett asked.

Connor started to answer until he realized that half of the class watched him eagerly, Sheena among them. His planned snarky remark dried up in his throat.

"I didn't mean to." Connor felt the pressure of their attention and tried to shrink into his chair. He'd been trying to prove a point, not get everyone's attention. "I wasn't really trying," he muttered quietly.

"That's it exactly!" Professor Skreed cheered. "Don't try. Let it happen. Connor, my boy. Come here a moment, will you?"

The professor led Connor over to the window where they stood wordless, looking upon the school gardens. The professor watched the flowers and the bushes sway outside with a content smile on his sunlit face. Connor alternated between watching the old elf and the gardens. He waited for further instruction, but the professor didn't offer any, and Connor knew his classmates were staring at his back.

"Professor?" he asked.

"What do you see out there?"

"Bushes?" Connor guessed. "Flowers? A fountain?"

"Wind. Air. Lots of it. Imagine what you could do with all that. Why, I'd wager just about anything."

Connor watched, really *watched*, the movements of the grass and plants outside. He looked for the point where a gust of wind began and followed it all the way to the trees in the distance and imagined he could see the contiguous stream of wind. The more he observed, the more he saw. Every twitch in the shrubs, every moving leaf on a tree. All of it moved by the wind.

I could do something. I could make wind so strong it could blow a person away, uproot plants, maybe even trees. Tornados are just wind, right? Now that's magic.

The wind picked up. Dark clouds gathered to block out the sunny sky. They roiled and twisted directly over the school. A sound like an old engine revving preceded the formation of a funnel cloud in the middle of the school gardens. A passing student going for a stroll outside dropped their bags and ran. The tornado ripped hedges into the air and tossed them away, too far to see. On the professor's desk, a phone rang.

"Hold that thought," he said to Connor. "Hello? Oh, hello, Headmistress. Nothing wrong here. Why? A tornado, you say. I'll see what I can do about it. Yes, a pleasant day to you too, ma'am." He hung up and smiled at Connor. "I don't suppose you know how to stop that? Ah, very well."

The professor winked at Connor, and the tornado dispersed as if it had never been.

"I hope you all see the power of idle thought and flights of fancy," Professor Skreed said, turning to address the class. "Many of you who succeeded before may not today. There are eight elements, and you will not be able to work with all of them. Do your best, but don't get discouraged."

Connor played with the air in the classroom, using his newfound talents to tease Ninette in particular. True to the professor's word, many of the students who excelled with earth and water struggled to make anything happen with wind. Garrett's roommate Julian, who had yet to do anything but cause disasters, thrust a gust of wind at Vern, the dour and doleful elf, powerful enough to knock his desk over. Gemma Perriwinkle, class know-it-all, could flutter individual papers hung on the wall by pointing to them. Ninette failed to do anything but huff and puff until she was red in the face. By the end of class, Connor could use the air to push anything in the classroom—including Garrett—around with ease.

Garrett took a more nuanced approach. He bobbed a book up and down on a swirling draft. He inspected the tome with bright eyes.

"This is actually a lot easier than using Will," he noted.

"Exactly," Professor Skreed cheered. "You're using the essence of the air instead of your own, and you're obtaining the same effect. You might have a better hold of something with Will, but is it worth the cost? Always a decision a Magi must make."

When the bell rang, Sheena grabbed her things, ducked her head, and bolted out the door without a single word to anyone, snide or otherwise.

"She was quiet today," Garrett observed.

"Fine with me. Little brat thinks she's so good and can't stop rubbing our faces in it. We deserve a break," Ninette said.

Garrett watched Sheena disappear out into the hall. "I never saw her get it to work. Maybe she couldn't."

"Serves her right."

"But you didn't get it either, did you, Ninette?" Garrett asked.

A sharp look from Ninette elicited a yelp, but then she grinned, and Garrett relaxed.

"Who needs wind? Check this out." Ninette clenched her fist, engulfing it in glowing red fire.

"No way!" Garrett gushed. He extended his hand towards the fire and then quickly snatched it back when he felt the heat. "You figured fire out on your own?"

"Lady Ariel may have helped a little."

"Cool," Connor said. He crossed his arms and frowned. He wanted to be happy for Ninette, but a nagging thought held him back.

Something I'll probably never be able to do unless I run into a forest fire. He shook his head to clear it and sighed.

"Hey, I'll catch up with you guys later. I want to ask Skreed something."

Connor waited in his seat until the class emptied before approaching the professor.

"Hello, Connor. Something I can help you with? Not Wind Magic clearly."

Connor reached into his back pocket and pulled out his focus glove. The beat-up, brown leather glove had sat idle on his desk since the first day of school. His nauseating first attempt had bred an abundance of caution, a rare thing for Connor, but he was willing to try anything to unlock the magic he knew he must be capable of.

"Do you know how to use one of these?" he asked. "I thought it might help me cast bigger spells, but the one time I tried to wear it, I almost threw up. I haven't tried it again since."

"A focus glove? May I?" the professor asked. He held it up to the light, examining each finger. "This is quality work. I used to have one a few hundred years ago. Handy things, if you'll pardon the pun."

"So, it might help me?"

Skreed frowned and shook his head. "I don't see how. Seeing essence is useful for a lot of things, but if you aren't interacting with it in the proper way, seeing it won't be much help. Lady Ariel has no skill with Nature. You could give her two focus gloves and sit her in a garden for a week, and she wouldn't grow weeds.

"Cheer up, my boy. You have a talent. You've shown equal comfort with earth, water, and wind. Most who can use earth especially have trouble with wind. You didn't. I wouldn't be surprised if you could cast a spell in five or six elements at this rate. A rare feat."

"Maybe." Connor took the glove back and stuffed it in his pocket. "It's just not how I imagined it. I wanted to duel. I wanted fire and lightning and…" he struggled to get his point across, finding the words as hard to come by as the magic.

"You may yet. Magic is a strange thing, Mr. McTaggart. You never quite know what you're capable of. I expect you will surprise us all, and perhaps even yourself." He smiled, and Connor's spirits lifted, if only slightly. "And be careful with that glove. I *did* throw up the first few times I used mine. Practice makes perfect."

Connor decided not to follow his friends and instead wandered the halls.

"Maybe he's right. Plenty of wind and earth and water. Dueling stadiums are outside, so at least there's that."

He was startled by a screech ricocheting violently off the lockers, a high-pitched cry of pure terror and pain. Before his mind caught up, his feet were sprinting in the direction of the cry. Another shriek sounded, the same voice, but weaker. Connor ran faster. He searched wildly for anyone that might be able to help, but classes had ended for the day. The students and teachers were gone, and the halls and classrooms were completely empty. Around a corner and down the corridor, a girl lay sprawled on the floor outside the bathrooms. He knelt beside her.

"Hey, are you okay?" he said, more a wish than question.

Her glazed eyes stared at the ceiling. Her veins stood out as thin rivers of ice under the pale skin of her face and arms. Connor gently shook her by the shoulders—she was cold to the touch.

"Come on, please wake up. You're okay. You're okay, right?" Then he saw the blood, and all rational thought vanished.

On the side of her stomach were dozens of tiny puncture wounds. Pinpricks of red welled up at each of them, forming a 'V' shape, but there was no blood anywhere else; she may as well have been asleep, if not for her wide-open eyes.

"Help!" Connor shouted. "Somebody help, please!"

There was no one in sight, and no one responded to his cries.

Down the hall, a door clicked, but when he looked up, no one was there. A dozen yards away, the door exiting the school swung closed.

"Wait!"

But the door clicked shut.

"I'll... I'll be right back, okay?" Connor said to the unconscious girl.

He didn't want to leave her; she looked bad. If only he knew how to heal. But he didn't, and there was no one else around. No one except whoever had just left. Connor's chest tightened, his heart raced, but he knew there was nothing he could do for the girl, not by staying. He got up, burst through the door, stumbled out into the gardens, and spun around frantically to find whoever had gone through.

"Hello? Anyone? We need help."

Panic rotted into suspicion at the silence around him. He was positive someone had left through the door. A guttural grunting behind him, a sound completely inhuman, was not the answer he'd hoped for. He got no other warning before something kicked him in the back and knocked him face down on the ground. He rolled over on his elbows, turning to see what hit him.

It looks like a pig, he thought. His mind processed the monster before him in scattered pieces.

It *did* look like a pig. A pig covered in needle-like bristles and as big as a lion. It stamped one cloven hoof in the dirt and tossed its head back and forth, snorting and grunting. Its eyes glowed orange like hot coals, and black smoke puffed from its snout. Four tusks, each almost as big as his forearm, protruded from its lower jaw.

Connor scrabbled backward; the pig-thing unfolded its wings. Leathery wings, like a bat, and tipped with razor-sharp claws, like a... Connor didn't know and didn't care. With a few mighty thrusts, the creature rose into the air. Its blazing eyes pinned Connor to the spot. Its forelegs were hooves, but its back legs ended in vicious talons. Connor tried to run, but his legs wouldn't respond. It squealed an ear-piercing noise, then dove, talons aimed at Connor's face.

"No, no, no, no!" Connor cried. He threw up his hands as if to block and dredged up a wall of stone between them without thinking, but the force of the creature's dive nearly shook it to pieces. It wheeled around and dove again. This time, it broke through and slashed Connor's arm.

I'm going to die.

He scrambled to get up and felt the focus glove, a beautiful lump in his pocket.

"Please don't throw up," he begged himself and tugged the glove into place.

Verdant greens swirled with muddy browns while smoky, gray zephyrs danced above. Splotches of aqua burst up and down in the distance and, settling to the ground in front of him, a mass of inferno red. The pig radiated the red light like a bonfire. The colors permeated his vision and turned everything before him into a surreal portrait of horror. Only adrenaline kept Connor's lunch in his stomach.

"I can do this," he groaned.

The visual onslaught settled into his mind. His lessons, few though they had been, started to take over, and he recognized the colors for what they were—magic. Magic he could use. The creature brightened, the red light intensified, and Connor knew to brace for Fire Magic. He grabbed hold of the earth below him and tore up another wall to deflect the gout of flame. The creature squealed and belched another blast. Blue caught Connor's eye and he connected his mind—his essence—to it. He pulled water from the fountains to douse the pig. Its skin crackled and hissed, and the fiery aura dimmed before roaring back, brighter than before. Connor tried to harness the wind to blow it away, but the pig ignored his best efforts.

Another fireball, and the barrier shook.

"Someone, help me!"

Another fireball and the wall exploded. Connor felt the impact reverberate through his bones. Dirt and debris pelted his face, and in its wake, the creature advanced. It snorted and grunted in deep, bestial growls. Smog and flame dripped from its maw.

The next blast came as a wall of red flame. He threw out his arms and the blaze stopped inches from his face. The heat of it licked at his cheeks and stung his eyes, but it didn't come closer.

"I stopped it? I stopped it!" Connor shouted, blinking the sweat away.

His celebration was short-lived. The pig charged him. Every hoofbeat reverberated through the ground. It bowled Connor over and pinned him to the ground. The creature's jaws were inches from his face. Its rough, jagged hooves dug into his chest and crushed him. Connor struggled to fill his lungs. He choked on its rancid breath. Its maw opened, flames burning in the back of its throat.

Connor tried to think of something, anything, but the fear of being cooked alive erased all thought but one.

I got to see a monster.

He was vaguely aware of the irony.

"Get off him!" Ninette yelled. She came barreling out of nowhere, her fists burning bright. Garrett trailed behind her, his eyes wide with outright panic. Ninette swung a crushing right hook into the monster's jaw and knocked it back. It roared in pain and spit a billow of flame at her. She fell to the ground, and the monster flapped its wings, taking off. Connor and Ninette both got up as the monster prepared to dive.

"I totally had that," Connor giggled, the fear and adrenaline leaving him giddy.

"Sure you did," Ninette smiled. Manic energy tinged her voice.

"You okay, Garrett?" Connor called out.

Garrett nodded shakily, standing a few feet back and darting glances at the school doors, hoping for help to arrive.

The pig monster came in low, belching flames. Connor had an idea. Water had slowed it down, he just didn't have enough. He pulled another stream from the closest fountain.

"Here you go," he called out. Using the motion of his hands to guide it, he channeled the flow of water to the muscly mer-girl.

Ninette amplified it ten times over and funneled a geyser into the pig's snout, extinguishing its flames and forcing it to veer away. It circled back and screeched so loud that they both dropped to their knees clutching their ears. Garrett's eyes rolled back in his head, and he collapsed to the ground. The pig looked ready to dive, but before it did, the Headmistress and Lady Ariel arrived. The teachers got between the kids and the monster, and it stopped short. The monster's eyes flashed for an instant, and it jolted in place before flying away toward the forest, deceptively fast for its bulk.

"Damn," Ariel cursed, tracking the monster in the distance. "What's a vesporcus doing here?"

"Headmistress! Lady Ariel!" Connor panted. "There was a girl! In the hall!"

"She will be fine," The headmistress said. "She is alive and in Nurse Poole's care. She lost a lot of blood, but I expect she will make a full recovery." The headmistress turned to Ninette. "Ms. Reefwalker, can you take Mr. McTaggart and Mr. Clarke to the nurse's office as well?"

Connor and Ninette helped Garrett to his feet, and Connor offered him a shoulder for support. The three of them hobbled to the school together without saying a word. Once inside, Connor's eyes fell to the spot on the floor where he'd found the girl. She was gone, but a few crimson drops remained, stark on the white tile. He swallowed a lump in his throat and looked back to see if the teachers were following.

They weren't, but he still whispered. "Someone set me up. I found a girl there, hurt pretty bad, and when I tried to help, someone was watching from the door. They lured me outside. I think they wanted me to be attacked."

"Are you sure you aren't being a little paranoid?" Ninette eyed him sideways. "You're probably just shaken up. That… vesporcus? It got you pretty good." She pointed to the blood stains on his shredded shirt.

Connor gripped his wounds and winced. "No way. Whatever got that girl, it wasn't the vesporcus. The bite marks were all wrong. Whatever got her had a lot of little teeth, not tusks."

"Do you think it's one of the monsters from the other night?" Garrett asked.

"I bet they both are," Connor answered. "Lady Ariel sure wasn't acting like this happens every day."

"Why would they attack you, though?" Ninette said. "You haven't done anything."

Garrett thought for a moment. "You saw someone. Maybe they saw you, too. Maybe they think you know who they are."

"But I don't! Now I know they saw me though."

"You wouldn't know anything if you were dead. You're welcome, by the way," Ninette teased through an elated grin. She still had a wild look in her eye.

"Yeah, thanks," Connor said, chuckling with her. "Why were you looking for me?"

"You didn't come find us after class," Garrett murmured. "We got worried."

"Garrett got worried. Then we heard all the noise coming from outside, and I thought I might get to hit something." She punched Connor in the shoulder and barked a laugh. "Turns out I was right."

Chapter 6

The Creature Compendium – Were-creatures
Were-creatures are the victims (or their descendants) of a curse that twists their essence pattern to mimic that of an animal. They may shapeshift into animal form at will, but, on the full moon, the change is involuntary, and they lose all control. They also become dangerously infectious.

Connor, Ninette, and Garrett walked alongside many of their schoolmates toward the dueling stadium on Friday afternoon. Fall had arrived, but the light chill in the air did little to cool the student body's excitement for the first duel of the year. Connor amused himself by casting gusts of wind to tug on Ninette's scarf.

"Stop it," she snapped, pulling it out of her face and tying it tighter. She carefully arranged it to ensure her neck was completely covered. "You're going to pull it off."

"So what?"

"Just wait 'til we get to fire," Ninette menaced. "Then we'll see who's laughing."

Connor smirked, but he did let the breeze die. "Garrett, why did you bring your tablet? Aren't you going to watch?"

Garrett looked up and pushed his glasses up his nose. "I don't know. I'm not that interested in it. I wanted to hang out with you guys, but Ariel has a quiz for us next week. How long is the duel again?"

"Six matches, five-minute time limit each, time to rebuild the arena between. Probably not more than an hour?" Connor guessed.

"Rebuild?"

"Well yeah, it's going to get rough," Ninette smiled hungrily. "They aren't out there tickling each other."

"We'll be safe right? I've had enough danger for the year." Garrett shivered. He lowered his voice and looked toward the forest on the horizon. "You haven't seen it again, have you?"

"No," said Connor. "And I've been looking. I don't think many people even know what happened. No one is talking about it." Connor patted the focus glove in his pocket.

This is the only reason I'm still alive. That thought bred a worse one. He glanced at the other students around him suspiciously. *Someone tried to kill me a few days ago. Should I really be out here?*

He forced a smile. "We'll be fine today. There will be a referee, and two of the teachers will be keeping a shield around the stands."

Most of the students around them wore the Mattson blue and gold, but ahead a second line of people in electric green and bright yellow entered the stadium.

The line formed mid-path, with more and more people joining seemingly out of thin air.

"What's that?" Garrett asked.

"A portal," Connor replied. "It's a doorway to another place. I bet it leads to the other school, Point Loma."

Garrett angled his head to peer through and caught a glimpse of palm trees waving against a cloudless sky. "That's California through there?"

"That is where Point Loma is," Ninette said. "Look, Borodin is holding it open."

Master Borodin stood to the side of the portal, bedecked in blue robes trimmed in gold. He looked through the portal, checked his watch, then looked through again, brow furrowed all the while.

"Guess he doesn't want to miss the duels," chuckled Connor. "Come on, let's go get seats."

"What's your hurry?" Ninette said. "The team isn't even there yet. See?"

Ninette pointed to a gaggle of swooning and sighing girls surrounding the clean-cut, dark-haired young man from the other day. He and the team jogged down to the field.

"Good luck!" Connor shouted to him, waving.

"Thanks, kid," the boy responded over his shoulder.

He didn't stop to look. He hardly acknowledged the crowd of adoring fans around him other than to wave or return a compliment. He led the team down the hill at a steady, confident pace, and they disappeared through the stadium gates. Connor hadn't realized he'd started jogging after them until Ninette caught him by the shirt collar and pulled him back.

"You're gross," Ninette said. She elbowed him hard enough to bruise, but her cheeky smile hinted she meant no harm.

Connor stuck his tongue out at her regardless.

As the three of them settled into their seats, a static whine signaled the stadium speakers coming to life.

"Grab your seats Mattson Manticores. The duels are about to begin. Welcome to all the Point Loma Krakens who came out today, and, as always, a big thank you to our volunteer teachers, Eric Masters and Speck the Bonecrusher, for keeping the audience high and dry during the bouts."

Mr. Masters stepped onto the field alongside the faerie teacher to take up positions by the stands, him on Connor's side and Speck on the opposite. He wore his usual Hawaiian shirt, and though he had traded cargo shorts for cargo pants, he still wore socks with sandals. Speck wore her long, grass-green hair in intricate braids, and a necklace of various skulls, some as large as her own, hung around her neck. She flitted from one side of the stands to the other, flexing her muscles and hooting and hollering with the fired-up crowd.

"Captains, come on out and shake hands."

The handsome boy left the Mattson sideline to meet a dwarven girl midfield. After the handshake, the third doubles teams took the field. The referee, a green-skinned goblin even shorter than the dwarf, stood between the pairs.

"Here we go." Connor leaned forward with an eager smile.

The ref blew one long tweet, and Connor lost track of everything but the match. The Mattson boys sent tremors through the ground to launch their opponents in the air, trying to set them up as easy targets for lightning bolts, but something deflected the electricity. The Point Loma kids retaliated with a volley of flaming arrows, also blocked.

"What's stopping those spells?" Garrett asked.

"Shields of Will," Connor answered, never looking away. "It's a Will spell. Basically makes you invincible."

Lightning and fire flashed back and forth; some of it ricocheted away, but none of it ever reached the bleachers.

"Why doesn't everyone do it?"

The audience gasped as the first arrow, then more, pierced the Mattson shields. Two connected and the boys limped back.

"Because it's exhausting," Connor explained. "It drains your essence proportional to the spell you're blocking."

The match degenerated into a shootout, but when the dust settled, only the Mattson boys were standing.

During the second bout, one of the Point Loma kids adopted a meditative pose while the Mattson duo filled the stadium with a storm of fire and burning stones. The meditation-enhanced shield knocked them all back. One of the flaming rocks veered in Connor's direction. He didn't think much of it until a girl in the front row screamed and ducked—the projectile pierced the barrier and soared straight for Connor.

"Get down, you idiot!"

Ninette bowled him over as the flaming rock detonated in Connor's seat. The sound rang in Connor's ears, and bits of debris rained down on his head. He pushed himself up to gawk at the burning wreckage of his chair until his eyes watered from the stench of smoke and melted plastic.

"I thought we were safe," Connor groaned in a daze. "What happened?"

Down on the field, the ref stopped the match and chewed out Mr. Masters, who cowered in response and looked rather embarrassed.

"Maybe we should leave," Garrett said.

"We're fine," Connor reassured him. "I'm sure it was an accident. We do need new seats, though."

When things settled, the match resumed. Fire filled the air, but the handful of errant blasts were held at bay by the much more alert Mr. Masters. Point Loma took the round. Mattson lost the next round as well due to a penalty on one of the Mattson girls—she took a shallow cut to the stomach and retaliated with a fireball bigger than a house, resulting in a forfeit and a heated warning from the ref.

"Come on, guys, get your heads in the game!" Ninette yelled at the team as they marched into the locker room at halftime.

"I'm sure they're trying," Connor said.

They looked amazing, and most of them weren't much older than him. Yet they weren't even winning. Doubt took hold of him.

"Do you think we'll make the team? I expected kids our age to be a lot worse than the pros, but, watching them now…" Connor turned to Ninette and waved his hand vaguely toward the groundskeepers filling craters in the field and casually regrowing the grass.

"We will. As soon as Skreed shows us a little bit more, we can really practice. I'll even go easy on you." Ninette flashed her wicked, toothy smile.

"Yeah, okay," Connor muttered.

Ninette poked him in the shoulder and continued to do so until he perked up.

"Hey now. Remember what I did when you tried to soak me," Connor warned, hefting his drink.

"You guys are insane. We almost got blown up just watching this," Garrett moaned. He pointed a shaking finger at the ruined seating. "You want to be in the middle of it?"

"We would have been fine," Connor said. "Even if we did get a little singed, we could get healed."

"That doesn't stop you from feeling the pain, right?"

"Well, no, but—"

"Shut up. Second half is starting," blurted Ninette.

The speakers buzzed.

"Okay, folks, we are back on. First up, we've got our own Van Fredericks against Point Loma's Throm Goodson."

Van bounded out onto the field, a smile so broad you could see it from the cheap seats. His shaggy brown hair blew in the breeze. He was tall and thin, and he swam in his large Mattson varsity jacket. He shook hands enthusiastically with Throm. Then the bell rang, and Van howled.

His hair grew, covering his body. He threw off the jacket and his limbs stretched and cracked, the bones elongating and the joints shifting. His hands twisted into brutal claws, and his mouth grew into a snout filled with crooked yellow teeth. Van took a step forward, now a foot taller, his skinny form replaced with lean muscle. He glared down at his opponent through golden, lupine eyes. The creature howled again; his powerful cry reverberated through the stadium. Throm backpedaled a few feet but braced himself and sized up the werewolf.

Garrett coughed up his popcorn. "Wait, what?"

"He's a werewolf," Connor explained. "We have those."

"But... what? Is that normal? Should we be worried? Should *I* be worried?" Garrett babbled. He leaned back in his seat as if the creature in question weren't a hundred yards away.

"Nah," Ninette said. "They're only contagious on the full moon. Only dangerous then, too."

"I'm sure they get locked in their rooms or something. That's how most people deal with it," Connor added.

Van lunged at Throm who erected a wall of stone between them. Van slashed at it and his claws left hot, red gouges in the rock. Throm's hands flew in deft swipes. Each one chipped pieces of the wall off and hurled them at Van, three connecting in rapid succession. Van flipped backwards to get some distance and re-evaluate. Throm didn't give him time to breathe, keeping the stones flying, so Van took off at a sprint in a wide circle around his opponent. Little flashes of light marked where the stone missiles hit the stadium shielding, but none got through. None that is, until Van ran past Connor's section.

A handful of sharp stones went right over Mr. Masters' head, careening straight at Connor. He ducked and covered, but the shrapnel stopped inches short by someone else's shield.

"Eric Masters, do I need to come down there and do your job for you?" Lady Ariel hollered. She passed her thermos to Master Borodin, who was belly laughing in the seat next to her, and cupped her hands over her mouth. "Me grandmother could do a better job."

The referee didn't stop the match, but when Throm hesitated, Van didn't. His dash brought him around behind the dwarf and a flaming kick left the boy unconscious. Van was declared the winner.

Connor could barely get excited about it. *One wild spell could be a fluke, but two? Aimed directly at me?*

Connor searched the stadium. Some of the crowd glanced his way with mild curiosity or concern, but most of them remained enthralled by the duels, either cheering for Van or calling for the next match to begin. No one seemed particularly interested in a minor accident, especially when no one got hurt.

"Something isn't right. How come that's only happening to us? Every other spell has been blocked, no problem."

"You still think someone is after you?" Garrett whispered.

"I still think you're paranoid," Ninette said.

Connor tried to shrug off his suspicions as the next match began. Codie stepped lightly onto the field, strawberry-blonde hair tied back tight and an open-backed top fully exposing her winged arms. The petite harpy girl jumped high in the air and glided to the center of the stadium. Nothing about her screamed "fighter," neither her size, nor her demeanor, but then Connor remembered something.

"I recognize her from orientation. I had never seen a Harpy before. She's just a sophomore, right? And she made second singles?"

"Then she must be good. See? Maybe we do have a chance," Ninette said, then covered her mouth after realizing she'd spoken out loud.

Codie flapped her wings and launched into the air to circle over her opponent. Every beat of her powerful wings rained down feather-shaped icicles, but they bounced harmlessly off a shield. Her opponent retaliated with a storm of wind and sharpened leaves, but she blew it back at him with her own, more powerful gusts. Gale-force winds slowly pushed him, step by step, toward the wall.

The Point Loma boy dug in his heels and raised his hands to the sky. Clouds gathered in angry clumps. Thunder rumbled. Codie dodged as lightning struck. Bolts continued to lance down from the skies, forcing Codie into an evasive pattern. Several strikes conjoined into the form of a bird. The animal shrieked and chased Codie, who faltered and wheeled around. The boy capitalized on her distraction and nicked her with a blast of arctic air, chilling one of her wings numb. She cried out in shock and surprise, and pinwheeled out of the sky. The crowd gasped when she hit the ground. The ref hurried to her side for first aid, but she made it to her feet, albeit unsteadily, and the match was called for Point Loma.

"The score stands at three matches for Point Loma and two for Mattson. All ties are settled by the winner of the first singles match, so this is it. Give it up once again for your captain, James Radimus!" The announcer roared over the speakers.

The crowd went wild. Everyone rose to their feet, roared approval, and pumped their fists in the air. Connor couldn't help but join them. This was the moment he'd waited for since he first saw James in the hallway. He hadn't even known that the boy was captain, but it made sense. How could he not be with the way people reacted to him? Someone that good, that talented—that was who Connor wanted to be.

I need to watch every move he makes.

James walked out with his hands in his pockets. His eyes were on the crowd, not the foe before him. His opponent, short even by dwarf standards, looked better prepared: feet set, hands up, eyes only for the Mattson captain. The whistle blew.

James waited. He waved to the crowd. He yawned. He turned his back on his foe and stretched in an exaggerated display of boredom. She did not rise to the bait but prepared several spells at once. Globes of flame and stone swirled around her waiting to be launched. She lobbed a fireball at James's back, and it exploded harmlessly against his shield. She tossed another, but this time it was a feint; the real attack coming from below. A sharp upward thrust of earth tossed James in the air. He used the spell like a springboard, flipping and catching himself mid-air, hovering above the fireball.

He turned and faced her.

"Not bad." He hopped down and waved her attack away. "What else you got?"

The dwarf bared her teeth. She conjured a streamer of flame from one hand. It circled halfway around the arena before taking the shape of a dragon. She placed her other hand on the ground which rumbled violently until a dragon of stone launched itself into the air and then back underground. Tremors and cracks appeared on the field as the spell burrowed through the ground toward James.

"Whoa," murmured Connor.

"What's with all the animals?" Garrett asked.

Connor noticed him leaning into the action once more and smiled. "It's a Point Loma thing. They study a lot of Nature Magic and animal spirits."

"I thought they did yoga," Ninette said absently.

"That, too. All the schools have specialties."

Garrett pulled a notebook out of his bag and scribbled down notes. "I didn't know yoga was magic. What does Mattson specialize in?"

Connor scratched his head. "I don't actually know."

The dragons circled and jumped around James, keeping him contained while pelting him with fire and stone. But he stayed calm, relaxed even, as his shield held off the continuous assault—until the dragons converged on him. Right before they smashed together James dropped through the ground and disappeared beneath the explosion of rock and fire.

His foe looked around frantically but didn't see him rise behind her. He appeared from her shadow as if it were a hole in the ground. In one clean movement, he dislocated her shoulder and kicked out her knee. She cried out and blasted the ground behind her, but he wasn't there. She wreathed herself in flame to purge the nearby shadows. James reappeared from the shadows on the other end of the stadium.

"You can concede any time you want." He walked toward her, hands back in his pockets as if nothing had happened.

"No chance," she growled. With her good hand, she whipped fireball after fireball at James, but he stopped them all, using small shields to deflect the spells and send them flying off in all directions.

"You don't think," Connor started, but a few of the flames floated down directly on top of him. Ninette grabbed his drink and tossed it into the air. She and Connor waved their hands to spread the liquid into a protective dome to extinguish the fire.

"I don't think you're paranoid anymore. No," Ninette said, "something isn't right."

James pressed forward. The dwarf continued her assault, each fireball smaller than the last. James smiled and, placing both hands together, let loose a blast of water. The torrent doused her flames and pinned her into the arena wall. The girl struggled but couldn't get away. She sucked down water when she tried to breathe. She tried to tap out against the wall, but the water trapped her arms. Finally, her coach intervened to surrender.

"Victory for James! Victory for Mattson!" the announcer blared. "An impressive display of Shadow Magic set the stage for a decisive strike. Congrats to our Manticores for a phenomenal come-from-behind win."

"Did you see that? He was amazing," Connor cheered. "She was, too, but, I mean, she didn't stand a chance."

"He's a jerk," Ninette spat. "He didn't have to break her arm."

"I thought you wanted to hit people," Connor argued. He couldn't believe she wasn't impressed. "People get hurt in duels."

"Yeah, but not like that." She clenched her fists, and the veins on her arms popped out. "He knew he could win. He should have ended it."

"I think you're jealous," Connor taunted.

Ninette whirled on him, ready to protest, but Garrett cried out to intervene.

"I think you're both forgetting we almost died today. Again." He fixed the two of them with a frustrated glare.

Connor and Ninette stared at Garrett, mouths hanging open. Their arguments died in their throats. He had a point. Their frustration evaporated into giddy smiles, and they settled back into their seats.

"Mr. Masters held the shield on our side. We should ask him what happened," Connor suggested.

Mr. Masters' gaudy attire made him easy to find. He was talking to Speck and the referee when they approached. Speck hovered inches from his face waving her stubby finger at him and the goblin ref glared upward with his hands on his hips and his lip curled up in a snarl to reveal pointy, needly teeth.

"…won't happen again. I promise. I swear I had the shield over the whole thing," Masters whined, waving his arms around. "Oh, and here they are. Totally fine." He pointed at the approaching kids and forced a smile. "Are you kids okay?" he whispered to them.

"Actually…"

"We're fine," Connor said, elbowing Garrett. "Just wanted to know what happened."

"I don't know. Everything seemed fine. Worked everywhere else. You weren't doing anything weird, were you?"

"You're blaming us?" Ninette said incredulously.

"No, no, of course not. Well, you're fine. That's what counts. Shouldn't you be heading back?"

"But we wanted to know more about—" Connor began.

"To your rooms," Speck boomed. Her deep voice was starkly at odds with her childish frame, but the threatening tone, combined with the skulls on her jewelry, lent extra weight to the command. "The duel is over. You've no more need to be out here."

Turning to leave, they passed an elf with black hair and facial piercings.

"Hey, I remember him," Garrett hissed. "He summoned some creepy spider thing at orientation. Master Borodin got pretty upset, remember?"

"He got in trouble for summoning something?" Ninette said. "And you just remembered that?"

"I've had a lot to process," Garrett protested.

"Didn't Master Borodin say the spider drank blood?" Connor whispered.

Ninette smacked Connor on the back of the head. "You *really* forgot *that*?"

Connor's face burned red. "It's been an exciting few weeks?" he suggested pitifully.

"Hey, look," Garrett whispered, pointing behind them.

The boy slipped some crumpled papers to Mr. Masters, who pocketed them and sent the boy on his way.

"That's weird, right?"

"You mean that the kid that summoned a blood-drinking spider talked to the teacher that almost let us get fried, days after a blood-drinking monster attacked someone, and then another monster almost fries you?" Ninette rolled her eyes.

"Definitely weird," Connor agreed. "I remember now, his name is Farrun something. We'll have to see what we can find out about him."

Connor rolled around in his bed, wrestling with the excitement of the first school duel and the stress of knowing one of his classmates might be trying to kill him. Neither was conducive to sleep.

Did I see Farrun that night? he wondered. *I don't remember. What did I see? Was it worth killing me over?*

Connor's head thundered from a pressure—like being deep underwater. He shook it clear. Everything went black. He pushed himself up on a beach—a black beach. He couldn't see anything. Sand crunched beneath his bare feet, and waves crashed against the inky shore. The water stretched out before him. An ocean of shadows.

"This is the same dream. This is the same bad dream, and any minute now, I'll wake up."

He touched his cheek and remembered the scratch.

But he didn't wake up. Time crept by at an abysmal pace. He finally decided to move, walking away from the water; something about the sound of the waves unnerved him. He hadn't gone far when the gritty sand gave way to cold black dirt, and unseen leaves brushed at his arms and face. He kept going, continuing in a straight line away from the eerie ocean. His head pounded more and more as he went. He heard voices not far ahead. His heart froze, gripped by a fear of discovery.

"YOU WILL BE DONE SOON," rasped a familiar voice.

The voice from my dream, Connor thought.

"Soon is relative. I'll be done when I'm done," responded a male voice.

"UNACCEPTABLE. YOU WANT OUR KNOWLEDGE. OUR POWER. YOU KNOW THE PRICE."

"Look, I don't need to draw any more attention." The voice sounded calm but annoyed.

"YOU DID NOT MENTION DISCOVERY."

"Just some kid. He won't be a problem for long."

Connor stepped back. A dry branch snapped under his foot. The sound was an explosion in his ear. He knew the voices heard him. He turned to run, but something grabbed him around the waist and hauled him off over its shoulder, dragging him in a hectic dash through the trees.

"Hey, let go!"

"YOU WISH TO LEAVE?" an echoing voice snarled in his ear.

"Obviously, yes!" Connor cried back.

Whatever held him stopped running and hurled Connor through the air. He landed so hard the breath was forced from his lungs. He sat up, gasping for breath, twisted in the sheets of his bed.

"I don't think these are dreams," Connor whispered.

Chapter 7

Magic 101 – Farsight
Farsight uses a faint essence copy to extend a Magi's sight to near-limitless ranges. Adepts in the skill give the appearance of clairvoyance, and, in some ways, it's not so different. They did, in fact, see it coming.

"Have you ever had a dream like that?"

"Oooh! Scaaarrry!" a ghastly voice wailed. Ninette tried not to laugh but failed miserably. "I'm sorry. It's just hard to take you seriously with all of this going on." She pointed to the wailing apparition.

As October rolled in, Halloween hit Mattson Academy like a haunted freight train. Perpetual twilight loomed in the park—the only light a spectral green glow. The ponds transformed into bubbling, murky swamps. The trees became bare and menacing, shifting in time with a silent breeze. Worst of all, a rank fog with a mind of its own pervaded the area, coalescing into ghostly forms that would occasionally moan and shriek.

"It's obnoxious," Connor complained. "But seriously, have you?"

"I haven't," said Garrett. "You're sure they threatened you? The human voice?"

"Positive."

Garrett looked over his shoulder as if expecting to be threatened himself. Getting used to the idea of magic had been hard enough. The possibility that someone might intentionally hurt him with it hadn't crossed his mind. He shivered as a chill ran down his spine.

"You should tell a teacher."

"Good idea," Ninette said, rolling her eyes. "Just march into the headmistress's office and say, 'Hey, I dreamed some other kid wants to kill me. Can you expel them, please?' I'm sure she'll jump right on it."

"I thought maybe they'd know something," Garrett said quietly.

"No, Ninette's right." Connor ducked under another pass of the fog. "Besides, I already told her we saw a kid doing the summoning. It's not like this is really new information."

He didn't add that the dreams felt dark, and not just literally. They felt wrong, and if he was controlling them somehow, even unintentionally, he wasn't sure he wanted the teachers to know. Not unless they absolutely had to.

Connor pushed the thoughts from his mind.

"We need to get proof first. I just don't know how."

"You saw this Farrun kid at the summoning demo, right?" Ninette asked. "Do you know anyone taking summoning?"

Garrett and Connor shook their heads. The three sat silently in the jagged shadow of a barren tree, wondering what to do when an announcement came over the PA.

"Happy Halloween! I encourage you to get in the spirit by partaking in seasonal events this weekend. Please find schedules posted around the school, or simply ask for directions."

Garrett's round eyes brightened, and he jumped up and looked at Connor and Ninette hopefully. They glanced at each other, and Connor broke out an eager smile. It wasn't like they would solve the mystery that morning. A little Halloween fun couldn't hurt. They followed him into barely recognizable hallways. Jack-o'-lanterns lined the halls, singing songs and cackling. Skeletons stood vigil, waving and beaming gap-toothed grins. The haunted fog groaned here as well, much to Connor's chagrin.

"Whose idea do you think that was?"

"Speck the Bonecrusher, of course!" giggled a nearby skeleton.

Connor jumped back and yelped, bumping into Ninette.

"Do you enjoy crashing into people?" Ninette shoved him back to his feet with a playful grin.

They joined a throng of students crowded around a screen boasting the list of seasonal activities. The events included candy conjuring, costume creation, seasonal creature care, and pumpkin enchanting.

"That last one sounds neat," Garrett said, smiling. "I'm getting pretty good at enchanting."

Ninette squinted at the screen and shook her head.

"Lady Ariel? Count me out."

Unable to convince Ninette, Connor and Garrett walked to Ariel's classroom, weaving around the thick webs—spiders included—and bouncing pumpkins hopping about the hallway. They arrived to find the class nearly full. Lady Ariel perched atop her worktable, legs dangling above the floor. She had ditched her practical overalls and apron for an orange sweater and black slacks, and seemed to be more relaxed than usual.

One of the last students to enter had a familiar face.

"That's him, right?" Garrett gasped. "Farrun Wallus?"

Connor nodded as the sour elf scurried in, grunted an apology to Lady Ariel for being late, and grabbed a seat behind them. He dressed like a bad impression of a punk rocker. He sported a torn-up denim vest covered top to bottom in iron-on patches, several mismatched chain necklaces. He even had a few facial piercings and spiky blue hair.

"Yeah, that's him. I wish we sat in back," Connor grumbled. "I can't watch him."

"You don't think he's going to do anything here, do you?" Garrett sat stiff-backed in his chair.

"Okay, class," Lady Ariel announced. "We're enchanting pumpkins, which you appear to be lacking. I don't believe many of you have met my fellow instructor, Soarra Witherroot."

She waved half-heartedly to an elf standing next to her. The woman was the most beautiful person Connor had ever seen. Ms. Witherroot had a round face with pink cheeks and a tiny nose. Platinum blonde hair trailed all the way down to her feet, with leaves and flowers strung throughout it. The dainty elf padded on her toes across the front of Lady Ariel's desk and shyly waved at the class.

"Um, good morning," she breathed. "So, you needed pumpkins?"

Ms. Witherroot tapped her finger on her lips and reached into a small leather pouch hanging off her belt. She pulled out a handful of seeds and tossed them up. They hung suspended in the air as Soarra made a series of slow, deliberate gestures, and the seeds sprouted into bulbous, lumpy pumpkins in a matter of seconds. Then they kept inflating. One of them burst, showering stringy pulp on a handful of students.

"Oh, goodness. I'm sorry," she mumbled. Her cheeks turned from pink to scarlet.

"Thank you, Soarra!" Ariel interjected, taking her by the shoulders and shoving her out of the classroom. "Looks like she made enough, regardless. Next, you'll need to carve them. Bear in mind that the carving can affect the enchantment. Happy faces make for happy pumpkins."

"That can't be right," Connor said to Garrett. "Can't we enchant them however we want? I'm making a scary face."

"I wouldn't," Garrett urged. "The material always affects the enchantment. That's rule number one." He shuddered at each of Connor's aggressive stabs into the orange canvas.

Connor stepped back, pleased with the fanged monstrosity glaring back at him. Garrett carved a dopey grin into his. Connor thought he had the meanest-looking pumpkin, until he looked at Farrun's—it bore the terrifying face of an eight-eyed beast with a hideous mouth full of spiny teeth.

"Enchanting starts with Will Magic," Ariel lectured. "You need to imprint the behavior from your own mind into the pumpkin. The stronger the imprint, the longer the enchantment will last."

Connor took the pumpkin into his hands. His knuckles whitened from his tight grip. He leaned in closer until his forehead brushed against the cool husk. The glaring face remained inanimate.

"C'mon, laugh, dammit," he muttered.

"Why did you make it so scary?" Garrett took one look at the gruesome expression on Connor's pumpkin and shuddered.

Connor ignored him. He looked his pumpkin in the eyes; it looked back at him—and winked.

"Huh?"

The pumpkin wriggled out of his hands and dropped to the ground. It growled at him, then bit his leg. Connor cried out, trying to kick it off. The pumpkin rolled away, laughing maniacally. Garrett covered his mouth and tried in vain not to laugh as well. All around the room, the other pumpkins sprang to life. Many giggled and shook but did little else, while some growled or shouted "Boo!" Lady Ariel's sang a lively tune, and she stood on her desk and sang with it.

Connor and Garrett heard a repulsive crack from the table behind them.

Farrun's pumpkin split open, its sides peeling outward to form eight spindly legs. It skittered to one end of his table, then another, before leaping onto his shoulders and chittering in his ear.

"Gross," Connor said. "Guy has got a thing for spiders, I guess."

"Spiders freak me out." Garrett gagged. His jack-o'-lantern mirrored his disgust, scrunching its eyes shut and making a gargling sound from within its hollow center. "You know how they eat, right? They liquefy your insides and drink it. Kind of like…"

Connor pretended to barf and nodded.

"He did summon a magical spider with an absurd amount of teeth."

"They're called mandibles."

"Teeth, mandibles, whatever. That girl was bitten by something with too many bite-y bits. We're following him after class." Connor was on to something. He knew it.

Ariel dismissed the class, but pockets of students lingered, awaiting her review of their work. Farrun lurked in the back of the class with his pumpkin-spider dangling from a web made of pulp. Garrett kept Connor between him and the horrid creature—the sight of it made his throat tight and threatened to bring up his lunch. When Ariel got to the two of them, she gave Garrett's pumpkin an approving pat.

"It mimics you perfectly, Mr. Clarke," she observed. "Was that your intent?"

"Sort of?" Garrett blushed, and the pumpkin turned a deeper orange. "I just wanted it to be friendly."

"Indeed," she murmured, stroking her chin. "I expect you will continue enchanting with me for the foreseeable future. Mr. McTaggart," she said, kicking away Connor's rolling menace. "I doubt this to be the first or last time you hear this, but greater caution and closer adherence to the instructions will serve you well." She furrowed her brow and flicked her wrist. Connor's pumpkin gave a final, defiant cackle before falling silent.

Behind them, Farrun took down his stringy spiderweb, collected his pumpkin back onto his shoulder, and said goodbye to Lady Ariel before ducking out the door.

"Absolutely, Lady Ariel. We gotta go, though. Right, Garrett?" Connor insisted, elbowing Garrett hard.

"Oh, right."

Garrett's pumpkin sighed.

"Can I leave him here and get him later, Lady Ariel?"

Ariel frowned disapprovingly at Connor but nodded as Connor dragged Garrett away.

The halls teemed with students excited to show off their projects. Many wore enchanted clothing that glowed or moved on its own. Others pulled candy out of thin air, munching away. Connor and Garrett kept a few steps behind Farrun to avoid notice. He was easy to follow thanks to the twenty-pound orange spider on his back and the wide berth the chittering gourd bought him.

"You didn't tell me you were so good at enchanting," Connor whispered.

"I just do what Lady Ariel says." Garrett avoided Connor's eyes.

"You're doing it better than anyone else, apparently. It's cool." Connor gave Garrett a playful shove.

Garrett finally met his eyes and smiled weakly.

Ahead of them, Farrun slipped inside a classroom and closed the door behind him. Connor and Garrett followed, lingering across the hall, and trying to look casual. They waited for several minutes, watching costumed classmates come and go, but no one else entered or left the classroom.

Connor pointed to the nameplate next to the door. "That's Mr. Masters' class. Something definitely is up with those two."

"But what are we supposed to do? We can't go in there."

"Why not? It's just a classroom. Middle of the day on a Saturday. No reason we can't pop in." Connor didn't wait for Garrett to argue and crossed the hall, but he hesitated at the door.

"Excuse me?"

Behind him stood Mr. Masters in a Halloween-themed Hawaiian shirt.

"Oh, uh, hey. Hi, Mr. Masters. I, um, wanted to see what you were doing today. I like your shirt," Connor stammered.

"Thanks," Mr. Masters said, "but this activity is full. Sorry." He paused to look Garrett up and down. Mr. Masters scratched his chin but ultimately shook his head "no" and slipped into his room.

Connor caught only a glimpse of a few serious-looking students seated around a table, dozens of papers splayed before them, and then the door slammed shut. He reached out for the door handle, then let his hand fall to his side. He knew there would be no point in trying to force his way in, and even if he did, there were so many people in there. The papers itched in his mind. What could they be? Farrun had slipped one to Mr. Masters as well. They had to be important.

"What do we do now?" Garrett asked. He leaned back against the lockers across the hall and let out a long sigh hoping Connor didn't have an answer.

Connor's eyes bore into the closed door. "We need a way in there."

Ninette retied her scarf and reached for her towel. The order was an intentional habit, even when alone. By now, almost everyone at school knew she was half-mermaid; anyone who knew anything about Merfolk could probably figure it out based on her teeth alone, but keeping her gills covered made her comfortable. She could at least pretend no one knew. After toweling off her hair, she wrapped herself and stepped out of the shower to inspect her teeth in the mirror.

"Ugh, fish bones."

She had enjoyed her quiet morning. She ate by herself, went back to bed for an hour, then hit the gym to lift weights. It was nearly empty, exactly how she liked it. Any morning she could get to herself was a good morning. Even with the whole ocean at her disposal, she could never get away from her full-blooded cousins unless she hid in her room. Huddled alone in a dark, damp cave wasn't exactly peaceful and relaxing.

"At least since that stupid dance, most people are keeping their distance," she chuckled. "I guess seeing how hard a mer-girl can punch will do that."

Still, Connor and Garrett were never far, and with them came Julian, Vern, and even Carrie. There were more friends than Ninette was used to, which proved overwhelming at times. Quiet mornings were a nice break.

The bathroom door opened, and Codie strolled in, humming to herself in her lilting voice. The contagious tune tugged a genuine smile out of Ninette.

"I didn't know you did that. Smile, I mean," Codie laughed. "You always look so serious in the gym."

"Yeah, well. The stink-eye keeps people out of my business."

Codie noticed Ninette's scarf and wrinkled her nose. "Most people here aren't like that. They don't look twice at girls like us," Codie added, fluffing her wings for emphasis. "You shouldn't hide it."

"Merfolk have it a little different."

"Well, suit yourself. But if you ever need to talk…"

Codie waited and watched her for a response. Ninette shifted her feet and silently turned back to the mirror to resume picking her teeth. Behind her, Codie opened one of the stalls and shrieked. The shrill sound pounded at Ninette's eardrums, and she squeezed her hands over her ears. One after another, the mirrors along the wall shattered into tiny pieces.

"You okay over there?" Ninette asked, barely able to hear her own voice over the ringing in her ears.

"There's something in there," Codie squealed. She fluttered back toward Ninette but never took her eyes off the slightly cracked stall door.

"Something in the toilet?"

Codie stared at the stall with big, unblinking blue eyes. "It had gross yellow eyes and a weird, hairy head. It-it tried to grab me."

Ninette tightened her towel and took careful, quiet steps toward the stall. Codie's bottom lip trembled, and she looked at Ninette with wide, pleading eyes. Ninette raised her finger to her lips and slowly grasped the handle. She flung open the door, and there, peering back at her from the toilet bowl, were sickly pale eyes under a tangled mat of sopping black hair.

"Yuck!" Ninette shouted, and fire leaped from her hands, detonating the toilet and leaving a spurting pipe in its place. Porcelain and tile rained down over her. Her hands aflame, she searched for any sign of the *thing*. Nothing remained but the ruined plumbing.

"I told you! What was that?"

"It was gross, whatever it was." Ninette peered inside the stall but found nothing—no hair, no footprints, no proof other than her skin still crawling from the feeling of those eyes on her.

The bathroom door burst open, and the two of them both jumped and spun to face it. Icy feathers swirled around Codie, all pointed at the door, and twin fireballs burst to life in Ninette's hands. Sheena stalked inside and brushed past them to look at the stall, then glared up at Ninette, hands on her hips.

"Did you do this?"

"Yeah, I did. There was a—" said Ninette.

"You shook half the school, you oaf. What, did you see a bug or something?"

"Excuse me? What is your problem?"

"My problem is you. Bad enough I have to ignore you in class. I shouldn't have to put up with you on the weekends, too."

"Listen, you stuck up, little—"

"It was a monster," Codie interjected. "Something in there tried to grab me. Ninette saw it, too."

All annoyance dropped off Sheena's face, and she went back into the stall, stooping down near the pipes and inspecting the floor. She placed her hands on the stall walls and looked up at the ceiling. Unsatisfied with what she found, Sheena stalked out, grumbling to herself while checking the other stalls, too. Ninette and Codie glanced at each other and shrugged. After completing her investigation, Sheena rounded on the other two girls with a barrage of questions.

"What did it look like? How big was it? Did it cast any spells? Did it touch either of you?"

Ninette could only gape in silence, but Codie tried to answer the barrage of questions.

"I didn't really see much. Just yellow eyes and black hair. I don't think it cast any spells, but we don't know where it went."

Sheena surveyed the destruction again, then stabbed Ninette in the chest with a well-manicured fingernail. "Why didn't you freeze it?"

"Huh?"

"Is your brain waterlogged? I've seen you freeze things. If you caught it, I could have figured out who summoned it!"

Ninette clenched her fists. She loomed over Sheena, bringing all her size and weight to bear. "I can think of something I'd like to freeze. Don't worry. The next time there's a gross monster lurking in the toilets, I'll be sure to ask him to wait while I fetch you from afternoon tea."

Sheena huffed. "You'd be better off if you did." She stormed out. The growing crowd, drawn by the commotion, parted to let her pass, as the semi-celebrity expected.

"She sure is pleasant," Codie giggled.

"She's a pain in the butt."

"Ninette! Ninette, are you okay?" A concerned voice called out over the general chaos.

Ninette peered over her amassing classmates and saw Connor and Garrett waving. Only then did it dawn on her: she was wearing nothing but a towel.

"Dammit, Connor, this is the girls' bathroom! Go away, I'll be out in a second!"

Ninette raked her fingers through her hair and sighed. She and Codie turned around and took a moment to fully appreciate the damage she'd done. The stall walls bent outward from the jagged hole in the ground. Water pooled on the floor and the remains of the toilet were scattered in a thousand pieces all around. Codie covered her mouth and giggled. She rested her slender hand on Ninette's shoulder.

"You're not half bad," she laughed. "I mean, you really let that toilet have it. Would you want to spar with me sometime? It would be good blocking practice if nothing else."

Ninette shrugged but forced an uncomfortable smile and went in search of her clothes.

Connor and Garrett were sitting on a bench under a peach tree when she approached them.

"You guys missed out. While you played with pumpkins, I got to see a monster," she boasted. "Sort of."

"Was it a spider?" Garrett asked.

"No. Why would you think that?" Ninette shuddered. "Ugh, I hate spiders."

"Farrun Wallus definitely has a thing for spiders," Connor explained. "He made a creepy spider-pumpkin today, and then went to Mr. Masters' classroom. Masters wouldn't let us join the activity though. We need to find a way in and figure out what's going on."

"Let's just bust into his classroom tonight. Maybe we'll find something there." Ninette rolled her neck and stretched.

"Isn't there a curfew?" Garrett protested. He fidgeted with his hands. "What if we get caught?"

"Detention isn't so bad," Ninette said, wrapping an arm around Garrett. "But, and hear me out, what if we don't get caught?"

They did.

"I thought you had more sense than these two, Garrett," Lady Ariel said sternly.

She watched them trim the hedges—by hand—for the entirety of the following day. She didn't allow breaks.

"I hate you both so much," Garrett grumbled, rubbing his shoulders.

"Well, now we know Lady Ariel patrols the floor at night. We won't make that mistake again," Connor said, undeterred.

"We could also try and catch the monsters," Ninette suggested. "We think they're after you anyway, right? That rich, brat Sheena said if she caught one alive, she could figure out who summoned it. A teacher could probably do the same."

"That's a good plan B," said Connor, "but it also involves me being bait which I am less than enthusiastic about. We'll figure something out and try again."

Garrett groaned.

On Monday, Ms. Ramona Ruiz stood at the front of the class, leaning against Seer Brokk's desk, and chatting with the Will instructor. The raven-haired teacher wore a fitted black turtleneck, slim black slacks, and a silver, chain necklace, putting her in stark contrast with Brokk's ratty attire. She had a well-earned reputation as one of the strictest teachers at Mattson, so Connor was surprised to see an uncharacteristic smile replace her usually grim expression.

"How long were you talking to the skeleton?" she teased Brokk.

"Foolishness! Blasted Speck and her tricks. I will show her when next we—" His ears twitched as he became aware of the entering students and never finished the threat. "To your seats!

"Halloween is a fool's holiday. Pure human ridiculousness. An entire season of trickery and deceit. No student of mine will be caught unawares. You have learned to use your Will to affect the world around you. Today you will use it to affect yourself. Using your essence, you will amplify your senses. You will hear a fly land on the wall in the next room. You will smell the fresh-cut grass of the atrium from across the school. You will see over miles and around corners. Vigilance in the extreme."

"He's going to teach us to see?" someone whispered.

"No, I am not going to teach you to see," Brokk snarled. "You, I am going to teach tact. The rest of you will learn from Ms. Ruiz."

"There are two skills," she said, sauntering to the front of the class. "Farsight and enhanced sight. Farsight allows you to see as though you were standing somewhere else, usually far away. Get it?"

No one laughed, but Ms. Ruiz didn't care. "Enhanced sight amplifies your eyes where you currently stand. I'll demonstrate both."

Ms. Ruiz placed her fingertips together and opened her eyes wide, as if to fill her face. Her dark irises expanded, leaving no white remaining.

"I can see Ms. Crowton is texting her father about skipping introductory-level classes. If you didn't feel me looking over your shoulder, girl, then perhaps you should rethink that."

Sheena's jaw dropped. She grumbled under her breath and crammed her phone back into her purse, then huffed and crossed her arms, at least pretending to pay attention.

"What's to stop someone from seeing into our rooms? Or the girls' bathroom?" Gemma said. She wrapped her arms around herself and eyed her male classmates.

"There are wards in place to prevent such things," Ms. Ruiz stated casually. "To exercise Farsight, you need to have a reasonable memory of where you wish to 'stand' assuming you cannot see it. I trust none of the young men in here are so knowledgeable." She glared at the class with her dark eyes narrowed and her lips pressed tight in a hard line. "Back on task. Enhanced sight."

Ms. Ruiz turned on Brokk's screen and brought up a diagram. It showed a stick figure with his hands on either side of his head. In front of him, a glowing brick bounced up and down in the air. This elicited a few chuckles.

"Don't laugh. That's what some of you look like. What you're doing with telekinesis is wrapping objects with your essence to control them. With enhanced sight, you do the same thing with your eyes."

Ms. Ruiz widened her eyes again. This time they turned solid white.

"I can see the grain on your desks, all the dirt and hair on the floor, and I know more about the pores on your faces than anyone would ever care to."

Connor concentrated on the pool of essence inside of him and took hold of the roiling source of magic, almost second nature after a month of practice. While he held it, he imagined himself standing in the back corner of the room. His perception of the classroom blurred and suddenly, he was looking at the backs of his classmates' heads. He could even see the back of his *own* head. He pictured himself up in the corner of the ceiling at the front of the class. Again, a blur, and then he was there, looking down at Brokk's desk. He glanced over at his seat and saw himself still sitting there with solid black eyes. A stack of papers on the teacher's desk gave him an idea.

Connor tried the other half of the lesson, the enhanced sight. He shrouded his eyes in essence, feeling his magical energy wrapped around them. Even though his eyes were back with his body, the effect still worked: he could see the papers on the desk clearly—except they were all in braille. The essence vibrated around his eyes.

He hadn't expected to feel it physically affecting him, but it led to another thought. He released the magic, and his perspective whipped back to his body in a dizzying blur of color and motion.

"Seer Brokk?" He called out. "If we can use our essence on ourselves, could we use it on someone else, too?"

"You speak of hexing. The headmistress teaches such a class." The bell rang, and Brokk called for attention. "You will thank Ms. Ruiz properly for her assistance. Tomorrow, we move on to enhanced hearing and smell. I will resume your instruction. Dismissed."

Connor asked Headmistress Mine about hexing as soon as he got to history, but she brushed him off, saying it was a sophomore-level class. Her Halloween lesson embraced the season, in opposition to Brokk's bitter rejection.

"Mattson Academy was founded by witches, my ancestor among them. Much of the portrayal of witchcraft you see today is a commercialized derivative of the truth. Witches, vampires, ghosts, and more all have a basis in reality. I wish to share those stories with you."

"Headmistress, are you saying ghosts are real?" Garrett asked.

The class burst into laughter, but the Headmistress didn't join in, waiting for silence before proceeding.

"It is a valid question and one worth exploring. In a literal sense, no. What most people experience as hauntings are mischief-making pixies and faeries. There is another phenomenon—what we call Essence Echoes.

"Every living being has some measure of essence. We cast spells by focusing our essence on a certain purpose. Even those who don't know how to control their essence, or don't have enough to cast spells, sometimes leave an imprint of it when they die. There is no sentience, but it's enough to leave an impression of some strong memory or feeling. Something important to them at the time of their death. It is the dying gasp of their essence—an echo."

"Headmistress, if these echoes are actually made of essence, could we use them for our spells?" Gemma asked. "Just like anything else in nature, right?"

The headmistress's lips pressed together in a firm line. When she spoke, it was in a taut, tense voice, as sharp as a blade.

"You have just defined Necromancy. Using the dead's essence is an utter ethical and moral violation. Furthermore, to do so is incredibly dangerous. Your essence is as much a part of you as your DNA. To mix in another would change who YOU are. You would become an abomination, something unnatural."

Chapter 8

A History of the Folk – Ancient Ones
Most Folk outlive humans, and most magic users live even longer. Beings who transcend even these exceptional bounds, like the Lady of the Lake, are classified as Ancient Ones. The longest-living Ancient One was Herrereor, the first dragon, slain after a life of over one hundred million years. According to the dragons, anyway.

Connor's head dipped and his eyes fluttered open and shut. He fought down a yawn and braced himself against the cafeteria table to avoid face-planting in his pancakes.

"You look like crap," Ninette observed.

"You could have tried a little harder at Farsight so we could take turns."

Hoping to improve their chances of a successful sneak-out, Connor had stayed up late using Farsight to watch the atrium. Lady Ariel patrolled every night, and Ms. Ruiz, Master Borodin, and Coach Kalett all took turns as well. He never saw more than one at a time, but he suspected another might be lurking. If they ever stopped patrolling, it was after Connor passed out from exhaustion. Even worse, more than once he saw Farrun and several other students returning to their rooms well after curfew. Each presented a note to the teacher on duty and got past without any trouble.

"We know Mr. Masters is involved," Garrett said. "He's probably writing them the pass."

"Ninette's plan is sounding better and better." Connor yawned and forced himself up so he could eat. "Except we have no idea when the next attack will be. Nothing's happened for weeks." Connor slapped his face to perk up. "At least we have the duel at Merlin Academy this week."

"How can you think about dueling right now?" Garrett groaned.

"He's always thinking about dueling," Ninette said.

"I'm still planning on trying out for the team. Also, learning some new tricks might come in handy if we end up fighting a monster again," Connor added. "Besides, this week, we get to go to England. You have to be excited about that."

"I guess." Garrett sighed and poked at his breakfast. "Just, at the last duel, we almost got blown up."

"Mr. Masters won't be doing the shields this time," Ninette pointed out. "Besides, now we're ready."

On the day of the duel, the three of them loitered outside the school, enjoying the crisp afternoon. Garrett sat against the stone walls with a book in hand while

Connor and Ninette passed a fireball back and forth. A steady procession of their classmates headed toward the stadium where Master Borodin waited with a portal. Through the tear in space, a torchlit, cobblestone path led up a hill to a shadowy, foreboding stadium.

"Remind me why we're waiting?" Garrett said.

"We might see Farrun," Ninette explained. "He was at the last duel, too. Easier to follow him than try to find him in the crowd." She amped up the size of the fireball and tossed it more forcefully at Connor. "Up for some sparring?"

"Sure."

Connor ducked under the blazing sphere and chuckled at the cries of surprise from behind him. Several of his classmates scattered and jumped to avoid getting singed.

They stepped off the path and put space between them. Garrett scooched further away. Ninette led off, shaping a fireball with her hands, expanding it to her full arm span and then launching it. The spell ground to a halt a foot in front of Connor. He twitched his fingers to help split his concentration, dividing the orange sphere into three smaller ones he sent zipping around toward Ninette from all directions.

"Stop taking my spells!"

"Stop letting me."

The projectiles landed harmlessly around Ninette, but Connor wasn't done. Using wind, he lifted Ninette up into the air and suspended her upside down, a trick picked up from Lady Ariel.

"Oh, now you're in for it," Ninette growled.

The ground opened and Connor dropped into a shallow pit. He lost his concentration, and Ninette fell on her head.

"That's awesome, you guys!" Codie chirped.

She and the entire Mattson team stood by Garrett, some even applauding.

"I hope you try out next semester."

"You mean it?" Connor clambered out of the ditch, smiling ear-to-ear.

"Yeah," Van said. He tossed his shaggy hair and flashed a toothy grin. "Fresh competition never hurts."

"You better watch out, Van," James laughed, jostling his friend. "Another fire specialist might be competition for *you*."

Van's jaw dropped—that hadn't occurred to him.

"And a counter spell should never be underestimated," James added. He raised his voice and eyed his team. "We've got this. Assuming we don't forfeit by being late. Let's roll."

"Good luck, guys," Connor called after them. He waved at them until they were well out of sight, imagining himself in one of the team jackets. It looked good.

Farrun was one of the last students to come out of the school. He slunk with his hands in his pockets and a dark hoodie pulled over his head, but Connor caught a glimmer of his piercings in the fading light. They followed him through the portal, and Garrett gasped when confronted with the Merlin Academy dueling stadium.

The towering edifice of stone stacked on titanic stone climbed high into the night. Smoky bonfires burned bright behind fortified turrets, and Mattson banners flapped proudly in the night air, alternating with the royal purple and yellow of the Merlin Sages.

"Told you it'd be worth the trip," Connor whispered.

They secured seats a few rows behind Farrun, and the tension in Garrett's shoulders eased slightly once they had their target securely in their sights. Connor and Ninette alternated glances between Farrun and the field, but Garrett's eyes were always on Farrun. The elf didn't make any sudden movements or do anything suspicious, and after a few minutes, Garrett settled back into his seat and released the breath he'd be unconsciously holding.

"How come their stadium isn't made of grass?" Garrett asked.

The dueling area resembled Mattson's in size, but instead of well-manicured grass, the field was a shallow pit of loose sand.

"There's no standard field. As long as it's equal for both sides, anything goes," Connor explained. "I saw a water stadium on TV once, lots of big lily pads floating around for the duelists to stand on."

"Sounds like my kind of field," Ninette said.

The teams paraded out and met in the center. The captains shook hands to the fanfare of the Merlin Academy Band. Mattson wore their standard varsity jackets, and the Merlin team wore flowing robes with starry patterns in the school's colors, matched by similarly patterned, conical hats that flopped down to the side.

"I can't believe they actually wear those," Ninette said. "You wouldn't catch me in a goofy bathrobe."

"I think they're kind of cool," Garrett murmured. "That's what I assumed wizards looked like until a few weeks ago."

The first three matches were a blur of action. A dwarf and faerie team used mushroom spores to daze and confuse the Mattson duo, followed up by eruptions of flame from underground. The Mattson second doubles used blinding flashes of light to get behind their foes, wrapping them up in ice and pelting them with a storm of small spells. First doubles kept their cool this time, using wild winds to keep the Merlin duo, both orcs, off-kilter. The Mattson girls dodged sandblasts and lightning bolts with ease and secured an easy win.

Connor stretched at half-time but had no intention of going anywhere. He didn't want to miss a thing, and they had to keep watch on Farrun. Except Farrun barely stirred either, so Connor took a moment to take in his surroundings.

The gray stones making up the coliseum were cracked and mossy. The seating was comprised of rows and rows of ancient wooden benches warped and smoothed by centuries of spectators. He swept his eyes over the crowd and caught a glimpse of the silhouette of the school in the night sky. Merlin Academy's dark spires pierced the night sky from their clifftop perch. The castle had stood since the Middle Ages, and countless Magi had walked its halls in the intervening years. Halls they shared with…

"Hey, isn't Excalibur supposed to be here?" he asked.

Garrett stared at Connor blankly.

"What do you mean Excalibur?"

"You know. Excalibur," Connor said. "It's the one you're thinking of."

"Right, but it's just a myth."

"Like mermaids?" Ninette teased. She playfully messed up Garrett's hair.

Garrett wrestled her away, all the while wearing a good-natured smile.

"Fine. But is Excalibur actually real? Like, we could go see it?"

"I dunno where it is," Connor said. "Hush, the matches are starting back up."

Van's opponent was a mer-boy, even taller than Ninette. He wore a scarf over his head and face, but the tall, spiked fin on his head stood out regardless. His robes dripped water, leaving a trail in the sandy pit. Van shifted to wolf form and exhaled searing blasts of flame. The mer-boy scrambled to stay away. He never got off a single spell.

Codie's match went similarly well. The girl she fought filled the stadium with lightning, but Codie never left the ground. She enhanced her speed with Wind Magic and dodged the strikes, then immobilized her opponent with a storm of wind and ice.

"James is up," Connor grinned. "This should be awesome."

"I still think he's kind of an asshole," Ninette said. "I don't buy the goodie-two-shoes, team captain act. He tortured that girl last month."

"Guys," Garrett said.

"You play to win, right?" Connor argued. He waved away her concern and tried to pay attention to the field. "She was talented. He didn't want to give her an opening."

"Guys?"

"I'm saying I don't like the way he duels. If you duel like that, I won't like it on you either."

Garrett nudged them both and pointed to the vacant seat. "Guys, Farrun is gone."

"Why didn't you say something sooner?" Ninette jumped up and looked around, ignoring calls from behind to get out of the way. "Damn. Black hoodie doesn't exactly stand out."

Connor pointed to a hooded figure leaving the arena. "Is that him?"

"Let's follow him."

Ninette grabbed Garrett despite his weak protests. Connor looked down in the direction Farrun went, then back to the dueling field. James stepped out, cleaning his glasses while the other team captain hammed it up for the fans.

"But James's match," Connor protested.

"Seriously?"

Outside, the grounds were completely abandoned. The trio stepped out into the night and down the uneven, cobblestone path toward the school. It loomed high above, a jagged shadow perched on a clifftop. Behind them, a cheer rocked the stadium. Connor grumbled but hurried onward.

Farrun walked briskly up the path to the castle, never bothering to look behind him. Connor and his friends stayed as far back as they could without losing sight of him. The torchlight along the path flickered and jumped. More than once, Ninette turned to make sure Garrett was still following.

Where Mattson sprawled, Merlin Academy climbed; heavy stones as tall as Connor stacked high into the cloudy night. Spires branched off at odd heights and angles, creating the impression of a chaotic candelabra—an image enhanced by the hundreds of small lights glowing in the tower windows. A stained-oak drawbridge spanned an empty moat, and a high-arched entryway, rusted portcullis raised high, stood dark on the other side.

"A moat? Seriously?" Ninette said under her breath.

"I like it." Connor smiled. "There he goes." Connor pointed at their hooded quarry. "Walking right in."

"Then so are we. Come on."

More torches hung in high sconces along the walls. Cool, stagnant air permeated the ancient halls. Their footsteps echoed as the three crept quietly after the elf. The walls were adorned with life-sized oil paintings of severe men and wise women, their unblinking vigil a presence all its own.

Farrun kept up his hurried pace, turning down side passages until he came to a small, iron door. For the first time, he checked around him for followers, but he thought himself alone and slipped through the door, shutting it behind him without a sound.

"How does he know where he's going?" Connor wondered.

"Maybe he's been here before?" Garrett said.

Connor narrowed his eyes at the door. "He's looking for something, and he knows where to find it."

"Stop gabbing." Ninette shoved the other two along. "We've waited long enough. Let's see what he's after."

Through the door, a cramped spiral staircase led in one direction: down. Far below, a bobbing light danced upon the walls. They tiptoed after, using the faint glimmer to avoid a nasty fall. Each step was carved into the wall, worn down in the center from ages of use. The air grew mustier the further they went. The creak of a door was the only warning before the light winked out.

They froze, afraid to take another step. Ninette conjured a globe of flame to get them safely to the bottom, where they eased open the rickety, wooden door and emerged into a narrow, unlit hallway, but Farrun's light glowed far ahead. Ninette let hers dissipate before continuing their pursuit. Bare stone walls pressed tight on either side—broken up by something much worse.

"These are dungeons," Garrett said when they passed the first set of iron grates. He ran his fingers along the bars, surprised to find they were deeply etched. As his fingertips traced the shapes of the grooves, his eyes lit up with recognition, and he gasped, "The bars have runes on them. These are Magi dungeons. Why does a school have dungeons? Does our school have dungeons?"

Garrett's breathing accelerated until Connor took him by the shoulders.

"Calm down, dude. Think about it: if a student got out of hand, especially a powerful one, you gotta put them somewhere, right?" Connor looked into the nearest cell; a cramped room mostly filled by the narrow cot along the wall. "Besides, look at the dust. These things haven't been used in forever. I'm sure it's a last resort."

"Yeah, probably only if a student brings in monsters to eat their classmates," Ninette cheered mockingly with a sarcastic thumbs-up. Her fake smile fell away, and she pointed down into the gloom. "He must have found what he's after. The light stopped."

They came to a final open door and peeked inside. Farrun stood at the center of a circular room. A warm presence filled the space—something tickled against the boundaries of their minds.

At the center of the room, the hilt of a sword jutted out of a pile of rubble.

"Excalibur," Farrun murmured. "With this, surely…"

He took one step forward. Then another. He approached the sword as if it were a wild animal. Mustering his courage, he reached out with both hands and braced himself with a foot against the stones. He pulled once, twice, but it refused to budge.

"Come to try your luck?" A melodic voice floated through the air from behind them.

Garrett yelped, and Connor and Ninette both spun around to face the new arrival. Farrun turned and did a double take at the sight of the speaker and his classmates.

The speaker stood patiently behind Connor and Ninette. Flowing white robes clung to her slender frame. Her skin was marble, her eyes pearl, and her long, unbound hair shimmered like mercury. She approached the sword as silently as she had appeared behind them.

"It is inevitable. My own students have usually given up by this time of year, but the duels always bring aspirants. For what purpose do you seek the sword?" Her voice echoed in the small room, her own personal choir.

"Who are you?" Farrun asked.

"The White Woman. The Lady of the Lake. Nimue. I have held many names over the centuries. Today most simply call me 'Headmistress.'"

A smile, barely perceptible, touched the corners of her mouth. She beckoned Connor and the others to join her in the chamber. A mural wrapped around the circular room, covering floor to ceiling with scenes of battles, throne rooms, weddings, and funerals. All with one thing in common: the sword.

"Can I try?" Connor asked.

"Dude!" Ninette hissed while Garrett groaned.

"Of course. For what purpose do you seek the sword?"

"Well, I want to be a famous duelist someday. I also suspect someone tried to kill me a few weeks ago." He shot a dirty look at Farrun; Farrun's face remained neutral. "Should help with both, right?"

"Power. It is always power," the Lady sighed.

Connor stepped up to the sword. He gripped the hilt with one hand and pulled, watching his friends for their reactions. It didn't move. He tried again, this time with both hands and his feet set squarely on either side of the weapon. He strained and tugged until he was out of breath but got no better result than Farrun. The sword wouldn't give an inch.

"Anyone else?"

Garrett and Ninette shook their heads.

"Good. Please leave. I detest being down here."

"Didn't you make the sword?" Garrett asked. He pointed to the first scene of the mural, the lady holding the sword amidst a radiant light.

She turned to Garrett, anger glowing white in her eyes, there and gone like a flash of lightning. The afterimage burned into Garrett's mind.

"It's the first picture in the story," he finished quietly.

"I did, and I will forever regret it," she said, withdrawing into herself and retreating to the shadowy corridor. "Wars have been fought over this sword. Countless lives frittered away. Over what? Power. Let me pass on wisdom I wish I possessed a thousand years ago. Seek not power for power's sake. Seek to do good and find power enough."

She left them standing there, slowly walking away, robes fluttering behind her.

"If it's so dangerous, why isn't it better protected?" Ninette shouted. She sounded annoyed at the lecture. "We walked right in here. What if one of us HAD taken it?"

The lady did not stop. "The sword chooses its wielder. When it is ready for another, I suspect there is nothing I can do to stop it."

By the time they got out of the school, the match had ended. Students and families were clearing out—the Merlin kids coming up the hill and the Mattson ones departing through a nearby portal. From the disappointed looks on the faces of the home team, James had taken the final match.

Before entering the portal, Farrun spun around, seething. "Why were you guys following me?"

Connor crossed his arms. "Why were you sneaking off? How did you know where to find Excalibur anyway?"

"None of your business. Just leave me alone." He pulled his hood back up and stalked away, hands in his pockets and shoulders hunched.

"That got us nowhere," Ninette said.

"We know he wanted the sword. What is it really? What does it do?" Garrett asked.

"I don't know," Connor said. "It's an artifact, like my glove. It's obviously powerful. So powerful that even non-magical people know about it. What would he do with it, though?"

"Also, is she really *the* Lady of the Lake? From the story?"

"I don't know why she'd lie," Connor said.

"So, she wasn't being facetious? She's actually over a thousand years old?"

"Why not?" Ninette said. "Merfolk live to two hundred or so. Same with dwarves. Elves longer than that."

"But then what is she?"

Connor and Ninette kept up their impromptu sparring sessions as much for fun as for the preparation, and the results showed. By the end of October, Connor's strengths were on full display—as were his weaknesses. No amount of class or practice resulted in the ability to create magical elements out of thin air. He could use them as he pleased, even co-opt others' spells, but when left to his own devices, he found only emptiness and frustration.

"It's not fair," he complained as he walked into Professor Skreed's class on Halloween day.

"Sounds like first-world problems to me," Julian said. Garrett's roommate brushed crumbs off his tattered denim jacket and sighed. "I still haven't been able to gain any ground with anything but… ground."

The others responded with facepalms and groans of disgust.

"Seriously, bro. You've got something cool going on, and everyone sees it but you."

"He's right," Vern agreed. His voice was stern and serious.

After almost two months of living among elves, Connor was getting used to reading the emotion in their solid, black eyes. Vern's narrow slits broadcasted obvious annoyance.

"You've shown talent with lightning, fire, water, wind, and earth. More than any other in our class." The elf swirled fire in his palm, then snapped his fist closed again. "You should not complain."

"I guess," Connor grumbled.

It didn't feel like magic. It almost felt like stealing. Whatever it was, it didn't feel like *he* was the one doing it, and that sucked.

Candles burned on each student's desk in the eerily dark classroom. Shadows climbed the walls like tiny claws scrabbling to gain purchase. A dense swatch of darkness stretched out from behind the professor's desk, elongating until it reached the head of the class, where it rose and took shape, forming into Professor Skreed dressed in a tuxedo and top hat.

"Who's ready to learn Shadow Magic?" he said. "It's not evil, though it certainly holds that reputation. But who among us does not cast a shadow? They are as much a part of us as any other."

"But, sir," said Gemma, hand waving in the air. "Aren't shadows the opposite of light?"

"No," he said with a vigorous shake of his head. "A shadow can only exist where there is light, but it can also only be banished by light. It is a unique relationship and the focus of our lesson today."

He tasked the class with manipulating shadows. The students created shadows in different areas of the room using different light sources. They made shadows larger or smaller, and all manner of shapes. The professor challenged them to eliminate all the shadows from the room, but even with candles blazing, the darkness remained.

Ninette growled, igniting her entire desk, and her neighbors', but she couldn't chase away the last of the lingering darkness.

Connor amused himself by making shadow puppets on the wall—dog, cat, rabbit, bird—and didn't notice the professor join him.

This isn't even magic, he thought. *Aren't we supposed to be controlling the shadows?*

A single black feather fluttered down from the avian shape, and the bird leaped off the wall and into the classroom. The slick, black apparition zipped around Connor's stunned classmates, weaving around flickering lights before flying straight through Connor's chest.

"Nicely done, my boy. Could you do it again?" Professor Skreed asked. He leaned over Connor's shoulder and pointed to the wall, watching it with a twinkle in his graying eyes.

Connor twisted his hands and fingers into the shape of a dog, but this time he really paid attention to it. The form on the wall smoothed from that of his conjoined fingers into something truly resembling a dog. Then it grew. And grew. Connor gasped and a smile spread across his face. The dog filled the wall, looked out at the class, and a low growl echoed in Connor's head. Professor Skreed clapped, and the lights came on. The students cried out in surprise, and when Connor's eyes adjusted, the shadow dog was gone.

"Shadows are slippery," the old elf said. He dimmed the lights and re-lit the candles with a flick of his fingers. Dark reflections of the students danced on the walls around them. "Think of every dark mood you've felt. We use the word 'dark' for a reason. We all have shadows within us as well."

"I thought you said Shadow Magic wasn't evil," Garrett said, eyeing his own shadow and leaning away from it.

"Shadows are not evil," Skreed responded, his voice taking on a strange, low tone and rhythmic cadence. "We seek cool shade on a hot day. When we are sad or ill, we seek the solace of silence and darkness. The shadows soothe us." He stood tall and raised his voice, gesturing with vigor. "Our darker emotions can be put to great purpose. Anger can grant strength. Bitterness can become resolve. Fear. Fear is the foundation of bravery."

The bell rang, but no one got up. The professor settled down and returned to his normal posture and voice, and folded his hands behind his back.

"It is all a question of perspective." He half-smiled, and his eyes twinkled with the reflection of the candles. His shadow flickered on the wall behind him, waving cheerfully to the students while the Professor remained utterly, perfectly still. "Class dismissed."

Chapter 9

Elemental Magicks – Fire
Fire has long been the key to man's survival. It is a powerful tool, short in natural supply but quick to self-propagate. Equally useful for creation and destruction, lesson number one of Fire Magic is not burning yourself.

Headmistress Leorra Mine's history class huddled together in small groups along the gravel path between the school and the stadium. The wide-open space on the side of the hill offered little shelter from the brisk November air; a cold breeze kicked up leaves and pierced coats. The sun hid behind racing gray clouds, befouling the students' moods as they waited for their instructor. Connor and Garrett stood close together, shivering.

"Wimps." Ninette stood apart, stoic in a light windbreaker.

"We can't all be used to ocean floor temperatures, can we?" Connor shot back.

Ninette opened her mouth, retort ready, but a tap on the shoulder distracted her. She looked behind her and found no one there. Another tap, and she spun the other way. Connor and Garrett burst into giggles.

"How did you do that?"

"He tapped you with your shadow." Garrett covered his mouth to hide his smile.

Connor had doubled down on his shadow spellwork after finding out he could create shadows. He could give them tangibility, and found all sorts of ways to practice this newfound skill, much to his friends' dismay.

"I'm going to tap you with my fist in a minute," Ninette sneered. A subtle smile emerged.

While Connor and Ninette needled each other, Garrett caught himself looking at the forest on the horizon.

This is where the vesporcus attacked Connor, Garrett thought. *It's the first thing I thought about when we came out here, but those two aren't worried. Hopefully, it left and never comes back.*

He shivered again and caught the other two staring in the same direction. Connor patted his back pocket; the fingers of the focus glove stuck out. Some of the tension in Garrett's shoulders melted away, and he turned his back on the shadowy woods.

"Here comes the headmistress," Garrett pointed out.

Leorra walked down the path side by side with James, chatting amicably. He smiled and laughed and even clapped her on the shoulder, more like he was conversing with an old friend than the head of the school, and she seemed similarly at ease with the dueling captain.

"Good morning, class. Today we will be taking a field trip to Atlantis. Mr. Radimus has kindly offered to create our portal there as practice for his ongoing studies."

"Isn't Atlantis underwater?" Connor asked.

There were more than a few snickers at this, none louder than Sheena. She stood a healthy distance away from the others, wrapped tight in a pink, fur-lined parka. When he made eye contact, she rolled her eyes dramatically and looked away.

"There's a dome over it," Garrett whispered.

"Yes, Mr. McTaggart, much of the old city *is* underwater, but if you did your reading last night, as Mr. Clarke has, you would know the inner city has been restored and is domed to provide oxygen for the inhabitants. For the rest of our expedition," she paused and twirled her finger.

Nothing happened that Connor could see, but his ears popped.

"What you cannot see is that we are surrounded by a bubble of air, completely pressurized to keep us dry and breathing on our journey. Mr. Radimus?"

James smiled and snapped his fingers. A portal ripped open between him and the class, revealing a dark, cobblestone road glowing with faint patterns of swirling light filtering down from far above.

"Have fun, kids," he said with a wave.

"I thought portals were supposed to be hard," Ninette said. "He snapped it open. Literally."

"I thought so, too." Connor gawked at the magical opening and his eyes drifted unconsciously to the young man who created it with such ease.

Leorra gestured to the class to follow her through the portal. Connor stepped through the opening and into a dreamscape. Faint rays of sunlight cascaded down to dance along the stone street. A procession of stone columns bordered the path, some standing and some crumbled down to nothing. Strange algae crept across the stone, casting a ghastly green glow over the area. A shining, bronze gate stretched between the final two pillars with climbing ivy wrought across its surface. Beyond it, the city shone bright against the ocean murk.

To his left and right, the ocean faded into deeper darkness. The waters were held at bay beyond the path, but curious schools of fish swam up to the edge and peered at the travelers before continuing on their way. Shifting shadows of larger creatures swam among the ruins of the ancient structures. Connor saw movement out of the corner of his eye, something fast and gray, but when he turned, he saw only fish and open ocean.

"Did you see that?"

"I see sharks," Garrett murmured. His eyes darted all around.

Connor looked closer and made out the distinct dorsal fins on some of the larger shadows patrolling alongside the path.

"Sharks aren't so bad," Ninette scoffed. "Little swat on the nose, and they'll leave you alone."

"You've punched a shark?" Garrett gasped in disbelief.

Ninette looked away and crossed her arms defiantly. "I wish. But that's what my old man always says. How tough can it be?"

The class approached the gate and beheld the city. Where the path they walked was rough and worn, covered with slime and sea waste, before them the stone sparkled a brilliant white. Incandescent globes hung from lamp posts to flood the streets with light. The gates swung open without a sound.

"Welcome to Atlantis," Leorra announced, facing the class. "Current population: about two hundred. The city was founded around 4000 BC. It contains the first recorded instances of humans intentionally harnessing magic and studying its use. The first and only Magocracy; its ruler was selected based on strength of essence and granted the title of Grand Magus."

She walked backward through the main avenue with a relaxed and practiced gait.

"The dome is projected by artifacts brought here after explorers rediscovered the city in 1922. Since then, it has been home primarily to academics and service personnel."

She gestured to an open-air pavilion, a tiered pit set in the center surrounded by ornate golden statues of trees, the canopies of which formed a roof of silver branches and leaves.

"This is believed to have been the first school of magic. The structure, as well as much of what remains of the city, was forged out of Will alone over hundreds of years. The city rests upon intersections of ley lines— natural veins of raw essence within the planet.

"Scholars of magic debated theory and practice to all who would hear it. We loosely follow a similar model today; you spend a year or two learning the basics, during which time we hope your natural skillsets emerge, and then we can direct you to the subjects at which you will excel." She descended the stairs into the center of the amphitheater. "Here, whenever a Magi puzzled out some new spell or ability, he would book his time as lecturer and instruct any willing to learn.

"As time went on, the people of Atlantis became obsessed. They were no longer satisfied with their natural limits. They devoted all their resources to finding external sources of essence. Children born without 'enough' magic were cast out of the city."

"Think you'd make the cut?" Sheena whispered to Garrett in a venomous tone.

Garrett sidled closer to Connor and tried to ignore her. Ninette reached out to grab Sheena by the coat, but a brief look from Leorra stopped her. The headmistress went on without missing a beat.

"Their pursuits led to the discovery of certain gems that provide subtle boosts in magical power, many used in artifacts today. They were the first to discover and use ley lines. Some recovered texts indicate their scholars believed there were dimensions of pure essence, waiting beyond the veil to be tapped for our use, much like we use the elements of our world."

They exited the other side of the theater, and the headmistress paused as they approached an intersection in the road. To the right, it wound deeper into the city, but to the left, it ended in a jagged tear in the street framed by two houses split down the middle. The dome ended just beyond. Seaweed idled in the current-worn and rounded foundations—the remains of an entire city district—stretched across an endless desert of seabed.

Connor stared at the ruined structures. "What happened?"

"We have guesses," the headmistress answered, "but nothing concrete. Most speculate that the Atlanteans opened too many portals to other realms, and the sheer concentration of conflicting energies destabilized the whole region, causing its collapse into the ocean.

"Your assignment today is to explore both the domed part of the city and the extant ruins. The only thing off-limits is the Grand Magus's palace. There are dangerous, unstable magics still at work there.

Otherwise, roam to your heart's content. I expect a report by the end of the week with a comparison of the architecture of the city as compared to its less magic-centric contemporaries, with an emphasis on functionality." She put her hands on her hips and adopted a matter-of-fact tone. "Now, who believes they can cast the air bubble spell I demonstrated earlier?"

Six students raised their hands, Connor among them, and they took turns demonstrating the spell to the headmistress. After each received her approval, she split the class into groups. Connor, Ninette, and Garrett clumped themselves together as quickly as possible. One unfortunate group was stuck with the headmistress as none of them could perform the spell to her satisfaction. That left Sheena. While her celebrity status had been exciting at the start of the year, her abrasive nature had done little to earn her any friends, and the prospect of being in a small group with the spoiled heiress left her the odd girl out.

"Ms. Crowton, you have a choice to make. Make it. I am eager to be off."

Sheena looked back and forth between Connor's group and the headmistress's. The gears of her mind ground as she calculated the lesser of two evils. She opened her mouth to protest, but all that came out was a frustrated squeak. Finally, she stomped over to stand with, but clearly apart from, Connor and his friends. She turned her back to them and gave a haughty huff. Ninette shot Connor a panicked look, but Connor had no answers.

"We meet back in one hour at the pavilion. I advise you not to wander too far from the dome. It's not a pleasant swim." She waved her arms to usher the groups of students away and then headed down a side street with her own group in tow.

"Where should we go?" Garrett asked. "It might be cool to find a market or something. Somewhere a lot of people would have gathered?"

"There has to be a dueling stadium, right?" Ninette suggested. "I mean, these dudes loved magic so much, they probably liked to show off."

"Pedestrian," Sheena yawned. "Shops and stadiums? Please."

"You have a better idea, princess?" Ninette growled.

"Obviously. We're going to the palace."

"The headmistress just told us it wasn't safe," Garrett whined. "Why would you want to go there?"

"In another time and place, I suspect my family would be living there," Sheena boasted. "The Magocracy. Can you imagine it? Talent for leadership instead of... whatever we have."

"There's probably a good reason it was the only one." Ninette pointed toward the nearest edge of the dome and to the ruins beyond. "Looks like a real big win for the Grand Magus. Come on, let's go see some stores or whatever so we can write our papers and get out of here."

"I don't know," Connor dragged out his words. "I mean, the palace would be cool. There's got to be some really old, powerful stuff there."

Sheena's lips turned up into a mischievous half-smile. "Maybe you're not as boring as you look."

"The headmistress said there was unstable magic there." Garrett tugged at Connor's sleeve. "That can't be safe. In fact, she explicitly said it wasn't."

"Magic isn't safe," Sheena sneered. She prodded Garrett on the shoulder. "I didn't see you sniveling when you got to play with lightning. I'm sure there's an ancient potted plant or something else you can take notes on."

"You can't seriously be giving in to her," Ninette hissed in Connor's ear. "She acts like a spoiled brat, and now we're just going to do what she wants? Hell no."

"You don't want to see the palace?" Connor whispered back.

"I didn't say that. I… ugh." Ninette balled up her fists and shoved them in her pockets. "She better knock off the attitude."

They followed the main avenue through the city. Elaborate manors with swirling conical spires earned only the barest glances. Sheena set her eyes on the palace and strode quickly in that direction, hurrying the others with snippy comments whenever they fell behind. Each structure they passed was crawling with archaeologists and tourists, but the closer to the edge of the dome they got, the fewer people they saw. The street went all the way to the palace walls, but the protective dome ended just short. They stopped at the edge; all eyes turned to Connor. He closed his eyes, took a deep breath, and tried to perceive the oxygen around him. A swirl of air whipped around the foursome, and he snapped it into place with an audible pop.

"Let's mosey." Connor tried to sound more confident than he felt. He forced himself to stand up straighter and set his shoulders back.

He took the first step through the dome—trying to subtly hold his breath, just in case. Somewhat sure his bubble would hold, he motioned the others to join him. He silently congratulated himself on not drowning everyone and continued forward. The main gate hung limp off a single hinge, but the walls stood strong. Mosaics, depicting historical scenes of Atlantean accomplishments, were displayed prominently on either side of the ruined entrance: On one side, a cluster of Magi built the trees comprising the school; on the other, a figure dressed in multi-hued robes, with his face hidden in the deep shadows of a cowl, held a carved white staff—its head twisted and warped around three spheres.

"If we're not supposed to be here, shouldn't there be guards or something?" Garrett asked.

"Exactly." Sheena slapped him on the back; the shock made him stumble. "If it was *really* bad, there'd be someone here to keep us out."

They followed her into the remains of a garden. The effects of time only served to enhance its beauty. The marble statues of regal men and women, blanketed with algae and seaweed, stood sentinel over the remains of flower beds given way to sand and shells and rocky growths of coral. The great silhouette of the palace cast a cold shadow over the once-welcoming space.

"Did you guys see that?" Garrett whispered. "Something moved. Over there." He pointed behind the nearest statue, a bare-chested, headless man who held a thunderbolt in one hand and pointed accusingly with the other.

"You're seeing things," Ninette said. "There are a lot of fish schooling around."

"I swear something moved."

"I think the fish-girl knows a fish when she sees one." Sheena smirked. "Let's keep moving. We don't want to be seen loitering."

They entered a grand foyer with a double staircase curving down from either side of a balcony perched over the open room. Behind it loomed an algae-covered statue of the hooded figure, arms outstretched and a halo of light emanating from behind him. Stagnant, murky water darkened the chamber; more of the pale, green growth along the walls provided the only light, a faint glow.

"That must be the Grand Magus," Garrett said.

All around them sat the remnants of fixtures for tapestries and the frames of pictures, the art long lost to the wear of the salt water and the ebb of the currents. They stayed closely grouped as they climbed the stairs to the second level. A faint light shone at the far end of the shadowy hall.

All of Connor's concentration was on maintaining the bubble, so Ninette lofted a globe of orange flame to light the way. They crept down the dim corridor toward the light. They passed one side passage after another, each consumed by the gloom of the water. Alcoves set into the wall featured vases and other clay sculptures floating above the remains of intricately carved pedestals. Garrett stopped to inspect one but blushed and hurried to catch up when Sheena snickered at him.

The hallway ended and opened into a spacious, circular room. Toppled columns littered the floor, but in the center of the room a throne stood untouched. Connor expanded the bubble until he felt it tremble against the water pressure, and the others spread out to explore.

The throne occupied a broad dais several steps raised from the floor; Connor felt it looming over him no matter where he stood. Behind it, a panoramic window ran the length of the wall. Once it must have been a spectacular view, but now it showed only the eternal twilight of the depths. Around the room, they found traces of finery: crumbled statues, shattered pottery, thin wisps of curtains. The floor was covered with the bones of unusual creatures—whole skeletons arranged in a macabre dance. The walls were carved and decorated with alternating mosaics and pictograms. Garrett traced a decorated column up to the arched ceiling and cried out.

Two sharks swam in lazy circles high overhead, their scarred bellies as pale crescent moons in a slow orbit. For the moment, they seemed content to patrol above, but Connor couldn't help glancing up frequently to make sure they stayed there. Sheena paid them no mind and made straight for the throne.

The heavy seat looked untouched by time and radiated a soft white glow. It was marble carved to look like wood, and its high back branched into representations of the eight elements. Sheena plopped into the seat. She rested her head in her hand along one of the seat's arms and draped one of her legs over the other, the very image of decadent royalty.

"It suits me, right?"

Ninette was thinking of a comeback when she caught the blur of something darting behind the throne.

"I saw it this time." She motioned for Connor to take the opposite side as she crept around the throne.

"You're messing with me," Sheena said. "Guys?"

The two ignored her, and as they were about to converge, something jumped over the back of the throne, landing square on Sheena's head. She screeched and abandoned her perch, leaving the creature to take her place.

It looked like a gray tabby cat—if cats wore tattered, hooded cloaks and Cheshire grins. There was, however, no humor in its yellow eyes. The cat's smile filled its face, and it pointed up in the air. Connor and his friends looked up; the sharks were descending.

"They… they wouldn't. Not into the bubble, right?" Garrett cowered behind Connor.

The cat laughed—a rasping, mirthless hiss. It bared its teeth, and its hackles stood on end. Glittering lights sparkled in its eyes, and it locked gaze with Connor, staring right at him, staring *into* him.

Connor felt a painful pressure inside his head, threatening to crush his brain. Before he could react, his essence was ripped away from him. An unseen force wrenched open his mental grip on the air bubble protecting them. The walls of air vanished, and the ocean collapsed onto the four of them, plunging them into darkness penetrated only by the searing yellow of the cat's eyes and the terrible whiteness of its smile.

Chapter 10

> The Creature Compendium - Grimmalkin
> Native to Scotland, the Grimmalkin is an omen of ill luck, doubly so for Magi. These intelligent, toddler-sized cats emit an essence-dampening aura that makes using Magic nigh-impossible. They are known to kill for essence and for fun.

Pressure crushed Connor's body. His lungs burned. He was vaguely aware of someone thrashing nearby. He tried to recreate the air bubble, but any thoughts of magic were like a TV with no signal—the harder he concentrated, the louder the static buzzed. He was running out of time. Something abrasive jostled him. With his lungs screaming and his mind growing dim, Connor remembered the focus glove waiting in his back pocket. He snatched it and slipped it on, and the black depths exploded into a world of colors.

He saw the rich blue of the ocean. He could see his friends, glowing outlines of them anyway, and the sharks as well. Garrett flailed his arms while Ninette deftly swam to position herself between the sharks and her friends. Sheena floated, unmoving, her light fainter than the others. The sharks slid calmly between them, one of them prodded Sheena with its nose; she remained motionless. A bright light from below caught Connor's eye.

Down below the floor, a hot, white rift vented scorching light upwards. In the distance were others like it, occasionally crossing this one's path, their intersections a fountain of lights and colors he could never have described even if he tried.

Most apparent in this world of color was the cat. The creature consumed the light, and everything around it faded to shades of gray. The cat's eyes were no longer yellow but deep black, abyssal pools sucking in light, and emitting tendrils of black energy. The beautiful rainbow of essence surrounding Connor flowed directly into those two black holes. He looked down at his hands and body—devoid of color as well—and found tendrils latched onto him.

With the edges of his vision going dark, Connor's mind settled lazily onto the white lights beneath him. The light comforted him, and he thought how nice it would feel to be closer to it. He reached out to it with body and mind, and searing heat coursed through him, shocking him back to wakefulness. With the aid of the glove, he saw a tether of light connect him to the ley-line below, and he became aware of a new source of essence within himself. He tried again to concentrate, grasping at that pool of power. He recast the air barrier, and this time it worked. He fell to his hands and knees on the stone floor, gasping for air. A second later, he heard a loud thud followed by annoyed muttering.

"Ninette! Can you give me a light?"

"What do you think I'm trying to do?" A brief flicker showed Ninette's face screwed into a grimace. She tried twice more. "I can't get it going. I can barely feel my essence."

It's doing something to our magic, Connor thought. *Ninette can't see the ley lines. She must not be able to use them.* They needed a fire, and he knew he couldn't make it himself, but…

"Try again," he urged.

Another flash sparked out of Ninette's palm, but before it went out, Connor grabbed it, connecting the white light from his body to the flame. The little light roared, painting the throne room in chaotic orange and red. Connor swooned, and his stomach turned, but he held tight to both spells. The cat still occupied the throne, sitting in its own smaller bubble. It stared at Connor and furrowed its furry eyebrows. Garrett paddled into the bubble, stumbling to his feet in the awkward transition from swimming to walking. He spat seawater and fell to his knees, whimpering and trembling. All the color drained from his face and his eyes were wide and full of fear. The flickering light revealed Sheena floating lifelessly, circled by the sharks.

"Grab her!" Connor called out.

Ninette dove headfirst into the water, and Connor gawked at the speed of her movements. She outpaced the sharks and reached Sheena in seconds. One shark swooped in close, and, true to her word, Ninette wound up and punched it hard in the snout. The shark snapped back, and Ninette recoiled. The two predators tightened their circle; both fixated on the livelier Ninette. Connor tried to expand the bubble to reach the girls, but it butted up against the dead area around the cat.

"I can't get it any closer!"

Ninette wrapped one arm around Sheena. She tried to move, but the sharks kept cutting her off. She flicked the wrist on her free hand once, twice, but nothing happened. Connor tried to cast a third spell, but between the air bubble, the fire, and the increasingly painful pounding in his head, it fizzled out.

"Garrett, you need to do something," Connor said.

Garrett didn't react at first, didn't move, didn't breathe. Then he shook his head, looking from Connor to the two girls to the sharks. He clenched his fists, and a few sparks of electricity crackled around him. Both sharks reacted instantly, circling away from the girls and directly toward Garrett. They stopped short of the bubble, fins cutting into the open air, and doubled back.

"What did you do?" Connor asked.

"They… they… hunt by…" Garrett sucked down air. "They hunt by sensing electromagnetic fields. I thought I could distract them."

Ninette burst back into the bubble, hoisting Sheena onto her shoulders. The cat stood up and stretched but never broke eye contact with Connor. It licked its lips and hopped off the throne. Connor's bubble faded when the cat approached. Water trickled in around the edges.

"Run!" Connor shouted.

He took the lead back down the corridor. The sharks followed closely behind, with the cat on their heels.

"Garrett, stop whatever you're doing!"

"I did!"

"Then explain that!" Connor pointed to the end of the hall.

Blocking their exit was another shark, so huge it nearly filled the hallway. It lunged straight for them, its teeth big enough to count. Connor skidded to a halt at the nearest offshoot from the main hall.

"This way."

The others scrambled after him, Sheena bouncing on Ninette's shoulder and Garrett bringing up the rear.

"She's not breathing," Garrett urged.

They continued down the narrow tunnel; the scratchy breathing of the cat echoed behind them. The way ended abruptly, cut off by a collapsed wall. Turning around, Connor increased the light. It illuminated the giant shark careening toward them. The only other option was a steep staircase spiraling deeper into the blackness.

"Hold on," Ninette said. She stepped between the boys and the shark.

With her free hand, she made a fist and pounded the wall beside the doorway. The ancient stone crumbled. Sand and gravel poured in from the outside, partially blocking the way back.

"We're trapped!" Garrett moaned.

"Yeah, but the shark is stuck over there," Ninette said. "Let's go!"

They descended the mossy stairwell. In the bowels of the palace, the darkness pressed in on them, resisting the light of the flame. They emerged into a narrow hall lacking the upper level's remnants of posh decorations. The few doorways they passed were long since caved in. They slowed to a brisk walk, searching for a safe place to stop. The floor was uneven, the sand having forced its way through eroded walls, and they were forced to move single file. Motes of debris floated in the water around them, catching the light and making it hard to see farther ahead.

The static in his head had gone, but Connor's temples throbbed. The hall sat directly over a ley line, and more of them snaked in from other directions. All the vivid colors strained his eyes, but his mind felt sharper than ever. The tunnel terminated abruptly at an intersection of three ley lines, a wellspring of unbearable color only Connor could see. He removed the focus glove, and the psychedelic lights receded into the murky ocean depths. He stayed above one of the lines and hung onto the warmth in his stomach to ensure the bubble remained.

The room was larger than he expected, almost as big as the throne room, but the walls were bare. A circle of stone tiles, big enough for a king-sized bed with room to spare, raised up from the floor. The tiles were eroded and covered with algae, but the remnants of pictograms remained. As Connor blinked away the last of the light, he realized the ley lines intersected at the circle's center.

Back the way they came, he saw nothing but darkness. "I think we have a minute. Can you help her?"

Ninette laid Sheena down. "Do either of you know CPR?"

The boys shook their heads. Ninette cringed before taking a deep breath and placing her mouth over Sheena's, forcing air into the unconscious girl's lungs, and beginning chest compressions.

"Why do you know it?" Garrett asked incredulously. "Mermaids can't drown, can they?"

"We all learn it." Ninette continued the rhythmic compressions. "Race relations thing. Humans don't like us, remember? Saving drowning idiots is kind of a freebie."

After a few moments, Sheena came to with a jolt, coughed up mouthfuls of salt water, and rolled to her side, continuing to retch. Garrett helped her to her knees, and they told her what happened.

"The ley lines saved us," Connor said. "Something about that cat kept me from casting any spells until I found them. That's why the bubble dropped."

"I can feel them." Sheena placed her palm flat on the floor and shuddered. "My skin is crawling. You don't feel it?"

Ninette and Garrett shared a shrug. Sheena looked impatiently at Connor.

"A little? It was easier when I could see them. I know they're here but... but where is here?" he asked, changing the subject.

Sheena crawled over to the tiles at the center of the room. "Give me some light." She ran her fingers along the stones, nose almost scraping the floor as she inspected. "These are runes I've never seen before."

"Runes?" Garrett perked up. "Let me see." He crouched down next to her and traced the lines. He pulled a dripping notebook from his jacket and consulted some notes. "They look sort of like some of the barrier runes we've learned."

Sheena moved further into the circle. "Aha! This I know. There were summoning circles here once. There are bits and pieces left. Not enough for me to make out what they brought, but..." she paused. "Eight circles?"

"I read about that," Connor chimed. "Eighth-level summon, right? Needs seven people, used for..." he trailed off under Sheena's withering glare.

"Yes, I know what it is," she huffed. "What I don't know is why you would want to do it or why you would do it all the way down here. And what are the barrier runes for? Anything that powerful wouldn't need protecting."

"Maybe it wasn't the one being protected," Ninette snorted. "Who cares? I want to know more about that damn cat."

"When it looked at me, my essence was completely blocked," Connor said. "With the glove on, it looked like it was eating the essence around it. The ley lines helped me get the bubble back up, but only barely."

"It's been following us," Garrett said. "But why?"

Connor thought he knew. This cat fit the bill for a level five summon. More proof someone wanted him dead.

Sheena screamed. Glowing yellow eyes leered out of the murk, creeping down the hallway. Connor and Ninette rose—Connor on unsteady legs—taking positions between the cat and the other two. The cat stepped fully into the light. It walked on its hind legs, wrapped in its smaller air bubble. Its gaze pierced Connor's mind causing a haze and exhaustion to wash over him. His bubble wavered. Ninette thrust out her hand and grunted, sending a wave of earth rippling through the ground toward the cat, but the churning stone stopped short of hitting it. The cat looked quizzically at the ground, prodded the upturned floor with a paw, and laughed. Connor tried to freeze the seawater into a spear, but the harder he tried, the more leaks sprang in their protection.

"I'm too tired. I can barely hold this up," he gasped.

The cat took another step toward them. Its aura exuded pressure against the bubble. Connor gave up all pretense of casting another spell. He let the firelight dwindle to almost nothing.

"Out of my way," Sheena sneered, stumbling past him. "Do you have any idea who I am?"

She whipped her hands in a slashing motion, and blades of ice shot through the ocean. Two of them dissipated before connecting, but much to the cat's surprise, one got through, ruffling its whiskers. It hissed at Sheena, looking away from Connor and settling on her. Sheena gasped indignantly and scowled at the cat when her next spell never materialized.

"What did you do to me, furball?"

Connor caught his breath—the noise in his brain reduced to a quiet buzz, and he refortified the bubble. He tried to open his mind to the essence seeping up from the ground below, but the thought of any more magic made him sick. The cat stepped into Connor's bubble. The space became concave, and leaks sprung around the cat; water spreading over the floor and rising.

"What do we do?" Garrett grabbed onto Connor with shaking hands.

The cat stopped and turned away from them. A bright light pierced the gloom. Headmistress Leorra ran into the room, her face flashing from relief at seeing the kids to fear and anger when she looked at the cat. Without a word, she drew a long, thin dagger from her sleeve and flung it at the cat, another appearing in her hand to replace it. The cat crouched low, avoiding the blade, and somersaulted over the headmistress, scratching Leorra's arm. Her light blinked out, and the water flooded over her. The cat gave Connor a wink and scampered away.

If being drenched perturbed the headmistress, she didn't show it. She calmly swam up to Connor's bubble and stepped inside.

"You kids had a more interesting field trip than expected, haven't you?" Her voice dripped with annoyance.

"Headmistress, are you okay?" Garrett asked, letting go of Connor and rushing to her side. "What was that thing?"

"A grimmalkin," Leorra responded. She rubbed her arm where the cat scratched it. The wound didn't look deep, but the headmistress glared at it. "They're faerie cats. They feed on magic. They're also venomous."

The kids gasped and stared at the wound on her arm with wide eyes.

"Calm down. I am in no danger. The venom reduces one's ability to use magic. Much like the field they emit."

"That's why we couldn't hit it," Ninette said.

"And why you used a knife," Sheena added. She pursed her lips, deep in thought.

"Yes. Anyway, I will need your help to return to the city, and I am afraid our trip will last longer than intended. I don't think I'll be opening a portal for some time."

Connor held the air bubble while Garrett helped Sheena walk, and Ninette provided the light. The weary group hobbled back out of the tunnels. There was no trace of sharks or the grimmalkin. Garrett and Connor explained what happened to the headmistress as they walked.

They made it back to the main city dome, and as Connor finally let down the air bubble, exhaustion crashed over him. The absence of adrenaline and ley lines left him completely sapped. He wobbled before catching himself on the side of a building.

"Let me have a look at you," Leorra said, placing her hands on either side of his head and staring deep into his eyes. "You've had a lot more essence rolling through your body than ever before. Most of it came from the ley lines, but it still takes a toll. A good night's rest will be the best thing for it."

Sleep never sounded better, but Connor shook himself awake instead. There would be plenty of time for sleep when they got back.

"Why did it attack us?" Garrett asked the headmistress.

"I don't know why it singled you out. Grimmalkin are native to the Scottish Highlands. They have certainly been seen in other places, but Atlantis is not one of them. I would wager it came with us from the school."

It was almost two hours before the headmistress could gather enough essence to create a portal back to the school. The students marched through, and if some of them were moving a little faster after hearing what happened, no one blamed them for it. The wind howled; the trees swayed violently. Lady Ariel and Mr. Masters waited outside the school, huddled together against the cold. They roused when the portal opened.

"Headmistress, thank goodness you're back," Mr. Masters whimpered. He paused, glancing at the students nearby. "We have a… erm… situation."

Leorra's back stiffened and she pinched the bridge of her nose. "Well, out with it."

"Another student was attacked while you were away," Lady Ariel announced. She lowered her voice. "All blood drained, same as before."

"Rooms. Now. Dinner will be delivered," Leorra shouted.

A few students shifted, but none moved. They looked at their teachers with faces full of unease.

"Now!" Ariel hollered.

Back in the atrium, Connor stopped the others. "The teachers still haven't caught the monsters," he said. "It's up to us to figure this out."

"Figure what out? What the hell are you talking about?" Sheena spat.

"Strange things have been happening since the dance," Garrett elaborated. "Monsters have been attacking students."

"And?"

"You were there! You know what happened. Don't you want to find out who did it?" Connor blurted.

"I almost did. No thanks to you. Now, I just want to stay alive. If you find out who it was, let me know. I have some questions for them." Sheena put her hands on her hips. "All I know is I'm steering clear of you clowns from now on."

She spun on her heel and walked off to her room.

"I saved your life!" Ninette called after her.

Connor caught Ninette's arm. "Let her go. We have bigger issues. You saw who reported the news: Mr. Masters. He has to be involved, and we're going to find out how."

Chapter 11

> Dueling – Rules and Regulations (High School)
> A high school duel consists of six matches—three doubles and three singles. A tie is broken by the captains' match. At this level, referees are quicker to intervene to promote safety, and any intentionally lethal attacks are grounds for immediate disqualification.

Garrett tossed in his bed. His sheets were clammy with sweat, and they twisted in knots around his legs. The night brought no rest, only visions of black ocean water and sidewinding sharks. He rolled to face his clock, groaning at the hour.

I may as well get up at this point. A cold shower before class probably wouldn't hurt.

He gathered his shower stuff and stumbled out of his room into the cool, foggy morning of the atrium. When he woke up at his usual time there were always a few students about, either heading to the bathrooms or enjoying the serene atmosphere of the sparsely occupied park. At this hour there was no one.

He pressed into the boys' bathroom door on autopilot. The door pressed back, and he hit it face first.

"Ow." Garrett pressed the door again. It gave an inch or two, but something blocked it from the other side.

Why would someone leave something heavy right there? He leaned his whole weight against the door but couldn't budge it.

"Hello? Is someone in there?" Garrett pressed his ear to the door to listen and caught only a faint splash followed by utter silence.

"Is someone in there?" he repeated.

"What's up, kid?"

Garrett jumped, catching his yelp in his throat before it got out. Behind him stood James, also carrying a shower kit, and looking almost as disheveled as he was.

"Sorry. Something's blocking the door."

"Huh. Well, let's see what we can do." James leaned his shoulder into the door. His face turned red from the effort, but the door slid, inch by slow inch, making room for Garrett to squeeze inside.

"We need a teacher," Garrett gasped.

"What is it?" James peered inside and hissed through his teeth. "Stay here. I'll find someone."

Without waiting for an answer James sprinted away. Garrett was left alone with the hulking form of Marck, son of Murk. The orc's eyes locked in terror, mouth stuck in a scream, and his entire body frozen in a block of ice.

Seer Brokk stalked the length of the classroom muttering to himself as Garrett arrived. He took his seat by Connor and Ninette and filled them in on what he'd seen, while Brokk growled at the trickle of arriving students and herded them to their desks. When the last student arrived, he slammed his door and spun to address them.

"Son of Murk will be fine," he said, his voice low and lacking his usual dry humor. "He foolishly attempted an ice-block spell—dangerous even to the adept—without knowing how to undo it. Even so, his foolishness may have saved his life."

Brokk balled both his hands into quaking fists. "This will not happen again. Today you learn to defend yourselves. The Shield of Will is a Magi's greatest defensive tool, and the most taxing," he said. "It requires razor-sharp focus. You must believe you are invincible. You must know this beyond doubt."

He turned to Ninette. "Reefwalker. Throw a fireball at me. Your biggest."

"Are you sure?" she asked, giving Connor a sly grin. Ninette's fireballs were growing bigger by the day, and Connor knew she wasn't even giving him her best anymore.

"I am sure." He waited at the head of the class. "I know what you can do."

Ninette stood up, hand lifted behind her back. A spark ignited, then ballooned to the size of a fist, then a beach ball, then kept growing.

"Last chance," Ninette said. She smiled with all of her razor teeth on full display, and the firelight glinted dangerously in her eyes.

"I asked for your biggest."

"You can't even see it!"

"Then make me." Brokk held his hands open in a welcoming gesture.

Ninette's smile warped into grim determination. Her fireball swelled, filling the air, and scorching the floor and nearby desks. The students behind her scrambled out of the way.

"Watch it, you oaf!" Sheena toppled from her seat to avoid being singed.

Ninette didn't notice; the muscles in her forearm strained with effort. She heaved the fireball with a mighty grunt. The miniature sun arced lazily through the classroom and collided with something invisible, inches from Brokk's face. The explosion incinerated everything and swallowed Seer Brokk within its furious light. The blast expanded until it hit another invisible wall short of the first row. Flame and smoke beat at the shield, dazzling the class with waves of red and orange and black.

The explosion subsided, and the smoke cleared to reveal the entire front half of the classroom reduced to a blackened, smoking crater. Nothing remained of the teacher's desk, or even the floor. At the center stood Seer Brokk, a single bead of sweat running down his forehead.

"As you can see, I believed myself invincible, and I was. Negating spells uses much essence. I admit I could not do it again, though, I suspect neither could she."

Ninette gripped her desk for support, but she managed to shrug.

"Pair off. I want you all to be able to do this by the end of the hour." He pointed at Ninette. "You'll work with me. The rest of you use something less destructive than fire. Ice or stone or wind if you can."

Connor and Garrett took turns creating shields and attacking each other. Connor used wind, not wanting to rip up the floor, and Garrett struck back with forked lightning from his fingertips. With every shot, yellow and blue lights crackled around Connor's shield. Connor could feel every hit taxing him, but he held firm against Garrett's attacks and remained unharmed.

"You're getting good," Connor said.

"Thanks." Garrett answered. He blushed and his next spell faltered before it reached Connor. "Lightning feels natural. Back home I was messing up our clocks and TVs, and I accidentally blew up a computer once. It's how the school found me."

They switched roles and Connor lashed out with blades of wind. An audible crack preceded one spell getting through and leaving a small cut in Garrett's shirt.

"Focus, Clarke!" the Seer called from across the room.

It turned out Brokk had spoken with the other teachers to arrange for an extended class session. By the end, no student was left standing, either from sheer exhaustion or the culmination of injuries from failed shields. The bell rang, and the weary teacher dismissed them, urging them to practice the new skill daily.

The trio trudged to lunch, too tired for words. In the cafeteria, the students huddled close over their tables, mumbling to one another. One attack was funny—crazy things could happen at magic school—two was disquieting, but three? Four? Even Connor had to admit learning self-defense was a lot less fun when it felt mandatory.

"When are we going to start looking for this thing?" Ninette said. A deep-fried lunch had perked her up considerably. "I don't want to wait until it finds us."

"Which one?" Connor asked. "Monster pig? Evil cat? Or mystery bloodsucker?"

"Bloodsucker," Ninette said with more certainty than Connor expected. "The pig's in the woods somewhere. We'd never find it. Cat seems like a pain. How am I supposed to fight something I can't blow up? The bloodsucker is here somewhere. I bet that's what Marck saw today. It came after Codie in the bathroom, too. It's in the school. That means we can find it."

"If we don't know what it is, how do we know we can handle it?" Garrett asked. "The cat almost killed all three of us, and even the headmistress couldn't catch it."

"First of all, it only almost killed you two." Ninette flashed a toothy smile. "Second, I'm sure she was just as surprised as we were to see that thing down there. In a fair fight she'd have gotten it. She knew what to do, just didn't have time to do it. Besides, you saw me in Brokk's class," she said, chest puffed out. "He can act tough all he wants. I had him sweating." Ninette crossed her arms over her chest and made a show of flexing her biceps.

"That's flawed logic," Garrett pointed out. "We don't know if brute strength—"

He paled at a glare from Ninette. "Raw strength," he corrected, "would work. We don't know what it is. Besides, something doesn't make sense."

"Lots doesn't make sense," Connor pointed out. "Can you be more specific?"

"It's Sheena. She wanted to catch whoever summoned the monsters. She knew before anyone. Why won't she help us? She must know more than we do."

"Right," Connor agreed. "She might know a better way to find the monsters. I'll ask her in Elements today, then meet up with you after."

Skreed's lesson plan mirrored Brokk's in its immediate practicality.

"I will say freshman year is not usually so… martial in nature, but I suppose it can't be helped." He furnished a sad smile.

He paced the aisles of the classroom with his hands folded behind his back. On either side students practiced erecting walls of stone, ice, fire, and vines. Connor made sure to pair off with Sheena, much to her dismay. The wall spells were easy enough, Connor had created one reflexively when the vesporcus attacked him. He weathered Sheena's hailstorm assault while trying to talk to her.

"So, how did you know someone was summoning that night?" he asked from behind a waist-high barrier of stones.

Sheena wasn't looking at him. Shards of ice flew in a steady stream from one hand while she idly swiped at her phone with the other.

"I told you my family wrote the book on summoning circles. Literally, my great-grandmother wrote the textbook. When you do it a lot, you can feel the essence gathering into the circle before it's even activated—it's a unique essence pattern. Why do you care?"

Connor added more stones to reinforce his wall, but it eroded faster than he could build. "You know exactly why. I think whoever drew the circles sent the grimmalkin after us. I need to find them first. You might be in danger, too."

"Don't care. Obviously, I can handle myself."

"But I know you want to know." He allowed the rocky barrier to fall and threw up his hands to call a roaring gale, redirecting the icy attacks upwards.

"I did want to know, and you blew my chance to find out. My dad doesn't even believe it was a student. He said whoever drew those circles knows their stuff. No kid should be able to do that. I can't even..." Her spell weakened as her voice trailed off.

"Wait, are you... jealous?"

Sheena's face twisted into a scowl. She dropped her phone to the floor and used both hands to collect and shape the frozen shards of her spell into a single, life-sized bull of ice. She thrust her hands forward, and the icy sculpture charged straight through Connor's wind barrier, slamming him in the stomach. He landed flat on his back; all the air burst out of his lungs.

"I need to know who did it. I need to know how. I DON'T need you getting in my way," she huffed, and stomped off.

Connor left class frustrated and sore. He gathered Ninette and Garrett in the atrium and they found a secluded spot near one of the ponds. Garrett propped open a book to work on homework while Connor collapsed in the shade.

While the trees' leaves reflected the changing seasons in their reds and yellows, the sun shone bright through the skylights, and the temperature remained the perfect warmth of late summer. Ninette sat on the edge of the pond with her back to the others and wrapped her arms around her legs. She gazed out over the glassy surface of the pond and sighed.

"She's not going to help," Connor told them. "Our best bet is to keep trying to catch Farrun and Mr. Masters. Until then we don't have a better lead."

"I told you, I think we could find the one that's in here," Ninette argued over her shoulder.

"Where though?"

"The school's not THAT big," she grumbled.

"We'll worry about it tomorrow," Connor insisted. "I'm fried."

"Too fried to practice?" Ninette said, jabbing him in the side.

Garrett groaned. "Do we have to?" He gestured futilely at the books arranged in front of him. "This has been a long day, and I'm still kind of freaking out. Can't we just go to our rooms and study?"

"We need to keep improving if we're going to make the team," Connor protested.

"And something might happen to give us a lead," Ninette added, smiling.

"That's the point. I don't WANT something to happen." Garrett lowered his voice to a whisper. "I'm scared, okay?"

"Anything trying to get you has to get through me." Ninette flexed her biceps and both fists glowed with orange embers. She stuck out her tongue at Connor. "Connor, too, I guess."

"Are you guys getting ready to fight?" A singsong voice called out from across the pond.

Two girls, one short and round, the other so petite as to look fragile, waved at the group. Carrie Kung jogged around the body of water. Her black pigtails bounced behind her. Codie took the more direct route and flew over it. She landed gently on the edge of the water next to Ninette, smiling warmly and waiting for Carrie to catch up.

"You guys are trying out for the dueling team, right?" Carrie asked. She paused to bend over and catch her breath. "Are you practicing already? I want in."

Codie covered her mouth with a winged arm and giggled. "I caught her trying to make a tornado on the other side of the atrium. It wasn't going well, so I figured I'd bring her down to dueling practice to get some pointers."

"I almost had it," Carrie protested. "Whatever. By the time winter tryouts roll around, I'll be set."

"I can't wait," Codie said. "A lot of the team are seniors right now, so even if you don't make it this year some spots will open up. No need to rush it." She teased Ninette by reaching up to ruffle her hair and winked.

"Thanks," Ninette said. "Connor and I have been practicing, though. We might surprise you."

"Oh?" Codie smiled at Connor. "If you can keep up with her," she tilted her head at Ninette, "I think you're a shoo-in. She's a toughie."

She turned back to Ninette. "You should try and relax a little though. If you're practicing with both of us, you must not have much free time." She checked her watch. "Speaking of time, I gotta get down there. Come watch some time!" she called as she ran off.

"No fair!" Connor protested, giving Ninette a futile shove. "I thought we were practice buddies!"

"She asked me after I blew up the bathroom. It's only been a couple times, I promise," Ninette laughed.

Connor tried to protest, but Carrie broke in first. "Well let's stop squawking about it and get to practicing ourselves. We'll catch up, right Connor?"

"Yeah, we will." Connor's eyes sparkled with excitement.

Garrett cleared his throat, and the two aspiring duelists both spun to face him with a mixture of surprise and embarrassment.

"Do you really think it's a good idea? I mean, considering this morning?"

"I almost… I mean… I still can't believe that about Marck. Somehow this monster stuff didn't feel real before, but we know him." Carrie's smile melted away and her shoulders sagged.

"I know," Connor murmured. "He's my roommate."

"Oh gosh, I didn't realize."

"He's okay, that's the important thing." Connor forced himself to smile, hoping it would rub off on the others as well.

"Dunno what it is with these monsters and trying to hit us in the damn bathrooms," Ninette harrumphed.

Carrie's eyebrows popped up. "What do you mean?"

Ninette explained about the day she blew up one of the toilets, and Carrie's cheerful expression returned, complete with a fit of giggles.

"I heard about that. Didn't know it was you." Carrie tapped her fingers on her lips. "The kid before Marck was in the showers when… whatever it is got him. You guys were on that Atlantis trip, right? Guess I need to find a bathroom buddy."

Silence settled onto them despite the attempt at humor. Garrett flipped through the pages of his notebook, staring at the words but failing to read them. Connor kicked at the ground and Ninette skipped a rock over the pond. Each hop came with a sharp *snap* as turbulent ripples upset the water's smooth surface. Carrie shivered and pulled her jacket tight despite the atrium's warmth.

"Well, I'm gonna risk it, I think. You sure you guys don't wanna come to the stadium? Keep me company?" Carrie's eyes darted toward Connor and her voice cracked. She cleared her throat and giggled nervously. "Tryouts will be here before we know it."

Connor took a step in her direction, but Garrett and Ninette both glared at him. He froze, stuffed his hands in his pockets, and shook his head.

"Well, suit yourselves." Carrie took a few steps backward before turning and strolling off after Codie.

When she was gone, Garrett shook his head and pulled at his hair while letting out an exasperated sigh. "You're all crazy. Monsters are in our school sucking us dry, and all anyone seems to care about is dueling."

"It's so much fun though," Connor and Ninette said in unison.

"I hate you both," Garrett declared. "You can't duel if you're dead."

"We aren't going to die," Connor exclaimed, hoping his enthusiasm was contagious. "I have a plan. We're going back out. Tonight."

Chapter 12

The Science of Magic – Potions
Potions are combinations of magical ingredients to produce equivalent magical effects. Many ingredients were discovered in the ongoing quest for new sources of essence. While potions may be used by anyone, many of the rarer ingredients are difficult to obtain without possessing magical abilities—or an abundance of money.

Connor lay in bed, pretending to sleep. Though he faced the wall, he monitored the atrium all evening using Farsight. He checked his clock—11:00 p.m.—and sought the first step in his plan. Pushing the limits of his Farsight, his magical eyes searched the shrubs until he found a slender, stoppered vial of bubbling, orange liquid lying on its side. He had planted it there after class, as far from his and Garrett's rooms as possible. An irksome thought popped into his head.

I wonder if I should have tried this before committing to it.

He was a hundred yards away from the miniature potion of liquid flame, and he couldn't technically see it. He concentrated on creating a telekinetic extension of his hands, reaching out to grab the cork. At first nothing happened, but after several attempts, the vial rolled to the left. A few more tries, and it hovered off the ground. Connor couldn't hear it, but he imagined a satisfying *pop*. Wildfire poured out, igniting the bushes. It leaped to a nearby tree and spread through the park.

Connor threw off his sheets and slipped out of bed. He felt glad for Marck's absence, then immediately felt guilty about it. He wore all black in an attempt at camouflage and opted to go without shoes for silence. He opened the door and crept out into the night.

Lady Ariel and Master Borodin rushed to the fire. Borodin summoned a purple-spotted, camel-sized toad. It spat torrents of water, but the potion did its job— unending flame. Connor kept low and close to the walls until he reached Garrett's door, never taking his eyes off the teachers. He reached into his pocket and pulled out a small stone. Connor held it to the base of the door and let his essence flow into it for a quick second. A bright, white light blinked into the room. He could hear muffled footfalls. The door cracked open, and Garrett peeked out.

"Do we really have to do this?" Garrett looked longingly back at his bed and sighed.

"Do you want to get attacked by a homicidal cat again?"

Garrett gave this more thought than Connor expected, then joined him—also dressed all in black— being careful not to make a sound when the door closed. That left Ninette. Her room was closer to the fire than

Connor liked, but it couldn't be helped, and he planned for this as well.

Creeping around the corner and onto the girls' row, Connor extended his essence into the shadows dappling the grassy park. He darkened and stretched them across the ground and wall to obscure Ninette's room. Connor lit the stone again, and the door opened. Ninette loomed over them with her eyebrows raised.

"Why are you dressed like that? Where are your shoes?"

"Oh yeah," Garrett said, looking down. "Do you want to go back and grab them?"

"It's so I could walk more quietly," Connor muttered. "Come on. We need to move."

"You realize if we get caught, you look like someone who snuck out of their room," Ninette stated. She leaned against her doorframe with a crooked smile.

"Shut up."

Out in the hallways, the sparse emergency lights reflected on the linoleum tiles and the dull, metallic lockers. The rustle of fliers taped to lockers and the whir of the heating systems roared in their ears. Without the bustling bodies to fill the corridors, the only smell was the faint, piney tang of cleaning solution. The sensation of loneliness in a place usually so crowded sent shivers through Connor. Every footstep echoed in the eerily dark hallways. They approached an intersection, and Connor signaled a halt before spinning around with a frown.

"Ninette, can you try and walk softer?"

"What are you trying to say?"

"I'm saying you wore boots."

Ninette gave her heavy, black work boots a passing glance, and then favored Connor with a toothy grin. "I'm saying you look like a doofus."

"That's mature."

Garrett grabbed them both and tried to pull them away from the crossing, but budging neither. "Shhh! I hear someone."

Dr. Greens hummed to herself while rifling through papers. She wore polka-dot pajamas, and was completely absorbed in her reading, but she was on track to walk right past them. One quick look would mean the end. Connor looked for a class or bathroom to duck into, but the stretch of hallway was all lockers on either side.

"What's the plan?" Ninette whispered. She dared a peek around the corner. Dr. Greens was almost on top of them.

"I don't know," Connor admitted, backing away slowly.

Garrett turned a queasy green, and for a moment, his glasses reflected the harsh-white lights. He scrunched his eyes shut and clenched his fists so tight they shook. A few sparks flew from his hands, and the lights gave off a few dying flickers, then blinked out.

Connor held out his hands to gather the ambient shadows around them. Darkness pooled at their feet and climbed the wall behind them until the three were all but invisible. They all held their breath as the teacher's shuffling footsteps grew louder.

She passed by, humming off-key and giggling to herself, and never once looked up from her papers. The trio didn't move an inch until they could no longer hear her slippered footsteps.

"Maybe we shouldn't be doing this," Garrett whined.

Connor scuttled ahead to scout the next intersection. "The hard part is over. Now that we're out here, it's all downhill. You can do that trick with the lights again, right?"

"I think so, but so could you," Garrett pouted.

"Maybe. Show me later."

They crept in silence, pausing every few steps to look and listen. None of them had forgotten their stint as gardeners, and they hoped to avoid a similar fate. At one such stop, after determining they were clear—for the moment—Ninette spoke aloud, more to herself than to either of her companions.

"Why aren't they dead?"

"Who?" Connor asked.

"The kids who got attacked," she groaned. "Who else?"

Connor stopped creeping. "Maybe they got lucky?"

"You have a weird definition of lucky," Garrett said.

"I don't think so." Ninette crossed her arms and looked up, deep in thought. "The monsters are being controlled, right? If they could take that much of someone's blood, they could have killed them, too. They're alive for a reason."

"Could be a vampire," Connor suggested. "They don't always kill."

Ninette shook her head. "Bite's all wrong."

Garrett's eyes ping-ponged between them. "There are vampires?"

He sucked down a deep breath and tried to keep his knees steady.

"You've met a werewolf, a faerie, a mermaid, and a pig monster," Connor ticked off on his fingers.

Ninette growled. "Half-mermaid. And don't put me on the same list as the pig monster. Rude."

"Sorry. Yeah, there are a few vampires." Connor squeezed Garrett's shoulder. "Magic is fun, huh?"

"Fun," Garrett grumbled.

After a few more minutes, they were standing outside Mr. Masters' classroom. Voices, some quiet, some animated, all unintelligible, buzzed from within. The lone wooden door stood between them and the answers they needed. Connor had yet to decide if he hoped to find a monster or not, but he knew whatever they found would establish them as school heroes. They stood outside, alternating turns with their ears pressed to the door.

"I hope you thought further than this," Ninette said. She let out a wide-mouthed yawn. "It's getting late."

Connor ignored her, pressing himself as close as physically possible to the door. He was listening so intently that he never noticed the spider drifting down from above. It landed softly on his shoulder, reaching out tentative forelegs to tickle his neck. Ninette gasped and jumped back, but Connor, annoyed more than anything, gave it a hard swat. All sound from within the classroom stopped. Connor bit his lip and held his breath, hoping it was a coincidence.

"Who's out there?" Farrun Wallus called from behind the door.

"Run away?" Ninette asked, positioned to dash, but the door flung open.

Mr. Masters filled the doorway, and behind him sat a bizarre group.

Several desks pushed together formed a loose circle. Six students sat around it, Farrun Wallus among them, all wearing mismatched robes, some hooded, some clearly bathrobes. Sheets of paper covered in scribbled notes and rough sketches sprawled around them. The six students gawked at the intrusion with varied expressions of annoyance and wide-eyed surprise.

"What is going on here?" Mr. Masters raised his voice in a failed attempt at intimidation. "What are you kids doing here? It's past curfew. You should all be in bed."

"We, uh, heard about your club and, um, wanted to see what it was all about?" Connor ventured. He backed away slowly, fumbling behind him to push Garrett down the hall ahead of him.

Mr. Masters' irritation evaporated into a bright smile. "You're interested in Dungeons and Dragons? Why didn't you say so? We're pretty full now, but with three of you, I could probably get a second campaign going."

The students behind him smiled and nodded. Even Farrun's dour expression lightened a shade.

Connor's excitement shattered into a million pieces. No answers. No monsters. Nothing remotely close. He tried to recover, to stammer out a response, but Ninette cut him off.

"No, we're not. Sorry to bother you." Ninette grabbed Connor's shirt and dragged him away.

"Wait, what?" Connor protested. He struggled for only a second before going limp and allowing himself to be dragged.

"They didn't do it," Ninette grumbled, stifling another yawn. "Back to square one."

"Didn't do what?" Mr. Masters called after them.

"They thought maybe you and Farrun had something to do with whatever is attacking the students," Garrett said absently. The stress of sneaking out and the burst of relief at *not* finding a monster, snapped something in him and he couldn't quite think straight.

"You thought what?" Mr. Masters squeaked, caught completely off-guard by the accusation. "Hey! Hey, you kids, come back."

The students behind him clustered to eavesdrop. Ninette dropped Connor, and the two looked at each other, then to the teacher, and deflated. They marched back, both glaring at Garrett.

"Why would you tell him?" Connor hissed between gritted teeth. "We could have just left."

"What makes you think I had anything to do with that?" Masters said, trying to regain his composure. His lips trembled in a sad pout. "I am a teacher, for goodness' sake. I don't want any of you to get hurt."

"Well, you did almost let us get blown up at the first duel," Connor pointed out.

Mr. Masters looked down at the ground and scratched his head. "I said I was sorry. Never happened before. One minute, everything was fine. The next, my head got all fuzzy, and all my spells disappeared. Just for a second, though."

Connor's chest tightened, and the sounds of crashing water filled his mind. "Like your magic was gone?"

"Yeah, how did you know?"

"The grimmalkin did the same thing to us in Atlantis," Garrett explained. He shivered. "I guess it really is targeting us."

"Okay, but what about me?" Farrun sneered, pointing an accusing finger at Connor. "What made you think I'd do something like that? You guys were the ones following me the last few weeks, remember?"

"Dangerous monsters were summoned into the school," Ninette said in a deadpan tone. "You got busted summoning a dangerous monster into the school on the very first day. A dangerous, blood-drinking monster. Why WOULDN'T we think it was you?"

Farrun's cheeks reddened, and he turned away and huddled in on himself. "Doesn't seem like much to go on," he mumbled.

"Okay, fine" Ninette growled. "You're kind of creepy. You have a thing for creepy spiders. Plus, you creeped off during the Merlin duel to try and take a magic sword from their creepy basement. Creep."

Farrun looked indignant, but before he could defend himself a timid voice behind Mr. Masters piped up.

"You tried to take Excalibur?" A squat dwarf with light brown hair done up in a high ponytail fluttered her eyes at Farrun, her cheeks flushed. "You're so brave."

"You think so?" Farrun laughed, turning a matching shade of pink. "I thought it was worth a shot, you know?"

Ninette gawked at the girl, then at Farrun, then slapped her forehead. "Can we go?"

"We're sorry to have suspected you, Mr. Masters," Connor admitted. "We'll let you get back to your game."

Connor and Ninette walked away, Connor with shoulders weighed down by disappointment and Ninette grousing about the dumb things boys will do to impress girls. The walk back to the dorms was less stealthy. Ninette stomped with her hands in her pockets, and Connor followed with his head hung low and his feet dragging while Garrett brought up the rear, shushing them every few steps. The night had started so well—his plan to sneak out had worked perfectly—and he had such high hopes they'd catch Farrun and Masters red-handed. He'd left no room for any alternative. Connor couldn't believe they were back to square one, and he had no idea where to look next.

"Monster hunting," Ninette proposed, obviously less deterred. "It's the only thing that makes sense."

"There are three of them. Any of them would be tough for the three of us," Connor countered. "We don't even know what the last one is. Our track record against the two we've met isn't inspiring either."

He stuck his hands in his pockets, frustration radiating off him.

"Maybe we do," said Garrett reluctantly. "It always attacks near the bathrooms, right? Think about it. Connor found the first girl right outside one. Ninette, you and Codie saw it in the girls' room. Carrie said the last boy was in the shower when he got attacked, and I found Marck frozen in the doorway to our bathroom, too. It's always near the bathroom. And what connects all the bathrooms?"

"Pipes?" Ninette guessed.

"Sewers," Connor realized. His excitement surged back in full. "A school this big has to have some sort of sewer access or something, right?"

"Are you saying what I think you're saying?" Ninette asked. She cracked her knuckles.

"Monster hunting it is. We start tomorrow. Good thinking, Garrett." Connor slapped Garrett on the back.

They slowed to a crawl when they approached the entrance to the atrium, trying to make as little sound as possible. Connor couldn't hear the teachers fighting the fire anymore.

With any luck, they wrote it off as a prank and went to bed, he thought.

He cracked open the door and peeked inside. The park was dim, the only light from the stars and moon. Crickets chirruped, the wind played in the trees, and nothing else made a sound. Connor turned to give the all-clear and received a shock instead.

Ninette and Garrett were facing away from him, staring at Dr. Greens, still in her pajamas, flanked by Lady Ariel and Master Borodin. Dr. Greens grinned ear to ear, but the other two did not look amused. Their clothes and faces were covered in soot, and they reeked of ash and smoke. Despite being at least a foot shorter than any of them, the deep-lined scowl on Lady Ariel's face made her the most intimidating of them all.

"These three. I should have known," she grunted. "Didn't learn your lesson the last time, eh? I've a mind to teach ye again."

"Did you make this potion, Mr. McTaggart?" Dr. Greens asked, completely ignoring the other teachers' irritation. She held up the vial with a few drops of orange residue remaining.

"Yes," Connor admitted. He folded his hands behind him, looked sheepishly at the ground, and tried to look apologetic. "I'm sorry, Dr. Greens."

"Sorry?" she tittered. "Don't be sorry. A masterwork, clearly. The perfect reduction without losing any of the potency. And the staying power. Goodness gracious, I daresay these two would never have gotten it out if I hadn't come along with a counter reagent."

Borodin and Ariel scowled at their fellow instructor.

"You're impressed? I'm not in trouble?" Optimism crept into Connor's voice.

"Oh, you're in trouble. Loads of it," Dr. Greens cackled. "Setting off a fire potion in the school? Very dangerous. Lucky I was around, really. It's detention for the lot of you." Dr. Greens turned to leave when something caught her attention. "Mr. McTaggart, where are your shoes?"

Chapter 13

> A History of the Folk – Dragons
> Dragons are rare and reclusive creatures known for their long lives, wisdom, and avarice. The wisdom is a byproduct of the long lives, but the avarice they come by honestly. Every dragon has a hoard, and they will defend it to the death.

The library was almost empty, as expected before sunrise on a Saturday. A chair creaked. Some pages rasped. A smattering of seniors—most half asleep—worked on research projects. Dr. Greens relaxed in a study nook, absorbed in an Alchemy text. A quiet reverence pervaded, broken only by a yawn passed around the room.

Connor's chin drooped. He felt like he was falling—because he was, from the ladder—and clutched the hand bar to catch himself. Their punishment, since they snuck out late, was to be up early. A few rungs below, Ninette nudged him in the ribs with another book.

On the ground, Garrett sorted through the remaining piles—piles taller than he was.

"Honestly, I'm not sure why they're punishing ME," Mr. Naegus complained. The librarian looked up from his book with a grimace. "This is my day off, yet I find myself taskmaster to impetuous youths." He returned to his book, content to let proximity pass for supervision.

"I hate you guys," Garrett said, not for the last time. He sent up another armload of books. "How many times are we going to get detention this year?"

"Three? Four?" Connor guessed.

Garrett muttered to himself and continued his dig through the books. Ninette hopped down and pushed the ladder to the next section. Her stomach rumbled and she hoped they would finish in time for breakfast.

"Where are we going to look for the monster?" she asked in a low whisper. "I haven't seen any 'SEWER ENTRANCE HERE' signs posted around the school, have you?"

Connor slammed another book into its spot on the shelf. "No, but there has to be one. I'm sure they do maintenance or something. We'll try the bathrooms and go from there."

"All the makings of a sound plan," Garrett said. He practically threw the next books at Ninette. "How do you think *that* will land us in detention?"

They finished the task in silence, under the not-so-watchful eyes of the librarian.

Mr. Naegus rose with languorous stretch. "You missed one," he droned, and tossed his book to Garrett. "Have a wonderful weekend."

Connor groaned and started up the ladder, but Garrett tugged his shirt to stop him. "This book. It's an architectural history of the school."

"That's exactly what we need!" Connor exclaimed and snatched the book away.

"What are the odds?" Ninette murmured. She watched the librarian saunter away until he disappeared from sight.

"Not important right now." Connor laid the book on a table. "This must have floor plans, right?"

Sure enough, the book contained comparative schematics of the school grounds throughout the years, from its early days as a commune of log cabins to its upgrade into a single facility in the mid-1800s.

"A bunch of sinkholes opened about a hundred and fifty years ago," Connor read. "It destroyed like half the school. Whole buildings were swallowed by the ground."

"So what?" Ninette said. "Everyone was fine, and they built the new school."

"Right on top of the old one," Garrett noted. "Right on top of the sinkholes. Sinkholes form when caverns and tunnels open up beneath the ground. Those tunnels are probably still beneath the school. Maybe they incorporated the tunnels into the school itself. Maybe the sewers connect to the caves somehow?"

"What better place for a monster to hide?" Connor said giddily.

"Okay, but where are the sewers?" Ninette asked impatiently.

"Here." Connor pointed to an architectural layout of the school. "This looks like the cafeteria, but I think there's a connection there."

"Perfect. I'm starving anyway. Let's go."

Warm, breakfast aromas floated through the cafeteria doors. Inside, a few small clusters of students hunched over towering piles of pancakes. Even after their morning labors, it was too early for all but the earliest of birds to be about. Connor peeked back into the serving area; enchanted kitchen implements ran things efficiently to the tune of rhythmic clanks and underlying sizzles, cooking and serving away, but a pair swinging double doors leading further into the kitchen presented a mystery.

"It must be back in the kitchen," he said when they sat down. "All the leftovers have to go somewhere, right? Maybe there's a garbage room or something connecting to the sewers."

"I dunno." Garrett glanced down at his untouched eggs. "Are we allowed back there?"

Ninette made a sweeping gesture of the open room. "It is 7:30 on a Saturday. No one is here or awake enough to care about anything right now. You're lucky I'm here."

Connor and Ninette wolfed down their food and went back to the buffet. There were no other students, just the clink and whish of knives and spatulas preparing food, and the hiss and spit of skillets frying up another round. With a final check for witnesses, the three ducked behind the buffet and slipped into the kitchen. Industrial-sized refrigerators lined one wall, each opening and closing to allow more food to roll out on carts. Opposite, a row of sinks overflowed with hot, soapy water—a parade of utensils and cookware bounced in and out and then floated back into the cafeteria. A fastidious mop patrolled the floor. There wasn't a single person in sight.

"Very Fantasia," Ninette said, mouth full of food. She shoveled down a second plate and dumped it into a nearby sink, only for it to pop back out, shiny and clean.

They split up and searched the pantries, fridges, and closets, but found no doors. Standing in the center of the room, they were about to give up when a cart rolled in carrying dirty dishes and half-eaten scraps. It scurried over to a bare wall where a small hatch slid open to reveal a garbage chute. The plates jumped from the cart to scrape leftovers into the chute and then danced away to one of the sinks.

"Nope. No chance." Ninette shook her head and stepped backward.

"Come on," Connor prodded. "You wanted to hunt the monster. The monster is probably in the sewers. This is our only idea."

"This is not an idea. This is a garbage chute." Ninette set her shoulders and crossed her arms. She took another full step back from the slot in the wall.

"It does probably lead to a maintenance area," Garrett reluctantly admitted.

Connor looked his two friends in the eyes. Garrett looked away, but Ninette met his stare.

He sighed and looked back at the chute. "Fine."

Connor dove in headfirst. He sailed down the greasy slide, nose filled with the reek of old food and spoiled dairy. The chute dropped down at terrifying speeds; Connor fought the urge to scream, knowing opening his mouth would be a huge mistake. He landed in a dumpster full of scraps and garbage bags, releasing his held breath in a gasp of surprise and pain. He climbed out and brushed himself off as best he could. There were two loud thuds behind him, followed by two sets of disgruntled complaints.

"If I didn't think someone was trying to kill you," Ninette growled, spitting and scrubbing at her face, "I'd be doing it myself."

"You're a true friend," he said with a smarmy grin.

He helped them out of the dumpster and Ninette conjured a globe of hot water. Connor waved his hands and directed the water in a quick wash for him and his friends, complete with a brief blow dry, and only then did they investigate the room.

An entire corner of the room was occupied by an iron furnace with low-hanging pipes spiderwebbing along the ceiling. It glowed a warm orange inside, and churned out stifling, humid air. There were two doors: the first led to a narrow stairwell they assumed climbed back up into the school; the second was labeled "Maintenance."

"We couldn't have looked a *little* harder for those stairs," Ninette grumbled. "No, we had to go dumpster diving."

The maintenance room was dark, almost as warm, and full of even more plumbing, heating ducts, and machinery. A healthy coat of dust sat undisturbed on the equipment. Working their way around, they followed the pipes to a padlocked hatch on the floor.

"I hear water below us," Connor said.

"You hear sewage below us." Ninette shuddered. She held up a hand to the lock. "Stand back."

A burst of light and fire flashed from her palm. The ground shook and the pipes rattled from the explosion. When the smoke cleared, the lock and most of the hatch were gone.

Ninette gestured to the jagged opening. "After you."

"Was that necessary?" Connor lifted the remainder of the hatch and, holding his nose, peered into the murk below. "Can you give me a little more fire?"

Ninette produced a smaller, tamer flame, and Connor lobbed it downward, letting it hover in the air. A short drop below, a slimy brick path ran alongside opaque, flowing water. They hopped down and gasped at the labyrinth of tunnels sprawling below the school. The arched, stone passage ran into blackness in either direction, and more pipes and ducts crowded the ceilings in a tangled nest of industrial metal.

"This is insane," Garrett said. His voice echoed down the brick walls and called back to them in a faint imitation. He winced and pointed above them. "I bet those pipes reach all over the school. They're not small either," he added in a more hushed tone, and let that sink in.

A scratching sound behind them caused Garrett to jump; a rat shot them a quizzical look while it nibbled an apple core. When Garrett's heart stopped thudding, he whispered to Connor.

"You have your focus glove? Just in case?"

Connor nodded and patted his back pocket to reassure both his friend and himself.

They explored the sewers, peering furtively around corners and frequently checking behind them. The steady burble of the water mixed with the odd clink or crinkle from random trash made it hard to hear anything else. Eventually, they came upon a widening of the tunnel where two paths intersected. The water roared as it churned and drained in the center in a voracious whirlpool. Grated walkways, wide enough to walk single file, extended across the gaps. Connor brightened the light and they tried to determine which way to go next.

"Over there, across the water," Ninette hissed, pointing to a rusty smear on the wall. It originated from a duct above and trailed off down one of the further pathways. "Blood. Has to be, right?"

They scrambled across the grates to inspect the wall. The smear continued into the darkness of the duct above them. Warm air billowed out of the murky opening.

"Must be the air conditioning?" Connor suggested. He lifted the flame upward to illuminate the duct but saw only the dull glint of metal where it made a hard turn. "Can't tell where it goes."

Ninette ran her finger along the wall and Garrett gagged.

"The blood looks old," she said. "At least we probably won't find any new victims down here." She followed the blood trail deeper.

"Wait, aren't we going to get a teacher?" Garrett asked. He took several hopeful steps away from the bloodstain. "We found a trail. Let's head back, okay?"

"We don't know if it's any good or not," Connor corrected. He followed Ninette and waved Garrett forward. "The blood is old. It could be from anything. We need more proof."

The trail didn't go far, fading into the stonework after only a few yards, but they stuck with the path. The tunnel's brick ended without warning; the water took a sharp turn through a barred grate and continued away unseen while the path continued straight ahead, the structured sewer giving way to a natural stone tunnel.

Water dripped from stalactites, coalescing into shallow pools along the ground. The walls were worn, smooth with time, rippling and flowing as though once made of water themselves. Connor led the way ever deeper with the globe of fire lighting the way, and Garrett brought up the rear as close to Ninette as he could be without tripping over her.

"This must be one of the caves," Connor said. "Could be the place."

"I don't know. Don't you think the teachers would have looked here? Seems obvious now that I think about it. We should probably go." Garrett's words tumbled out from his chattering teeth.

The tunnel expanded the further they went. After a short hike, it became a high-domed cavern, easily big enough to fit the dueling stadium with room to spare. The walls climbed high with no ceiling in sight, only an array of stone daggers stabbing down from the impenetrable gloom. Unlike the rest of the tunnel, the cavern was curiously dry, not a drip or puddle to be found, and even more unnerving, glowing stones lined the walls at regular intervals and filled the space with soft, yellow, almost cozy light. As they stepped deeper inside, a keening note filled the cavern. Even Ninette shivered.

"P-p-probably wind?" Garrett stammered, wishing it to be true.

The sound rose higher and then cut to silence. The ground shook. No one moved. Something shifted in the darkness beyond. Something big.

"What is that?" Connor whispered. His throat had gone dry, and it was a challenge to squeak out the question.

The ground rocked. Tremors ran through their legs. Pebbles skittered across the cave floor. The pounding continued, mounting, until a gigantic shape lumbered out of the shadows and straight toward them. It was a hundred feet long, from its massive head to its vicious spiked tail. Long, jagged teeth crowded its mouth, each a blade warped by frequent, violent use. Broad silver scales covered it like a segmented coat of armor. It had four legs, each tipped in wicked black claws. It stood before them, unfurled pale wings like the tattered sails of a ghost ship, and bellowed, knocking Garrett to the ground while the other two fought to stay standing. The primal sound resonated in their bones.

"That's a dragon. Oh my god, we're gonna die, we're gonna die," Garrett screamed and flailed backward.

He ran for the entrance, but the dragon lashed out with its tail and blocked their exit; then it locked onto Connor with its smoldering, molten gold eyes.

"Run!" Ninette yelled.

Flames leaped from her palms and scorched the dragon's face. It tossed its head back and forth and snorted, annoyed but unscathed. Connor scanned the room for anything he could use for magic and his eyes caught the deadly rock formations above. He reached up to the stalactites, connected his essence to the earth within them, and pulled, causing a shower of stone spikes to crash onto the dragon's back. The rocks broke apart against its steely hide, and it screeched in anger.

Garrett babbled incoherently. Connor's legs trembled. Ninette gritted her teeth and put herself between the dragon and her friends. She slammed her fist into the ground and a fresh wave of stone shook loose, crashing onto the dragon's head.

Connor watched her with his mouth hanging open. He couldn't back down either. There was nowhere to run, and he refused to die as a dragon snack before he finished high school. He grabbed hold of the shadows surrounding them, twisting them into ropes to bind the dragon. The mammoth lizard cried out again. It twisted and contorted to shake off the dark bonds, but made no move to attack the kids.

"Impetuous youths!" it bellowed in a deep, smooth voice.

"Wait a sec," Connor said. The voice, and the memory it triggered, almost broke his concentration on the binding spell. He hoped he was right. He lowered his hands, freed the beast, and motioned for Ninette to do the same. "Mr. Naegus?"

"The last student who dared attack me in my home has not forgotten it," the dragon rumbled. The words carried only a hint of humor. It used its wings to brush dust and debris off its shoulders and then sat on its hind legs, almost like a dog. "I presume I am not what you expected to find down here, but you are looking for something, yes? Few students have the stomach to wander the sewers."

"That's what I said," Ninette mumbled.

"You lead us down here," Connor protested. "You gave us that book."

The dragon lowered its head to look more closely at them. The heat of its breath washed over them like a moist blanket. The dragon looked from Connor to Ninette and then to Garrett, who was still shaking.

"Yes, I suppose I did, but I didn't want you disturbing *me*." He shook his head and glanced sideways at Garrett. "Well, I don't want to give the boy a heart attack, do I?" he said with a throaty growl of a laugh.

He rose to his full height and then curled in on himself, coiling his neck and tail tight, and then cocooning himself with his wings. He continued constricting inwards, shrinking down to his human size. With a flash of silver light, the dragon was gone, and in its place stood their librarian.

"Follow me," he instructed and then walked away without waiting to see if they would.

He led them further into the cavern. Connor and Ninette each took one of Garrett's hands and dragged him. Books littered the cavern floor. It began with a few here and there, but before long, they passed shelves as high as houses and piles of haphazardly stacked tomes like miniature mountains. The school's library was expansive, but there had to be ten times as many books down here.

"You like my collection? It has taken some time to accumulate," Naegus said, "but then again, I have nothing but time. I have been the librarian at this school for well over one hundred years."

They followed him into a narrow tunnel at the far end of the cave and into a cozy parlor with two plush maroon armchairs, a worn leather couch, and a deep-set, stone fire pit in the center. He gestured to them to sit.

"Tea? It will only take a minute." He busied himself with lighting the fire and filling a kettle, then sat in one of the chairs. The three took the couch across from him. "So now you know. I am a dragon. Few students ever find out. This cave has been my home for as long as I can remember. I settled down to nap for a hundred years or so, and when I awoke, a school had been built above me. I am… not much of a morning person."

His eyes gleamed in the firelight.

"You caused the sinkholes," Garrett said, and then yelped and covered his mouth.

"I did," Mr. Naegus admitted in a gentle, reassuring purr. "Bit of a land dispute with the residents, but we came to terms. I have been on the faculty ever since. They provide me with things I want, and I remain here, a more or less obedient servant of the headmaster. Or mistress."

Garrett pushed himself back as far as the seat allowed. "Do they feed you students? We found blood. Right outside. Was-was that you? Please don't drink my blood."

"Heavens no. They find me rare books for my collection. The administration is a tad more responsible than that," he chided. "The blood stains were not my doing, although I did see the culprit. I thought to give chase, but those tunnels do not accommodate my normal size, and my visitor made their getaway while I changed." He tilted his head, pondering for a minute.

"But that is why you are down here, is it not? Three adventurous monster hunters plumbing the catacombs for the nefarious kappa."

"Kappa?" Connor asked. "What's a kappa?"

"River child," Ninette whispered. "A water demon."

"Indeed," Naegus said. "And quite rare in this part of the world, but then it is not from this part of the world, is it? So, you seek the summoned monster and the summoner as well, unless I miss my guess. Knowing it is a kappa might help you, though it has not helped the faculty."

"They know?" Connor asked. "Why haven't they told us?"

"Perhaps because such knowledge might have naïve students down in the sewers looking for it," Naegus answered with an arched eyebrow. "The kappa has no small magic at its command, and it is physically stronger than our maritime maiden here." He gestured casually toward Ninette. "Why would they encourage such reckless behavior?"

"Why are *you* telling us?" Ninette asked.

"As I said, my position here is… contractual. I find myself less concerned with your safety. Besides, I see something in you three. Maybe you will succeed where they cannot. As long as you're trying, you are welcome to visit. I do occasionally long for company. Come, I will grant you access to a less odious entrance; however, I advise discretion in your visits. I don't want my home to become a tourist attraction."

Mr. Naegus rose and led them to a staircase, a rusty, metal spiral climbing sharply up a cramped chute. They followed close behind, climbing through total darkness. After a long while, three small slits of light appeared above. Naegus peered through one of them, then pressed a button set into the wall. The door popped open with a metallic creak, and he ushered the kids into an empty hallway. They turned to find an ordinary student locker.

"Here you are. You'll note we are right outside the headmistress's classroom. The combination is 9-10-21. Do try not to forget it." The librarian turned to leave them.

"Wait, what about the kappa?" Connor asked. "Are you going to help us?"

"I suspect not," Naegus responded. "I gave him quite the scare. He's been scurrying about the sewers since, but I doubt he'll come my way again. Best of luck to you. Let me know how it goes, yes?"

He closed the door behind him, leaving the three students alone in the hallway. They stood stunned, silent. An hour ago, they were grasping at straws, and now they possessed a wealth of new knowledge, all of it interesting and shocking by degrees, and some of it relevant to boot. Garrett opened his mouth to speak, but he was cut off by an ear-shattering screech. Connor and Ninette shared the briefest of looks before they barreled down the school corridors in search of the victim. They passed a girl's bathroom and Ninette stopped. Without hesitating, she charged in with Connor close behind.

"Hello? Anyone in here?" Ninette shouted.

There was no reply, but they found a girl sprawled on the wet floor. She had the same bite marks on her stomach as the first girl. Ninette had barely checked for a pulse when wet slapping noises and the sound of the door opening drew their attention.

"It was still in here!" Connor cried. "Garrett, get help."

He and Ninette sprang to their feet and ran after the monster.

Chapter 14

Elemental Magicks - Lightning
Lightning magic is potent but unpredictable. Effective use requires an understanding of the physics involved in electrical discharge. Whether for Weathermancy or the budding field of technomancy, the effects are always impressive, but lightning never strikes the same place twice, unless the Magi behind it is just that good.

Connor's pulse thundered. He raced after Ninette while Garrett's cries for help echoed behind them in the empty halls. They chased a trail of watery footprints on the ground and the wet *slap slap* of the Kappa's feet. Ninette caught a glimpse of it as they turned down another empty hallway, but it disappeared through a door. Right on its heels, they followed it into a classroom. The monster, with nowhere left to run, slowly turned to face them.

The creature was small, maybe three and a half feet tall. Its beady eyes glowed a jaundiced yellow from behind scraggly, wet black hair. It had slimy, mottled green skin, like weeds in a swamp. A hard, turtle-like shell, darker than the rest of it, protected its back. Sharp scales stuck out at dangerously odd angles. Its hands and feet were webbed, but all of its digits ended in pointed claws. A shallow dent in its head contained a small pool of water. Most importantly, dozens of needlepoint teeth—all stained crimson red—filled its beak of a mouth.

"Gross," Ninette gagged and covered her mouth.

"It just ate. Let's hit it while it's full." Connor pulled the focus glove out from his back pocket and tugged it into place on his left hand.

The rush of colors hit him full force, but he only swayed a little. Outside the window, gusts of gray wind swirled. The vibrant green forest splashed the horizon. Far away, he saw the familiar white of ley lines. The kappa's distended stomach held a roiling, pale yellow light. Ninette blazed fiery red, and he knew she itched to unleash her Fire Magic. The kappa raised its webbed hands in their direction and a radiant, cerulean aura surrounded it.

"Watch out," Connor warned, preparing a shield, "It's going to use Water Magic."

A jet stream of crystal-clear water shot out from the monster's palms, hitting Connor hard enough to send him flying, shield and all, into the classroom wall. It turned its gross gaze on Ninette, redirecting the flow of water. The blast hit her in the chest, but she leaned into it using her heavy boots for traction.

"That all you got?" she grunted.

She tried to cast flames, but the torrent of water extinguished them too quickly. She pressed through the stream, step by slow step, into striking distance when the kappa ended its spell, and she stumbled forward. She got her footing and kicked at its head, but it caught her leg, stopping her completely. She didn't have time to fully register her surprise before it punched her in the stomach. She sailed through the air like a discarded toy. Connor dragged himself to his feet and caught her on a cushion of wind. They stood side by side. The kappa made no move to run.

Connor watched the creature closely. Its aura maintained a steady bright blue.

"More Water Magic," he said.

He scanned the room and spied a sparkling, yellow light running through the ceiling and walls. With the aid of the focus glove, he could see charged ions in the air as sparkling, neon yellow motes. His mind and essence connected the two. Plaster and drywall exploded as he threw one thunderbolt, then a second, drawing directly from the school's wiring. The creature waved its hand, and a sphere of water materialized between them.

Connor's lightning bolts stopped in the water, crackling wildly around the orb. In one smooth motion, the kappa launched the supercharged water at Ninette. She couldn't react in time; the combined spell blasted her through the wall and out into the hallway.

"Ninette!"

Connor searched for something, anything he could use, but the walls were dim—he had shorted the power—and nothing else was close at hand. Professor Skreed's words echoed in his head.

Always plenty of earth and wind.

Connor inhaled, and the windows of the classroom exploded inward. Catching the shards of glass in the wind, Connor fired them at the kappa. Cuts opened all over the creature's skin and it belched a tortured groan. It tried to move but found its legs shackled by shadows. It glared at Connor and knocked him over with a geyser of water, followed with a blast of ice, freezing him to the ground. The kappa closed in on him, beak open and teeth glistening with the blood of its victim. Connor's mind went blank with fear, and he lost all connection to the elements around him. The kappa leaned in, its mouth gaping, dripping with pinkish blood and saliva.

Flaming spears whizzed past and struck the ground between them.

"Not another step!" James yelled, running into the room. "Kid, are you okay?"

"Fine," Connor replied. His teeth chattered against the words. "Can't get up."

James waved his hand without looking, and the ice melted. "Leave us alone," he stated. He stared down at the creature and his voice was solid, commanding. "Last chance."

The kappa cocked its head, then raised its hands; whirlpools of water gathered around them. James lunged at the kappa. Jets of flame erupted in his wake, propelling him like a missile into its stomach. The kappa croaked, coughing up blood, and the two soared out the window.

Connor staggered up, looking first at the broken window and then at the hole in the wall left by Ninette. *I'm sure he's fine.*

Trusting the dueling captain, he ran out into the hall and found Ninette slumped against the lockers, which she had completely smashed inward. He hurried to her side; her breathing was slow but steady. Relief flooded him at the sight of the headmistress and Lady Ariel sprinting down the hall with Nurse Poole in tow.

"Here!" Connor shouted, waving them over. "I think she's okay. James and the kappa went out the window." He pointed into the ruined classroom.

With the teachers on the scene, Connor felt safe enough to slip his glove into his pocket. The riot of magical colors disappeared in a dizzying snap. He closed his eyes and shook his head, trying to steady himself.

"Mr. McTaggart, why am I not surprised?" the headmistress muttered as she swept past.

Nurse Poole knelt and placed her hand on Ninette's forehead. "Must have been hit pretty hard," she deduced. "It's not easy to knock out a mermaid, even half of one." Her hands lit up a glorious white, and Ninette's eyes twitched and fluttered open.

"Let me at him," she slurred, trying to stand.

"The only thing you're being 'let at' is bed rest," Nurse Poole warned. "You had a concussion and three broken ribs. I've patched up most of it, but I still want you on observation for a day."

"I'm fine," Ninette protested, but her wobbly knees gave her away.

"And I'm the nurse. Now sit."

Lady Ariel walked out of the classroom with a bruised and bleeding James hoisted over her shoulders. Nurse Poole helped set him down on the ground. She grabbed his head in both hands and pure, brilliant light flooded the hall.

James's eyes shot open. He screamed as his lacerations sewed themselves shut, and the splotches of purple and black bruises washed away like paint. His breathing came in short, ragged bursts, and he looked wildly from the Nurse to Lady Ariel. He flailed, trying to pull away, but the sturdy dwarven instructor held him tight. When he came to his senses, he stopped thrashing and his breathing slowed. He laid back down and closed his eyes.

"That never gets easier, does it?"

"No, it doesn't, and you ought to know better than most," the Nurse scolded, though she smiled at him. "Certainly well enough to avoid foolish risks."

A moment later, the headmistress returned, a scowl on her face and annoyance in her brisk stride. "Is Mr. McTaggart fit to come with me?" she asked, not waiting for the answer.

"Moreso than these two, but go easy on him," the Nurse called after her. She gave Connor a pitiful glance. "Off you go."

"Good luck," Ninette said. She gave him a feeble thumbs up, then closed her eyes and rested her head against the locker.

Connor followed the headmistress down the halls toward her office. They encountered several groups of students en route to the site of the commotion, but the headmistress sent each one retreating with a level glare. Once there, he sat down in the chair opposite her desk as he had on his first visit, and hoped he looked apologetic enough. She collapsed in her chair with an explosive sigh and rested her head in one hand, staring at her desk. Behind her, a coffee pot burbled to life.

Connor fidgeted. The headmistress ignored him; she seemed content to stare at the empty space on her desk. Finally, he broke the silence.

"Did you get it?"

Leorra snorted. "No, I did not. It found water by the time I caught up to it. I am not so foolish as to challenge a kappa by running water, and Mr. Radimus required medical attention." She raised her head and met Connor's eyes. "This is going to be a regular occurrence, isn't it? You go looking for trouble, don't you?"

Connor bit down his first protest. "I wasn't looking to be drowned in Atlantis! I didn't go looking for the vesporcus either!"

"I'll note you did not say you weren't looking for trouble today," Leorra said. "And I believe twice you have received detention for being out when you should not be? Just this morning, in fact?"

Connor looked away defiantly but said nothing. She paused to pour coffee, sat sipping for a moment, then asked him to tell her exactly what happened. Connor admitted they were looking for a monster but omitted any mention of their encounter with Karronus Naegus and his subterranean study. He stopped at the point where Leorra found him and waited to see what she would say.

Leorra laid her hands flat on the desk and her expression softened to one of gentle concern. "Look, Connor, I get it. I, too, was young once, if you can believe it. I'm sure if I were your age, I'd be right there in that seat getting chewed out by my headmistress. But I'm not. I'm here, and I'm trying to give you the benefit of hard-earned wisdom." She traced her finger along the faded scar running the length of her cheek, tapping it for emphasis. "These are dangerous creatures. This isn't some adventure, at least not one you want. Skulking about is going to get you, or one of your friends, hurt. Possibly killed."

That stung, made no better by a vision of Garrett's fear-filled eyes. He stuffed it down. "I'm sorry, headmistress. I wanted to catch it before someone else got hurt. I'll be more careful."

"It's not 'I will give up on actively seeking my doom,' but I suppose it's the best I could expect. Why don't you see if Ms. Reefwalker is comfortable in the nurse's ward? I expect Mr. Clarke will be there, as well. He was rather shaken up."

Connor stood to leave. As he walked out the door, the headmistress called out to him.

"Mr. McTaggart, one more thing. You will be trying out for the dueling team, yes?"

Connor's mouth hung open, but no words came out. The headmistress casually glanced at the trophy on her shelf—a dueling trophy.

"I saw evidence of your resourcefulness. Quick thinking will serve you well out there." She rested her head on her hand and smiled at him. "I hear you are showing much promise to Professor Skreed. Perhaps dueling would be a safer outlet for this mischievous energy."

With a wave of her hand, she dismissed him and shut the door.

The Nurse's ward was sterile white: the tiles on the floor, the paint on the walls, the curtains, the sheets, even the uniform—it hurt Connor's eyes. The room boasted two cushioned benches for those waiting to be seen, and a handful of empty beds lining the wall underneath the windows. Two doors led further back. A small metallic desk—white, of course—sat inside the doorway. A student medical volunteer in white slacks and an apron greeted him as he entered.

"Connor, right? Ninette is waiting for you. Right this way."

They entered one of the doors and into a smaller room containing only two beds. A dim overhead light warmed Connor through to his bones. The tension in his body melted away and his eyelids grew heavy.

The volunteer noticed and explained. "This is our primary recovery room. It's enchanted with a low-level healing spell. Just being in here will help you recover."

He stifled a yawn. "It also acts as a mild sedative, so don't stay too long."

Ninette turned away from Garrett and pointed an accusing finger at Connor. "And then THIS guy blasts me with lightning bolts for no good reason."

"I am SO sorry," Connor apologized, bowing his head. "I didn't know it could do that."

"I'm joking. Mostly," she laughed. "I didn't know it could hit like a sperm whale."

"Is that girl okay?" Connor asked. The other bed was empty.

"She's in the other room. Intensive care," Garrett added in a somber voice. "I stayed with her until the teachers came. She-she never moved."

Connor squeezed Garrett's shoulder firmly. "You did all you could."

Garrett looked up at him and stood a little straighter, and the beginnings of a smile appeared on his face.

Connor put his hand on his hip and pressed on. "Well, at this point, I think we can safely say the bathrooms aren't safe. Pattern established. Now we need a way to catch it."

"The bathrooms are a coincidence," Ninette said firmly. "The kappa is a water demon. They can move freely between bodies of water, aqua-teleportation. I never saw one, but we were always warned about them growing up."

"So, you weren't exaggerating?" Garrett asked. "It came up out of the toilet?"

Ninette shuddered at the memory and nodded.

"Well, I'm never going to the bathroom again."

"Not alone anyway," Connor agreed. "What else do you know? Is there some way we could lure it out? We could set a trap. Give us the advantage."

"You're not serious." Garrett backed toward the door. "You guys almost got killed! Again! The headmistress just told you to leave it alone."

Connor shook his head. "Mr. Naegus said the teachers know it's a kappa, so it's probably avoiding them. But it's not scared of us."

"It should be. I'm ready for a rematch," Ninette said. She tried to sit up and had to stifle a pained grunt. "Or I will be soon enough. Here's everything I know."

Chapter 15

> The Creature Compendium - Kappa
> The kappa is an aquatic demon resembling a mixture of frog and turtle that is native to eastern Asia. Kappa possess an indent on the top of their heads that they must keep full of water, or they rapidly lose their strength. They will suck the blood of anything from humans to horses, but they are also inordinately fond of cucumbers. They will never back down from a direct challenge.

As the days marched into December, Connor and Garrett did more research on the kappa, but avoided putting themselves in overt danger, which meant always going to the bathroom together. As eager as Connor was to end things once and for all, he knew the two of them were no match for it. Their best bet was to wait for Ninette. Ninette remained exhausted for over a week. All the while, the teachers ramped up lessons and homework to prepare for term finals.

With just two weeks until winter break, Professor Skreed introduced his final subject: Light Magic. He studied the class in complete silence as if waiting for some expected reaction, smiling as though he knew something they didn't. He even looked directly at Gemma to see if she would ask a question to help set the tone for his lecture, but she remained silent—though the ferocity with which she twirled her pigtails indicated strong resistance.

"Very well," he said with a dismissive wave. "If the ever-inquisitive Ms. Perriwinkle won't oblige me, I will tell you straight out. Light Magic is not *good* just as Shadow Magic is not *evil*. It is often thought of as such. The comforting warmth of the light. The light at the end of the tunnel. Those who gain wisdom have 'seen the light.'" He rattled off each example in a bored drone. "But the light blinds us. The light burns. The light reveals that which ought to remain hidden. Think of all the atrocities performed in the name of the light. It is the Magi who determines whether it is good or evil. While shadow is the element of fear, doubt, and confusion, light is the element of courage, confidence, and unfailing certainty.

"We begin today with globes of light. While you may compare them to globes of fire, you will find them challenging to produce. Are you positive you want to see what the light reveals?"

He snapped his fingers and the shutters over the windows came crashing down, the lights flipped off, and the classroom went black. An orb of light floated from his hand, coming to rest above the center of the classroom.

Connor held out his hands and pictured a lightbulb between them. Nothing happened. He pictured a lamp. Nothing. He strained and squinted and squeezed but didn't get so much as a flicker. He thought smaller, trying to imagine a single mote of light on the tip of his finger. Not even a hint of a glimmer. He groaned and dropped his head into his hands. He knew he should have expected this initial stumbling block, but after his recent shadowy success, his hopes had been raised that his elemental affinities may have just come last in the curriculum. With no small resignation he leaned back in his chair to observe his classmates and wait for a chance to try and manipulate their lights in lieu of creating his own.

The other students set to work lighting up the rest of the room, though few got far. Sporadic flashes sparked and faded. Others produced persistent sparks no bigger than a firefly. Frustration and discontented grumbling mounted. No element had eluded so many.

"How about I show them how it's done?"

A dazzling light flooded the classroom from somewhere in the back row, banishing shadows and washing out everything it touched. Connor already knew the source, but he squinted his eyes to look anyway.

Proudly displaying her sphere of condensed brilliance was Sheena, smug satisfaction painted across her face. After letting her revel for a moment, the professor asked her to let it fade.

"Ms. Crowton has shown the requisite attitude to master the light. She has no doubts in her mind. This is how you must be in order to shine today." He chuckled at his little joke. For once, he was the only one.

Garrett and Ninette continue to try, but neither of them created a single flash. Connor doubled down, hating the idea of being outdone by Sheena once more, but nothing happened. In a moment of desperation, he dragged himself to Sheena's desk.

"Can you show me how you did the light spell?" he asked, barely audible.

"Come again?" Sheena laughed. "I can't hear you."

"Look, I just want to see you do it again. Maybe if you make a light, I could at least control it," Connor said, a desperate plea hiding behind his words.

"Knock yourself out," Sheena taunted.

She relit the air, leaving Connor seeing nothing but splotches of color. When his eyes cleared, he forced himself to look at the light. He tried to take control of it like he did with Ninette's fire spells, but it wouldn't budge. He couldn't move it, change it, or interact with it. He probed the space with his essence as he had with all the other elements but failed to make even the smallest connection.

"Are you still concentrating on it?" Connor asked from around the glare.

"What are you talking about?" Sheena asked. She flipped through articles on her phone, only half listening.

"Never mind."

Connor dragged himself back to his seat, fell into it like a sack of rocks, and began counting the minutes until class ended. When the bell rang, Sheena remained the only person displaying any level of competence. Some produced a few more fireflies and Vern created what could best be described as a child's nightlight. No one jumped up from their seats to leave. Students and slackers alike waited, hopeful for some further guidance from Professor Skreed. Connor was not the only one to take the failure personally.

"I see a lot of dejection," the Professor said. "You should not feel so. There is a reason this is the last lesson. It is the hardest. Especially for children. The day I meet a classroom full of self-confident teenagers will be a frightening one indeed." He paused, offering them his most earnest smile and finally earned some begrudging laughter. "Furthermore, you are not required to master this element. Very few display talent with all eight elements. You will have another week or so to practice before the final exam. To pass, you need only demonstrate proficiency with two elements, and competence with two more. Play to your strengths. I will see you all tomorrow."

Connor rose from his seat, still trying to get a light going. Someone brushed past him, blinding him with a flash to the face. By the time the stars cleared, Sheena was parading down the hall ahead of him. He asked Ninette if she felt like practicing, but she wasn't over her bout with the kappa. Garrett wanted to study for history finals. He tried a few others, but they wanted to focus on their end-of-semester studies as well. No one was concerned with one element, and why should he be? He knew he'd pass Skreed's class. Maybe *he* should be studying history, too. Instead, he found himself moping on a bench in the atrium.

He was lost in a daydream—a rematch with the kappa in which he emerged sufficiently bloodied but triumphant—when he became aware of someone sitting next to him.

"Tough day?"

James lounged on the bench with the same look about him as Ninette: only the faintest scars remained of his battle, but his skin was paler, and heavy bags hung under his eyes. Healing could only do so much. Connor leaned back, attempting to mimic the upperclassman's relaxed attitude.

"Yeah, I guess. How are you feeling?"

"Like I could take on the world," James boasted with either a smile or a wince, possibly both. "Nah, I'm pretty wiped. Sucker really stuck it to me by the water.

Pretty dumb to knock him out the window." He shrugged. "Just glad you're okay." James gave Connor a more careful appraisal. "Are you okay?"

"Yeah. I blew it in Skreed's class today. Light Magic." Connor made a half-hearted attempt, flicking his wrists and wishing for lights to appear, but all he saw was the after image of Sheena's lights seared onto his retinas.

"Light Magic is tough. You can't have a single doubt in your mind or heart." He pointed first to his head then to his chest for emphasis. "That's why I stick to Shadow Magic. Fear and doubt are easy. And if you aren't afraid, your opponent probably is." He smiled and closed his eyes. He appeared to sink into the shade of the tree.

"It's so frustrating." Connor looked at his hands as though expecting them to do something. "I feel like I got screwed out of the best magic. My elemental magic feels so lame. I was starting to get over it since I could at least *use* the other seven, but I got nothing with light. Not a glimmer."

"Seven is a big deal. There are probably only three or four other kids in the whole school who can do that. You need to learn to use what you've got. Speaking of, I heard you might try out for the team." He opened one eye and tilted his head to the side.

"I'm going to make the team," Connor blurted, then blushed. "I mean, I think I have a chance. Right?" He held his breath, waiting for the captain's response.

"Kappa didn't kill you. Probably a good sign," James joked. "Well, I'll see you out there then." He slapped Connor's back and left.

Connor looked around; he was completely alone. Afternoon had faded to twilight and the many students using the park for studying, practicing, or other less studious activities had dispersed for the night. A cloud wandered across the skylight plunging the atrium into deeper shadows. Connor shivered and decided to go back to his room and study after all.

Connor continued trying to think of a plan to catch the kappa, and inspiration struck a few days later in Dr. Greens' lab. The recent rash of exsanguinations had left Nurse Poole's transfusion stores rather low.

"Fortunately, I have a fantastic source of cheap labor to remedy this shortcoming." Dr. Greens cackled. "You. You're it. We're making blood today," she clarified. "A lot of it. Search for 'blood' in the file and you'll find it. Only one in there. You'll see, you'll see!"

Connor and Ninette pulled up the recipe for the Elixir of Multiplicative Blood. Ninette read the description aloud.

> After all other ingredients are prepared the final addition of biological matter will cause the elixir to become a universal blood type, as well as multiply one hundred times over.

"Biological matter," Connor read with her. "Dr. Greens? Does this elixir work for non-humans?"

"Of course it does," the doctor answered. "Everything has blood. That's why the final ingredient says, 'biological matter' and not 'human bits.' I would think a budding potion master like yourself would read between the lines."

"Yeah, Mr. McTaggart," Ninette sniggered.

"Shut up." Connor shoved her. "Are you thinking what I'm thinking?"

"I'm thinking I would be failing this class if you weren't sitting next to me."

"I'm thinking we need to find a bit of horse."

Ninette frowned, but only for a second before understanding lit up her eyes.

The elixir required three leaves of redthorn mixed with four ounces of iron filings, boiled in equal parts water and chimera saliva, followed by a simultaneous infusion of Wind and Fire Magic. Connor handled the wind and Ninette added the fire. They stood on opposite sides of the burner and funneled their magic into the flask until the concoction clarified.

The doctor made her rounds of inspections and plucked up five of the prepared bottles. "These will all do," she stated returning to her desk. "The rest of you, I would encourage a little more practice on your own time before finals. Encourage strongly. Insist, even. It will be on the test. Now, I will demonstrate the final result."

She poured one of the bottles into what looked like a medical-grade garbage bag, then plucked a hair from her head and dropped it in. The elixir roiled and the bag clouded with condensation. It changed from clear to black to white to green, all the while bubbling and expanding. It finally settled on a familiar—if discomforting—crimson.

Ninette and Connor lingered after class, taking more time than necessary to clean their workstation.

Ninette studied the supply cabinet—already locked up again. "How are we going to get the stuff we need? I don't keep chimera saliva in my room," she whispered.

"I have an idea," Connor snickered. "You're not going to like it." He waved his hand in the air to get the teacher's attention.

"Yes, Mr. McTaggart, what can I do for you?"

"Well, ma'am, it's my lab partner," he said, leaning close but speaking in a stage whisper. "I did all the work for her today. I think Ninette could use the practice of doing this elixir by herself."

Dr. Greens lifted up her goggles, revealing red indentation lines in her round face. She stroked her chin and looked Ninette up and down—mostly up considering their difference in height.

"I see, I see. I hoped working with you would help her improve, but you are probably right. Ms. Reefwalker? Please take the requisite ingredients and practice this over the weekend. I recommend smaller batches. Don't know what you'd do with that much blood. Oh, and put a tarp down."

"You are a grade-A jerk, you know that?" Ninette scowled once the teacher had left. She punched Connor in the shoulder.

Connor crashed through a desk and toppled over a chair. He collected himself up off the floor and dusted off his clothes. *Guess she's feeling better.*

Chapter 16

A History of the Folk - Holidays and Celebrations
Each community of the Folk keeps their own traditions, and while some have assimilated to human holidays, few of them embrace Christmas. They know Santa Claus as "The Kringle," an ancient being and a spiritual protector. He sees them when they're in need; he knows when they're in trouble.

"Are you guys sure you want to do this?" Garrett's voice wavered as he pleaded with his friends for the tenth time.

"Yes," Connor insisted. "Be ready with the cucumber."

Garrett and Connor hid in bushes in the atrium. They crouched low, and Connor gathered up the shadows around them for extra cover. Not that they needed much—it was past midnight. They crouched a dozen yards from one of the ponds, prepared to spring their trap. Ninette stood in a clear space at the edge of the water completely exposed. She wore all black, including her heavy black boots—she intended to use them. She held a corked jug of dark red fluid over the water.

"Are you sure we're not going to get busted again?" She looked over her shoulder and waited to empty the jug.

"I really, REALLY hope not," Garrett said. "I guess it would be my fault if we did. But I know Ms. Ruiz and Master Borodin told Lady Ariel they would see her at the stadium tonight. I heard them tell her after enchanting class."

"That's three of the four," Connor said. "I watched for two hours before we came out. I didn't see Coach Kalett anywhere. Theoretically we should be clear. You know what to do, right Ninette?"

"Yes, *professor*." She glared at the container in her hand.

My lab partner doesn't know what she's doing, Ninette thought in a mockery of Connor's voice. *Do I know what to do? Hah!*

During her first attempt at the elixir, she overdid it on the saliva, and it turned into a shifting mass of sludge. The second, she didn't measure correctly, and it multiplied too fast, spilling blood all over the room, to her roommate's displeasure. Third time was the charm, and she came with a gallon of fresh, steaming horse blood.

"Alright, let's do it." Connor retreated further into the bushes and pulled Garrett back with him.

Ninette dove into the water making only the barest splash on the surface. The water was cool and as clear as glass. She swam a lap around the edge, looking for anything out of the ordinary, making sure to keep well below the surface. She'd never seen anyone else swimming in the atrium, which meant doing it would bring attention she didn't want or need.

Panicked whispering coming from above interrupted her thoughts. Ninette swam back to the edge and clambered out of the water. Connor and Garrett both exhaled in relief.

"What is it?" she asked, annoyed at the unnecessary interruption.

"You were down there for a while," Connor said. Some of the tension in his shoulders dissipated. "We couldn't see or hear anything. We got worried."

"If I was struggling, it wouldn't be quiet," Ninette smirked. "Let's do this thing."

She popped open the jug and spilled a little into the pond and the rest on the shore. The blood clouded the water, billowing outward. The puddle on the shore gleamed, almost black in the moonlight. They waited.

Seconds ticked by. Ninette held her breath and let it out slowly. She tried not to tense up. She knew she'd only have a fraction of a second to react when the time came. Minutes passed, and Connor shifted positions, his legs cramped from squatting. An hour crawled by, and Garrett started to nod off. Ninette did pushups to stay awake. Connor stifled a yawn. The sky above was crystal clear, and the moon cast a tranquil glow on the lush grass.

"Okay, I think this is a bust." Ninette pointed to the cooling, congealing pool of blood on the ground. "I'm thinking we made a mess for nothing."

She didn't see the dented head and beady yellow eyes emerging from the pond behind her.

Connor and Garrett pointed wildly. Ninette spun as it crept out of the water. Its eyes never left her as it scrabbled on the shore on all fours, inspecting the blood, lapping it up. While it drank, Garrett tossed the cucumber onto the ground as close to it as he could. The kappa croaked in excitement and pounced to snatch it up.

"I can NOT believe this is working," Ninette uttered.

The kappa downed its prize in a single gulp while watching Ninette, never noticing the other two. Connor reached into the ground, felt the connection between where he hid and the soil beneath the kappa's scaly webbed toes, then swung both hands upward like he was flipping a table. With an effort, he heaved the earth, toppling the kappa forward and spilling some of the water from its head.

The creature squeaked and grabbed at its head. Its yellow eyes dimmed and its slimy skin paled. It turned to dash for the water.

"Hey, ugly!" Ninette called out. "You and me. One on one."

It stopped cold on the edge of the water. Slowly, as though against its will, the kappa turned its head to make eye-contact with Ninette. It stood up and rhythmically slapped its chest, rasping another croak.

"What do we do?" Garrett whispered to Connor.

"Hope Ninette wins," he answered with more confidence than he felt. "If we interfere it might run." Connor clenched his fists and ran through spell options anyway.

Ninette raised her arms and circled the kappa. It matched her step by step in an odd dance. It shot water at Ninette, but she batted it away without flinching. She threw a fireball, but the kappa extinguished it with another water burst. She tried to shake the ground, but the kappa jumped away. It launched a volley of icicles, but they deflected off her shield of Will.

They continued to sidestep around each other. Ninette moved in closer. The kappa didn't back away. She lunged and they locked arms. Its claws dug into the backs of her hands, and it tried to throw Ninette to the ground. Her muscles strained and screamed, but she held on tight and struggled to remain upright.

"Not so strong now, are you?" she hissed.

The kappa revealed its needle teeth and hissed back.

They wrestled, neither gaining the upper hand. Garrett gripped Connor's arm tight enough to bruise it while Connor resisted every impulse he had to join the fray. His fingers itched, and he knew that together he and Ninette could win, but with so much water around he doubted they'd get the chance and they'd have wasted their opportunity.

Ninette ignited her hands and the kappa tried to disengage, but she squeezed tight. It screeched in agony and tried to bite her arms, the pain lending it new strength. She contorted to stay out of reach while holding on, trying to do as much damage as possible. Unable to dodge any longer, she let go and landed a flaming punch into its gut. The kappa squealed and thrashed. Its flailing claws left deep gashes on Ninette's arms and legs, and she limped back a step. They eyed each other warily.

Suddenly, Ninette leaped on it and tackled it to the ground. The kappa bit and scratched. Ninette pummeled and burned. They rolled around, struggling to pin each other. Ninette's breathing came in short bursts. The ground grew slick with fresh blood. Connor stepped out from his hiding place. Shadows swirled around him, tendrils raised from the ground and poised to strike, but he didn't have a clear shot.

"Don't you dare!" Ninette yelled. "I can do this."

The kappa sensed opportunity and pinned Ninette to the ground. It gave a triumphant belch and opened its beak wide—a rush of foul-smelling water poured over Ninette's face.

"What is it doing? Is it trying to drown her?" Garrett asked.

"It must be. It doesn't know she has gills!" Connor let out a giddy laugh.

Ninette concentrated on the water flowing from the kappa and froze it in the creature's throat. Its eyes bulged and it clawed at its neck, leaving jagged bloody streaks in its wake. Ninette threw it off and, swinging her fists up, encased its entire body in a pillar of stone, leaving its head and neck exposed. Only then did she thaw the water allowing it to breathe.

"You did it!" Connor and Garrett shouted.

They burst from the bushes and ran to her. Garrett squeezed Ninette in a hug, barely containing sobs of joy. They ignored the croaking and screeching of their prisoner.

"I'm okay, I promise," Ninette wheezed with a thumbs up. "Nothing to it." She wobbled and fell to the ground. "Okay, there's a lot of blood loss. Still probably fine though."

"Garrett, find a teacher," Connor instructed. "I'll make sure it doesn't get away. Get Nurse Poole, too."

Garrett ran toward the main area of the school. He stumbled over himself while looking back to ensure the kappa remained in place.

"Remind me why I didn't kill this thing?" Ninette said. She laid on her back and closed her eyes. "I don't think it can talk. Did you want to put it on a leash and see if we can return it?"

"It was your idea," Connor said, looking it over. "You said Sheena could track the summoner if she caught it alive."

"Oh, right." Ninette slapped her cheeks to try and shake off the wooziness. "That's the kind of thing you forget when you're wrestling for your life. Do you know how to do the tracking... whatever?"

"I do not," Connor admitted with a goofy grin. "But the teachers will! More importantly, we caught one of the monsters! The only one that's actually hurt someone so far."

The kappa stopped making noise and watched them, staring pure hatred from its sickly eyes. Its head remained utterly still.

"Maybe you're right. We caught it. It's someone else's problem now," Ninette said, drawing ragged breaths. "Hey, uh, Connor? Maybe I'm not doing so good. It's getting real foggy all of a sudden."

"It's not just you, that's real fog."

Thick, opaque clouds rolled in across the hills and filled the valleys of the park. They swirled and circled the two kids and their captive. Connor pulled on his focus glove, ready to defend Ninette, but the haze of blue and gray essence comprising the fog obscured his view. He could barely make her out next to him. He put his back to the kappa and paced circles around it, on guard for whoever, or whatever, was making the fog.

A blur to his left. A solid impact to the chest bowled him over, but he caught the barest glimpse of someone—someone in a blue and gold jacket.

The kappa's final croak turned into a wet gurgle. A howling gust of wind tore through the atrium, dispersing the fog. Garrett ran to them with Master Borodin and Nurse Poole in tow. Connor jumped to his feet, but it was too late. The kappa's throat had been torn open. Blood flowed in rivulets to paint scarlet streaks down its stone prison. Its yellow eyes were dim and vacant, and its beak hung slack.

The nurse ran to Ninette to administer healing magic. She wasted no words and squeezed Ninette's head in her hands. White light surged through the nurse, down her arms, and into Ninette, and she shrieked as her wounds zippered closed and vanished.

"Holy crap, why does that hurt so much!" she gasped.

"To discourage future stunts like this one," the Nurse grumbled. "That's the feeling of your skin stitching and bones setting—without anesthesia." She ran a hand through her wild black hair, still trying to wake herself up.

"You did this?" Master Borodin said, gesturing to the lifeless creature.

"Yes. I mean, no. We caught it, we didn't kill it," Connor stammered out.

"I see. You were right to catch it, though I would have suggested letting a teacher do that," the Master lectured dryly.

Connor fought the urge to point out he would have preferred that, too.

"A summoned creature will usually have a tint of the summoner's essence as long as it is under their will. Impossible now that it is deceased. I suspect someone is covering their tracks."

"Mr. McTaggart, Mr. Clarke, please help me lug Ms. Reefwalker to the infirmary," the nurse said. "We can leave the rest of this to Master Borodin."

Connor and Ninette both tried to protest but she silenced them with a fierce stare.

"Tonight was nothing short of total idiocy on your parts. None of you are excused from classes tomorrow."

The week ended quietly. The teachers announced that the kappa had been responsible for the attacks and was no longer a threat. The relief in the air was palpable, and a sense of normality returned to the school. That relief quickly gave way to stress as the last few classes before finals wrapped up. Students were told to spend the weekend and any free time they had preparing for their exams. Freshmen in particular were warned that their initial performance would dictate the courses available to them as they progressed through school, and any slacking would severely limit their options.

Professor Skreed's exams were a breeze for Connor. He demonstrated a proficient level of all the elements except light; the fact that he needed the professor to supply most of the elements wasn't held against him. Ninette exceeded all expectations with earth and fire and earned a proficient at water. She scraped out a "competent" at lightning, earning her pass. Garrett passed by the skin of his teeth, proficient in lightning and wind, and only showing competence at fire and nature.

"Mr. McTaggart, I am impressed," the Professor said to him. "I hope you're over your initial doubts about your abilities. Few are so versatile, and I dare say you will only improve with time. You may even master light one day. I do not often tell my students what classes in which they should enroll, but I would encourage you to take my Intermediate Elemental Magic class next semester. You will further develop your versatility, learning to combine the elements in new and interesting ways. I believe you would do well there."

Even more than Professor Skreed, Dr. Greens heaped praise on Connor. "Your work in—and out of—the classroom is top notch. You have an attention for detail. I very much look forward to continuing your instruction. You'll be in here a great deal in the coming years, Mr. McTaggart. Mark my words! I may even let you take Mad Science early if you keep it up."

While Connor basked in her praise, Dr. Greens suggested to Ninette that her time would be better spent on other areas of study.

The three met for dinner after the last exams. The cafeteria boomed with noise and excitement. Pass or fail, most students were just glad classes were over. The kitchen anticipated this, and there were far more sweets and treats on order than usual. Ninette managed to fit all of them onto her plate.

"What are you going to take next semester?" Garrett asked. "I'm taking enchanting with Lady Ariel again." He paused. "She didn't really make it sound like an option. I think I could do some cool stuff for my parents, though. I might even learn how to get near a computer again without blowing it up. I was also thinking about Folk History. I feel like there's still so much I don't know."

"That's funny. I was thinking of taking human history," Ninette said.

Connor laughed until she glared at him. "Wait, you're serious?"

"Yeah, so? I mostly grew up with my dad. I didn't get a lot of exposure to you people. Not nearly enough considering I'm probably going to be up here more often than not from now on." She thought a bit. "He'd send me up for local fairs and stuff. Things where

I could get lost in a crowd easily. It wasn't exactly a comprehensive education."

"What about your mom?" Garrett said.

"She died. I was five. Even then I didn't get out much. One look at my gills and people would poke me and laugh. Or worse." Ninette looked down at her food. "It was a long time ago. It's whatever, right? Anyway, I just wanna brush up a bit. Change of subject. I'm taking Intermediate Elemental Magic with you. I'm also gonna take Intermediate Will Magic. You in?"

"Maybe. I want to leave room in my schedule for Introductory Summoning," Connor said. "We need to know more about how it works. I might learn something that'll help us catch whoever's out to get me."

"But we got the kappa, right?" Garrett asked. "Things should be fine now."

"No." Connor shook his head. "We still don't know who brought them here." He leaned in and lowered his voice. "I didn't get a chance to say it, but whoever killed the kappa was wearing a dueling jacket."

Garrett choked on his food, and Ninette's fork fell from her hand.

"So, someone on the team is behind all this?" Ninette asked.

"Seems that way, but why? Why would they bring a vicious bloodsucker into the school?" Connor stared down at his plate as if it had the answers. "And why hasn't anyone died? Who tells a monster to suck out someone's blood but not kill them? Sure, one person might have gotten lucky, but four? They were left alive on purpose. We still have no clue what's going on, and there's still the vesporcus and the grimmalkin. They're not gone."

"Connor's right," Ninette said. She resumed shoveling snacks into her mouth. "As long as those two are around, we're all still in danger."

"Makes me glad to go home for two weeks," Garrett shivered. "Never thought I'd say that, but two weeks of boring sounds really great. TV and books. No school. No homework. No monsters."

"I don't want to go home, but my parents are insisting. 'Christmas is a family holiday,' they said. I guess I need them to sign my permission slip for dueling, so I should try to kiss up a little bit. What about you, Ninette?"

She smiled and gestured to the open cafeteria with her arms wide. "This is home 'til the summer. We don't celebrate Christmas. No reason to go back. Also," she pulled a slip of paper out of her back pocket, "signed and delivered this morning. Permission to kick asses and take names." She waved it in Connor's face.

"No fair! I'll probably have to spend half the break begging and pleading with my dad while my mom laughs and doesn't help at all." Connor slumped in his seat.

"I'm sure it'll be fine. Your mom sounds cool," Ninette reassured him.

"Yeah, we'll see. No Christmas, huh? What do Merfolk celebrate?"

"Hurricane season."

They laughed and ate and talked the evening away. Others joined them as the last exams concluded. Marck, fully recovered from his own run-in with the kappa, was going home to work at his dad's restaurant over the break. Julian was heading home as well to help on his parents' farm. Carrie and Vern were both staying at school—their families didn't celebrate either. Everyone's presence at the table stifled Ninette for a moment, but after a few months of socializing, she was starting to get the hang of having actual friends and managed to loosen up and crack a few toothy grins.

  Fat, wet snowflakes coated the patio outside, forming fluffy white pillows atop the tables and benches. No one noticed the hooded gray cat standing just outside of the warm glow of the cafeteria lights. Its yellow eyes watching. Its white teeth bared in a wide, menacing grin.

Chapter 17

Magic 101 – Shields of Will
The shield of Will is a barrier of pure essence able to negate almost any spell. Cast by the belief that the Magi is invincible, any wavering of that notion and the shield crumbles. Though powerful, the essence expended is directly proportional to the spells blocked, so it is rarely the most efficient means of protection.

The sun was high by the time Ninette woke up. Her roommate was an early bird and usually kept her from dozing late, but Ninette had the room to herself over winter break. She lay in bed for an extra half hour, soaking in the warmth of the blankets and solitude before finally rising. She stumbled down empty halls to the almost empty cafeteria to find Carrie and Vern lingering over breakfast. Ninette piled a plate high and joined them.

"'Sup," she greeted through a mouth full of bacon.

"Well look who's up," Carrie teased. "Vern and I have been here for an hour."

"How come? Food's not THAT good." Ninette heaped more into her mouth regardless.

"Hoping to run into you actually," Vern answered matter-of-factly. "Well, Carrie was. Since you're here, I think I'll head to the library and find a quiet spot to read."

"Oh. Okay. Good to see you?" Ninette took Vern's empty seat across from Carrie while eyeing the half-full plate he left behind. "Weird guy. Why were you looking for me?"

"Well," Carrie drew out the word, "It's basically the worst kept secret in the school that you and Connor killed the kappa. I want to try out for the dueling team, and I wanted to score some one-on-one practice with our resident monster slayer."

"Well thanks, I guess. I'm heading to the gym after breakfast. Do you want to come with?"

"Let's meet after." Carrie's black pigtails bounced as she jumped up from her seat. "I hate to work out on a full stomach. Or ever. Come find me after?"

"Sounds good," Ninette agreed. Connor, Codie, now Carrie. Ninette watched the bubbly girl leave and sighed. "Maybe I should skip tryouts and apply to coach."

When she entered the gym, she inhaled sharply at the sight of a wolf sprinting on the treadmill, but it was just Van. He was the only were-student she ever saw transformed in public. There were others, she was sure, but they kept a lower profile. She rubbed at her neck, felt the ridges of her gills beneath the ever-present scarf. The school was supposed to be a tolerant place, but as she knew, "supposed to be" didn't always work out.

Good for him, I guess.

She focused on her routine, content to ignore him. Lifting weights usually relaxed her, but not today. She couldn't help thinking he was watching her. Whenever she snuck a look at him, he seemed occupied, eyes forward and headphones—comical on his wolf ears—thumping away, but she had prickles on the back of her neck and arms. She was laid out for the bench press when his wolfish face appeared over her.

"Need a spot?" he huffed, out of breath.

"I'm good. You didn't need to stop running," she snipped. Annoyance crept into the edge of her words.

"I was wrapping up anyway. Thought you might need a hand. Gonna see you on the team next semester, yeah?" He flashed a lupin grin.

"That's the plan." She hoisted the bar. He didn't leave. She made sure to emphasize how little help she needed, performing each rep with deliberate and clean movements, then racked the weights without breaking a sweat.

"Cool, cool," he barked. He closed his eyes, and a shiver ran through his body. The shaggy brown fur on his arms and legs seemed to melt away and with it, no small portion of his mass as well. The lanky boy left behind whipped his mop of hair out of his eyes. "Well, hope to see you. I've heard the stories, too, yeah? Gave old Brokk a scare. Besides, anyone who could catch a monster when the teachers couldn't? Pretty badass." He left the gym whistling to himself.

Ninette was glad to finally have the place to herself. Something about the werewolf boy annoyed her. He hadn't been quite what she'd imagined. He seemed… nice. Too nice maybe? She wasn't sure, but she didn't stop mulling the feeling over until she was finished lifting. She cleaned up and went to knock on Carrie's door. Vern answered.

"You're here," he droned. "I guess I'll leave then." The dark-haired elf nodded to Carrie and strode off.

"You and Vern, huh?" Ninette teased. She stepped into the room and jostled Carrie with her elbow. "I can see it."

"It's not like that." She waved her hands in front of her. "I'm just not used to being away from home. My parents decided to take a second honeymoon, so I got stuck here. He doesn't show it, but he's homesick, too, and we're just keeping each other company. Besides," she added, blushing, "I don't think he's interested."

"Uh huh. Well, let's get out there. We're burning daylight."

"Out there?"

"Yeah, we're going to the stadium. There's no practice today, so we may as well use it."

Ninette threw on a light jacket while Carrie wrapped herself head to toe in a puffy, down jacket and matching knit cap and gloves. Together, they marched out to the dueling field. Icy winds cut through the air under a cold, gray sky, so they weren't expecting to see anyone else, much less Sheena Crowton alone on the field, eyes closed and sweating from exertion. She stood in the center of three arrays of complicated, red rings. Ninette and Carrie waited in the tunnels, unable to speak a word. They could only watch.

Swirling lights coalesced around Sheena. Even from where they stood some yards away, Ninette and Carrie could see the strain on Sheena's body—her muscles tight, tendons straining, veins pulsing like thunder, her breathing staggered. With a desperate scream her eyes flew open and rolled back into her head. The ground around her exploded with prismatic light and a rush of wind whipped through the stadium. The sound of her cry hung in the air long after the lights faded, and the wind died, and she collapsed to the ground. Ninette and Carrie ran over to her. She was still breathing, but her arms were covered with blood, and she was cold and clammy to the touch. Nearby, circles and symbols painstakingly painted in wet crimson marred the grass.

"Sheena, holy crap, are you okay? Sheena?" Carrie shook her by the shoulders.

"What the hell were you trying to do?" Ninette cried, looking around for help.

Sheena frowned where she lay and groaned. "I had to try. I still don't know how they did it. Even with blood. I couldn't do three at once." She could barely get the words out through her chattering teeth, but she pushed Carrie away and rolled to her purse. She pulled out bandages and wrapped her wounds.

"Why would you want to?" Ninette said, still incredulous.

"You wouldn't understand." Sheena gathered her things and stormed off in a cloud of haughty superiority that was somewhat lessened when she got dizzy and Ninette had to help keep her from falling on her face.

"You could explain. Because it looks like you nearly killed yourself to bring more monsters to the school."

"I don't have to explain anything to you," she snapped. She yanked free of Ninette and crossed her arms defiantly even as her cheeks reddened. Then she looked at Ninette and her eyes widened with some realization. "Maybe you could… no, you're too stupid. But if it's just…" she spat. "I needed to do it, okay? And… and I… well, I'm going to find who did it and I'm going to learn how they did it and then I'm going to do it." She stalked off like a wet cat, her stride stiff and her back straight but with her head held defiantly high.

"Intense," Carrie said, watching her leave.

"I think you mean insane." Ninette shook her head. "If she wants to work out her inferiority complex alone, she's welcome to it." Ninette bent over to touch her toes, falling into her pre-workout routine. She stretched out her arms and shoulders and then jumped up and down to get her blood pumping. "You ready?"

Carrie turned back from where Sheena had left and jumped back in surprise. "Huh? Oh yeah, I guess so."

Ninette crossed the field and took a stance opposite Carrie. "So, what's your plan?"

"What do you mean?" Carrie asked.

"Your strategy. James distracts people with his creepy shadows. Codie moves really fast. Van makes people uncomfortable by wolfing out. A lot of the doubles do a one-two punch of snare and attack." Ninette gestured to herself and smiled. "My plan is to hit people. Very. Hard." To emphasize her point she charged up a fireball bigger than the one she used in Seer Brokk's class. The whirling flames scorched the ground even from where she held them over her head.

"Oh, okay." Carrie tried not to look intimidated. "I think I would wear people down. Wait for an opening. I have a little trick I've been working on. Why don't you lay it on me, and I'll show you what I can do?"

"Are you sure?"

Carrie nodded, so Ninette pitched her fireball toward Carrie. The blast stopped short against Carrie's shield of Will, and then, to Ninette's surprise, bounced back instead of exploding. She prepared her own shield to spare her from the explosion, but the effort of blocking her own attack left her gasping for air afterward.

"Okay, that's pretty cool. I've never seen a spell bounce off a shield." Ninette brushed some debris off her shoulders. She caught her breath. "Try this."

Ninette raised both hands and prepared a torrential blast of saltwater. Carrie faced it down confidently, but the blast connected, bowling her over and drenching her.

"What the hell?" Her teeth chattered and she shivered inside her drenched coat.

"Why didn't you block it?"

"I swear I did. Okay, payback time," Carrie retorted between shivers. She rubbed at her temples but got back up and mirrored Ninette's ready stance.

"If you're sure."

"Oh, I'm sure." Carrie grit her teeth. She sliced the air and a blade of wind screamed across the arena, picking up dirt and grass as it went. Ninette deflected it easily. Carrie slashed her hands in front of her and let loose a flurry of air blades. Ninette blocked them all with minimal effort, but then one got through leaving a shallow cut on her shoulder, the next a gash on her side. Something wasn't right; static filled her head.

"Hey, Carrie? Carrie, hold up!" Ninette shouted.

But Carrie was lost in the moment, putting the finishing touch on her barrage with a swirling gust. It slammed into Ninette tossing her spiraling into the wall with a horrendous crunch.

"Oh no!" Carrie hurried to Ninette's side. "Are you okay? I thought you'd be able to manage."

"I thought so, too." Ninette stared at her hands. "My shield… poofed. I still can't make one." She flicked her fingers. Realization hit her like a tornado in the face. "Grimmalkin."

"What's a…?"

Ninette cut her off with a finger to the lips and scanned the area. A pair of glowing, yellow eyes stared out from the darkness of one of the entry tunnels.

"Come out," she called to it.

The grimmalkin hopped out from its hiding space and took a bow. The closer it got the more Ninette's head hurt.

"What the hell do you want?"

The grimmalkin shrugged, an oddly human gesture from the cat.

"What is that?"

"It's called a grimmalkin. It eats magic, and it's what stopped our shields from working. I can't feel my essence, can you?"

"Um, yeah, I think so." Carrie tried a slashing motion and another air blade whizzed at the cat. It didn't twitch a whisker, but the blade stopped a few feet short of it. "That should have been bigger."

"Magic doesn't work on it," Ninette remembered. She looked around and spotted a chunk of broken wall. Hefting it over her head, she chucked it at the grimmalkin. It missed, but it must have been closer than the creature expected because it narrowed its eyes and hissed at her.

"Can it use magic, too?" Carrie asked.

"Let's find out," Ninette growled.

She picked up another rock and charged the cat, ready to clobber the thing. She got in close and swung at its head, but her punch reflected off a shield. The impact reversed all her momentum, staggering her backward.

"That was different."

"My shield," Carrie whispered. "It's using my shield."

The grimmalkin fired off one of Carrie's air blades. The girls jumped aside. The grimmalkin watched them both, smiling and waiting. Its whiskers twitched, and it extended and retracted its claws. Minutes passed, but neither side made a move. The grimmalkin stretched in an awkward mimic of Ninette's warm up, then yawned, turned, and pranced away.

"Wait," Ninette called after it. "That's it?"

The grimmalkin looked over its shoulder and winked, then left the same way it came.

"What was that all about?" Carrie said.

Ninette wished she knew.

Ninette spent the rest of the week sparring with Carrie. Carrie's reflective barriers provided a new challenge that she was determined to overcome. She practiced working around them with spells targeted around Carrie instead of at her, and she helped Carrie practice being more offensive by chaining her own attacks to follow up on reflecting her opponents'. They both looked forward to the daily practice, but Ninette never convinced Carrie to join her in the gym.

She didn't see Van in the gym again—not strictly a negative, as something about him creeped her out, though she still couldn't put her finger on it. She never ran into Sheena either, mixed feelings there. There was something else going on with that girl.

She probably would *be helpful if she could get her head out of her butt.*

On Christmas Eve, with nothing better to do, Ninette paid Karronus Naegus a visit. She snuck through the hidden locker door and felt her way down the dark stairs, wondering how he would react to her dropping in.

He must have been forewarned because by the time she reached his study he had set out a pot of tea and two cups. He sat cross legged, filling his couch and beckoned her to sit in one of the chairs opposite him.

"I suppose thanks are in order for quieting my tunnels. Quite the feat, even after handicapping it."

"I don't think we would have figured it out if you hadn't told us what we were looking for," Ninette admitted. "Why DID you tell us?"

"Because you wanted to know." He smiled over his cup. "And because youth is brash where age breeds caution."

"You knew we'd fight it."

"And you would either succeed, and rid the school of a nuisance, or you would fail, probably horribly, and the staff would be forced to take more decisive action."

Ninette's stomach turned. "That's kind of messed up."

"Isn't it?" He laughed and his golden eyes glimmered dangerously in the firelight.

"It… it really is," Ninette protested. "What kind of teacher are you?"

"The kind who honestly doesn't care if you live or die," he responded in a painfully flat tone.

Ninette spewed tea everywhere, and the librarian laughed even louder.

"Dear child, I wouldn't have done it if I didn't think you had a sporting chance. Mr. McTaggart is wicked clever. I've known since I first met him. You are uncommonly powerful. Mr. Clarke was also there, I assume."

Ninette laughed. "Be nice. Garrett is great."

"He is indeed. He certainly has a greater sense of self-preservation than either of you, and I suspect the boy has talents he does not yet realize." The dragon spaced out for a minute. "So. One down. Two to go."

"Don't suppose you have any other *helpful* hints," Ninette said, sarcasm dripping off the word.

"No. At this point you know as much as I do. The vesporcus is out in the woods. I can tell you for certain it is still there; I can smell it. I suspect the grimmalkin is residing on the school grounds, but it will not be found unless it wishes to be. That is the way of them, and tracking it is worse than futile. Any tracking spell you might conceive of would falter before it connected."

"It wanted to be found the other day. It harassed me and Carrie while we were practicing."

"Did it now?" Mr. Naegus pursed his lips and leaned back on the couch. He stared up at the ceiling as if he could tell what was happening on the other side. "The cat toying with the mice, perhaps. I would watch your back. You know how that ends."

Neither of them said more while they finished their tea.

Ninette went back to her room still unsure what to make of the librarian. *He sort of acts like he wants to help, but he's also a smug jerk face about it. He and Sheena would probably get along great.*

Thoughts of Sheena only annoyed her further. Why couldn't people just say what they meant and do what they said? It wasn't a big ask. At least Connor seemed mostly on the up and up. He was a little too single-minded to be playing games with anyone. And Garrett was polite to a fault and sweet to boot. In the end, she supposed some people didn't suck. At least, not quite as much as all the rest.

Ninette awoke on Christmas morning to find two presents at the foot of her bed: one disheveled, the paper wrinkled and torn; the other wrapped neat and tidy with a crisp bow. Ninette hadn't celebrated Christmas since her mom died, and it hadn't entered her mind that someone might send her something. The nicer package was from Garrett, a US History book with a plain card saying, "Merry Christmas," in his tidy handwriting. She picked up the second; the wrapping paper fell apart with minimal effort revealing a shoe box containing a scarlet scarf. The note was in Connor's barely legible scrawl:

> If you're going to wear one all the time
> you may as well have more than one.
>
> Merry Christmas,
> Connor

Ninette buried her face in the scarf and cried, a giant smile splitting her face.

Chapter 18

> Elemental Magicks – Healing Spells
> "Healing spell" is a catch-all for magic used to restore physical injuries. Commonly used elements are nature, water, and light. All heal the body in different ways, but none is more or less effective than the other. Many of these effects can also be captured within the standard healing elixir. This draught provides ready-made if lesser effects and is a mainstay in Magi hospitals.

Connor's left arm hung limp at his side, chilled numb. He awkwardly tumbled to the side as the earth below him erupted. Nearby, Carrie struggled to free her legs from their stone prison, but she found the energy to summon lashing, thorny vines to protect herself. Across the pitch, Ninette stomped and caused a tremor to toss Carrie in the air. A vine whip across the back knocked Ninette forward and left a bloody gash along her shoulders. Connor tried hitting her with a wind blast, but Ninette pulled a boulder from the ground to block, then rolled it at him.

Carrie caught herself with a cloud and bounced in front of Connor. She used her shield to reflect the boulder back at Ninette. Connor plunged his fingers deep into the dirt; a stream of liquid shadow bubbled up beneath Ninette while Carrie cast three blades of air that shredded the ground as they converged on Ninette from all sides. Ninette threw her hands out to the side and braced for the impact. Her face contorted with the effort of stopping the spells, and she just managed it. Exhausted, she collapsed to the ground.

"Let's call it a day, shall we?" Nurse Poole declared, stepping in between them. The sharpness of her voice commanded enough attention to stop any further casting. She nodded with satisfaction and set about patching them all up. "It's nice to see you taking safety as a concern for a change."

Connor had returned to school with a few days left in the holiday break, itching to get ready for dueling team tryouts. Upon hearing about the grimmalkin attack, he dove back into practice headfirst—now with multiple motivations. Carrie continued to join in the sparring matches, and they discovered Ninette usually won until they started teaming up on her. Ninette lost, but not as decisively. After a day or two they recognized the need for post-practice medical attention. Fortunately, Nurse Poole and Coach Kalett were willing to supervise. Though they couldn't prove it, there were no further incidents with the grimmalkin, and they hoped the presence of the teachers would keep it that way.

He also followed through on his plan to take Introductory Summoning. The class was held in the gymnasium just as the demo had been at the start of the year, which Connor thought surprising as there were only twenty or so kids. But the bleachers were pushed back, and rows of chairs and desks were arrayed to face a portable chalkboard. Sitting in the back row, looking huffier than usual, Sheena Crowton shot a narrow-eyed, tight-lipped, death glare at anyone who so much as looked at her.

"Find a seat," Master Borodin said as he marched to the head of the class. He tugged at his red and gray goatee and his dark robes swished behind him while he paced. "We will begin shortly. We have much to cover."

Connor swallowed and steeled himself for an awkward conversation. Ninette had told him what happened over the break, including Sheena's botched summoning attempt. He knew Sheena could help them catch the other monsters, he just needed to convince her. He took the chair next to her, careful to avoid eye contact. The look she gave him could punch a hole through steel; he could feel it boring into him. He kept his eyes forward and his mouth shut.

Maybe I'll wait a few minutes to talk to her. Maybe a few days.

Master Borodin clapped for attention. "Welcome to Introductory Summoning. In this class, you will learn the art of producing and commanding magical creatures. This is a hands-on class," he said, pausing for effect. "If you are afraid of a little rough play, I advise you to withdraw. Still plenty of room in Soarra's Nature Magic Studies." He laughed derisively while he waited to see if anyone took him up on his offer. "Does anyone know the first rule of summoning?"

From the front row, an orc girl with uncharacteristically light hair in a long ponytail raised her hand. "Kaern, daughter of Krane. Don't summon what you can't control."

"Correct," Borodin said.

Kaern's chest swelled with pride, but the master gave her an unsettling look.

"But how do you know what you can control?"

Kaern chewed her lip while she thought. No one else had a clue. Sheena picked at her nail polish, mumbling to herself.

"You fight it?" Kaern finally offered.

"Simple and to the point, not incorrect. The better answer is experience. If you have tamed a creature before, or one like it, you may be confident you can do so again. If you have done sufficient research and know both your target and yourself, you may summon comfortably. For our purposes, I will act as your experience. I will also fulfill the second rule of summoning, which is…?"

Connor wished he had read the chapters, but all his free time went into training, and also, he never did the reading. Sheena sighed loud enough to be heard in the halls. All eyes turned to her.

"Don't summon alone."

"Thank you, Ms. Crowton," Master Borodin said with a smile. "Summoning is best done in groups. Even the most prepared summoners occasionally bite off more than they can chew. A partner is a wise precaution."

He turned to the chalkboard and drew a single, perfect circle with three runes inside. "This is a level one summoning circle. Best used for summoning docile creatures or familiars. The circle, when imbued with your essence, serves two purposes: it locates the intended creature, and acts as a magical leash. Put a leash on a tame dog, and you can take it for a walk. Put a leash on a feral tiger, and you will be horribly mauled.

"Most wild creatures must be subdued before you can expect them to obey you. More intelligent creatures can be bargained with instead, but this is a tricky proposition. Summoning a creature with any degree of intelligence will result in a much weaker bond, subject to breaking at any time."

So, whoever summoned our monsters has beaten a vesporcus, a kappa, and *the grimmalkin? Which one is the most powerful? We barely beat the kappa, and we cheated.* Cold sweat clung to Connor's shirt.

Master Borodin took a piece of chalk and drew another copy of the circle on the ground. "Today we practice familiars. Rats, bats, weasels, and the like. In most cases the circle alone is enough to ensure obedience. You may banish these creatures with the same circle you summoned them with—the opposite process—but this will only work if they are indeed obedient. If you haven't tamed them, they may resist being sent away. They may grow angry."

His circle glowed a fair lavender hue, and a rather obese ferret materialized. It sniffed the air and scurried up the master's robe, resting on his shoulder. "As a treat, and because I know she's going to do it anyway, Ms. Crowton, please step forward."

Sheena tilted her head, contemplating whether or not to humor the teacher, but ultimately rose from her seat and stalked to the front of the class with her head high and her back straight. She crossed her arms in front of Master Borodin and stared up at him. He met her stare with a haughty one of his own.

"Ms. Crowton is going to demonstrate an advanced technique. If she can," he added.

Her nostrils flared and she spun around to put her back to him.

"A summoner who has perfect mastery over circles and runes, who can picture it perfectly in their mind and knows the meaning in their bones, this person may create the circle from sheer Will. Level one only, please," he finished, stepping aside to give her room.

Not one to back down from a challenge, Sheena snorted and then slammed both palms onto the air behind her. With a snap like thawing ice, two circles—perfect replicas of the one on the board—appeared instantly in the air. They lit up the same purple color, and two identical ravens fluttered out of them to perch on her shoulders. A brief glimmer of purple shined in their eyes, and they bowed their heads in unison.

Master Borodin chose not to acknowledge the extra bird. "You may return to your seat. Split into pairs and practice your circles. There is an index of level one runes in the class module."

Connor caught Sheena's attention as she walked back. "Hey, Sheena. That was pretty cool. Do you think maybe you could show me?" He smiled so wide it almost hurt, even as his heart thudded nervously.

She scoffed. "It takes complete mastery of the circle to do it with your mind. Perfect knowledge. I could draw a circle and runes before I could write my name. Remind me how long you've been studying them?" Her cold voice echoed in the gym.

No one spoke, but the class moved as one, desks and chairs scraping as everyone found a partner that was not Sheena. Everyone except Connor. She groaned in exasperation.

Connor got out his tablet and picked the first three runes, not wanting to disappoint. He knelt on the ground to draw, deliberate and slow. He had barely finished when Sheena snapped at him.

"That's not a circle. That's an egg. This is a precise art. Try again."

"Yeah, sure. Sorry." He erased his first attempt and tried again, going even slower. "Why are you taking this class? I would think you could skip it."

"I thought so, too," Sheena pouted. She deflated into her chair. "That's why I didn't waste time with it last semester. My dad argued with the headmistress for weeks, but the stubborn bat wouldn't budge. Said I had to prove myself on the basics before they let me advance." She stamped her foot and grunted.

Come on. You can't be that good. Connor wisely kept the thought to himself.

He reversed position quickly, though, as it took him ten tries to draw a circle to Sheena's standards. She stressed perfection, but she and Master Borodin made it look simple. Finally, she gave him a curt nod, and he continued to the next step.

While he sketched the runes, she knelt beside him. "Look, you guys killed the kappa, right? So, you're not total morons. Maybe I could use some help," she whispered.

"Huh?"

"That grimmalkin thing was watching me over the break," she hissed, looking over her shoulder as though she expected to see it.

"Ninette saw it, too," Connor said. "Right after she ran into you, actually."

Sheena's cheeks reddened, and she looked away from Connor. "Told you about that, huh?" she mumbled.

"Whoever summoned the monsters must know you're looking for them. That's why it's watching you now. The vesporcus is still out there, too. The teachers haven't found it yet. I don't even know if they're still trying. Between that and the grimmalkin, we've got our hands full, but I'm sure one of them will turn up again eventually. Whatever is going on at this school, I don't think it's over yet."

Sheena considered this while she coached him through the runes. When he finished, he looked to her for approval.

"Yeah, that's close enough," she sighed, still deep in thought. "Go ahead."

Connor poured essence into the circle, feeling it flow from his core, down his arms, and through his fingers into the shapes on the ground. He pictured the animal in his mind. The runes lit up, and a tiny, blue and gray swallow appeared. It hopped in a little circle and looked around, then alighted onto Connor's finger and trilled a few notes before its eyes flashed purple. In the back of Connor's mind, like it took up a small physical space, he could feel the bird's presence, and he knew if he asked it to do something for him, it would obey.

"Not bad. A little small, but whatever. First try, right?" Sheena said. "So basically, you guys are waiting for the next awful thing to happen, and you're going to take it from there?"

"Yeah, that's kinda what we've got." Connor laughed. "It sounds dumb, but I guess it's worked out so far, right?"

"I was wrong. You guys are morons." The next comment came with no small amount of reservation. "But you're morons with one more notch on your belts than anyone else. I'll let you know if I see the cat again."

Connor smiled and held out his hand for a fist bump. Sheena rolled her eyes and ignored it.

Master Borodin made his way over to them and inspected Connor's new friend. Connor instructed the bird to hop from hand to hand, then to land on the teacher's head and sing. Master Borodin approved and moved on.

"I hoped I might learn something in this class that gave me an idea of where to go next," Connor added, "but I guess that's a lot to expect from the first day."

"You need to catch them alive. Then you might be able to trace the essence link, the magic connecting master and summoner. Until then, there isn't much more you can do."

"That's not quite true."

Connor knew where he could find the one behind everything. He'd seen the jacket, the puffy-sleeved blue and gold of the dueling team's varsity uniforms. One of the nine team members was the summoner who brought the monsters into the school, but the only way he could get close enough to figure out which one it was, would be to make the team himself.

Chapter 19

> Elemental Magicks – Nature
> Nature Magic covers manipulation of plants, animals, and even people. Uses range from Agrimancers growing rare ingredients for potions to shamans and berserkers entering trance-like states to harness the abilities of wild beasts. Other practitioners claim to be able to speak with plants and animals.

If anyone asked Connor what he learned on Friday, he could not have answered. Headmistress Mine called on him to explain what led the first master to leave White Lotus Academy and start their own school. He stammered and stalled until she shook her head in disappointment and assigned him extra homework. Even the punishment failed to register. He drummed his fingers on his desk and bounced his leg up and down at a manic pace. At lunch, he wandered automatically through the buffet to collect a random assortment of food, but once they sat, Garrett had to remind him to eat.

"You okay? You haven't touched anything."

"Just nervous," Connor answered. He forced himself to take a few bites but feared he wouldn't keep it down. "I mean, what if I don't make it? What if I should have practiced more? What if I…?"

"Hey." Garrett gave him a shake. "You're freaking out. You got this."

"WE got this," Ninette corrected, dropping in next to him. "Show them how many elements you can use. You're, like, the only one who can do that."

I'm not the only *one,* Connor's thoughts taunted. *James and Professor Skreed both said there are others.* He tried to shove those thoughts away and focus on his food.

The rest of his classes went about as well as history. In potions, he mixed up the order of spring rain and elm ashes, and his Lightning in a Bottle exploded—the resulting thunderclap deafened the whole class and earned him a rare rebuke from Dr. Greens. In summoning, he added an extra line a rune, and the swallow he summoned had three heads and breathed fire. It still listened to him, but Master Borodin strongly disapproved, and Sheena refused to acknowledge his existence for the rest of the day. Only after the final bell did he realize he'd spent all of Intermediate Elemental Magic staring out the window. Professor Skreed caught him as he shuffled out.

"Good luck today, young man." His words were warm and reassuring.

Ninette grabbed Connor by the shoulders and escorted him out of class. "Okay, Sleeping Beauty, time to wake up. Don't leave me hanging out there." She pushed him halfway down the hall before he shook off his stupor. "There you are. You with me?"

I can *do this. We've practiced as hard as anyone. I have to make the team. It's all I've ever wanted.* A second, less exciting, thought surfaced. *Also, it's probably the best lead on whoever is trying to kill me.*

He bit his lip and nodded, allowing Ninette to escort him down to the stadium and onto the field. Carrie was already waiting, bundled up head to toe against the bitter January cold, and they were joined at the last minute by a dwarf boy Connor recognized from his math class.

"Good to see some new blood," Coach Kalett called out when he entered the field. He was accompanied by Nurse Poole, James, Codie, and Van. The four of them wore warm workout clothes and they lined up across from the assembled dueling aspirants. "We're going to be evaluating you on a couple different things, so I hope you're ready to sweat." He rubbed his hands together with excitement. "Let's not waste time. First: raw strength. Not the be-all end-all, but important nonetheless."

He surveyed the four assembled students and read the first name off the list. "Carrie Kung."

The coaches and the three duelists took seats at the edge of the field, notepads in hand. Connor and Ninette and the other boy sat down on the bleachers behind them. Coach Kalett called out each of the eight elements and instructed Carrie to cast the most powerful spell she could in each. She threw a small fireball, created a weak rain of hail, passed on lightning and earth, then ripped up the ground with large blades of wind and summoned a giant Venus fly trap. She passed again on shadow and light.

"Not bad," the coach said while scribbling down notes. "Do you have any sort of unique spell?"

"I do, but I need help demonstrating it," Carrie responded, smiling.

Van hopped off the bench. "Got it, coach." He ran out to the field to stand opposite Carrie. "Whatcha need?"

"Toss a spell at me."

Van looked to the coaches for approval, then shrugged. He leaned back, took a deep breath, and then spat a blast of fire in Carrie's direction. Hands in her pockets, Carrie waited. The spell bounced off her shield and careened back twice as fast toward Van, who yelped and jumped out of the way.

"Reflective shield," the coach noted, voice even.

He told Carrie she could sit and then went through the same exercise with the next boy. He had amazing talent with earth; he created two towering stone golems that lumbered around pounding on things, but he only managed three other elements—and nothing impressive. The crestfallen look on his face said he knew he hadn't made it. He didn't even wait to watch the others.

"Ninette Reefwalker, you're up."

Ninette sauntered out to the field. Her fireball left a crater ten feet deep and would have demolished the nearby stands if Nurse Poole hadn't shielded them. She seemed torn between scolding Ninette and praising her. Ninette filled the crater with water in under three seconds, flash froze it, then shattered the ice and rained crystalline lances down around the area. She passed on lightning and then slammed the ground with her fist sending spikes of stone like miniature mountains exploding out of the ground. When the coach called out air, she shook her head and cut him off before he could go on.

"That's all I can do," she said.

"Any special or unique spell?" he asked.

"Do I need one?" She rested her hand on her hip and waited.

His face remained neutral as he told her to take her seat. He asked James and Codie to go out and restore the field before they continued. Connor observed the repairs with a lump in his throat. His heart pounded out the seconds while they smoothed the earth and regrew the grass until the field was good as new.

"Connor McTaggart," the coach read off the list.

Connor stood up, legs trembling and heart racing. He felt a little light-headed. Ninette slapped him on the back, almost knocking him onto his face, and gave him a thumbs up. Carrie smiled up at him and mouthed, "Good luck." The coaches watched him; he felt like they were already evaluating him. Connor swallowed hard to try and settle his stomach. He stepped out onto the field. A gentle breeze ruffled his hair. The sun warmed his face despite the winter cold. The grass beneath his feet was bright green, and the soil gave ever so slightly. Everything happened in slow motion.

"Fire!" the coach shouted.

Connor hesitated. His heart stopped. They were waiting for him to do something, and he couldn't.

"So, um, I can't make fire," Connor admitted. He broke out in a sweat when both coach and nurse started scratching notes. "I can use it, though!" he added. "I can use everything but light. I just… can't make it," he finished quickly.

"He's really good at counterspells!" Ninette supplied from the stands.

"Counterspells," the coach muttered to himself. "James, help him out."

James rose from his seat and walked slowly out to join Connor, giving him a sly wink. "Same order?" he asked the coach, who nodded in agreement. "Roger. Here we go."

James waved his hand to create a bonfire between himself and Connor. The flames called to Connor, and he mentally forged a connection between them and his own essence. He pulled four streamers of flame from it and converged them on a single point from multiple directions. James formed a raincloud. Connor used the water to create an ice slick across the grass, then turned it into a bed of frosty needles. James created a steady flow of electricity that danced between his hands and Connor redirected it into the sky then brought it crashing down in a devastating thunderbolt.

How many can he do?

The more he cast, the more comfortable he became. He could almost pretend James was Ninette, and they were just messing around like they had all last semester. He manipulated the ground without assistance, casting three furrows through the field to upheave the soil. Pulling the wind around himself, he made a barrier of shifting gusts, then launched it across the field to pummel against James's shields. He grew blades of grass into thorny vines as thick as a man's leg and lashed them about. Shadow next; his silhouette darkened into an inky blot and tendrils snaked out from it. They crisscrossed as they traveled, piercing in and out of the ground before terminating in sharp points halfway across the field. Before the coach could call out "Light," Connor held up his hand and shook his head.

"Okay!" Coach Kalett cheered, writing notes as fast as he could. "Still, seven elements. Not something we see every day. Right, James?"

James smiled and shook his head, never looking away from Connor.

"Okay, kid, anything special to show us?"

Codie had warned them about this part of tryouts a week ago. Connor spent every waking minute since trying to come up with something to secure his spot on the team. *Ninette thinks she'll get by on her essence alone. She's probably right. No such luck for me. Man, I hope this thing works.* It was now or never.

"Can James help? I need a victim," Connor said, substituting weak humor for confidence.

James smirked. "Am I blocking this? Letting it hit me? This is your show, I'm merely a player."

"You can try and block it," Connor taunted, though it sounded hollow. "If it works, you won't be able to," he added under his breath.

Connor hunched over, placed his hands in front of him, and zeroed in on the space between them. He blocked out the rest of the world except for the palms of his hands. Essence flowed from every point in his body to converge into a dense mass of pure, unshaped magic between his palms. To all outward appearances, nothing happened, but Connor was shaking when he straightened, and he fired the invisible ball directly at James.

No one saw or heard anything, but they all felt it; a wave of pins and needles passed over them like every muscle in their bodies had fallen asleep. James got it worse. He staggered back, and his face twisted through discomfort, confusion, and rage, and then returned to a cool, collected smirk in a fraction of a second, but his shoulders remained tense, his jaw tight.

He snapped his fingers. He opened his hand and flexed. He moved through several rapid, frantic hand motions. A few tortuous seconds later, fire and lighting sprang out of his hands and water poured from the sky above while a gust of wind swirled past, fluttering his jacket.

"He silenced me," James observed. "He silenced me," he repeated louder, so the coaches could hear. "It only lasted about three seconds, but I was dead in the water. What did you do?" he asked, looking again at his hands, not clearly addressing Connor at all.

"I threw essence at you," Connor gasped between sharp breaths. "Like, a lot of it. Condensed into a ball."

"Is that all?" James said, raising an eyebrow.

"Well, there's a game-winner," the coach exclaimed, jumping to his feet. "What do you call that?"

Connor tried to catch his breath. It took him a minute to register the coach's question. "Essence bomb?"

Coach Kalett told the remaining applicants to get some water and take a break while the coaches and team members conferred and prepared for the second portion of the tryout. Connor headed toward the locker room tired, sweating, and unsure how he would muster the energy to keep going. Ninette ran up behind him and put him in a headlock.

"Where you been keeping that one, huh?" she teased while jostling him around.

Carrie hurried to catch up. "I didn't know you could do seven elements. And I've never heard of anyone doing something like *that*."

"I don't think anyone has," Connor boasted. He squirmed free from Ninette. "I figured it couldn't be good, right? I thought a lot of essence in one place would be *something*? I didn't know for sure what it would do—I've never gotten it to do anything before," he added sheepishly. "I just couldn't think of anything else to do with my essence since I can't create elements like you guys." He tried to suppress his smile, but nervous excitement forced it out of him.

By the time they returned, Coach Kalett paced the center of a *mostly* repaired field with Nurse Poole standing stoically at his side while the three team members each stood in a separate corner.

"We're going to have you do some real dueling. Don't try to kill each other but take it seriously. Carrie, you're with Codie. Ninette, you've got Van. Connor, I want you with James."

I guess this is good, right? If I'm sparring with the captain? It either meant they thought James would be his best match-up or that he didn't have a chance, so the match-up didn't matter. He made his way across the field, optimism and nervousness warring for dominance within.

"Neat trick you pulled," James said. "You'll have to show me sometime. Now," he put up his hands in a mock boxing stance. "You ready to rumble?"

Connor was not, but he nodded anyway.

There was no fanfare, no whistle, nothing to signal the start of the sparring match. James waved his hand and released a fan of lightning bolts. Connor deflected it upward, retaliating with a straight bolt from the sky. James sidestepped it. They exchanged fireballs and icicles, gusts of wind, and more. Connor managed to take about half of what James dished out and send it back while attempting to shield himself from the rest. His counterattacks narrowly missed their mark while each spell of the captain's left cuts and bruises—never anything serious, but Connor felt it adding up over time.

"Don't block if you can dodge," James shouted. He rolled out of the way of a stone projectile. "It puts you on the defensive and uses more energy than you can afford." He tore up the ground and tossed Connor into the air, then hit him with lightning from above.

Connor landed on his back, sore and winded, but not overly hurt. He was amazed by James's control. Not only could the captain manage to control the flow of the battle completely, but he also evaded Connor's attacks with the minimum movement necessary, sometimes no more than an inch. On top of that, he managed to play teacher at the same time.

"Think three moves ahead."

Vines sprouted from the ground to snare Connor. He cut himself free with sharp stones and kept dueling.

Across the field, Ninette traded blows with Van in full wolf mode. They exchanged a flurry of fire spells—she grazed him once or twice, but Van's reflexes were on another level. He ducked and dipped around her firebombs, whipping smaller explosives at her while closing the distance between them, then exhaled a blast of flame that threatened to engulf her. She blocked the worst of it, but when the fire cleared, Van was in her face swinging a giant, flaming wolf claw at her head. Ninette stumbled backward, desperately erecting a wall of stone between them, and toppling it onto him. Van backflipped away, giving her space to throw more fire and boulders, but Van dodged them all. She decided to try something clever and dropped her guard. She prepared one of her signature gigantic fireballs behind her back; the flaming sphere burst into being and roared until it was taller than she was. Van snarled and lunged, sensing opportunity. He moved in close and fast to strike. Ninette abandoned the fireball and caught Van in the chin with a plain, old uppercut.

James rolled a boulder at Connor, and Connor blasted it back with wind. James dodged aside as his own spell rocketed past him. Seeking to capitalize on the initiative, Connor used the little essence he had left to concentrate the air around him into a screaming vortex, but before he could launch it, a dark shadow loomed over him. Another James stood behind him, grinning from ear to ear and holding a ball of lightning. Connor closed his eyes and tensed up as James slammed thousands of volts right into his chest.

He felt nothing. When he opened his eyes, James remained, his hand flat against Connor's chest. He winked.

"Checkmate," James announced from his original position. The attacking James melted away until it was nothing more than a patch of shade on the grass. "Just a shadow. I can give it enough essence to throw a punch or hold you down, but it can't cast magic. Without a substantial amount of essence, it's just an illusion."

The coach's whistle blew, and then blew again, and again, and once more, each one an increasingly desperate call for attention. Ninette and Van scuffled on the ground, oblivious. It looked more like a bar brawl than a high school sport. Ultimately, the coaches physically separated them, but the kids were grinning ear to ear despite their bumps and bruises.

"I want to thank you all for coming out and giving it one hundred percent," Coach Kalett said. "It takes guts to try out, and we all appreciate that. Right, team?"

James, Van, and Codie agreed. Codie subtly waved at Ninette and beamed a wide smile at her.

Nurse Poole held up her clipboard. "We've gotten a lot of good info. Coach Kalett and I will be talking it over amongst ourselves this weekend. We'll have the results posted in the cafeteria on Monday. You can head back to your rooms and get some rest."

Connor, Carrie, and Ninette walked back up the hill to the school, none of them in any particular hurry. Connor knew he wouldn't be able to sit still until he knew if he made it. Every couple of steps, he looked over his shoulder at the stadium. He'd done his best, at least he thought he had. He hoped it would be enough. It had to be enough. His heart started racing. He needed a distraction. He turned to Carrie and Codie and realized they'd been talking all along.

"Codie is so fast," Carrie gushed. "I could barely keep up with her. I don't know that I hit her more than once, even with air when she was *in* the air."

"Yeah," Ninette agreed. "I try to hit her from above to keep her on the ground."

"Oh, good thought." Carrie considered a moment. "I can probably make wind blow down."

"Well, I think I made it," Ninette said. She stretched her arms over her head and let out a wide-mouthed yawn. "I know I'm stronger than most of the kids at this school. I may not have someone's fancy tricks," she looked sideways at Connor, "but I think I can hold my own in a knockdown, drag-out duel."

"I'm not sure," Carrie said. "I'm hopeful, though. You did great, Connor. You'll make it for sure."

"Yeah, we'll see." He tried to put on a smile. He didn't want to be a downer. Sure, Carrie and Ninette lost their sparring matches—though Ninette would never admit it—but Connor felt completely defeated.

I never touched James. I guess he's the captain for a reason.

Carrie and Ninette invited him to dinner, but Connor wasn't hungry. Deprived of adrenaline, he couldn't keep his eyes open and went straight to his room.

How am I supposed to wait all weekend? he thought as he fell into a restless sleep.

Connor opened his eyes to nothing but darkness. "Oh, come on, really? Again?"

He sat up on the black beach beside the black ocean. Sweat trickled down his back. He tried to see if there were any of the creatures he encountered before, but his eyes couldn't make out much.

"It's a dream," he said in a scratchy whisper. "It's a bad, Magi dream. I should ask the nurse about it tomorrow. I'm not going to go anywhere. I'm not going to look for anything or anyone. I'm going to sit here and wait to wake up."

Connor lowered himself to the sand; it scratched at his legs through his pajamas. Minutes passed, and then what felt like hours, but nothing happened. He tried to pinch himself, to shake himself awake, but he remained on the obsidian beach. He screamed into the black nothing.

"How do I get out of here?"

"THIS PLACE HOLDS POWER. YOU DO NOT TRULY WISH TO LEAVE," a voice rasped right in his ear. Long fingers with sharp nails gripped his shoulder, securing him where he sat.

"I do. I want to leave. Please let me go," Connor pleaded, voice trembling. He tried to move, but whatever gripped him didn't allow him to budge.

"WE COULD HELP YOU. WE KNOW MUCH OF YOUR WORLD. SECRETS LONG FORGOTTEN. GREAT POWER LOST TO THE FAR CORNERS OF YOUR HISTORY. MANY COME HERE AND GIVE US THEIR ANSWERS. ASK THE OTHER. WE HAVE SHOWN THEM JUST THE BEGINNING." Each word echoed painfully around Connor's skull. The voice rumbled like an earthquake.

"I'm good, I promise," Connor stammered. He tried to gather the wind around himself, but the air didn't respond. The dry breeze wafted by heedless of his attempts to use it. "I didn't want to come here to begin with. Just let me go. I'll figure it out, and I won't come back." He strained his mind to force a connection, but the air around him refused to obey.

"YOU CAME WILLINGLY. YOU WILL COME BACK," the voice said with certainty. "THE SHADOWS CALL TO YOU. WILL YOU ANSWER THEIR CALL?"

"No!" Connor shouted. "I don't want anything to do with... whatever this place is!"

Connor landed in his bed with a jarring thud. He sat upright on top of the sheets, and his legs still itched with the feeling of rough sand. The sound of his entrance roused Marck in his bed on the other side of the room.

"Connor, you're back," Marck grumbled.

"Back?" Connor ran his hands over himself and his bed. He blinked as his eyes adjusted to his moonlit dorm room. Everything was just as he'd left it.

Another dream.

"I never left. I've been here since this afternoon." Connor's voice wavered. He needed it to be true.

"A poor joke," Marck growled, rolling over. "You were not here when I returned. You were not here when I went to sleep."

Chapter 20

> Elemental Magicks – Creation
> Just about everything is comprised of essence, and a Magi that knows how can make just about everything. The advantage is flexibility at an increased cost. Using an existing element is always easier than making it from scratch, but it's better to spend a little extra essence to make a fire than to wait for one to start on its own.

Connor remained awake for the rest of the night, afraid of what more sleep might bring. Marck's snores made the room unpalatable, so he threw on a t-shirt and jeans, and went in search of a distraction. He checked the clock before he left. It was a little after five am, so he knew he wouldn't get in trouble for being out. The last thing he needed was another round of detention. He tried exercising in the gym but gave up after just a few minutes on the treadmill. He went for a walk in the gardens outside despite the freezing cold. Practicing spells in the atrium reminded him of tryouts, which stressed him out almost as much as his nightmares. He returned to his room to get rid of his coat, and checked the time.

Only 7:30. On Saturday. Still two whole days.

He rolled around in bed for an hour or so, hoping he might find sleep again. No luck. Grumbling to himself, he got back up to search for his friends. Ninette wasn't in her room; her roommate said she'd gone to swim laps or something. No one answered at Garrett's room.

Probably in the library. Connor meandered in that direction. *I guess I could ask Mr. Naegus about my dreams, but I'm not sure how helpful he'd be.*

The school hallways were quiet. He passed the cafeteria, and though the smells wafting from inside were enticing, he didn't have much of an appetite; all the stress of the previous 24 hours occupied his stomach in a giant lump. He hoped whatever Garrett was working on would take his mind off things for a bit. On the way to the library, he ran into Julian and Vern. They wore their coats and gloves and were headed in the opposite direction, which meant their plans were more exciting than studying on a Saturday. Julian, in particular, was usually good for some entertainment, though his magical experiments weren't always safe—or legal.

"Hey, guys!" Connor waved them down. "What are you up to?"

"I was on my way out to the gardens," Julian said. "Dr. Greens is holding an Agrimancy seminar. Do you want to come?"

"I plan to observe," Vern added. His face remained placid, but his long ears reddened. "Nature Magic is a failing of mine I would like to address."

Nature Magic hadn't appealed to Connor, though he recognized it as another element he'd be able to use with some frequency. While there was always plenty of earth and air to be had, plants and animals weren't exactly rare either. Grass, trees, even moss or dormant seeds were well within a Magi's control. His successes with Shadow Magic gave him some more confidence in his casting, enough that he had almost gotten over his other shortcomings, and so he hadn't felt the need to explore this branch of magic. Controlling the shadows felt like a powerful tool that he'd seen few people, other than James, make use of. But his recent dreams, if dreams they were, made him wonder if maybe he should focus his attention elsewhere. At least for a while.

"What are you growing?" Connor asked.

"Mushrooms," Julian beamed. "They're an ingredient for loads of different potions and elixirs and, you know, stuff." Julian giggled mischievously.

Connor weighed this option. Sitting outside in frigid weather to watch fungus grow somehow rated below studying in the library.

"I think I'll pass. Count me in next time?"

The library was busier than Connor expected—it was always the warmest spot in the school, and Connor now suspected he knew why. Many students cozied up against the cold with a book or their tablets, and some even studied at the desks tucked into corners or at the ends of shelves, all unaware of their proximity to a dragon. The librarian likely leveraged his position to keep the temperature to his liking. Mr. Naegus manned the desk, fingers drumming as though he would rather be anywhere else.

"Good morning, Mr. McTaggart," he said in a slow drawl. "How can I help you? Looking for Garrett? Please say it's for something exciting."

"Actually, I had a question," Connor said, trying to decide how much to reveal. "Have you ever heard of someone… going somewhere else while they slept? I thought I was dreaming, but Marck says I wasn't in our room last night."

"Magic is all in the mind," Mr. Naegus said. He tapped the side of his head. "Anyone who knows how to do something well enough while waking can do it while they sleep. Some people sleepwalk, others sleep cast."

"But I don't know how to teleport or open portals. How could I…?" he trailed off under the librarian's hungry, golden stare.

"Where, pray tell, did you find yourself?"

"Never mind, it's nothing," Connor said, suddenly queasy. "You said Garrett was here?"

"He is brushing up on his enchanting, I believe. I'll take you to him." Mr. Naegus grabbed a book off his desk and told Connor to follow.

Garrett occupied a wide table all by himself deep in the library. He sat barricaded behind a fortress of books. Some piled high, the protective outer perimeter, while no less than three tomes lay open in front of him. Garrett scribbled furiously in his notebook, occasionally taking a break to turn a page, but he appeared to be working through all three at once. Mr. Naegus pat him on the shoulder and dropped the new book onto a pile.

"Oh hey, Connor," Garrett said, looking up from his reading. "We missed you last night."

"I was wiped out from tryouts," Connor explained. It was partly true. "What are you working on?"

"Lady Ariel's homework." Garret turned back to his books. More pages of notes sprawled over the table around him, each covered top to bottom in dozens of angular runes and symbols. "We're getting to more complicated rune combinations. Did you know runes aren't all one language? Different symbols come from different cultures. It's like learning to read all over again but in several languages simultaneously. But look," he gestured to one of the open books next to him and then to a sheet of paper he set to the side. "Does this look familiar to you?"

Connor shook his head. It looked like someone had given a pen to a crazy person. None of it meant anything to him.

"I think these are the runes we saw in the Atlantean palace."

Connor leaned in until his nose was inches from the paper. "What are they?"

"Some of them were barrier runes, more advanced than I thought, but these," Garrett pointed back to the book, "definitely aren't." He opened the book Mr. Naegus brought him and skimmed through it. "Yep, here. These other ones are for essence stabilization."

"What do those do?" Connor asked.

Garrett could hardly resist slapping his forehead and stared dumbfounded. "They… stabilize essence. Make spells last longer without using as much power, and keeps more chaotic magic manageable. It fits with what the headmistress told us. They were opening portals left and right to study other worlds. Maybe they opened one they shouldn't have?"

Other worlds, Connor thought. *I have no idea how, but that must be it. Too bad I can't take Portals for two more years.*

Garrett watched him, waiting for him to say something.

"Right, maybe. That's interesting. Hey, you wanna go do something other than this or…?"

Ninette glided through the lukewarm pool with slow, easy strokes. She approached the end at high speed and, without slowing at all, tucked into a flip, and kicked off the wall to speed back in the opposite direction. It wasn't the ocean, but swimming reinvigorated her. She didn't miss home, but swimming… She missed swimming. She'd avoided it as long as she could. She thought distancing herself from the water made sense, but now… She climbed out to check the time. Three hours had passed. She dove back in, thinking ten more laps would be plenty, but when she surfaced, she heard a splash behind her.

Van's grinning, wolf face stared back at her, tongue lolling and dripping water. His fur was drenched, and he looked more like a wet wererat than a werewolf. He shook it out, which only made it stick out in wild spikes, and paddled over toward her.

"No hard feelings about yesterday, yeah? Gotta go all out to see if you'll make the cut."

"Please," she snorted. "I just hope I didn't rough you up so bad it'll affect the next match. You here to work on your dog paddle?"

"Sort of," he grinned. "I need to work on my Water Magic. Never been great with it. Never been great with anything but fire, really. Thought a little swim would be a good warm-up. Wanna help me out?"

Ninette eyed him cautiously. "Yeah, why not. I don't have anything else going on. Unless you want to tell me if I made the team or not?"

"No can do. Don't know. We gave our opinions, but Coach and the Nurse have the final say."

"I figured. Alright, see if you can keep up."

Ninette felt more at home in the water than she remembered. While water wasn't her preferred element, the entire pool still moved at her command. With concentration and flowing movements, she could raise waves ten feet high, emptying half the pool only to bring it crashing back down. She conjured whirlpools and directed currents to turn the pool into a watery obstacle course. Van tried to keep afloat, but Ninette controlled every drop of water in the pool, dunking him mercilessly.

An hour later, they clambered out, both gasping for breath.

"You're incredible," Van marveled. He crouched on all fours and shook himself dry, then reverted to his human shape. His fur shrunk back into his body, and his bones snapped back to normal size with a sickening crunch, leaving him scrambling to retie his swimsuit over his skinnier frame. "I guess being half mermaid will do that, huh?"

"Guess so," Ninette grunted, toweling off. She pointedly wrapped her red scarf around her neck and finished drying off.

"Oh hey, I didn't mean," Van stammered. "I mean, I don't care. I'm the last one to judge, yeah?"

"It's whatever," Ninette grumbled. "People are jerks. Mermaids are jerks. Fitting in is easier."

"Maybe, but where's the fun in that?" Van said. He gave her a halfhearted howl. "We are who we are, so why not embrace it? You're a badass, and being half mermaid is a part of it. I think it's cool."

"Easy for you to say. No one has to know your deal unless you want them to. You could go anywhere and be a normal guy. You get to pick and choose who knows your secret. You can wait until you trust someone. Until you're sure they'll be okay with it."

"But I don't," Van pointed out. "Who you are shouldn't be a secret." He bit his lip and looked down at the ground, avoiding her eyes. "Look, I'm not trying to be in your business, yeah? I think you're cool, and really good at dueling, and pretty. And I hate to see someone feel bad about who they are is all," he babbled. When he finished talking, he covered his mouth as if surprised by his own words, and his cheeks flushed with color.

"Thanks, I guess," Ninette said, rubbing absently at her neck. She looked away, blushing herself, and refusing to show it.

"Well, thanks for the practice," Van ventured. "Hopefully I'll see you around?"

He's kind of cute when he's not drooling, Ninette thought. She smiled and finished getting dressed. *Time to go see what Connor and Garrett are up to. God knows they'd be in trouble without me.*

Connor dove headfirst into classes on Monday—it gave him a welcome distraction from bad dreams and dueling tryouts. Professor Skreed's intermediate class centered around creating the basic elements from raw Will and manipulating them in creative ways. Connor didn't have much hope for making much of anything, but he hoped the creative part would balance it out. Ninette, on the other hand, had a talent for creation. On day one, she conjured mounds of earth and swollen water clouds from the minute Skreed said, "Go." The professor described the process as incredibly taxing; Ninette made it look easy.

"You should use what is available when you can," he lectured, "but that's not always practical. Sometimes you need what you need. So, if you can't find it—make it."

Monday's class opened—as it so often did—with minimal instructions. Two words: "EARTH" and

"FIRE," were written in blocky letters on the chalkboard. Connor took his usual seat next to Ninette. The professor waited at the door to wave in the last of his students. He never failed to greet each one with a warm smile and comforting small talk. Only once everyone was seated did he begin class.

"Today, we work with earth and fire. Surprising, I know," he said, half glancing at the board. "Does anyone have any ideas on the uses these two could be put to?"

"Volcanoes?" Ninette suggested. "Lava?"

"That's just hot earth," The professor tutted, eyebrow raised. "A bit literal if you ask me. Anyone else?"

"Heated shelter?" someone in the back chimed.

"Blowing stuff up?" suggested another.

"Yes, that's all well and good," the professor said, waving them down, "but you're still thinking rocks. Earth Magic includes every mineral on the planet. Ignite magnesium for a blinding light. You might use lithium, sodium, or calcium to make fireworks. You could fire up some clay for pottery on demand or even use fire and ore to refine metal out of thin air. You need to think like the Magi of old. What did they use magic for? What technology, or lack thereof, did it seek to emulate?"

To demonstrate, the professor held out both hands. First, he created an oblong hunk of reddish-gray rock. The old elf's hands glowed, and he superheated the ore. Bright white and orange metal melted out of the stone. It shimmered and morphed in his hands, shaped by his mind. The professor blew chilly air onto his creation, and when it cooled, he held a flat, gray sword.

He deftly slashed at the air once, twice, and then nimbly stepped back and held the sword perfectly straight up in front of himself. "You never know when you may need one of these."

The professor turned on a screen to display a comprehensive amount of information about iron: locations, chemical composition, appearance, weight, the works.

"Much like you cannot use elements you do not understand, you cannot create what you do not understand completely. Creating iron is essential for making a tool, so you must know it to your core. Get to it."

Connor copied notes from the board. He knew if he was going to have any shot at this, he had to do it right from the get-go. A few of his classmates tried to dive right into creation—with mixed success. Some made rocks with no ore. Others melted their ores too fast, or the metals weren't sturdy enough for shaping. Ninette didn't write anything down, but she didn't try anything either. She sat, eyes closed and arms crossed, leaning back in her chair.

"Are you thinking or sleeping?" Connor asked. He swiped through the class module for ores.

You never know, a sour voice in his head said. *This might be the one you figure out.*

It didn't fill him with confidence.

"Thinking," Ninette answered after a long pause.

She opened her eyes and held out her hands. She bit her lip and stared like she wanted to burn a hole in the air. A few seconds passed. The air over her desk shimmered and stretched and twisted around itself. A hunk of ore the size of a cow forced itself into existence and then dropped, reducing Ninette's desk to splinters. She wavered in her seat and leaned on the newly-formed rock for support.

"Please be more careful. I have to rebuild those myself, you know," the professor chided. His smile dipped and his long ears twitched.

Ninette didn't acknowledge him. She maintained her focus on the stone in front of her. Steam erupted out of the cracks; bits of rock fell away until all that remained was an orb of liquid metal. Ninette worked her hands above it like she would a piece of clay, and the metal morphed along with her movements. Its glow dulled until it came to rest as a titanic maul as tall as Connor. Ninette hefted it with little effort, taking a few swings and slinging it over her shoulder.

"I wanted iron, I made iron. Easy."

Easy for you. Connor turned away from her, not wanting to spend the rest of class looking at the evidence of her success.

He tried Ninette's advice and thought "iron" over and over, concentrated hard on the air in front of him, pictured the rust-colored stone appearing in front of him, but all he got was a headache. More of his friends and classmates got the hang of it, so Connor doubled down. He looked at his notes, he double-checked the board, he searched everywhere for some critical piece of instruction he might have missed. The sounds of triumph assaulted him from all sides.

Iron. Fe. Ferrum. Iron oxidizes making rust. Iron combines with carbon to make steel. I know this. I can do this. He cycled through every fact he knew or learned about iron. Finally, he gave up. *Same as everything else. I'm sure I could work with it if I had some, I just can't make it.*

As if reading his mind, Ninette materialized another fist-sized chunk and handed it to him.

"Don't look so mopey. It makes me want to hit you," she said.

"I need the fire, too," he mumbled.

No sooner had he said it than Ninette tossed a small flicker his way. With the stone in one hand, Connor caught the fire in the other and merged the two together to create an ornate knife. It only took him a minute. He turned the blade over in his hands, but the rapid success did little to soothe his ego.

Professor Skreed returned to his lectern.

"Today's lesson is twofold. One: you can make anything you know how to make. Some people have a knack for it," he said, gesturing to Ninette. "Two: the more complex the thing, the harder it is to make. While most of you have no trouble creating a plain old rock, this specific one proved more difficult. Imagine the difficulty of conjuring a rare flower or a precious gemstone. It can be done, but how efficiently? Think on this."

"Hey, do you want to carry my giant metal club for me?" Ninette snickered. She held out the heavy weapon to Connor.

"Showoff," Connor retorted, sticking out his tongue.

"Oh, right. Almost forgot." Skreed snapped his spindly fingers and the metallic items vanished from around the classroom. "I don't need another lecture from Nurse Poole about students impaling themselves running down the hall with swords," he mumbled. He returned to his desk and fell into his chair with a satisfied smirk.

When the bell rang, Connor sprinted to the cafeteria, all thoughts of scholastic failures chased from his mind. The dueling team list had to be up by now. A small part of him didn't care if he'd made it or not. He just needed to know. He pushed through the crowded halls, heedless of who he might bump into, even tripping over one of his goblin classmates. He stumbled ahead, calling out a weak apology, but he had to know.

He practically bowled over Coach Kalett in his mad dash.

"Results are up," the coach said in a neutral tone. He walked away without another word.

Inside the cafeteria, Connor found a small crowd pressed tight around a piece of paper pinned to the wall. He shouldered his way to the front. The paper read:

> Mattson Manticores Spring Semester Team
> First Single: James Radimus
> Second Single: Codie Singleton
> Third Single: Van Fredericks
> First Doubles: Connor McTaggart and
>   Ninette Reefwalker

He didn't read the rest.

Chapter 21

Elemental Magicks - Sustained and Released Spells
A released spell leaves the Magi's control once casting is complete. It is the most efficient use of essence and frees up concentration for whatever comes next. A sustained spell remains connected to the Magi. They can better control it and protect it from interference or counterspelling, but it will steadily drain their essence until they ultimately release it.

Practice began the next day and, after getting over his initial shock, Connor read the rest of the depth chart. Michelle and Clara, the two previous first doubles, had shifted down a spot, and Carrie had replaced one of the third doubles.

"We have a lot of work to do before our matchup at Rasputin Hall next Friday," Coach Kalett announced. He stood with his hands on his hips and made eye contact with each of the students. "I expect the senior team members to help the newbies get accustomed to the routine. Enough chit-chat. Let's warm-up."

Tuesdays were for solo workouts and drills. The coaches—or James, the captain—would call out one spell after another and summon a target dummy for the team to strike at. This became Connor's favorite day of practice. No one but James could use as many elements as he could, and he picked up a half-dozen new spells, including fire arrows, wind fists, and chain lightning, on the first day. Van even taught them how to breathe fire.

"I mean, it's magic, yeah?" he said, cocking his head to the side. "It's all in your mind, your essence. You never have to *throw* a fireball. People have it stuck in their heads because that's how everyone else does it. Helps 'em focus or something?" He shrugged. "Someone ties up your arms or whatever, just blast 'em in the face." He threw back his head and howled gouts of flames in the air.

Wednesdays were sparring practice. The doubles teams played against one another to practice working together. Connor and Ninette almost exclusively practiced against Michelle and Clara, the seniors they displaced. The athletic girls immediately took a shine to Ninette, who they saw as a kindred spirit, and Connor often felt like he was getting pulled along for the ride.

"We've been on the team for three years but never climbed out of doubles," Clara said during a break. "It's still fun to come out and throw down."

"You guys made it on as freshmen," Michelle added. "I'm a little jealous, but hopefully that means you'll get up into the singles eventually."

The team spent Thursdays watching tapes of their opponent's previous matches. Each duel was recorded, and Nurse Poole insisted there was something valuable to be learned from even the lowest level players. Connor drank in each match, amazed by what kids just a year or two older than him could accomplish, and felt a compulsion new to him: the desire to take notes. He also appreciated the chance to see his upcoming opponents in action. He couldn't rely on Ninette to supply him with elements forever. Their best chance of winning was for him to turn his opponents magic against them, something he was uniquely qualified for—as long as they didn't use Light Magic.

"Ice and earth," Michelle pointed out. "That's their specialty. They'll try to slow you down and then hit you hard. As long as you can stay warm, they shouldn't cause too much trouble. Try this. The Fire Aura." She wrapped her arms around herself and a halo of soft, glowing flames, like a small candle, surrounded her.

Connor and Ninette spent the afternoon practicing the Fire Aura and working out a counterplay for their upcoming opponents. Michelle and Clara helped them practice, especially on how to not burn each other. By the end of the afternoon, Connor felt confident and excited while Ninette was already proclaiming their victory. The next week followed the same pattern, except on Wednesday, the coaches set Connor and Ninette against Van and Codie. Even though the two weren't used to working together, they outclassed Connor and Ninette in terms of skill and experience. Van's magic fell short of Ninette's in raw power, but he made up for it with speed of movement and casting. Ninette would still be winding up a fireball, while Van could hit her with three of his own. Connor could cast more spells than Codie, she was primarily limited to wind and water, but he could never hit her, and she never missed him. Plus, with Ninette tied up in a knockdown, drag-out brawl with Van, his own arsenal was limited. No one walked out unscathed, but Connor and Ninette were the clear losers.

"Nothing wrong with that," Coach Kalett reassured them. He patted Connor and Ninette on the shoulders and tried to cheer them up. "They've got age and experience on you. My advice: Ninette—protect Connor. Connor—try to keep your cool. Don't react. Stay alert and wait for Ninette to give you an opening. You guys do that, and you can't fail."

"So, who do you think it is?" Garrett asked.
"Huh?" Connor said.
"The mystery summoner?" Garrett prodded. "Person trying to kill you? Pretty sure they're on the dueling team you are also on now?"

Connor stopped himself from saying, "huh?" again. In the excitement of being on the team, he'd totally forgotten his other, much more practical, reason for joining. His blank expression and vacant stare made this apparent to Garrett, who slapped his forehead and sighed. Garrett waved down Ninette as she walked away from the buffet, chatting with Van. She split off and joined them, wearing an unusually cheerful expression.

"Do you have any idea who it is?" Garrett asked her, not sounding optimistic.

"Don't say 'huh?'" Connor warned as she opened her mouth to do just that.

"I can't believe you two," Garrett moaned. "Someone on that team is trying to kill you both, also probably me, and all you care about is beating each other up."

The two thought it over.

"Ideally, we'll be beating up other people," Ninette argued and stuck out her tongue.

"I mean, it can't be someone lower than us on the team, right?" Connor suggested. "Certainly not someone we bumped off the team, I would think. We're talking lots of essence to do the summoning *and* the fact that, one way or another, they got all three of those creatures to obey. Ninette could barely handle the kappa after we weakened it, and we still have no idea how to deal with the other two."

"But that leaves Codie, Van, and James," Ninette pointed out. "It's not Codie. No chance. And if I'm being honest, I think I don't think it's Van. I kinda like the guy now, but I can't picture him drawing a summoning circle in crayon, much less blood. Complicated stuff isn't exactly his strong suit."

"But I don't think it's James," Connor argued back. "Sure, he might be powerful enough, but what does he gain from it? He's already popular, smart, and powerful."

"If you say 'good looking,' I'm going to barf."

"Well, I mean…" Connor plowed ahead. "Seems more likely it would be Van."

"What does *he* have to gain?" Ninette asked, eyebrow raised.

"He's a werewolf," Connor blurted. His eyebrows scrunched down while he thought it through. "I'm sure that's not easy. Maybe he's angry or… what?"

Ninette stopped chewing and watched Connor with her eyes narrowed into threatening slits. Her lip curled into the beginning of a snarl. "So, he's different? That makes him more likely to do something like *this*? To hurt people?"

"That's not what I meant!" Connor sputtered.

"It's what you said."

"If it's not one of them, then we're back at square one," Garrett interjected.

Connor and Ninette jumped, having forgotten he was there. When they looked at Garrett their expressions shifted from annoyed to mildly embarrassed.

"You can at least keep an eye on them." Garrett rubbed his forehead and sighed. "Maybe you'll find out something."

Connor sat in the visiting team locker room. His hands trembled. Churning and twisting in his stomach had him feeling queasy. All his friends were out there waiting. Waiting to watch *him*. His mom and dad were there. Watching. They had sent him a letter earlier in the week saying they planned to make his debut duel. He huddled inside his brand-new team jacket—the one he'd dreamed of wearing the minute he'd seen it. Coach handed them out moments before the team took the portal to the match. Holding it filled him with a jolt of excitement and pride. A very temporary jolt. Now, the thick-padded varsity coat hung over his shoulders like a weight threatening to crush him. He got it; now he had to earn it. Ninette shook him roughly by the shoulders.

"Showtime," she said. She sounded calm, confident, normal.

It helped. A little.

The team stepped out onto the field together to the introduction of Rasputin's announcer. Fluffy snowflakes coated the ground and continued to fall. That didn't bode well, but Connor and Ninette were ready for it.

High spires and minarets gave the stadium the profile of an ancient crown. The field was all stone, a blank gray slab filling the space between the seats—seats full of puffy, bundled students and parents, most bedecked in the crimson and yellow of Rasputin Hall, but there were blue and gold pockets of Mattson supporters, too. Down on the ground, the chatter and cheering sounded like a dull roar.

"Match one. Third doubles report to the field," the announcer stated.

With a last look at the team and a few fist bumps for good luck, Carrie and her partner Thane, a junior boy lanky by orc standards, jogged out to the field. The bell rang.

Carrie and Thane waited for the other two to make the first move. They weren't waiting long. One of their opponents blanketed the stadium in dense, pea-green fog. In seconds neither Carrie nor Thane could see more than a few inches in front of them. Carrie stepped in front of Thane—she hoped—and prepared her reflective shield. A spiked boulder rocketed out of the gloom, bouncing harmlessly off Carrie's shield and granting Thane his opportunity. He cast two icicles to trail on either side of the boulder. Carrie counted to three and then used her essence to detonate the boulder while Thane shattered his spells.

There was utter silence on the other side of the stadium. Carrie waved her hands, and a gentle breeze dissipated the fog revealing both Rasputin boys lying prone.

"Round one: Mattson," confirmed the announcer. "Second doubles report to the field."

Clara and Michelle ran out, high-fiving Carrie and Thane on the way. They stood across from a tall elf girl and a young-looking dwarf boy.

As soon as the bell rang, Clara rained down fire from the sky. The dwarf held a shield of Will over him and his partner, who performed an instant summon. Connor's mouth hung open as a towering, level four circle materialized over the arena. Out of the lavender opening scrabbled a twelve-foot-tall pumpkin, belching eerie blue flames from a carved mouth full of jagged teeth, and flailing dozens of vines covered in thorns the size of butcher's knives.

"Go, Pumpking!" The girl shouted. She pointed a slender finger at Michelle.

"What the—" Michelle started, but she never finished the thought, having to duck under one of the vines.

Clara gave up on her first spell and sliced at the air around the giant gourd with swords of flame, severing a few of its vines, but more grew to replace them. No longer on the defensive, the dwarf boy circled around. He heaved wavering globes of water at them. Michelle blocked one with a shield of Will, but when she did, the boy turned the water to ice, completely encasing her.

Clara dodged a spray of blue flames from the roaring Pumpking. Its gaping maw gave her an idea. She ignited the air around Michelle to free her.

"Michelle, follow me!" She held her breath and dove head-first into the Pumpking's mouth.

Michelle barely hesitated and followed her partner.

The crowd hushed; even the announcer wasn't sure what to say. The Pumpking bobbled around for a minute looking for more food, then the light in its eyes dimmed and its body bulged, contorted, and exploded in a shower of seeds and steaming stringy orange goop. All that remained were the two girls, covered in muck and shrouded in fire. The Rasputin girl sagged, exhausted from the effort of summoning the Pumpking. Michelle and Clara battered their remaining opponent with fire and lightning. He couldn't withstand the spell barrage and tapped out. Victory for Mattson again.

Connor and Ninette were up.

Ninette got to her feet, and Connor forced himself after her. He walked out to the field, wooden and numb. His legs felt heavy, and his stomach roiled. The wide-open stadium seemed huge, and he felt small, insignificant. The world spun around him, and it felt difficult to breathe.

"You guys got this!" Codie cheered.

Michelle and Clara gave them a thumbs-up. Van waved and grinned. James nodded approvingly.

"Just like we planned, right?" Ninette said.

Glad she sounds confident, Connor thought. He gave her a limp fist bump.

With the ringing of the bell, the snow intensified into a howling blizzard. Connor could barely see his hands; he could barely *feel* his hands. Ninette shouted something, but he couldn't hear her over the wind. She glowed a dim orange, her aura ablaze to fend off the cold. Connor reached out until his mind brushed against the fire essence surrounding her. It bent to his touch, and he borrowed some to forge his own aura. They weren't going to freeze, but they still couldn't see anything. He may as well have been completely alone in the middle of the snowstorm. James's advice floated in his head.

Don't block if you can dodge.

Connor had watched the tape of his opponents enough to commit their opening gambit to memory and prepared for what came next. He hopped to the side as a spire of stone burst out of the ground. Ninette jumped away, dodging another. They bounced around, avoiding stony projectiles. Ninette hurled fireballs blindly across the stadium.

"You know, in hindsight, I think we make easier targets like this," Ninette shouted over the wind.

Connor pointed to one of the spires near Ninette, then ducked behind the one nearest to him, and they let their flames wink out. He fought back a shiver, wrapped his arms around his chest, and focused on the wind tearing at his jacket. The air essence was wild, powerful, but completely uncontrolled, and he formed a connection immediately. An arena's worth of air converged into a screaming funnel cloud of snow and ice. With the air cleared, their opponents were sitting ducks. The two Rasputin boys separated to opposite sides of the pitch to become more difficult targets. With a mental shove, Connor sent his new creation veering toward one of them.

The tornado pinned one of the opponents against a wall, and Ninette lobbed three mighty boulders into the sky at the other. He attempted to protect himself from above, and Ninette followed up from below, heaving the ground—and him with it—upward. Stone met stone in a mid-air collision with the duelist in between. He shielded the blow and tried to slow his fall with wind, but Ninette was on the ground waiting for him with a fireball in each hand. A one-two explosive combo left him unconscious.

Their other opponent wrestled control of the snownado from Connor and dissipated the spell, and all the snow and ice that came with it, but before he could retaliate, Ninette pinned him against the wall with a fist of stone. Connor's wind gusts were ready to fire, but the Rasputin boy surrendered.

They had won.

The crowd roared. Connor's felt lightheaded. He stood in the center of the field, stock still, arms hanging slack at his side. The Mattson folks cheered and shouted, overpowering the dismal sounds of the home crowd, but it didn't register. Connor didn't understand. His heart still thundered in his ears, and his skin felt on fire from pins and needles. Ninette led him off the field. He followed in a stupor.

"We did it, dude! We won!" she whispered in his ear while urging him along.

By the time they made it to the bench, Connor had a stupid grin plastered across his face.

The half-time break came and went. Van ran circles around his opponent, literally and figuratively, using wind to speed up his already fast wolf form and peppering his foe with firebolts and powerful fists of air. Codie's Ice Magic, enhanced by the wintry weather, froze huge swaths of the stadium in a single blast—the teachers on shield duty worked overtime to protect the audience from her frigid casting.

James marched out with a wink at Connor. When the bell rang, flowers blossomed all around his foe, spitting sizzling acid. The Rasputin student tried to dodge but couldn't, penned in by walls of wind. Shadows bubbled up from the ground and wrapped around their legs, further snaring them. Fire, ice, and lightning pelted the helpless young duelist. James hadn't moved.

He makes it look so easy, Connor thought. *I'm literally half as useful as he is.*

The bell rang. A complete sweep for Mattson.

After the standard handshaking and well-wishing with their opponents, the team returned to the locker room. The coaches congratulated them on victories well earned, especially the newbies. The older team members jostled and hugged and high-fived them as well.

Connor finally started to relax, feeling as if he was waking up from a thick, hazy dream. Being on the team finally began to sink it. He won. *They* won. He'd had his first official duel, and he'd won. He deserved to be here.

Coach Kalett opened a portal, and the team stepped through to find the sun setting on their home turf, painting the grassy field in rosy pinks and oranges. A throng of students and family swarmed them as soon as they arrived, Connor's parents among them. His dad burst from the crowd and crushed him in a tearful bear hug.

"I knew you could do it," his dad whispered. He held Connor tight with shaking arms. "You were amazing. I'm so proud of you. Please never, ever do it again." He squeezed Connor so hard he threatened to crush bones.

His mom swept in, adding her own hug to the pile.

"What your father means is we're both so proud, honey," his mom added. "I'll make sure to remind him that dueling is perfectly safe. You just make sure you don't get hurt too badly. Your father had a hard enough time watching you win."

Chapter 22

> Magic 101 - Curses
> A curse uses Will Magic to interrupt or alter the pattern of another's essence. One's essence pattern is like a spiritual fingerprint; changing it can have devastating effects. The most common curse is the Were curse which forcibly twists the essence pattern into that of an animal. Other curses result in illness, frailty, or death.

Connor spent the following weeks watching James, Van, and even Codie for clues. It wasn't hard since he practiced with them three times a week, functionally lived in the same building, and saw them occasionally on the weekends. Team activities on Saturday and Sunday weren't mandatory, but Connor wouldn't miss them even if he didn't have an ulterior motive. Through it all, James was nothing but supportive. Super helpful, even. Codie's cheery nature never wavered for an instant. And Van was Van—dopey, happy, and chaotic, but nothing overtly evil. Ninette continued her workouts with Van and Codie, but she only confirmed Connor's assessment: no apparent shadiness.

Connor continued to push himself in summoning. If he could learn more about how the monsters were summoned and the connection to their master, he knew he'd find the key to their investigation. While he didn't excel the way he did at potions, he felt like he was making progress now that he and Sheena were on civil speaking terms. She wasn't a bad teacher once she started talking and stopped glaring. He moved on from level one circles, and his level two work steadily improved.

"You are really not good at this," Sheena chided over his shoulder.

"Come on, this is a lot better!" he whined.

He inspected his concentric circles for mistakes, hoping to stay in Sheena's good graces by discovering his errors before she pointed them out. He wanted to keep her around, maybe even get her involved in the search. She knew so much they didn't.

The two chalk circles on the ground appeared as well drawn as he could manage, and each of his seven runes were crisp and clear. He gave up.

"What did I do wrong?"

"Here, here, and here," she pointed. "You used the runes for a magical creature instead of a normal one."

Connor erased the faulty runes, and Sheena helped him pick the correct ones from the listings on their tablets. Garrett hadn't been kidding—there were hundreds of runes, many almost indistinguishable from each other. Sheena seemed to have tons of them memorized, but Connor couldn't draw a single one without having a reference in front of him. After a few minutes of careful illustration, he received her approval.

"That will probably work," Sheena said. "What are you going to summon?"

"Giant killer bee?" Connor said hopefully.

"Magical. Wrong runes. Try again." Her flat tone was a slap in the face.

Connor thought for a minute. "Wolf?"

"Just be ready to stop it. The circle will make it more inclined to obey, but it will still be wild until you assert your dominance." Sheena crossed her arms and retreated to a safe distance.

Connor poured his essence into the circles. Lavender sparks leaped from his fingertips and powered the circles one after the other. The inner circle spun clockwise while the outer circle rotated opposite. The light brightened. In his mind, he envisioned a lean, gray wolf prowling in a snowy forest. The wolf appeared in the center of the circles, just as Connor imagined her. She looked around, getting her bearings. Unsure of her other options, the wild animal raised her hackles and lunged at Connor.

Connor reacted on instinct, forming his shield of Will. The wolf bounced off with a whimper, shook her head, and lunged again.

"Yeah, hide from it. That'll show her who's boss." Sheena's eyeroll was practically audible.

Connor locked eyes with the wolf and stood up straight, hoping to look taller than he was. He didn't want to hurt her; he needed to convey authority. While she considered a third lunge, he used Nature Magic to twist the wooden floor, trapping all four of her paws. She struggled and snapped at the floor to no avail, yowling and biting at the air. Connor used Shadow Magic to create an illusion of himself doubling in size. He loomed over the wolf and used wind to amplify his voice into a thunderous rumble.

"Down," he boomed.

The wolf looked up at him, whimpered, and lowered her head. Her tail fell between her legs. The runes of the circle glowed brightly in the wolf's eyes.

"You should have her," Sheena said with a hint of approval buried in her voice.

Connor dispelled the illusion and released the wolf. He called her over and she sat next to him, nuzzling his leg. A gentle scratch behind her ears rewarded him with an affectionate growl. Connor sent the wolf to Sheena, who gave it a begrudging pat before shooing it away.

"I think she likes you," Connor smiled. He knelt and placed his hands on the summoning circles once more. The wolf disappeared in a purple flash. "So, I can summon her again and she'll obey me?"

"Yep, she's all yours," Sheena affirmed.

"Aren't you going to work on the level two?" Connor asked while he cleaned up his circle.

Sheena responded with a haughty huff, and, with a familiar open palm gesture, created a flawless level two circle in the air. Out of the opening floated a Somnoth, a glowing moth, fat and fuzzy like a cotton ball the size of a cat. It flapped around, humming softly. The soothing sound vibrated throughout Connor's whole body until he felt like he was under a pile of blankets. His eyelids drooped and his legs turned to jelly. Sheena banished the moth.

"Fair enough." Connor slapped his cheeks to try and wake up. "Can you go higher?"

"Level three," Sheena said in a clipped tone. "I'm close to level four. My father can go up to seven."

Sheena's eyes lost focus, and her mouth moved though she made no sounds.

Now's my chance, Connor thought.

She liked showing off, and clearly, something else was on her mind. With the right question, he might be able to get more info out of her. He brushed his chalky hands on his pants and thought.

What are we missing? What do we not know that might help us figure out who the summoner was? Whoever they were, they had to be powerful. They summoned three monsters at once. But they hadn't done the instant summon the way Sheena could. Their circles were still on the ground when Sheena and I arrived. Connor shuddered at the gruesome memory, and then it hit him.

"Why would someone use blood for their circles? We use chalk in class, and you use essence?"

"Huh?" Sheena snapped back to the present and tilted her head toward Connor. "Oh, I guess I never told you. Blood amplifies your essence. It takes a lot out of you to summon larger creatures. You don't really feel it with the ones and twos, but the higher you go, the harder it becomes. Blood can also serve as an offering. You show the creature you're willing to sacrifice for it, and it will obey more easily."

"Would that only work on creatures that drink blood?"

"No, that's stupid. Your essence is in your blood. All living beings need essence. It binds us to the Earth and the Earth to us. All creatures recognize its power." Her condescending tone made it seem like this was a kindergarten-level lecture he should have long since gotten.

Connor ignored her bad attitude and pressed on. "Wouldn't using your blood make you weaker?"

"Physically, sure. But a circle of blood is basically a circle of essence. Essence into essence is essence squared. You might leave yourself in a bad spot later, but for the purpose of summoning it would be a net gain." Sheena looked at her arms, healed without so much as a scar. "It wasn't enough. The circles required too much blood, and I didn't have enough essence to finish. Whoever did this is powerful, blood or not."

"I meant to ask how you were doing. You haven't seen the grimmalkin anymore, have you?"

"Once or twice," Sheena admitted, not meeting Connor's eyes.

"What?" he gasped. He leaned in close and lowered his voice. "Why didn't you say anything? Did it attack you? Did it follow you? Did it say anything?"

Sheena pushed him away. "That's exactly why I didn't say anything. Relax. It didn't try anything. It follows me around like a little creeper until I find more people, and then it disappears. It's annoying, but it's not life-threatening."

"Still," Connor protested, "you could've been hurt. We can help you. We want to. I promise."

Sheena turned her back to Connor to try and hide a coy smile. "I'll think about it."

Garrett closed the Runes module, set his tablet aside to charge, organized his notes and his homework, and tidied his desk. He leaned back in his chair and stretched his cramped muscles. The clock on his desk said he'd been studying for over three hours, well past dinnertime. He wasn't hungry, but some company would have been nice.

He flipped open the book on advanced runes he had borrowed from Mr. Naegus, hoping to discover more about the runes they found in Atlantis. The more he learned in class, the more the ancient mystery nagged in the back of his mind. Each new rune was a puzzle piece, but he couldn't see the full picture and didn't even know if the pieces he had went to the same puzzle. His extracurricular research turned up a few handy protective runes he'd have to show Connor and Ninette later, but nothing of substance on Atlantis. He pulled out a sheet of notes he'd set aside and added the shielding runes to it.

Learning runes excited Garrett. The instructions were clear and specific, not the subjective nonsense he got from some of the teachers on other magical applications. The only drawback was the need to do the runic engravements well before their use. All the other magic could be used on command, but runes needed to be prepared carefully, and required tools and materials. Even the most basic runes needed to be drawn on something, a far cry from a flick of the wrist or the feats of concentration his friends performed.

"I just need to start making things," he stated to the empty room. "That way I'll be ready. I should have made some runestones or something before we fought the kappa. Next time then." Garrett stopped and looked around. "Now I'm talking to myself. I definitely should have gone to dinner."

The next book on his desk was Connor's Creature Compendium. *There are so many cool things in here. How come we only run into the scary ones?*

He flipped to the chapter on the vesporcus and reread it. He didn't see anything they didn't already know—breathes fire, resists magic, mean, reaches maturity in less than a year, average size is ten feet long and two thousand pounds.

"Wait, what?" He reread it. He rubbed his eyes and read it again. It still said two thousand pounds.

Garrett grabbed the book and burst out of his room. *How did we miss that? I have to let Connor know.*

In his haste, he ran into someone, tripping over them and landing flat on his face. Collecting his glasses and his book, he turned to apologize and found himself staring straight into a pair of familiar, cruel, yellow eyes in a furry, gray face. The grimmalkin smiled at Garrett and waved while its tail twitched in anticipation.

It took some persuading, but Sheena agreed to at least eat dinner with Connor and his friends. He followed her through the food line like a mute attendant while she gathered a dainty assortment of foods and then steered her toward their usual table. Ninette and Carrie were chatting about the match at Rasputin Hall. When Sheena sat down, Carrie babbled, star-struck by the minor celebrity. Ninette was a study in not caring. Connor and Carrie maintained most of the conversation while Ninette and Sheena actively ignored each other. Eventually, Carrie—oblivious to the tension—hopped up and headed back to her room with a tray of snacks to munch on while doing homework.

The ensuing silence was painful.

"So, Ninette," Connor prodded, trying to get some conversational traction, "you and Sheena are both pretty good with Water Magic. How do you practice?"

"Hmph," Ninette grunted. She refused to look directly at Sheena.

"This was a dumb idea," Sheena snorted. "If I wanted to be safer, the last place I'd be is with her. She's as likely to blow *me* up as anything else."

"Come on, that's not cool," Connor protested, waving a placating hand at Ninette. "Ninette is really powerful, but she's totally got it under control. Right, Ninette? That reminds me, uh, Sheena, do you like dueling at all?"

She looked up slowly from her food. She met Connor's eyes, opened her mouth as if to speak, then violently stabbed at her salad and took a bite. Connor wiped a drop of sweat off his forehead.

"I've never been particularly interested, no," she said at last, waving away the idea like a buzzing insect. "My father says it's a lot of sound and fury signifying nothing." She finally deigned to look in Ninette's direction and offered her a sickeningly sweet smile. It was not a positive development.

"It's not like that. You should come to practice sometime," Connor offered. "It's fun to watch. You might like it."

Sheena opened her mouth to express how much she would probably *not* like it, when the cafeteria doors opened with a crash, and Garrett tumbled inside. His wide eyes located Connor and Ninette, and he scrambled over.

"Connor! Ninette! Sheena!" he wheezed, then shook his head and looked again. "Sheena? Never mind. Grimmalkin. Outside. My room." He doubled over and finally remembered to breathe.

Connor and Ninette jumped up from their seats—upsetting their trays of food and ignoring Sheena's irritated cries—and sprinted down the halls to the atrium and the dorms beyond. They cut through the park in a mad dash, dodging around their confused classmates enjoying an otherwise pleasant evening. Cresting a hill, they came to Garrett's room, wind and fire spells ready in hand. No one was there. On the floor outside Garret's door lay a note. It read:

Watch where you stick your noses. You can't all take care of yourselves.

They stood in shock, reading it over until Garrett and Sheena caught up. The note suddenly glowed bright and, with a brilliant flash, incinerated itself, leaving nothing but crumbling ash.

"That reminds me," Garrett squeaked, staring at the remnants of the threat. "I think the vesporcus is way bigger now. It must have been a baby when it attacked you."

"That makes sense," Sheena pointed out. "And sort of explains things."

"What are you talking about?" Ninette snapped.

"Babies are easier to subjugate, typically," Sheena lectured. "Small animal. Easy to control." She enunciated slowly with a nasty grin at Ninette. "Lock it down once, and you have a loyal friend for life, even when it gets bigger. If this thing matures as fast as you said, then it was a smart play to nab a baby."

"Must be tough having such a smart summoner around," Ninette fired back. "Someone better at the thing you're supposed to be good at."

Sheena and Ninette glared at each other with such intensity that sparks almost literally flew. The few other students in the vicinity decided to relocate as quickly as possible.

"Guys?" Garrett interjected, pointing to the ash. "What are we supposed to do now?"

The two girls ended their staring contest to follow Garrett's finger to the little, gray mound. Ninette subconsciously stepped toward Garrett and wrapped her arm around his shoulders. Connor understood the threat behind the note. He and Ninette were becoming more capable combatants, but Garrett—if he were ever caught alone—wouldn't stand a chance. The three of them shared a smile, two confident, one only mildly reassured. One by one they turned their attention to Sheena.

"What? I don't need help. I can take care of myself just fine."

And yet, Sheena found herself regularly eating lunch and dinner with Connor, Garrett, and even Ninette. It was begrudging at first, yet she kept coming back.

The next day when Sheena stepped out of the shower before morning classes, the grimmalkin was waiting for her. She screeched and sprayed a burst of light beams from her fingertips at it to no avail; they fizzled out inches in front of the cat. Thinking quickly and putting more distance between them, she summoned a giant killer bee. With an incandescent, purple flash, the colossal insect appeared. Buzzing its war cry, it launched itself at the grimmalkin. The cat extended a paw, and a spray of brilliant projectiles perforated the insect. Sheena screamed again and tried to summon something else, but the grimmalkin locked eyes with her and her magic slipped from her grasp.

Fortunately, her screams attracted several other girls into the bathroom, Ninette among them. Ninette ripped a brick out of the wall with her bare hands and chucked it at the cat's head. The grimmalkin ducked, gave a final, gruesome smile, and scampered out the door.

On Saturday, it caught Connor and Sheena as they walked to lunch. It crossed their path in the hall and waited, resting on its hindlegs with its forepaws held casually behind its back.

"What can it do if we don't attack it?" Connor whispered.

"It can annoy the hell out of me," Sheena whined.

They stared it down, neither saying a word nor casting a spell. Footsteps sounded from down the hall as more hungry students made their way to the cafeteria. They turned to see who was coming, and when they looked back, the cat was gone.

It would pop out of nowhere to unnerve them. It tried to catch them when they were alone, but they were increasingly going about in pairs or more whenever possible. They even buddied up to go to the bathrooms—Connor and Garrett minded far less than Ninette and Sheena. Sometimes it still approached, and, against better judgment, someone would sling a spell at it, but the grimmalkin returned them all with interest. After a few days of this, everyone was on edge. Garrett jumped at shadows. Ninette snapped at anyone who spoke to her. Sheena was sullen and uncharacteristically quiet, even when easy insult opportunities presented themselves. Connor itched to blow off steam in sparring practice.

It all came to a head one afternoon while Connor and Ninette practiced amplifying spells. Connor wasn't capable of the raw power Ninette was, but he could take her power and apply it with greater precision and speed. Together they could pull off far greater magic than either could separately. Ninette wound up a fireball, and Connor filled it with oxygen, swelling the spell into a raging inferno as big as a house. She reached back to toss it, but before it left her hand the searing flames disappeared into nothingness.

"Oh no," Connor gasped.

Seconds later, the blast went off across the stadium in the stands. Screams of pain and panic broke out. The coaches and students ran across the field to help. Clearing away the rubble, they were surprised to find Garrett holding a steel plate the size of a small book. It glowed with warm, white light and emitted a protective shield over himself, Sheena, and a handful of other students. They seemed no worse for wear, but Nurse Poole insisted on checking over each of them.

When the situation was under control, Coach Kalett pulled Connor and Ninette aside. He looked to be wrestling with himself, and his voice came out caught between anger and confusion.

"What happened out there?"

"The spell disappeared right out of her hands," Connor said. "It had to be the grimmalkin. It's been harassing us for a few days."

The coach cursed under his breath. "Why didn't you say something?"

"Would it help?" Ninette blurted. She got eye-to-eye with the coach. She set her jaw defiantly, and her arms tensed as if she were going to shove him. "The headmistress has known it's been around for months. I assume you knew, too. No one has done anything yet, so I guess we're stuck with it."

His lips curled as if he were about to shout, but only for a minute. His shoulders sagged, and he scratched his head.

"I suppose you're not wrong." He looked up at the sky, then down at his watch. "Van, pack it up. Grab some dinner and then back to your room."

Van nodded sharply and waved goodbye before jogging off. The coaches shooed the student bystanders back to the school while the rest of the team helped clean up the field and put the stadium back together. No one said much while they worked. It was dark by the time they were done.

"Hey, why did the coach send Van back and not the rest of us?" Carrie asked.

"Full moon tonight." Connor pointed up at the sky. "He's contagious."

"Oh, right," Carrie grimaced. "It's easy not to think about, you know?"

"Yeah. I don't think there are many werestudents here, and Van is the only one who's even open about it. I guess the others don't want to make it a big deal." Connor could understand why. Here Van was, being singled out. It couldn't feel good, and that feeling had to build up over time.

"I think Van is pretty brave for being out about it. I could see someone catching a lot of crap for being different here," Ninette said pointedly. "Imagine if he wasn't a popular jock. Someone might suspect him of being up to no good," she added, staring daggers at Connor.

The appearance of the headmistress along the path spared Connor a response. She approached them with a smile and wave.

"Ms. Reefwalker. Ms. Kung. Please continue to your rooms. I require a word with Mr. McTaggart."

The girls spared Connor pitying glances, but retreated nonetheless. Connor watched them go, finding no excuses for his own escape.

"I didn't do anything." He pouted.

"I didn't say that you did. And yet here you are, at the scene."

Connor threw up his hands. "So what if I am? No one else is doing anything! People keep getting hurt, and nothing is happening!"

"This is a magic academy. Think about the injuries you've gotten from dueling practice. Think about the damage Ninette does every day in her classes. I once turned the entire gymnasium to ash over a disagreement with my professor. Gregor summoned a

Shade-Wraith and it gave people fever chills for a month before it was caught. If each incident shut the school down, we'd never get around to teaching you.

"You are children with extraordinary abilities. They are wild and dangerous, and many of you are going to do extraordinarily stupid things with them before you leave school." Her hand rose to her face, and she rubbed the scar on her cheek.

She squeezed Connor's shoulder and gave him a small smile. "We will find the culprit. You seem to think you need to get involved. You do not. You find yourself in danger because you go looking for it. Focus on your studies, and you will remain safe. Trust me."

"You're wrong," Connor asserted, his defiance surprising them both. "The grimmalkin keeps coming after my friends and me. Just us. This isn't something I can ignore."

Leorra sighed and reached into her pocket. "I had a feeling you wouldn't be deterred." She placed a smooth, gray stone into his palm. It was inscribed with a single twisting rune. "If you channel your essence into this, I can find you anywhere. Please, just call for help next time?" She squeezed his shoulder again and went down to the stadium.

Connor watched her go. He touched his own cheek, smooth and cool. *How did she get her scar? What did she do?* A part of him hoped he would never find out.

Chapter 23

> Magic 101 – Old Magic
> Old Magic commonly refers to spells that have gone awry over long periods of time. Whether powerful enchantments that lasted longer than intended, or spells reapplied repeatedly by different casters, the end result is powerful, unpredictable, and sometimes feral.

The four students met early the next morning. Ninette lounged against a smooth tree trunk, and next to her Garrett fiddled with his notebook. Connor and Sheena scouted the base of the hill and the dorms surrounding them, searching for anyone, or any*thing*, that might overhear. Confident no one was nearby, Connor held out his newly acquired stone to the group, and Sheena snatched it for examination.

"That's a summoning stone," Sheena turned the flat stone over in her hands and traced the carving with her perfectly painted fingernail. "She must be worried."

"What do they do?" Garrett asked. His voice nearly squeaked with enthusiasm. "Lady Ariel hasn't taught us that one yet."

"Ariel couldn't teach it to you even if she wanted to. That is Leorra Mine's personal rune. The magic of that symbol is tied directly to her, so only the headmistress could carve it. If Connor activates it, she's going to have warning bells going off in her head telling her exactly where to find him."

"What are you going to do with it?" Ninette yawned.

"I don't know." Connor looked down at the rune. "I think maybe the next time we're in trouble I'm going to use it. Until then, we're still on our own."

"What do you mean 'next time?'" Garrett groaned.

"I said I'd call for help. I didn't say we were done looking."

"But, where?" Sheena asked. "You've searched the whole school and then some. The only thing we can find is that stupid cat, and only when it wants to find us."

The four sat in the shade of the tree and thought. While they did, a crowd of students gathered nearby. They huddled together and whispered excitedly. More and more gathered, the newcomers all exhibiting expressions of surprise and shock. Their conversation got louder as each one tried to talk over the other.

"What's going on?" Connor called out.

"You didn't hear?" One of them shouted. "Van broke out last night. The teachers had to beat the fur off him to get him back into his room."

Before anyone else could react, Ninette was on her feet. Connor looked up at her.

"Where are you going? You think he was trying something last night? I'll come with you."

"I was *going* to see if he was okay," she snapped back. "He was out last night helping us until the last-minute, remember? This is kind of our fault."

"I don't think that's—" Connor argued, but Ninette was already striding away.

Ninette peered into the nurse's office. Nurse Poole leaned on the desk and breathed in the scent of her coffee. Her normally styled hair was a tangled mess, and her eyes were bloodshot. A wrinkled white coat was draped over her shoulders. She leaned heavily on her hand, barely awake, and didn't react until Ninette greeted her.

"Oh, good morning, Ms. Reefwalker. Who are you here to see?" she made a weak attempt at eye contact.

"Is, um, Van here? I heard about last night." Ninette's heart pounded in a slow, heavy rhythm.

"Poor Mr. Fredericks. He has a severe concussion and six broken ribs." The nurse winced "You can go see him if you like." She indicated the door to the left.

Ninette crept into the recovery room. Van laid still, a quilt of bruises and cuts covering his body. Bandages wound around his head and chest. His eyes fluttered open as she approached.

"Hey, man," Ninette whispered. "How you doing?"

"Never better." Van's chuckle gave way to a pained grimace. "I feel like I could take on the whole school."

"I think you did," she laughed. "The teachers anyway. Do you have any idea what happened?"

Van closed his eyes and sank into his pillows. "Nah, I never remember. I go to bed and then wake up on the floor, usually. Today I woke up here. Coach filled me in. I'm just glad no one else got… hurt." He rolled onto his side, facing away from Ninette.

"No one thinks it's your fault," Ninette lied. She sat down next to his bed and reached out for his hand.

"I know it's not my fault," he snapped. He glared at her over his shoulder. "Doesn't help. I could have hurt people, or worse."

Van fell back onto his pillow and closed his eyes. "I'm sorry. I'm exhausted. I thought I was over the whole guilt thing. This brings up a lot of painful memories though." Van's eyes watered, and he let out a weak sniffle. "We don't have a lot, back home. It's just me and mom. She left my dad because he didn't tell her he was… he was like this. It was too late though."

"Van, you don't have to…"

"No, no it's good. She thought she knew what to do, but I got out once, when I was ten. I hurt another kid. Turned him." Van's tears flowed, but the words kept pouring out. "They forced her to turn me over every month for professional lockup. She hasn't looked at me the same since." He wiped his eyes, grabbed a tissue, and blew his nose. "You don't want to hear all this though. My sob story. My problem. I'm fine now, usually. I try to embrace it, yeah?"

"I'm sorry," Ninette sniffled. She wiped away tears of her own. "It sucks. Being different." She placed her hand on his arm and this time left it there.

Van flinched at her touch, but he didn't pull away.

"Shouldn't you go to class?" Van asked after a while. "First period has to be starting soon."

"Meh, I can skip it."

By lunch, most students knew something of the night's events, and the cafeteria buzzed with speculation. What they didn't know, they guessed or just made up. Depending on who you asked, Van either got busted pulling off a legendary prank, staged a protest for werestudent awareness, or tried and failed to spread his curse to someone out of spite. None was a good look for him.

Ninette found the others in a corner by themselves.

"Where have you been all day?" Sheena asked.

Ninette narrowed her eyes. "Not that it's your business, but I was trying to cheer up Van. He had a rough night."

"Don't you think he kinda asked for it?"

Ninette slammed her tray on the table. "You mean because he was late for lock up because he tried to help clean up *our* mess?"

"The grimmalkin isn't *our* mess," Sheena corrected. "It's kind of pathetic that we're the ones cleaning it up, honestly."

"May as well be ours." Ninette growled at her plate. "Weren't you supposed to be helping us find these things?"

"That vesporcus thing is the size of a minivan. Have you tried just looking for it?"

Connor found his voice in time to stop Ninette from responding. Half the cafeteria was already watching in hopes of a fight breaking out.

"It's in the woods. I don't know what kind of chance we'd have at finding it."

"It's a big, fire-breathing pig," Sheena declared incredulously. "I doubt it's hiding."

"The woods have a lot of ground to cover," Connor argued.

"It. Breathes. Fire." Sheena jabbed her food with her fork at every word. "The woods are made of wood. It can't be hard to find."

"I bet the teachers thought that, too," Ninette shot back, taking a gigantic bite of her sandwich.

"I don't know if you've noticed, but the teachers at this school are incompetent. I am not." Sheena smiled with all her teeth and leaned toward Ninette.

"Oh, did your daddy tell you that? You hear from him lately?"

The two girls got within inches of each other, both smiling, neither amused. After the longest second in Connor's or Garrett's lives, the girls stormed off simultaneously in opposite directions. Garrett let out the breath he'd been holding the entire conversation.

"You were no help there at all," Connor sighed.

Professor Skreed acted as if it were any other day, his normal, cheerful self despite the rumors that he had led the charge against Van. Even so, he remained seated at his desk, reclining in his chair less energetic than usual. All he asked was for each student to show him a unique combination of two elements—bonus credit if it was something new or exciting for him.

"I've been around longer than you think," he said. He leaned back and closed his eyes. "I've seen a thing or two, but try your best regardless."

Connor spent all of class worried about Ninette. She stared forward blankly, never looking in his direction. He'd never seen her like this, and he felt at least partially responsible—adding Sheena to the group was his idea—but he hadn't been the one to argue. He didn't understand why she wasn't talking to him. Halfway through class, several of their classmates had met the professor's test before Ninette shook her head vigorously and turned to face Connor with her jaw set and a dark frown.

"It wasn't Van."

"That means it must be James. That's scarier."

"So what? We do what we have to do. Find the proof and take him down." Ninette stretched her arms, flexing. "I bet I could take him. I mean, with a little more practice," she added quietly. "I just don't think it's Van. You believe me, right?"

"Yeah. If you say so." Connor swallowed, afraid of what disagreeing might mean.

The professor issued a ten-minute warning.

"Okay, uh, what are you doing?" Connor asked Ninette, desperate for inspiration.

"My toolbox is limited." Her eyebrows jumped and she grinned. "Professor! How's this?"

Ninette conjured up a hunk of black stone, and then squeezed it tight with both hands. The air shimmered and distorted around the stone as Ninette superheated it, creating intense pressure, and forged it into a raw diamond. Not content to stop there, she shaped the diamond with her Will into a slender, glittering blade.

"I like the iteration on my previous lesson, Ms. Reefwalker. It's been some time since I saw someone create a diamond. Your talent for making is most impressive." The professor turned to Connor and gestured for him to proceed.

Connor groaned. He was the only one left. Unease filled him. His thoughts turned to shadow. If Shadow Magic truly fed on uncertainty, then this was his chance to show off.

"Ninette, can you light my fire?" he joked with faux confidence.

Connor concentrated on his doubt, the gnawing sensation in his stomach that he was about to come up short yet again. Ninette passed him a handful of fire. The flickering tongue smoked in his palm. Gradually, the fire shifted and twisted from warm reds and oranges to a dense, oily black. It drew the light and heat out of the room, instead of providing it. Connor didn't like it one bit, but it was new to him at least, so he lifted his hand up and displayed his creation for all to see.

The professor stared into the black flame for a long time before abruptly dismissing the class. The bell hadn't even rung.

"That was weird, right?" Connor said to Ninette after they stepped into the hall. "I've never seen him not... talkative."

"Maybe. Whatever you did gave me the creeps, too." Ninette rubbed the goose bumps on her arms.

"I haven't been using shadow much lately. I know James uses it a lot, but he's the only one." Connor thought for a minute. "If it is him we're after, it can't hurt to get better. Besides, I do want to try and take his spot someday."

"Only if I don't beat you there."

"Then it's a race to the top."

The camaraderie didn't last. Ninette's mood soured when she saw Sheena waiting at their usual table. Sheena looked up to see Ninette and wrinkled her nose, adjusting herself to face away. Garrett noticed the exchange and sighed. He dropped his tray onto the table and fell into his seat, then pulled a book out of his backpack and pretended to read.

"You guys are sure?" Connor asked once more. "James is a straight-A student, he's the school dueling hero, and everybody loves him."

"Maybe he thinks he can get away with it," Ninette suggested, wolfing down her pizza. "Macho power trip kind of thing."

"You'd know all about that," Sheena said. "So what? We stalk the creep until he slips? We could be waiting a while."

"We don't have time to wait," Connor argued. "The grimmalkin attacks are getting worse. He's building up to something."

"But we don't know what," Sheena shot back. "And I'm still not satisfied. James is powerful and talented, but he's still a kid. He's not working alone. He at least had help with the summoning, and Van is his best friend."

"Van wouldn't do that," Ninette growled. "If you just knew him better, you'd…" She trailed off into a growl under Sheena's skeptical stare.

Sheena didn't take the bait and instead went digging through her purse for her phone. The casual shift in attention stoked Ninette's ire further. She gripped the cafeteria table until the cold plastic cracked in her hands.

After a few minutes, Sheena spoke again, sounding bored. "Then we only have one option. You said the vesporcus was the size of an SUV, right? Even in the woods, you could probably find a sign of it."

Connor's eyes lit up and he leaped halfway out of his seat. "Sheena's right. If we find it and catch it, then the teachers can trace it to whoever summoned it."

"Oh no. We?" She held up her hands in protest.

"Yeah. Rest up. This weekend we go into the woods."

The next day Professor Skreed caught Connor by the arm and asked him to stay for a word after class. Connor told Ninette he'd catch up with her and hung back. He stood by himself, fidgeting at the front of the classroom, while the professor made small talk with the few remaining students. When the room emptied, the professor closed his door and invited Connor to sit.

"I wasn't sure I should say anything at all," Professor Skreed began, "because I don't know if you could do it again if I asked you, but I wanted to speak with you about shadowflame."

"Did I do something wrong?"

"Not in the technical sense, no." Skreed shook his head. "You performed the spell correctly and kept it under control, but it is one you should not do again. It is dangerous."

Connor's stomach sank. The last thing he wanted was to disappoint the kind, old elf. "I thought you said Shadow Magic wasn't bad?"

"I didn't say bad, I said dangerous." He paused, choosing each word deliberately and slowly. "You could use Fire and Nature Magic to create a nuclear reaction if you possessed the knowledge and the power. It wouldn't be bad, but it would still be dangerous.

"Fire provides warmth, comfort, energy, but it can also cause physical injury or widespread destruction.

Shadowflame provides nothing, it only consumes, and it does not burn the body, but the mind. The mind is not so easily healed. For this reason, the use of shadowflame is strongly… discouraged."

"So, you're saying don't do it again?"

"I am saying that would be the safest course. Not until you have a better understanding, and even then, I don't see a use for it. Plenty of healthy uses for Shadow Magic beyond this." The Professor turned and offered a sly wink. "I'll be happy to show you more next year. Now be gone. I don't want your tardiness on my conscience." His smile crinkled the corners of his eyes as he escorted Connor to the door.

Connor sulked out of the classroom. *I wish I could use Light Magic. That probably wouldn't get me into trouble. Why did Shadow Magic have to be the one I'm good at?*

Garrett walked into enchanting early and excited as usual. Enchanting provided a quiet break from the chaos in his life. For one thing, there were only ten kids in the intermediate session. He scanned the empty worktables around the room.

I don't know why more people didn't take the next level. It's not that much homework. I guess Lady Ariel can be strict, but she's not as scary as Brokk. Whatever the reason, it helped Garrett feel less self-conscious.

He took his seat in the front and pulled up his notes, but a movement by the forge distracted him. Lady Ariel emerged from within, covered in sweat and grime.

I guess no one got detention this week.

"Good morning, class. I've got a fun one for you today. The Rune of Return."

She sketched an example on her tablet and then flipped on her screen to show them. The rune looked like an imbalanced triangle with a downward arrow through it.

"The Rune of Return, originally used to help seaward explorers find their way home, works as a sort of compass. They are made in unique sets, best done with similar ingredients. When activated with essence the runes seek out their mates, tugging in the right direction, as so."

She held up a small, flat stone with the rune engraved on it in rich red-gold, and trickled her Will into it. The rune emitted a golden light and jerked forward. The class turned to see an identical stone inching its way toward her from an unoccupied table behind them.

"Traditionally, one of the two would be set into a more solid position, a lighthouse perhaps, or another permanent harbor structure, like the Colossus of Rhodes. These stones were both found in the same area of the gardens, and the runes have both been glazed with an identical mixture of gold and other dyes. Continuity is key. The rune seeks to find its mate. If they are not in tune, they are not nearly as effective." She went to the back of her room and pulled out a lumpy, burlap sack. "I have saved you the trouble of finding suitable stones. When you have completed the engraving, I will instruct you in the next steps."

Garrett stood in line to collect stones, and when he got to the front, he asked Lady Ariel if he could take four instead of two.

"Looking for extra credit, Mr. Clarke?"

"No, ma'am," he replied, "I just want the extra practice."

"Don't bite off more than you can chew," she warned, handing him four of the rounded stones.

"Voluntary extra work will be no excuse for failure to complete the assignment."

Garrett returned to his table, got out his stylus and acid, and set to work. The stones were easy to work with and in no time, he carved out four runes, all receiving the "okay" to proceed from Lady Ariel.

"The second step is to paint the rune with alloy and magic. You are striving for a unique combination. It is possible for similar runes to attract each other and lose all usefulness. You have access to all the materials, metals, and dyes in my stores. Be creative."

Garrett settled on a bronze inlay for his runes and used Water and Air Magic to oxidize it to a neat, green color. For the final touch he imbued all four with Lightning and Wind Magic, with a trace of Water as well. He placed the stones into one of the forges to allow the magic to settle, and went back to his table to read peacefully while he waited.

He retrieved his stones from the forge and, to his delight, all four clicked together like magnets. "Lady Ariel, look. All four work together."

"Expertly done, Garrett," the little teacher said, inspecting his work. "Cleanly drawn, and I see no trace of interaction with the others. I suspect you and your friends will find them effective." She smiled and patted him on the back while he fumbled for a response.

In between classes, Connor prowled the school gardens to familiarize himself with all their leafy twists and turns. Much of the ground between the school and the forest was flat and open. Slinking through the high hedges of the garden would provide cover for their initial escape, but at the garden's edge, there remained about a hundred yards of open field. They would have to make a break for it.

His other main focus remained on dueling practice. Despite the fact that someone on the team wanted him dead, he still wanted to improve. A part of him felt that winning his first match was a fluke, and he was determined to keep getting better to make sure he won again. Getting better might also increase his chances of survival the next time a monster, or worse the summoner themselves, decided to attack him. Unfortunately, the people best able to help him improve were also likely the ones who wanted him dead. Connor decided to take his chances with James. The captain was the only person he knew besides Professor Skreed to use Shadow Magic with any regularity. Connor's recent mishap with the only element he had an affinity with left him wanting to know more.

"Hey, James. Looking good out there," he said during a water break. "I was uh, hoping you could help me with something."

"Oh yeah?" The captain removed his glasses to wipe sweat from his forehead and clean up the part in his hair. "What's up?"

"I wanted to get better at Shadow Magic. My last attempt didn't go so well. I sorta, accidentally made shadowflame. I think I freaked out Professor Skreed."

James shivered. "Nasty stuff. I did the same thing once. Skreed really let me have it."

Connor's lips curved into a smile.

"I stick with the vanilla stuff. Illusions, shadow walking, bindings, those things."

"Right," Connor said. "But your shadows are always so powerful. How do you do it?"

"Fear." James looked right into Connor's eyes for a long time. He broke contact to take a swig of water, and Connor wondered how long they had been staring at each other.

"What do you mean?" Connor finally choked out. "You're not afraid of anything."

"Everyone is afraid of something," James said without looking at him. His voice lost some of its typical swagger. "Afraid of losing. Afraid of not being good enough. Afraid that at the end of the day you don't matter." James hung his head and sighed. When he lifted it, he wore a cocky grin once more. "You'll figure it out. I'm sure."

It wasn't a smoking gun, but something about the way James looked at him gave him chills. Whatever just happened was no ordinary pep talk. But maybe shadow users were just a little weird. Professor Skreed wasn't exactly normal. Connor couldn't tell if he was imagining things or not.

He chatted up the other team members, but they only confirmed what he already knew.

"What can I say about James?" Codie thought aloud, pulling her hair back and tying it up in preparation for practice. "He's always helpful. A great captain." She looked over her shoulder at Van and James rough housing with each other. "James is James. He can be a butthead when someone loses, but I think he just takes it personally. A captain thing, you know?"

"Yeah, James is the best," Thane echoed while they traded spells in a sparring match. "He taught me how to shatter my icicles and keep control of all the parts. He's not in it for himself. Dude wants us all to win."

That was the clear message. James wanted to win, and no one harbored any suspicion or resentment toward him for it. A few more mentioned James's temper when he, or anyone, lost, but that wasn't new or helpful.

James seemed to light up the lives of everyone he encountered. The more Connor heard it, the more suspicious it sounded, however badly he wanted it not to be true. There was one other constant.

Wherever James went, Van was never far.

On Friday night, Connor, Garrett, Ninette, and Sheena met in the gardens. A light breeze whistled through the branches, cutting the otherwise warm evening. Ducked behind a hedge and out of sight of the school, Garrett handed out the runestones he'd made. They huddled close to go over the plan.

"We spread out, as wide as we can while still seeing at least one other person," Connor instructed. "This is a big pig, so hopefully it's obvious where it's been. The book says it prefers swamps and marshes. I don't think there's a ton of that up here, but if you find any water just shout and we'll look around there."

"And you really think, in a massive, magical forest, we're going to find this thing?" Ninette snorted. "This is the best plan we have?"

"I'm open to other ideas. What's yours?" Sheena snipped back.

Connor tried to cut off the brewing argument. "We can't find the grimmalkin. I don't really know how to handle it anyway. This is all we have if we want to put a stop to… whatever James is planning. It's worth a look, right?"

"I'll just be glad when this is done and things can go back to normal," Sheena sighed.

"If anyone gets separated, the stones point you to the closest one of us," Garrett reminded them. "Charge them with essence and they'll do the rest."

He held his stone out and demonstrated. The rune of return lit up with an ethereal, green glow and the stone jumped from his palm and fell on the ground in front of Sheena. All three of them broke into a fit of silent, stress-induced giggles.

"Make sure you hold on tight," he added.

Connor checked his pockets. He touched his focus glove and the headmistress's rune stone for reassurance. They skulked through the garden paths, staying low to the ground and sticking close to the bushes and hedges. A half-moon hanging in a clear sky provided enough light to see the paving stones. It reflected off the ponds, the fountains, and oddly, the rose bushes. The flowers, a blue so faint as to seem white, scattered the moonlight like starry petals floating on the air.

After a long, slow crawl, they made it to the final row of hedges. A broad expanse of open grass separated them from the forest. No one moved until Ninette, with a brief glance back at the school, crouched into a sprint, took off across the field, and disappeared into the woods. A minute later she peeked out from the trees and beckoned them to follow. Connor and Garrett went next, with Sheena not far behind. They took a moment in the tree line to catch their breath and make sure they hadn't been seen.

"We're getting really good at this," Connor grinned. "We should sneak out more often." He forced out a small laugh.

Dark shadows layered over each other like blankets on the forest floor. Only the faintest trickles of moonlight made it down through the dense canopy. The four of them turned around, but the clearing and the school were barely visible through the branches and trees. Garrett took a step back to the school, but Connor caught him by the wrist and shook his head. They had to do this. Spreading out as planned, they began their search; Sheena to the left, then Connor, Garrett, and Ninette on the far right.

"Stay within eyesight," Garrett called out. "I'd rather not have to find out how well these stones work."

They slogged through the forest. The scent of damp earth filled their nostrils. At first it was easy to stay together, but the deeper they went the more they found the tangled undergrowth made pacing uneven. More and more they encountered thickets of thorns and weeds. Ninette was quick to remove an offending snarl of roots and branches with a casually tossed fireball, but even as the smoke from the explosion began to clear, the plants regrew thicker than before.

"That's not right," Ninette said.

She tried again, conjuring a fire blast that left a smoking ruin in front of them, but before any of them could pass through, the forest groaned and the ground shuddered, and a full-sized, new tree grew to block the path.

"Let me try," Sheena said.

Sheena formed a circle with her fingertip and a searing white light formed in the center. It sprang forth in a solid beam, obliterating everything in front of them and punching a man-sized hole through the tree. Sheena prepared to claim victory over Ninette, but the tree twisted and expanded, filling the hole and growing even wider than before.

After an hour without seeing so much as a squirrel, much less a monster, the soft trickle of running water brought a smile to Connor's face. He went to flag Sheena down, but couldn't see her anymore. He called out. He waited a minute then called again. No response. The forest swallowed his voice whole. As far as he could tell there were no signs or sounds of movement where she should have been. Connor took a step in her direction when Garrett grabbed his arm, panic awash on his face.

"I can't see Ninette. I can't hear her either. She didn't answer when I called." Garrett held Connor's arm tight and squinted into the gloom beyond. "Oh no, you lost Sheena, too?"

Garrett fished in his pocket for his rune of return and charged it. The rune glowed and he stone jumped straight to Connor. Connor's jumped back and the two clicked together and fell to the ground. They looked around: abundant, green-black foliage pressed in on them from all sides. There were no footprints or any kind of path indicating which way they came from. The girls were lost. *They* were lost. They were alone in an enchanted forest with no idea how to get out.

Chapter 24

Advanced Will Magic – Portal Making
A portal is a magical gateway to connect any two locations, however far apart. The foundation of the technique is to magically stitch the two spaces into one. A clear mental picture of the destination is essential. Portals require a great deal of both focus and essence, and even the most talented Magi cannot hold a portal open indefinitely.

"Connor, you douche, where are you?"

Sheena had only gone a few feet to skirt a broad oak tree, but when she came back around, she couldn't see Connor anymore. She called out at a reasonable volume, then decided screaming was more appropriate. She ran in the direction she'd last seen him but tripped on a root and landed face down in the cold dirt. She pulled out the stone Garrett gave her and flooded it with essence. It spun like a top on her palm.

"Fantastic," she muttered, climbing to her feet. "Leave *one* thing to someone else."

The dark forest pressed in on her, smothering her outburst. The only light was the twinkle of stars breaking through the tightly packed leaves above. Through fall, winter, and even now in early spring, the forest foliage remained full; the same lush wall that shielded the school from prying eyes prevented her from seeing more than a few feet in any direction. She was alone in a magical forest created for the sole purpose of keeping things hidden. The trees were fat-trunked behemoths, and their branches were low and plentiful, ready to further obstruct her movement.

She listened for Connor, for Garrett, even Ninette. Nothing but oppressive silence. She strained to hear anything: twigs snapping, birds chirping, water running, or hopefully people talking.

There must be some bugs or something, right?

Not a peep. The heavy trunks and rich undergrowth swallowed all sound. The sudden thought of an army of deathly silent bugs surrounding her was more than she needed at the moment.

"Well, I'm not going to sit here alone," she grumbled to herself.

Palm splayed, she let out a burst of Will to conjure three concentric, lavender circles in the air. A flash of purple light and brilliant runes exploded, leaving in its wake a slender figure the size of a child. It had pale brown skin with mossy green freckles, bright green eyes filling its face, and hair-like leaves and flowers flowing down to its ankles. The wood nymph barely had time to blink before Sheena grabbed it and swung it around so they were face to face.

"Do we have any questions about who's in charge?" Sheena menaced.

The creature shook its head "no," and Sheena released it.

"Okay then, get me out of here."

The nymph chirruped at her and bobbed its head. It floated up into the canopy, circled around in the leaves, then climbed higher. After a minute it zipped back down, exploring the immediate area before hovering in front of Sheena. The nymph let out series of titters and tweets and cocked its head in a questioning manner.

"What do you mean there's no end to the forest?"

The nymph burbled a response.

"You are the worst wood nymph I've ever seen."

It stuck its tongue out at her and made a series of high-pitched squeaks, like an irate squirrel.

"You're not off the hook. Let's see if we can find our way out the old-fashioned way."

Sheena tromped through the forest while the nymph led the way and pointed out the worst of the underbrush, so Sheena didn't trip and fall again. The trees stretched on forever. As they walked, the nymph continued to babble at her. It marveled at the unique flowers and interesting leaf shapes unlike any it had ever seen, and it gushed over the hues of bark and berries. Sheena couldn't care less if she never saw another shrub as long as she got out alive. Pushing through bushes and clambering over logs, they made their way in what Sheena hoped was the right direction.

"You're saying there's something unusual messing up your senses? We're in the woods! You're a wood nymph!"

The nymph's eyes twinkled as it smiled and shrugged unapologetically.

"You're incredibly useless, I hope you know that."

Sheena trudged onward. The nymph continued to chatter in its odd, singsong voice, and Sheena tuned it out. This was not how she expected her first year of school to go. She planned on getting through with as little engagement as possible. Her tutors assured her she would ace her classes.

I thought being rich and famous made life easier. Dad never has to deal with this crap.

Everything came naturally to her father. He was smart, talented, well respected. He had it all. All her life Sheena believed herself to be the same. Until she saw the bloody summoning circles.

I guess I should have expected I wouldn't be the best right away, I am only fourteen, but no one was supposed to be that *much better, and now I'm mixed up in this mess with those losers and... and...*

She stopped walking to rub her eyes and take a deep breath. The wood nymph turned around. It tilted its head and put its finger to its lips.

"I'm not crying, you're crying," she snapped. She sighed, searching her surroundings once more. "Still, I hope those losers are okay. Even the oaf."

A twig snapped.

Ninette stomped around the forest, shouting for Garrett.

This was a dumb idea. I should have said so. Just once it would be great if a plan went right. The kappa plan almost *went right.* She smiled. *That was fun.*

She had tried the trinket Garrett made, decided it wasn't going to work, then tried blowing up chunks of the forest at random. Not only did no one respond, but the forest restored itself almost instantly.

So much for blasting a path out, she thought, pushing aside another tangle of twigs and leaves.

She kept her eyes and ears open for hints of water as she slogged ahead, pausing occasionally to blow something up. It didn't work, but it made her feel better, and maybe it would eventually signal the others if she got close enough. No wonder the forest kept the school hidden so well. Ninette hoped it didn't keep her and the others hidden forever.

"I had to come," she grumbled to no one. *Connor is pretty helpless without me, and don't even get me started on Garrett.* She stopped walking to lean against a tree and think. *But that's not why I came, is it?*

She was looking for a fight, and she knew it. Ninette felt at her best when she was beating the salt out of something or someone. She'd wanted to duel from the minute she got to the school, and she'd jumped at every chance they had to fight a monster.

I sure didn't come for that rich twit Sheena.

Coming in and asking *them* for protection, then having the gall to complain about it? If she was going to complain, why tag along? She could afford protection, heck she could probably afford to be privately tutored. She was rude, she was uptight, and she was generally unpleasant to be around.

We should have asked Van for help, except... except they were searching for his best friend. She doubted that would go over well. Being different had hurt him, arguably more than her, but he embraced it. He flaunted it, and Ninette was a little jealous. She rubbed at her gills beneath her ever-present scarf.

As a kid she spent most of her time on land with her mom, but any time someone noticed her gills, or really looked at her teeth, they pointed and stared. When she broke things because she didn't know her own strength, the kids called her "freak." Then her mom died, and she went to the ocean. She couldn't hide down there.

They were just as bad. And when they weren't teasing me, they ignored me. Acted like I didn't exist. Somehow that was worse.

Her dad tried to help. He taught her, played with her, everything. It hadn't been the same. Connor and Garrett were amazing friends, the best she'd ever had. The only ones she'd ever had. They didn't get it though. None of them could. None of them, except Van. Van actually understood how she felt, and that was special.

Ninette slapped her cheeks a couple times and gave herself a vigorous shake. She ran full speed ahead, no longer concerned about the prickly foliage.

"Man, I want to hit something!" she shouted into the darkness.

She needed to find that oversized pig and barbecue it. Her next step landed her ankle deep in mud, and she growled incoherent anger at the forest. She took out the frustration on another nearby tree with a blast she hoped might do permanent damage. It didn't, but another burst of flame answered back not far ahead.

"Connor? Garrett?"

No response but grunts and squeals, and the sound of something big sloshing through the mud. Something angry.

"Did you hear something?" Garrett whispered. He stopped and listened, but it was gone. It sounded like a slow-motion car crash. Maybe the overgrown foliage dampened it, or maybe it was far away, or maybe his ears were playing tricks on him. Connor, daring only to be a few feet ahead, stopped as well, but he shook his head "no," and they pressed on.

Connor had spied a sorry excuse for a creek a while back, and when they decided they weren't going to find the girls, they chose to follow the water.

"We may as well keep going," Connor had said. "They know what we're after, they'll probably keep looking, too." His explanation made sense.

Garrett hoped he was right.

The eerie stillness of the woods wrapped tight around them. Even the creek grew silent after they found it. It was narrow, and running so slowly it could have been frozen, but it *was* moving, so it must have a source somewhere. They hiked along the side of it, going presumably deeper into the twisted woods.

Garrett pulled the runestone from his pocket and squeezed it tightly. *I should have seen it before. This is probably why you usually make them in pairs.* Being so close to Connor made their pair effectively useless, other than as beacons for Ninette and Sheena.

"Why do you think they haven't found us?" Garrett called out.

"Why haven't we found them? It's a big forest."

"No, I mean the runes." Garrett waved his stone in Connor's face. "Ours don't work, but we're right next to each other. Theirs should still reach out to us. They should have used them by now unless—"

"Don't even start," Connor cut him off. "Ninette and Sheena are both fine. They're probably safer than we are." He chuckled. "Here, let's try something. I'm going to go ahead some more. Shout when I get out of sight. We'll try them out."

"Are you sure that's a good idea?"

But Connor jogged away and disappeared around a leafy shrub.

"Connor, I can't see you. Connor? Connor!"

Garrett took out his rune and charged it; the stone spun wildly in his palm. "Crap, crap, crap." Fear gripped his chest with icy fingers. *I don't want to be alone out here. I don't want to be alone. I don't want to be out here at all. I need my friends, I need...* his thoughts came in a panicked jumble.

Then he heard them. Something rustled ahead of him, but further out someone shouted. Then an explosion, and the sound of something smashing through branches and twigs. The rustling sounded safest. His stone stopped spinning and pointed ahead. He ran, slapping at the leaves barring his path and plowed right into Connor.

"What. The. Hell!" he panted. "Where did you go?"

"I was right here," Connor said. "You never said anything, so I stopped walking. I called you, but you didn't answer. My stone stopped working, too." He held it out for emphasis, but it jumped at Garrett.

"Something is not right here."

"Oh, figured that one out, did you?" Connor teased. "Come on, the stream gets wider up here. I think we're close."

A passing thought took hold of Garrett. "What are we looking for, Connor?"

Connor hesitated. "The vesporcus, I guess. Why else would we be out in the woods this late?"

"Well, I don't know. There's that, but we also don't know where the grimmalkin is. We don't know what James is actually planning at all. We could be looking for a lot of things out here."

"'Anyone who goes in not knowing what they're looking for has a way of getting themselves turned around,'" Connor gasped as he remembered his mother's words. He took off at a sprint, leaving Garrett stuttering.

Connor tore through the brush, scratches burning on his arms and face, but he didn't care. It made total sense. The forest didn't hide the school. It hid everything. He cleared his mind. He wanted this to be over. He wanted to know what was worth killing him and his friends. He wanted to know who was behind everything. That last wish burning in his mind, he pushed through a clump of leaves and burst into a clear glade.

He stumbled into the huge, open space, perfectly circular, and illuminated more than the moon could account for. From the center rose the thickest tree Connor had ever seen, but squat, dwarfed by the other trees of the forest. Its branches sprawled out in a tangled web to create a solid, green dome as dark as the night itself. From the base of the tree flowed the creek. It sprang from the roots and ran past Connor into the forest behind him. Sitting against the trunk, half asleep, was James.

Connor growled, but Garrett grabbed him by the arm and yanked him back into the cover of the brush. They remained hidden and observed. Floating in the air above James, a globe of red fluid undulated, growing by the second. A thin ribbon of red connected it to a cut in James's arm. The blood flowed out for a minute more before James ran his other hand over the cut and healed it. He froze the blood into a sparkling red crystal and set it down beside him.

"Oh. Hey, guys," he called out, turning to face them. A vicious smile crept across his face.

The vesporcus squealed and charged again, tusks glistening in the moonlight. Ninette waited until the last second and jumped aside. So far it hadn't hit her, but she hadn't hit it either. When it first noticed her, she conjured a fireball that should have left her with a lifetime supply of ham. Instead, it merely veered off and crashed through the trees.

She sent blast after blast of fire at it, and even hit it with a combination of iron and fire, peppering it with explosive shrapnel. Nothing pierced its hide or caused it to hesitate. It was twice as big as before, and easily twice as aggressive.

If I knew it was this tough maybe I wouldn't have charged it the first time.

Ninette ducked for cover behind a tree while the beast recovered from its last assault. She drew in a breath and held out her hands, willing rough stone to appear. It melted into a broadsword as long as she was tall. The vesporcus snorted and snuffed, and she knew she was out of time. She came around the tree and ran headlong at the giant pig. She swung hard; the blade scored into the side of its snout. The vesporcus missed goring her with its tusk and bellowed furiously with a gout of flame that lit up the dark forest. Ninette scrambled to put distance between them. The cut on its face appeared pathetically shallow.

Not much better than magic, and I don't want to get that close again. It might be time to run.

The vesporcus stomped and smoke rose from the ground. Its hooves scorched the soil, and it charged again. Ninette hurled her sword at it and jumped out of its path—too slow.

She screamed as a searing hot tusk pierced her calf. Excruciating pain overwhelmed her senses. She rolled to the ground, clutching her leg to her chest and biting her lip to hold in another cry. Hot blood soaked through her pants and a metallic scent flooded her nose. Without thinking, she froze her leg into an icy cast.

I'd hate to bleed out before it ripped me to pieces.

She pushed herself to her feet and limped away as fast as she could, which was not fast at all. The mammoth pig made a horrible, whimpering squeal. She risked a glance over her shoulder. One of its eyes was gone and it rubbed its face in the dirt.

"I can pat myself on the back later," Ninette mumbled.

She continued her frantic hobble, but dragging a frozen leg meant lots of snapped twigs and crunched leaves. She didn't get far before the vesporcus heard her. It rooted around, found her, and geared up for a stampeding charge.

"Get ready to jump!" a voice yelled. "Now!"

Ninette sprung forward in a lopsided dive while behind her, a flash of lavender light erupted. The impact of the vesporcus hitting something behind her made the ground tremble and the air shake. A luminous white wall stood between her and the monster. Ninette looked around for her savior. To her dismay, it was Sheena.

"Did you summon a wall?"

"It's called a Nurikabe," Sheena huffed. "It's a wall demon. I have no idea how long it can hold. Can you walk?"

"I can move. We need to find Connor and Garrett and get out of here."

"No way." Sheena held up her hands to stop Ninette. "We need to get *you* help. We might not have much time to worry about them anyway."

The wall shuddered again, cracking. On the other side, sounding a world away, the vesporcus roared, and the canopy glowed orange.

"Fine," Ninette grumbled. "We go, but we get help and we come back for them."

"Works for me."

They hobbled together, Ninette leaning on Sheena for support.

"You looked pretty cool with that sword," Sheena added after a minute.

"Yeah, I did," Ninette beamed.

Connor pushed Garrett back and drew on his focus glove; pure essence suffused the glade, but he couldn't say what element. The colors shifted constantly—green, then blue, then yellow, then red. James radiated intense black smoke—shadow essence.

"It really is you. But… why? Why hurt people like that?"

"No one is dead," James responded. "At least, not yet. I thought I was being generous. You would never have known anything was amiss if you hadn't kept nosing around. It's been a little obnoxious to be honest."

"What are you doing with your blood?" Connor tried not to gag when he glanced at the sphere.

"Oh this?" James gestured to the scarlet crystal on the ground. "I don't know that it's any of your business." He rose slowly and dusted off his pants, then looked Connor squarely in the eyes. "Look, I like you. I think you've got talent. This is getting old though, so let's make a deal." He hefted the frozen blood. "This here is my show of good faith. This blood is mine and mine alone. I won't hurt anyone else, but I need you to *back off*."

"What do you mean?"

"Just that. Stop trying to catch me, and I'll finish up on my own. No more monsters. No more attacks. It's that easy."

Connor wanted to believe it. He wanted to survive to graduation, or at least make it through freshman year. Then he remembered the sight of that poor girl lying on the hallway floor, pale, bloodless. He remembered the fear in Garrett's eyes upon finding the threatening note. He knew he couldn't let it go.

"Finish what up?"

"You don't need to worry about it. But if you keep pushing," James turned his steely gaze on Garrett and his voice turned to ice, "he's next."

"Connor?" Garrett moaned.

Connor wanted nothing more than to wipe the smirk off James's face, but he couldn't let Garrett get hurt. He spun up a dust devil as a distraction, found the headmistress's stone in his pocket, and channeled his essence into it. The stone warmed, then grew hot—too hot. He threw it to the ground before it burned him. It lit up the night with a blinding, blue-white fountain of sparks.

James snarled and snatched up the frozen blood and melted into the shadow of the tree. "Fine. Just remember, I gave you a choice." He uttered, before he disappeared.

Above the stone, a vertical line split the air and widened into a doorway-shaped portal. Out stepped Headmistress Mine. She wore a loose bathrobe and her hair hung down her back, but her stance and expression were that of grim readiness. She held the same dagger she drew against the grimmalkin in Atlantis.

"You can't do these things in the middle of the day, can you?" she hissed at the boys.

She spun around to take in her surroundings and runes of pristine white light burst into the air all around them. Connor marveled at the rapid display of defensive magic; he almost forgot the danger they were in. When she was satisfied they were safe, the headmistress relaxed a fraction and her expression turned from serious to seriously annoyed.

"Thank you, Headmistress," Connor said with genuine gratitude. "I don't know what we would have done. James was getting ready to attack us before you showed up."

"James?" Leorra said, sounding confused. "James Radimus? Surely, you're kidding."

"It-it's true, headmistress. I saw him, too," Garrett assured her.

"He was here. He was… collecting his own blood. He didn't say what he was going to do with it," Connor continued. "I think he summoned the grimmalkin, too. All the monsters."

"Connor, I want to believe you," the headmistress said, "but I need some proof. Where was he? Did he cast any spells? Where did he go? I can tell you the only portal used recently here is mine."

"He jumped into that shadow." Connor pointed to the base of the tree. He tried desperately to recall every detail of the brief conversation, but he could tell it wouldn't be enough. His cheeks burned. He should have tried to stop James himself.

"I will speak with James tomorrow. I want to get to the bottom of this as much as you do, but you must understand my skepticism. James is a student in good standing. Not so much as a slap on the wrist in three years." She sighed and finally took in her surroundings.

The look on her face barely changed, but she spent a long time studying the tree at the center of the clearing. "Do you boys want to tell me where we are?"

Upon learning they were in the forest, the headmistress launched into a tirade about the dangers of the enchantment on the woods and how easily they could have been lost forever. She navigated them out, and when they exited not far from where they entered, they ran into Ninette and Sheena making a slow crawl toward the school.

"I suspected you weren't far, Ms. Reefwalker. Though, Ms. Crowton, you are an unlikely addition to this band of troublemakers." She indicated they should all keep walking. "I expect a brisk hike on that leg might remind you why these escapades are a bad idea."

When they got to the school, she escorted Ninette to the infirmary, then personally dropped each of the others at their rooms, Connor last. She stopped outside his door and fiddled with the belt of her robe for a moment, searching for the right words.

"I'm glad you called for help. It shows a maturity I didn't have when I was in school." She caught herself tracing her scar and stuffed her hand back into her robe pocket, retrieving the runestone. "Hang onto this. I suspect you'll need it again unless I spend the rest of the year sitting on you, something I have half a mind to do. I will speak with James. I want this nonsense ended." She frowned and pursed her lips. "Please, stay in your room for the remainder of the evening. I would like to get a little sleep." She ushered him inside and pulled the door shut behind him.

Connor never made it back to sleep. He spent the rest of the night staring at the ceiling. James *had* given him a choice. What would it cost him?

Chapter 25

Elemental Magicks – Shadow
Shadow Magic bears a stigma from ages when its practitioners were shunned for consorting with ancient evils. Its users enjoy a better reputation today, but not by much. Shadow Mages manipulate both literal and figurative shadows: darkness in the waking world, and darkness in the heart and mind. What's not to like?

The next morning, Connor, Garrett, and Sheena met in the Nurse's office to check on Ninette. Nurse Poole looked up from some paperwork on her desk and welcomed them with a cheery smile.

"Here to visit my number one customer?" She pointed to a bed by the window.

Ninette sat upright with a tray of food in her lap; a white sheet covering her to the waist. The pristine bedding glowed under the full sunlight from the windows, and Ninette waved them over eagerly.

"Hey, guys," she said through a mouth full of food. "You know, I'm fine, and I'm not necessarily saying I want someone else to get hurt, but I would also like to not be the one in this bed next time."

"For sure," Connor promised. He grinned and firmly clasped her hand in his. "Next time I'll make sure to take the hit and you guys can come visit me."

"That's all I'm asking." Ninette attempted a demure smile. "I am a delicate lady after all."

Sheena snorted, and Garrett covered his mouth to hide a smile.

"Oh, come on. I'm not that bad. So, what happened out there with you guys?"

Garrett glanced over his shoulder, but Nurse Poole appeared absorbed in her work. He lowered his voice. "We saw James. He was draining his own blood."

"That's a nice change of pace," Ninette joked.

"He said if we left him alone, he'd stop stealing it from other people, but then we called the headmistress and…" Connor looked down at the floor.

"I'd have done the same thing," Ninette reassured him. "Or just hit him in the face. But what's with all the blood?"

"He froze it," Connor added. "He's saving it for something. Something big."

Ninette chewed her lip. She set her plate on a table next to the bed and folded her hands in her lap. She took a deep breath but couldn't look them in the eyes. "Was Van there?"

"No, just James," Garrett said.

Ninette flopped back on the pillow and closed her eyes. A small smile spread across her face.

Nurse Poole cleared her throat. She stood up from behind her desk and deftly ushered Connor and the others to the door.

"She'll be fine, but she does need her rest. A Friday night goring is no excuse to miss class on Monday, bad limp or no."

Connor thought he'd feel good about the results of their excursion, but all he felt was drained. They now knew, beyond all doubt, that James was the summoner. He brought the monsters into the school to steal blood. All they needed was evidence. Knowing it was him only brought more questions, more danger. And instead of taking the easy way out James had offered, Connor plunged him and his friends in deeper. Garrett and Sheena went to breakfast, but Connor wasn't hungry and said he'd catch them later. He didn't feel like being around anyone.

I'm scared, he finally admitted to himself. *I'm scared I'm in over my head.*

Monster hunting seemed like a fun adventure at first, something every kid at magic school should do at least once. He'd thought… what? He'd slay the dragon—or pig, or cat—and then go on with a normal school life? Maybe. What he didn't dream was that another student, a teammate, someone he idolized not long ago, would openly threaten him and his friends. Hearing the malice and flat seriousness in his voice, Connor believed James to be capable of anything.

Connor spent the rest of his day hiding in his room curled up in bed. He turned his friends away, feigning exhaustion from being out all night, and only opened the door for Headmistress Mine. She confirmed Connor's fears: there was no evidence to suggest James had anything to do with the attacks. Connor thought again about James's offer.

Maybe I should have listened. He hasn't *killed anyone. But now he might.* Ninette kept getting hurt. Garrett was a sitting duck. And Sheena… *Okay, she involved herself, but she's my friend now—more or less—and I don't want her to get hurt either*. He lay in bed, not sleeping, but not truly awake, as the rest of the weekend passed him by.

The sun shone through his window Monday morning, warm and comforting. Connor woke from a deep sleep he didn't remember falling into. He yawned, stretched, and was surprised to find a warm sense of determination churning within him.

Connor gathered his friends and sat them down out in the atrium. Spring sang in the air. The trees and flowers bloomed in vibrant affirmation of the season. A soft breeze whispered of a pleasant day to come. Connor looked at each of his friends in turn. He thought he had made a decision, but he needed to be positive they were on board, too.

"James threatened me and Garrett. I have to imagine you guys are in danger, too."

Sheena placed her hands on her hips. "Is that a surprise? He's been trying to kill you all year." She tapped her foot and checked her watch. "If you're holding up breakfast for that news flash, then I'm gonna go."

"No, it wasn't… it was different," Connor said. He shivered at the memory of the look in James's eyes. So calm. So rational. "He was only trying to scare us before. Get us to give it up. If we died, whatever but that wasn't the goal. Things are different now."

"We can get the teachers now, right?" Garrett asked. His voice rang hollow, as if he knew the answer.

"No," Ninette said, staring at the ground. "You just did that. He's covered his tracks too well. If the headmistress looked and didn't find anything, then tattling on him again will get us nowhere."

"But, if the teachers can't find anything, how will we?"

"Are you all forgetting dog-boy?" Sheena asked. "He's the weak link in that brain chain."

Ninette's fists clenched, but she said nothing.

"I say we tail him. Maybe lean on him even. You're really going to tell me the psycho's best friend doesn't know *anything*?"

"Maybe we don't even have to do that." Connor locked eyes with Ninette. "What if we talked to him? What if you talked to him?"

"I'm not asking him that."

"Sheena has a point. Maybe you're right, and maybe he's innocent, but he has to know something. How could he not?"

"Why? What makes you say that?" Ninette raised her voice and stabbed her finger in Connor's face. "James has covered his tracks perfectly. Why would he risk that by telling anyone anything?" She glared at Connor.

He bit his lip and frowned. This wasn't going how he'd planned.

"He'd tell a partner," Sheena said flatly. "Someone who helped him with the summoning, maybe? He didn't do it alone. He couldn't have."

"Just because you couldn't, princess? Screw you."

"Screw you!" Connor shouted back. "You can't just ask the question? Just because you've got a crush? Are you *that* afraid of the answer?"

Ninette punched Connor in the gut. He flew back several paces and landed flat on his stomach. She froze and her mouth hung open. She backed away, slowly at first, then ran away without looking back. When Connor caught his breath several minutes later, Sheena helped him limp to the infirmary. Garrett didn't speak for the whole day.

The following weeks felt like they happened to Connor, like he was an observer of his own life.

Connor and Ninette rarely spoke. She and Van officially became a couple. They were rarely separated outside of class and held hands in the halls whenever they could. With Connor and Ninette butting heads, Garrett withdrew from the group, slowly but surely. Unable to decide where to sit at meals for fear of further hurting anyone's feelings, he took his food back to his dorm room. He buried himself in his enchanting studies, spending all his time in the library or Lady Ariel's workshop. Garrett didn't explicitly say he wanted to end their pursuit of James, but he always found an excuse not to help with surveillance, and Connor didn't force it.

That left Sheena. She continued to help Connor understand more about summoning beyond the scope of the introductory class. She also convinced him to follow Van. They took turns using Farsight to spy on his room at night. Connor interviewed the team again, this time only asking about Van, but none of their answers changed. The guy was lovable to a fault. Connor expanded his quest to include teachers. They said much the same as the students. Van's reputation—though not as sterling as James's—included nothing malicious or suspicious. Doubly impressive considering his werewolf status.

Through it all no one else got hurt. No one saw the grimmalkin creeping around. The vesporcus remained in the woods. There were no more summonings, no more monsters. A whole month passed without incident. Things almost felt normal. Almost. Connor started to believe James was giving him a second chance. Part of him wanted to take it. Yet, James remained a specter over dueling practice, smiling, laughing, helping the coaches, and being the perfect captain. He even offered to practice with Connor every week without fail. It was miserable, particularly because Ninette opted to practice with Van, which left Connor no excuses. Connor and Ninette's teamwork suffered for it, and it wasn't long before they regularly lost to Michelle and Clara. Losing pissed Ninette off even more, but she refused to talk to him about it, or anything else.

It all came to a head on Monday before the final matchup of the year against the Tikal Observatory. Coach Kalett pulled Connor aside before practice.

"Look, Connor, I don't know what's happening with you, but you're slipping. Is everything okay?"

Connor wore a wooden smile. "I'm fine," he answered automatically.

"I know today is solo practice, but James has agreed to spend the day working with you. I think he can help you get your head back in the game." The coach gave him a gentle nudge toward the waiting captain.

Connor's shoulders slumped and his stomach turned inside out. *How am I going to make it through this?* Was James going to taunt him? Humiliate him? Threaten him some more? Connor looked around—half for an excuse he could make to get out of it, half making sure there were witnesses.

"You ready to work, kid?" James said with no hint of menace.

"Why? Why would you even bother?"

"Because I hate losing. If my team doesn't win, I don't win," James explained as if that made perfect sense. "We're going to have a perfect record this year. You get me?"

Connor stared slack-jawed. "So, we're going to pretend we're cool, and you're going to get me ready for the match?"

"That's the plan. You don't want to be a blood sacrifice, do you?" James said with a wink.

Connor's stomach hit the ground, then leaped back into his throat. He spun around in a panic to make sure someone was watching. "What?" he choked out.

"Relax." James placed his hand on Connor's shoulder, which only made Connor flinch. "Mayan joke. We're playing Tikal Observatory? They used to sacrifice the losing team or something."

"I-I don't think that's right," Connor stuttered.

"Whatever. Let's go. I want to show you something."

James pushed him to the far end of the stadium. The afternoon sun dipped low, and long shadows groped across the field, bringing a spring chill to the air. Connor let James navigate him without much resistance. When they reached the darkest corner of the field, James turned Connor to face him and then gestured around them. "Well?"

"It's dark and chilly over here," Connor observed dryly. "Did you want to show me how shadows work?"

"That's exactly what I wanted to show you."

James smiled and grabbed Connor. The ground vanished beneath them. Connor dropped like a stone through the shadow and his world turned black. Connor closed his eyes. Then opened them again. Nothing but darkness. Immense pressure weighed down on his mind. Sand crunched under his shoes. Somehow, he knew if he stayed here much longer, his consciousness was going to be crushed by it.

This feels familiar.

"It's intense, right?" James sounded far away, but his hands were still there. "You're in the shadow world. What we're doing is called shadow walking. You can feel we don't belong. Open your eyes, really open them. Perceive the shadow world."

Connor tried to open his eyes wider. Gradually things came into focus, not by color, but by texture, and somehow, he could see. He stood on grainy black sand, being lapped by a silent, oily, black ocean. Black wind whistled through the dry leaves of black trees. On the horizon, something like slimy black tentacles broke out of the water, writhing against the void of a black sky.

It's the same as my dreams.

"You build a tolerance to it if you come through enough; of course, you're not supposed to stay for long. If you do, they find you."

"Who is 'they?'"

"The shadow creatures," James said. "They've attacked me more than once. Immense power. I can't tell you how many times I've almost died in here."

His casual tone and cool demeanor chilled Connor to the bone.

"Something is wrong with you." Connor backed away, still trying to process. *I came here. I came here on my own somehow.* He felt exactly the same as before, which meant those other times weren't dreams at all. That meant there was a way out. Unfortunately, he didn't know it. "So, how do we get back out? How did we even get in?"

"You just ask a question," James explained, as if it were obvious. "The shadow's domain is uncertainty. When you admit your uncertainty, they let you in."

"And you get out by…?"

"Answering one of theirs." James's voice echoed away into nothingness.

The sudden absence rattled Connor. Psychic pressure squeezed his skull and panic crept in. James's cryptic instructions meant absolutely nothing. He took a single step and his foot splashed in the water. He jumped back and yelped, remembering the tentacles.

Connor took a deep breath. Then another. He closed his eyes and listened. *I've done this before. I can do this.*

At first, all he could hear was the breeze rattling dry leaves and the crunch of sand beneath his feet, but somewhere between those, he caught a trace of a familiar voice. The sound of it sent tremors through his mind, even as the words sought to put him at ease.

"YOU HAVE RETURNED TO US. LIKE THE OTHER, WE CAN GIVE YOU WHAT YOU SEEK." The voice turned insistent. It grew louder. "WE KNOW THE SECRETS OF YOUR WORLD. HE HAS ONLY SCRATCHED THE SURFACE OF WHAT WE OFFER. HE WILL HELP YOU." The voice paused, and the silence that filled Connor's skull was painful. "WILL YOU JOIN HIM?"

The ease of the answer was a relief. "Nope, sure won't." Connor flashed a big smile, then remembered no one could see it.

"DISAPPOINTING. YOU BELONG TO THE SHADOWS. YOU BELONG TO US. WE WILL HAVE YOU."

The world around him lit up. A hundred different portals appeared, some above, some below. They opened into blurry images of green grass and hard plastic seats and the cool concrete walls and even his teammates, over and over and from different angles.

These are the shadows in our world.

He located the one where James stood waiting, arms crossed. James looked up with a smarmy grin.

Somehow, he knew Connor had figured it out. Rather than give him the satisfaction of stepping out in front of him, Connor found a place in the stands. He exited there and stepped into the warm embrace of the afternoon sun. Happiness and light returned, filling a space Connor hadn't noticed was empty. He whistled at James.

"How's that?" he bragged, trying to sound smug.

"Not bad. Didn't take as long as I expected," James answered, unimpressed. "What did they ask?"

Connor didn't answer right away. He descended the stairs and jumped back down onto the field. "They asked if I'd help you."

For the first time, James looked surprised. His cocky expression was replaced with uncertainty. He frowned and leaned ever so slightly toward Connor. "And you said…?"

"I dunno. Tell me your plan."

"I'd think it was obvious." James shrugged and shook his head dismissively. "I'm looking to secure a new source of essence to ensure I am the best duelist the world has ever seen."

Connor couldn't immediately find the words to respond. It was so… ordinary. It wasn't big, or evil, or anything like he'd assumed. And it just didn't make sense. "You're already the best duelist at the school. Everyone knows you're going to go pro as soon as you graduate. Why risk that?"

"This school," James scoffed. "I am a big fish in an exceedingly small pond. I am the best duelist in *most* schools, and *this* school, if you hadn't noticed, isn't even that good." He rolled his eyes. "I am going to go pro the minute I graduate. And what then? What am I supposed to do when I'm faced with the other best duelists from the other, better schools? Or the professionals with years of experience and mountains of time and money behind them? What then?"

Connor had never thought that far ahead. For him, getting into the professional leagues at all would be a dream come true. The idea that it wouldn't be enough was insane.

"I mean, at that point you just do your best, right?"

"Hah! You sound like my parents," James snapped. The outburst drew the attention of some of the others on the field. He lowered his voice. "People try their best every day, and they get nothing for it. History is rife with the ghosts of people who tried their best every damn day of their lives, and we will never know their names because they amounted to nothing." He bent over, inches from Connor's face. "How are you supposed to know if your best is good enough until it's too late?"

Connor tried to back away, but he'd unknowingly already backed against the stadium wall. Before he could stammer out an answer, James spun around and sauntered away.

"Not me," James declared. "I'm stacking the deck in my favor from day one. Now, are you ready to continue the lesson?"

Connor's head spun from the abrupt change in tone, but despite everything, he still wanted to learn what James had to offer. "So, do I need to do this whole question thing every time I want to shadow walk?" When James did it, he jumped in and out of shadows like a prairie dog. *He moves too fast to be playing twenty questions.*

"Nah. One answer buys you some time. Why don't you pop on down and see for yourself? You still need to practice."

Connor sighed and sat down on a shadowed bench, but no questions sprang to mind. What kind of question was he supposed to ask? James stared at him like a hawk eyeing a mouse. He let out a half chuckle, a sound of pure condescension.

What's he really planning? Connor thought. The shadow below him softened. His body sank the barest amount. He knew he could drop through with a thought.

He fell into the shadow world, but this time under his own power. All the openings from before remained. Connor decided not to overstay his welcome and picked the closest to jump through, landing in a crouch back on the field. James slow clapped.

"I'd give you a B, but you pass. 'Grats."

"There has to be a catch," Connor said, casting James a sideways look. "Why don't more people do it?"

"People find the shadow world… unpalatable. Besides, not many specialize in shadows."

"Because it's dangerous," Connor prompted.

"All magic is dangerous. Your fishy friend there could level half the school with Fire Magic if she wanted to. Probably with her head depending on the day."

Connor flinched and then glared at James. He knew exactly how Ninette would feel about that. He clenched his fists, and a low growl escaped his throat.

"Like I said, I don't know exactly what's in there, and yes, clearly, it's unhealthy to stay there for long. Figure it out, man. Unlike me, you need all the help you can get." He walked away, leaving Connor alone in the cold shadows.

Practice ended, but Connor remained sulking in the shade. He sat with his back against the smooth wall and his knees hugged to his chest. The shadows stretched further and further across the grass until someone loomed over him. He looked up to see Ninette glaring down at him.

"Are you ready to talk?"

"There's nothing to talk about. Let's just worry about the match," Connor snapped.

"I am. Especially with you being so out of it—you can't tell a fireball from a firefly until it hits you in the face."

"What do you care? You don't want to hear what I have to say."

"You're right. I don't care what you have to say. I want you to listen, dammit! I want you to trust *me*."

"I want to, Ninette." Connor's chest hurt. *I do trust her, it's just...* just that, in this one particular instance, he didn't think he could. "I really want to. I can see... that you're happy."

"We know it's James, right? You literally saw him and no one else. That's all there is to it. Van and I... I don't know." Ninette paused. She inhaled slowly, started to say something, but then changed her mind and sighed. She blushed. "I like him a lot, okay?"

Connor slumped, but he forced most of a smile. It had been weird not talking to her and Garrett. Spending so much time alone with Sheena wasn't great for his self-esteem.

"So, what do we do?"

"I'm glad you asked," she beamed, and she looked almost like her normal, overconfident self. "When have things gone right for us?"

Connor thought back, but nothing sprang to mind. Other than the kappa, it felt like very little had gone right for them this year, at least where James and the monsters were concerned.

"When he's been trying to kill us," Ninette beamed. "Whenever *he* reacts to *us*, we get more clues. We need him to react."

"You *want* him to try and kill us?"

Ninette bobbed her head enthusiastically. Connor couldn't help snickering. Now *he* felt like his normal self, too. In fact, her recklessness gave him an impish idea.

"Okay, let's do it. By the way, he called you fishy today."

Ninette's eyes darkened, but her expression was one of wild glee. It scared him a bit, but he was glad for it, and he wrapped her in a tight hug. After a second with her arms awkwardly raised, Ninette returned it.

"You're going to punch him in the face, aren't you?"

"One hundred percent."

Chapter 26

Advanced Magical Concepts – Astromancy
Astromancy is an advanced offshoot of Light Magic that uses the light of cosmic bodies as its essence source. It can only be used by those with sufficient knowledge to know what light is available and from where. Astromancy spells could only be countered by another Magi with the same intense depth of knowledge, and the odds of that are… astronomical.

The next day at practice, as the team hit the field, Ninette called out to James in a voice dripping with honey. "Hey, captain, I *need* you for a minute."

James swaggered over with a smarmy grin. Ninette asking for help was enough to get the whole team watching, and James soaked up the attention. He stepped up close to Ninette—way too close. Van stuffed his hands in his pockets and huffed an annoyed grunt.

"And what can I do for you, miss?"

Ninette's surprise punch to the face sent him flying ten feet through the air before crashing in a tangle on the ground. Audible gasps and cries followed, none louder than Van. He yo-yoed back and forth between the two of them, holding his stomach and turning a sick shade of green. Nurse Poole rushed to James to check for signs of concussion. Coach Kalett grabbed Ninette by the shoulders and positioned himself between her and her victim. He tried to yell, but words failed him. He only managed a series of angry and confused sounds before he sent her off the field and suspended her from practice with the promise of a week of detention to follow. Ninette walked away with her head held high, and a concerned Codie fluttering after her, bubbling with questions.

James woke up under Nurse Poole's care, rubbing his already bruised and swollen jaw. He laughed it off, but the stare he shot Connor when no one else was looking said it was anything but funny. That dark glare was a promise, loud and clear.

Ninette missed dinner, apparently busy cleaning out the locker rooms by hand, which would be her evening plans for the next week. Connor went to check on her in her room later that evening. She answered the door looking tired, dirty, and incredibly satisfied.

"Looked like a mean punch. Worth the detention?"

"It was. Thanks."

They took a walk around the atrium. Connor hadn't spent much time exploring it in the evenings, only in the full dark of their midnight escapades. The trees shimmered, full of more fireflies than could possibly have been natural. The paved paths gave off an opalescent glow. Nearby, a bird warbled a relaxing tune.

"How did Van take you punching his best friend?" Connor asked.

"Better than you'd expect." Ninette chuckled. "He said it was probably a little overdue. Asked me not to make a habit of it. He's a pretty good boyfriend."

Connor didn't know what to say to that, so they walked in silence for a bit. They passed a few other students, mostly couples out for a stroll.

"We talked about James while I cleaned the locker room. Van helped me get it done faster." She gave Connor a withering stare.

Connor tried to meet her gaze but couldn't. The idea of helping hadn't occurred to him. A sour pit formed in his stomach. "What did he say?"

"Said James is a good dude. Had no idea what I was talking about. Look, I still think James is our guy, but Van isn't guilty of anything but bad taste in friends. Talk to him yourself. He's sweet. He's nice." Ninette's eyes glistened. "He gets what it's like being different."

"Ninette," Connor fumbled for words, "you know I don't think of you as different. None of us do."

"I know. And that's great. But I *am* different, and you can't know what that feels like sometimes, but he does. He's not involved. End of discussion. Let's get through the match and then deal with James. We know he's rotten."

Connor was about to respond, but Ninette held up a hand to stop him. Her watery eyes and trembling bottom lip said she knew exactly what he was going to say, and she wanted none of it. She turned and walked back to her room. Alone.

Match day. The clouds were fluffy, white, and scarce. The sun beat down in full strength from high in the azure sky. The Observatory stadium was a fully restored ballcourt, a long narrow strip of grass between towering tiers of stone seating, resting in the sprawling shadow of an ornate, gray pyramid. More squat pyramids and ziggurats comprised the entire campus.

What is it like going to school in such an ancient facility, Connor wondered, wiping sweat from his forehead. *Do they even have air conditioning?*

Fans filled the stands, as they must have centuries ago. Connor sat with his team and listened to the school announcer introduce the Observatory students one by one. In the meantime, the school's mascots, a sun and moon, cartwheeled around the field with cartoonish smiles stitched permanently on their faces.

Round one, and the players took to the field. Thane and Carrie versus two boys, a small freshman and a towering, but lanky, junior. A ringing gong set them off. Thane countered their water with ice, and Carrie rebuffed fire spells with overwhelming wind for an easy victory. Up next, Michelle and Clara against a musclebound orc boy and a slim elf girl. The Mattson duo was too predictable, their usual offensive tricks too easily countered by a hardy, earth-bolstered defense. A knockout on Michelle preceded a quick surrender.

"We're up," Ninette said, voice flat.

Connor had tried to apologize, but Ninette wasn't hearing it—especially since he apologized more for hurting her feelings than suspecting her boyfriend.

"Yeah. Let's go out on a 'W.'"

Their opponents, both dark-haired boys of a similar build, waited for them downfield. They sported the Observatory uniform consisting of loose gray shirts and trousers complete with golden bracers on their wrists and ankles. They stood back-to-back, exuding an aura of calm competency. The opposite of how Connor felt at the moment.

"So, on the tape, it looked like they like to—" The gong cut him off.

"I'm going to hit them very hard," Ninette growled.

Connor resigned to follow her lead. Ninette crafted her signature overlarge fireball and launched it, but halfway through its arc Connor divided it into a shower of whizzing sparklers. Their opponents scattered, taking several hits in the process. They both closed their eyes and held their hands up to the sky. Connor threw a wind blade at one while Ninette launched a spiraling streamer of flame at the other. Both shots connected, and the boys went flying in opposite directions. Connor smiled; this was a cakewalk.

"Connor, look out!" Ninette cried, pointing up.

Connor dove aside, narrowly avoiding being smashed by a pillar of raw heat. The air wobbled behind him. The grass burned black, and the smell of smoke filled the air. The shimmering beam inched in his direction.

"It's astromancy," Connor called back. He sprinted across the field. "They're channeling the light of the sun into a laser!"

"Which one?" Ninette looked from one boy to the other. Both their faces were scrunched in concentration.

Connor took a shot at the closest one; a shockwave rippled through the ground and knocked the boy off his feet, but the inferno kept getting closer. Ninette tackled the other, blasting him into the ground with fireballs, but he maintained his hold on his spell despite the pummeling. Every hit he took came with a dull flash of pale light. Connor's opponent was back up and called down flaming meteors at Ninette. They caught her in the side and continued to pelt her, driving her down into the turf. Connor lashed out with whips of shadow. The weaponized sunlight stayed hot on his heels, and he had to keep moving. The darkness struck the boy in the chest, and again a pale light glinted. The Observatory duelist somersaulted backward and sprang to his feet. Ninette screamed in pain and anger, blasting away with a rapid barrage of fireballs, sending her foe flying high but unharmed. Up in the air, he closed his eyes and Connor's opponent did the same.

"Ninette, close your eyes!" Connor shouted, but not fast enough.

The flash of light was so brilliant Connor saw spots, even through his eyelids. He blinked them open to a blurry world, shapes distorted and colors all wrong. The heatwave scorched his back, and he stumbled forward to avoid it. Ninette spun in a chaotic circle, firing off fire and earth spells blindly. The refs threw barriers around the stands to absorb the shots and protect the audience.

How are they taking these hits? They aren't using shields of Will. The heatwave was solar. Astromancy was all Light Magic. *But what else could they be...* Barely visible in the sky, the half-moon floated, its pale light washed out by the bright afternoon sun.

"Moonlight! Ninette, they have shields of moonlight!"

Ninette didn't hear. She continued her rampage, launching golf ball-sized hail, geysers of flame, and jagged boulders in wide arcs. Connor could only keep running, trying to figure out how to dispel their defenses. Fortunately, with Ninette providing a distraction, his only worry was the inexorable heat wave behind him.

The boys were busy trying to evade Ninette's wild assault and bring her down at the same time. It gave Connor just enough time to look for an out.

James watched Connor, expression hard and analytical. His stern glare gave Connor an idea. The low sun cast a sizable shadow from behind the pyramid. The shade had gradually reached across the grassy stadium as the duels progressed. Connor's chest felt tight as he reached down and felt the darkness become tangible under his fingers. He looked again at James and let his fear spur him on. Whipping the shadow like a sheet, Connor shrouded the arena with it, erasing all but the faintest traces of light. Both boys glowed faintly before winking out, one after the other.

"Ninette, keep doing what you're doing," Connor said, half to himself. "I need a second." He started to collect his essence into the palms of his hands. It coalesced into a small ball of writhing, undulating essence, every ounce spent left him wearier by the second.

The Observatory duo focused on Ninette, bobbing and weaving around her spells while more flaming meteorites fell from the sky around her. Ninette's spells weakened, the gaps between them grew. Her insane bursts of magical power took their toll, but some of her shots connected, and each packed a punch.

"Any time now, Connor," Ninette wheezed. She fell down to one knee but pounded shockwaves into the ground to deter approach.

The ray of sunlight pierced the shadowy veil as Ninette collapsed from exhaustion. The opposing team turned hungry eyes toward Connor, grinning at what they thought was an easy win. Connor's hands were empty. Connor smiled back and pitched his spell.

The essence bomb exploded, and the boys panicked in the aftermath. Connor knew roughly what it felt like, having lost his own magic to the grimmalkin more than once. The mental static, the futility of touching essence of any sort. He doubted they'd be familiar with the feeling, but he wasted no time. James hadn't blinked. He watched Connor thoughtfully. Weighed him.

I need to win. This is my only chance. Connor dug deep to find the last vestiges of his essence and combined them with the warm, dry air to focus hurricane-force winds at the temporarily silenced team, but instead, a smoky blackness poured out of his hands and screamed across the ground. The grass paled. The sound clawed at his ears. Connor fell to his knees and covered his head, desperate for it to stop.

The Black Wind screamed at the two boys, powerless to defend themselves. It picked up both like feathers and hurled them at the bleachers, and Ninette's unconscious body as well. The referees tried to catch them, but the essence bomb interfered, and all three kids were tossed into the stunned audience.

Connor sprinted across the field to help Ninette. *What did I do? What did I do to Ninette?* He vaulted over the wall and into the stands. He pushed and shoved horrified audience members aside until he found her. Her bloodshot eyes searched wildly, and cold sweat drenched her pale skin and matted her black hair to her face.

"Mom!" She cried in a raw voice. "Mom! No… Connor? Huh. A nightmare? I didn't even know I was sleeping." Slowly her memory returned. "The match. Why was I asleep? Did we win?"

Connor stood up and glanced over at the refs. They weren't far, inspecting the Observatory boys who looked even worse, both trembling and shaking despite being unconscious. The refs shared a look of concern but called the round for Mattson. Only a meek smattering of applause followed, swallowed whole by the uncomfortable tension from the onlookers.

"Yeah, we won," he whispered. *I need to find out what the hell I did. How can I not do it again when I don't know how I did it to begin with?*

He helped her to her feet, and she leaned heavily on him. Van ran out to meet them, and, brushing Connor aside, lifted Ninette. He fussed over making sure she was alright and got her onto the nurse's stretcher for healing. He didn't leave her side for the entirety of halftime. The rest of the team murmured quietly. They offered congratulations but made no further effort to speak to Connor. All but one.

"Black Wind, huh?" James sat down next to him, grinning ear to ear. "Gross. Whatever it takes to win, I guess, but you're not going to make any friends that way." He leaned in close to whisper in Connor's ear. "You sure you don't want to see things through with me? Might be good for you."

"It wasn't on purpose. I don't even know how… I don't have to explain anything to you. I don't want any part of what you're doing," Connor growled without looking at him. "I'm going to stop you. I'm going figure this all out, and I'm going to stop you."

"Well, good luck. Hey, watch my match closely. Might take a cut out of some of that unearned confidence."

The rest of the matches were quick, but not painless. Van was in a state after seeing Ninette hurt. He stormed onto the field full wolf before the gong finished reverberating. Fur smoldering red, he pounced on top of his opponent and bathed them in flame. The refs stopped the match almost instantly and issued Mattson a warning. Codie dropped the temperature of the air to nothing, and the elf girl she faced shivered violently. Her Nature Magic offensive stalled out—all the plants she grew withered and froze, rendering them ineffective. Codie pinned the girl flat with wind to end it.

The final match being only a formality, James chose to let his opponent make the first move. His foe, a senior, performed a rather speedy triple summon: Dire Wolf, Thunder Hawk, and Owlbear—all level threes. The wolf charged while the Owlbear cast Ice Magic, and the Thunder Hawk called lightning. James caught the wolf with telekinesis and blocked both magic attacks with it before hurling the wolf back at its owner. The Observatory captain blocked it, but didn't expect James to be right behind it, fist crackling with electricity. A thundering uppercut from below coupled with another bolt of lightning from above resulted in a total knockout.

The Mattson team ran out to celebrate with their captain for putting a decisive cap on a, by all accounts, terrific season. Connor and Ninette followed with more measured enthusiasm. There were hugs and cheers, claps on the back and high-fives. The Mattson students and families managed to fill the stadium with the roar of victory. A space in the crowd opened, and James and Connor were left to glare at each other.

"Good game, captain," Connor said through a grimace he hoped looked like a smile. He extended his hand.

"You, too, kid," James replied. His smile looked more natural, easier.

Connor wondered how he did it. The handshake he returned threatened to break bones.

A surprise awaited when they returned home—a twilight stadium filled with even more students and the entire faculty, Headmistress Leorra Mine at the center.

She let the team bask in the applause before raising a hand, gaining immediate silence.

"Welcome back, Manticores!" she announced. The wind carried her words swiftly for all to hear. "Congratulations on a hard-fought season. It looks to be an exciting beginning for some of our newest team members." She gestured specifically to Codie, who bowed her head and blushed. "And it is a triumphant, perfect season for Mr. James Radimus."

The crowd exploded with adulation. The headmistress allowed them a moment and then beckoned James to join her. He walked toward her, hands in his pockets and flashing his oil-slick smile. When he reached Leorra, he waved to his fellow students, eliciting even greater excitement.

"I won't put you on the spot, Mr. Radimus," she said, "but a perfect season *is* a special thing. You will have plenty of time to prepare a speech for when we celebrate it fully at the End of Year Dance."

James looked relieved, bashful even. Somehow, he managed to blush. "Thanks, Headmistress. I don't know what to say. Thanks for coming out and believing in us. Let's all have an even better season next year!"

The reaction was deafening. Students conjured impromptu fireworks in blues and golds and summoned showers of confetti. The sound shook the very ground beneath Connor's feet, and it didn't fade. The crowd screamed and hollered until he was sure some of them must have fainted.

This is how he gets away with it. They love him. He's completely above suspicion. How did I think I could convince anyone without catching him with literal blood on his hands? Connor's fists balled up at his side and his jaw set in grim determination. *If that's what it takes…*

Chapter 27

The Summoner's Art – Introduction
Summoners use combinations of circles and runes to call across space and bring all manner of magical creatures to heel. The creatures materialize instantaneously and are often feral until the summoner establishes dominance, after which the creature remains loyal for life, even if banished. A practiced summoner is unpredictable. There is no knowing what they may pull out of their hat.

Immediately following the duel, fliers for the dance appeared all over the school. They promised live music, spell-casting competitions, and of course, a celebration of the dueling team's success—particularly James's perfect season. Classrooms and hallways were abuzz with questions of who would ask whom out, who would be voted king and queen of the dance, and which teacher would be visibly intoxicated first—the safe money being on Lady Ariel or Master Borodin.

With the dueling season over, practice ended as well. The coaches encouraged unofficial workouts, but they didn't want to interfere with the students' preparations for finals. This proved to be a mixed blessing; Connor didn't have to see James as often, and he did need the extra time to study, but he and Ninette drifted further apart. She and Van remained inseparable. Connor knew this because Sheena convinced him to tail Van in the intervening weeks. Sheena wasn't content with the "wait to die" plan, and Connor didn't totally blame her.

One afternoon, the week of the dance, while Ninette and Van were catching up between classes, Connor and Sheena watched them from around a corner. The new couple cuddled close by Ninette's locker and whispered to each other. Crouched low to avoid being seen, Connor leaned closer to hear, stretching as far as he dared. He was balanced on the balls of his feet when Julian came sprinting down the hall from behind him, holding a bubbling concoction emitting a powerful, antiseptic smell. Dr. Greens scuttled after him, shouting for him to stop. Julian was too focused on the doctor to watch where he was going and collided with Connor at full speed. The two sprawled out on the ground in front of Ninette in a damp, smelly heap.

She froze, her eyes wide. She held Connor's gaze as the space around them in the hallway grew. Dr. Greens picked up Julian and levitated him away, chiding him for creating such a vile brew. Connor and Ninette continued to stare at one another as the hallway emptied, the tension so thick that the other students decided they had somewhere else to be. Tears sparkled in the corners of Ninette's eyes, but her expression shifted from sadness to a dark scowl. Ninette told Van to go ahead without her. He curled his lip into a snarl at Connor and stalked off. Connor hesitated but ultimately picked himself up off the ground and approached her. Sheena didn't follow him.

"I thought we had a plan," Ninette growled. "Piss off James then wait. What happened to that?"

"That's still the plan," Connor protested. "I just... Sheena thought we should also... I mean, I'm sorry, okay? We'll back off."

"Yeah, you will. If I see you following me again, I'm going to make sure it doesn't happen a third time." Ninette cracked her knuckles methodically. She looked over Connor's shoulders and winked at Sheena. Connor turned around, but Sheena was nowhere to be found.

The next morning at breakfast, Garrett called out to Ninette, but she ignored him, stuck close to Van, and left the cafeteria with her food. Garrett stared after her like a kicked puppy until Connor and Sheena explained.

"What did you guys think would happen? Of course she's upset. She's made it pretty clear how she feels about him. Do you really think driving her away is good for anyone but James?"

Connor had the decency to feel ashamed. Sheena, on the other hand...

"We don't have time to play love and politics," she scoffed. "Van is the dumb one. If he knows anything, he'll be the one to slip. I don't feel bad in the slightest."

"Unless Ninette's right," Garrett pointed out. "James is smart. He probably knows Van would say something."

Connor and Sheena didn't have an answer for that.

Things did not improve in first period. Ninette took a spot in the back of the class by herself. Connor searched for a seat near one of his other friends, but each one was taken, and he ended up next to mousy Gemma

Perriwinkle. All around him, a cacophony of conversation—most of it focused on the upcoming dance—drowned out his dour thoughts.

Professor Skreed entered, rubbing his hands together in excitement. "We're coming to the end of the semester," he cheered. "It's time for a treat. Today we will work on combining nature, fire, and wind."

Ninette immediately dozed off—nature and wind were no good for her, but Connor was interested. Anything to take his mind off the mess he'd made.

"The key to using Elemental Magic is to understand it, yes? It takes time. It takes knowledge. But you have that knowledge now. The basics, anyway. One often hears a little knowledge is a dangerous thing. I say too much knowledge is equally dangerous. You overthink, paralyzed by your options.

"Today I ask you to craft a spirit companion. Wind and fire provide the body, as it were, and Nature Magic will shape them into the form of a beast by mimicking its essence pattern. I intend to provide as little instruction as possible, only this demonstration."

The Professor held both hands in front of him. A small breeze whistled through the class, coalescing into a tiny tornado in his hands. A flicker of flame, no more than a candle, burned at the heart of it, then diffused into a sunset glow throughout the vortex. The magic took the shape of a house cat. The cat arched its back in a luxurious stretch, yowled like the wind in a mountain pass, and curled up on the windowsill to sleep.

"Cats. I suppose I should have expected that," the Professor chuckled with a shrug. "To your work."

Connor grumbled and tried to figure out the spell. Frustration warped into a desire to show off, to do the *big* magic he still dreamed of. He knew he'd messed up with Ninette, but he couldn't help wanting to beat her somehow, at something. Household pets materialized on the desks of his classmates—cats and dogs, a few birds, and even a snake.

Not big enough.

Connor opened his mind until he connected his essence to all the air in the room. He whipped up a swirling storm that sucked in papers from nearby desks and distorted the forms of the other spirit animals, tugging at their edges until they were almost pulled away. Without asking, he snatched Gemma's flame and stoked it into a bonfire. Connor thought big, then bigger, and the firestorm took on the shape of a raging red and orange grizzly bear. The bear looked around, puzzled at its surroundings. It turned its ember eyes to Connor, issued a guttural challenge, and slashed Connor's desk in half.

Connor toppled over backward, trying to get away. The bear took a step toward him, its paws left smoking black footprints on the tile floor. It reached back its blazing, clawed arm and prepared to swipe.

And Ninette was there, her arm encased in ice all the way to the shoulder. She caught the spirit bear's arm mid-swing. She thrust her other hand into its chest. The searing wind buffeted her, but she held firm despite her shirt starting to smolder. Her fist ignited, hotter than the bear, and she pumped more and more fire into the spirit beast. The bear swelled like a balloon, then wavered and lost consistency. With an echoing growl, the flame became too great, and the bear dispersed into the air.

"Thanks," Connor uttered from the ground, caught between shock and embarrassment. Ninette grunted and returned to her seat.

"Impressive, Mr. McTaggart," Professor Skreed said. "But more restraint in closed spaces, yes? These constructs are still wild. You would need to exercise your Will on top of the three elemental powers to control them. A bit more advanced." He bowed and addressed Ninette. "Quick thinking on your part. Unbalancing the ratio of elements was the easiest way to get rid of it."

"That was so cool," Gemma whispered to Connor while he magically reassembled his desk. "I'm serious! I could barely make a parakeet, and you conjured a freaking bear? And Ninette! Wow!" she gushed. "I wish I had half the essence you two did."

Connor started to say something about working hard and practicing until he remembered Seer Brokk's lecture—people have intrinsic limits to their essence—and the dominoes started to fall. He thought all the way back to the trip to Atlantis.

People have been trying to push their limits forever. Essence is in your blood. Blood. More essence—bigger spells. The headmistress's Halloween lecture echoed in his mind. *Necromancy is really just using dead people's essence. Nothing says you have to use your own.* And of course, Sheena's snide lecture. *Essence is in your blood. James has been stealing Magi blood.*

The truth hit him like a flaming bear: James would use the other students' blood to exceed his natural essence level.

Gemma blinked big, spectacled eyes at him, and Connor realized he'd never acknowledged her.

"Oh, huh? No, it's not. I mean, you're really smart?"

His mind whirled in another direction. Fortunately, the bell rang and saved him from embarrassing himself further. He thought about telling Ninette, but decided it best to save some dignity and leave quietly.

Connor spent potions class searching through all the modules available to him for anything involving blood as an ingredient.

I guess they don't want students going around trying to get each other's blood for their experiments.

He resisted the urge to ask Dr. Greens, knowing the answer—if he even got one—would draw attention he didn't want.

He spent summoning class sharing his theory with Sheena while she helped him navigate the level three summoning circle.

"It makes sense," she admitted, while correcting two runes in his outer circle. "But what is he going to do? He's going to use it to do something specific. It'll be easier to stop it if we know what." She pointed to his circle. "You should be good."

Connor empowered his circle, the runes beginning to glow the familiar lavender hue. Inside materialized a baby Owlbear, the size of a toddler. White fur covered its lower half down to its stubby tail and paws, while pale blue feathers adorned its winged arms and owl-like face. It squawked at him, breath frosty in the warm gymnasium, and conjured a little snowball in its arms.

"Don't you get sassy with me," Connor snickered, catching the snowball and winging it back.

The little creature stumbled backward and fell on its round, fuzzy butt, looking puzzled and unhappy.

Connor reached into his pocket and pulled out some trail mix. "Eat up, little fella."

The Owlbear munched the snack with gusto and then looked up at Connor; its eyes glowed lavender.

"That's one way to do it," Sheena said. "He'll still obey you when he's bigger, assuming he's still alive."

That's morbid. Connor picked up the small, furry creature and held it tight against his chest. "It wasn't exactly an original idea," he admitted, thinking about the vesporcus. "I'm surprised we only got as far as level three this semester."

"Big talk. You'll be lucky if you pass without my help." Sheena tapped the runes she corrected with her pointed shoe. "Did you think we'd go straight from one to seven in a few months?"

"You mean eight," Connor corrected her. He grinned, eager to gloat. "Remember? Summoning circles go up to eight."

"If you're going to correct me, you should at least try to sound intelligent. Level eight summons require seven people." Sheena sneered. She gestured to the class. "Interest in summoning is too limited—it's complicated and time-consuming. The next session of this class will be half the size and likely only get as far as level five. The difficulty increases exponentially. After that, I'd be surprised if there were more than two or three people besides me in the class. So, no, this school will not teach you how to do a level eight summon because there won't be enough people with the intelligence and talent to fill the circle. Besides, I doubt they want students summoning dragons into the school anyway."

"Dragons?" Connor asked, but his mind surged ahead. "Never mind. What if you didn't need seven people?"

"But you do," Sheena said. "You need that much essence to…" Her mouth hung open as she trailed off.

"He *has* that much essence," Connor finished for her. "He's going to do a level eight summon."

"No," Sheena whispered, trying to process. "No, it won't work. He's one person short. Besides, for one person to coordinate so much…"

"Couldn't Van help him?"

Sheena laughed so loud the other students turned to look at her. "Hell no. Like I said, you need seven people who actually know what they're doing. I don't know how he thinks he's going to do it by himself, but wolf boy isn't going to be any use to him unless James takes his blood, too."

"I know someone who might know more."

When class ended, Connor led Sheena down the hall toward Headmistress Mine's class.

"I thought the old witch didn't believe you," she said.

Connor ignored her and looked around the row of lockers outside the history classroom. The halls emptied after last period; they were alone. Connor spun the combination lock and popped open the locker. He pointed to the passage inside and the rickety stairs plunging into the darkness.

"What? No. Absolutely not."

"Fine," Connor sighed. "Then you can wait here or find something else to do."

He entered the hidden staircase but left the door ajar. Sheena looked around again. The halls were empty, quiet, unnerving. She looked down into the blackness. Connor's footsteps faintly echoed up to her, then faded away. Sheena stamped her foot and cursed before she followed him down and slammed the locker door behind her.

"Where are we going? Connor?" Her voice rang down the narrow steps.

"You'll see in a minute."

His voice bounced off the wall and she couldn't tell how close or far away he was.

After a few moments of silent descent, they emerged into the warmly lit study of Karronus Naegus. A pile of warm coals burned in the stone firepit and cast a soft, shifting glow on the smooth cave surface. Mr. Naegus wasn't there, though his chair had an open book resting on the arm, so Connor and Sheena took seats next to each other, sinking into one of the plush, well-worn couches and waited.

"Are you going to tell me where the hell we are?" She asked.

"Mr. Naegus's room," Connor answered.

"The librarian?"

"He's also a dragon."

Sheena's lips moved silently, many questions fighting to get out and none succeeding. Before one did, the door creaked open, and Mr. Naegus entered.

"Good afternoon! I am so glad to have visitors. It's been some time." The dragon's golden eyes lazily settled onto Sheena. "Ms. Crowton, it is an honor."

"You're a dragon?"

"Oh, secret's out," Karronus chuckled, placing a finger to his lips.

Sheena struggled to process the new information while the dragon bustled around his cave, preparing a pot of tea. He handed each of them a steaming, aromatic cup, then settled into his chair. He crossed one leg over the other and steepled his fingers.

"Now, since I do not believe Ms. Crowton knew of my location, I have to assume you had a reason to seek me out, Mr. McTaggart."

Connor nodded. "Mr. Naegus, if someone had access to the blood, the essence, of six Magi, could they perform an eighth-level summoning by themselves? What sort of thing would they be trying to summon?"

"Besides a dragon, you mean?" His sly smirk filled his whole face. "I suppose it would be possible, but you would have to be genius, and I mean no hyperbole. The Magi attempting it would be directing the flows of essence seven different ways, all of them beyond complicated. As for what they might summon…" He tapped his lips in thought. "My best guess would be something from another world. You are, in effect, summoning the realm itself and bridging the gap with our world. Otherwise, the creature wouldn't be able to pass through."

"But we can go to other realms. I've been to the shadow world," Connor pointed out.

"Have you now?" The old dragon raised his eyebrows. "Then you know how taxing it is on your mind and body. A prolonged stay means eventual death unless additional steps are taken—say, a proper summoning. I would wager our blood thief plans to bring over something that doesn't belong."

"The dance," Connor blurted out, expecting them to know what he meant. When they stared blankly, he elaborated. "He's going to do it at the dance on Friday. Think about it. This all started at the first dance when the whole school was distracted. What could be a bigger diversion than the end-of-year party?"

"He's the guest of honor," Sheena said with no shortage of sarcasm. "How could he possibly get away?"

"I don't know." Connor looked at Mr. Naegus who shrugged. "We need to be ready for anything."

On the evening of the dance, Connor took one final look at himself in the mirror. His hair refused to cooperate, despite attempts to tame it. He donned a plain white button-down shirt and an old paisley tie his dad must have thrown in with his clothes.

I wonder what they would say if they knew what I'd been up to. Mom might laugh. Dad might drop dead.

Rolling up his sleeves, Connor checked his pockets one more time: Headmistress's rune stone in the left, Garrett's rune stone in the right, focus glove in the back.

Marck had left some time ago to pick up his date, and Garrett always ran early, so Connor headed out alone to pick up Sheena. He arrived outside her door and knocked once. While he waited, he fiddled with his tie and glanced up and down the row of dorms. The rest of his classmates were appearing in their finest evening wear. Along with the usual dresses and suits were traditional orcish formal skins, fancifully enchanted dwarven mail shirts, and elven robes that seemed woven out of sheer magic. His wrinkled shirt and crooked tie felt shabby in comparison. Then Sheena's door opened, and his jaw hit the floor.

Her hair was done up in a high bun, accented with an array of jeweled ornaments that twinkled when she moved. She wore a high-necked, purple gown that bared her shoulders and accented it with her usual gold jewelry dialed up to eleven. Bangles, big hoop earrings, rings on almost every finger, she positively sparkled.

"Wow."

"Yeah, I clean up nice. The same can't be said for you," she responded, eyeing him up and down rather critically.

Connor pouted and gave up on his tie. "You made it clear that, while we were going together, we were not going *together*, and it was in no way to be misconstrued as a date."

"You could at least have tried not to embarrass me. Oh well. Shall we?" Sheena said airily, giving him her arm.

Connor escorted her through the atrium where the trees twinkled with magical lights and the gardens overflowed with new flowers. The halls were packed as the entire student body flowed at a crawl into the gymnasium. Connor and Sheena made small talk while they walked until they were interrupted by a murmur rippling through the crowd. A space opened up with the whispered commotion.

The item of interest was Ninette. Her long-sleeved gown was iridescent green and skimmed the ground behind her. She wore earrings, a necklace, and bracelets—the first time Connor had seen her in any jewelry at all—made of fine fishbones. A far cry from her normal baggy attire, and, for the first time all year, she wasn't wearing a scarf. At her side, Van slouched and grinned. His shaggy hair was as unkempt as ever, but he wore a tie and a suit that was a size too big.

"Talk about cleaning up nice," Sheena muttered through tight lips. "Still don't see what she sees in him, though."

"I think I get it. I just hope we're wrong about him."

The gym was awash with balloons and streamers, disco balls and strobe lights. It possessed all the requisite kitsch required of a high school dance. The bleachers were pushed back to make room for a sparsely occupied dance floor, and young students milled about, making awkward conversation and casting furtive glances at the empty space, as though daring themselves to do a coal walk. Teachers mingled, all of them present for the big event. Some danced, some supervised, others were... less vigilant. No school dance would be complete without the wallflowers, a group who, through their own unique series of misfortunes, ended up without dates. Truly, Connor belonged with them, but he and Sheena had business, so he at least got to look the part tonight. He scanned the wall for Garrett but couldn't find him. Oddly, he did see Codie. He walked over to join her.

"Surprised to see you over here. How many guys did you turn down?"

"Enough," she chuckled, cheeks flushing. "Didn't get the right offer, I suppose. I'm sure I'll get out there and strut my stuff in a while."

"Fair enough," Connor said. "Have you seen Garrett?"

"I have," Codie laughed. "Have you not?" She pointed behind him.

Out on the floor doing an adorable slow dance, Garrett and Gemma stepped nervously around each other. Garrett looked sharp in a navy-blue suit and tie, and Gemma wore a simple yellow dress and shoes to match.

Connor gawked. *I can't believe Garrett got a date.* Connor hadn't given much thought to getting a real date, but somehow he expected Garrett wouldn't have one either. *Good for him.*

When they made eye contact, Connor gave Garrett a conspiratorial glance, and Garrett half pulled his rune stone out of his pocket. They nodded to each other. Connor went to get Sheena a drink while she stalked around the gym, doing little to hide her stress. While he waited in line, he noticed Ninette and Van dancing and gazing into each other's eyes. When he got back to Sheena, she jumped in surprise.

"How are you so calm?" she asked with a shiver. "Something awful is going to happen tonight. How are you drinking punch?" She snatched the cup and gulped it down.

"What's the other option? I don't want to start anything. I haven't seen James yet, it's his move. We just need to wait."

So they waited. As predicted, it wasn't long before Lady Ariel's face turned red, and she and Master Borodin huddled together giggling into their punch cups like a couple of the teenagers they were supposed to be supervising. James arrived, stunning in a perfectly pressed tux with a giggling senior draped on his arm, and the two of them hit the dance floor like trained professionals. Connor asked Sheena several times if she wanted to dance, but she scoffed at him and responded with "as if's" and "what do you think's".

After an hour the band stopped playing, and Headmistress Leorra ascended the stage.

"I hope you are all having a good time tonight," she announced. "But not too good. You do still have finals coming up." This was met by boos and jeers, but she smiled a patient teacher's smile. "Tonight, I want to celebrate Mr. James Radimus and his impressive achievement of a perfect dueling season. Mr. Radimus, will you join me?"

James waved away the students around him, lowering his head and looking appropriately embarrassed as he joined the headmistress. He approached the microphone to increasing excitement from the other students, spent an obnoxious amount of time adjusting it, and opened his mouth to speak.

Then, the wall behind them exploded.

Chapter 28

The Summoner's Art – Eighth-Level Summoning
RESTRICTED INFORMATION

Brick and plaster showered over the stage. The lights flickered hazily in the dust and smoke. Through the wreckage stamped the vesporcus, one eye scarred over, the other blazing red. The headmistress lay sprawled on the stage, unconscious. The creature's terrifying gaze settled on James. It bucked and reared and knocked him across the room. James sailed through the air like a ragdoll and smashed through a brick wall on the other side of the gymnasium. The vesporcus turned and glared down at the dance floor.

    Its normally earthy-brown fur was pale and bristled, and its remaining eye burned with a crazed intensity. Connor slipped on his focus glove. Through the faint whorls of magic in the air, the vesporcus radiated the deep black of powerful Shadow Magic. Oily black tentacles whipped and lashed from inside the beast like some eldritch nightmare. With the glove on, its single eye shifted from red to a deep pool of jet black.

The stunned crowd all awakened from their shock as one. Teens and adults alike blasted away at the monster. Fire and ice, stones and lightning, wind and leaves poured forth from every corner of the gym. The vesporcus charged through the sorcerous storm, wings tucked back and black flames bellowing from its maw. Seer Brokk launched a volley of wind spells that clattered away to no effect before it trampled over him. Speck flew in from behind, shrouded in a crackling ball of lightning, but the vesporcus kicked her through the roof with its jagged hooves. Ariel and Borodin never got a spell off in their stupor. The giant monster's charge scattered teachers, its flames seared students, and bodies littered the floor, groaning in both physical and mental agony.

"Run!" Mr. Masters shouted.

He and Soarra and Ms. Ruiz worked together to corral kids out of the gym. Coach Kalett expended all his effort on rebuffing the vesporcus's flames away from the exits with a shield so dense it seemed impenetrable. Streamers of healing light burst out of Nurse Poole. She revived as many kids as she could and led them to safety. The vesporcus unfurled its wings and launched into the sky. It squealed so loud it shook the walls.

"Round three!" Ninette called to it.

She spread her hands and light shifted and warped in front of them into the form of a diamond broadsword, longer than Ninette was tall. The vesporcus tucked its wings and dove like a missile at Ninette. She hefted her blade, prepared to meet it head-on, but Van lunged and pushed her out of the way, taking the full force of the blow. The vesporcus carried him up into the air in its jagged jaws before tossing him through the stacked bleachers.

"Van!" Ninette spared only a glance in his direction before returning to the more immediate issue.

From high up in the gym, the vesporcus bellowed its challenge before exhaling another torrent of shadowflame. Garrett stood between Gemma and the blast. He squeezed his eyes shut, turned his head away, and threw up his hands. His shield of Will stopped the blast, but black miasma seeped through the barrier, and they both fell to their knees, coughing and gasping for air.

"Hang in there, Garrett," Connor grunted. He held his breath and ran into the dark cloud to grab Garrett under the arms to drag him away to safety. Once Garrett got his feet under him, Connor sucked down a breath of fresh air and went back in to grab a now unconscious Gemma and pull her out as well. Garrett knelt down next to her to check her pulse and breathing. Meanwhile, Sheena hurried to Ninette's side and sprayed ice blades upward. The vesporcus buffeted most of them away, but one struck home, piercing its wing.

"Nice shot." Ninette funneled a stream of flames skyward to no effect.

"Focus on the wings," Sheena directed, swinging her arms in wide arcs to hurl more icy blades.

The vesporcus dove again, washing the floor in deadly darkness. Sheena and Ninette split while Connor held up a barrier of wind to protect himself, Garrett, and Gemma from the flames and its side effects.

What is wrong with it? His thoughts raced. *What are all those shadows coming out of it?*

The creature wobbled and beat its injured wing frantically, struggling to stay airborne.

Connor looked back to check on Garrett and was momentarily stunned by what he saw. Hands reached up from below the floor to grab Garrett around his waist and drag him through the shadows, down into the floor.

"I'll be taking this," James hissed.

"Garrett!" Connor dropped to his knees to grab his friend, but his hands met solid wood.

Ninette and Sheena spun around, but the shadows had already swallowed Garrett. They were too late. Connor scrabbled in vain at the floor, pounded his fists against it. He turned his eyes above and found a suitable target for his rage.

With the aid of the focus glove, Connor could see every draft coming into the gym, every vent pumping in air, even the rapid, terrified breathing of his classmates like puffs of gray on a frosty day. He bit his lip and let his essence explode out to become one with all of it. He converged a storm of wind blades at the vesporcus from every conceivable angle. Many of them hit the body to no visible effect, but enough caught its wings and ripped them to shreds. The injured monster awkwardly fluttered and fell to the ground.

Connor joined Ninette and Sheena, and the three faced the flightless monster at the center of the ruined dance. It stamped and snorted; its single, working eye never left Ninette. The darkness around it intensified.

"Get ready," Connor warned.

Ninette erected a six-foot-high barrier of stone, and it held fast against the oncoming flame. The vesporcus grunted and charged. It crashed through the wall without slowing. Ninette waited until she could feel its moist breath and swung her blade like a baseball bat. Pained squealing shook the room as it veered away, missing Ninette and crashing behind her. A deep gash hung open from snout to flank, but rather than bleed, black fog seeped out of the wound. The flesh puckered and closed, sewn shut by a throbbing, black scar.

Ninette gawked in disbelief. "That's new."

"How the hell is it using magic?" Sheena gasped.

"I don't think it is," Connor said. Through his enhanced eyes he watched the shadows around it writhe, like they were wrestling to contain the wound. "James did something to it, I just don't know what."

"He pissed it off is what it looks like," Sheena grumbled. "That's fine. I'm pissed, too." Extending her palm, Sheena collected light from around the room and fired a laser that punched a neat hole in the side of the vesporcus. More oily blackness poured out to plug it up. "We're not going to get much done while it can do that."

Connor took a breath and held it, trying to calm himself; he tried to look through the vesporcus, to see the source of the shadowy essence within. The vesporcus got its footing and turned to face them.

If it's shadow essence, maybe I can…

Connor concentrated on the black energy—the monster's mangled face and black scars gave him plenty of fear to work with. He held onto that feeling while he tried to unravel James's spell. His mind brushed against the essence of the vesporcus; Connor grabbed it.

The rush of emotion threatened to consume him. He felt wild, terrified, the world spun around him. He couldn't focus. He couldn't breathe. He was breathing too fast. His heart screamed in his chest. Visions of fire and fear flooded his brain. He knew only fear. Connor staggered back, emptying his stomach all over the floor.

"Gross," Sheena gagged. She took a step back and covered her mouth.

"Really?" Ninette snapped at her. She helped Connor steady himself. "Are you okay? What happened?"

"It's scared," Connor gasped. "It doesn't know what's wrong either. James screwed with its essence. He cursed it." Shakily, Connor got back up. "He infected it with nothing but fear. I could see what it felt. It was awful."

"Well, you're the shadow guy," Sheena said. "Fix it, so we can put it out of *our* misery."

"We need to hurry," Ninette urged. "We need to get Garrett back. Van's hurt, too." She placed her hand on his shoulder. "You can do this."

The vesporcus tossed its head, but it hadn't moved since Connor last touched it. Pushing through his own fears, Connor grabbed the shadows within it once more. The rush of emotions—fear, anger, pain—ran wild with his senses. Connor steeled himself against the sickness, and pulled the blackness out of creature, slowly at first, but more came and fast. His knees buckled, but Ninette held him upright while the negative energy crashed over his mind, threatening to wash him away.

It was over in seconds, but it felt like hours. Connor sank to the ground, gasping for air. The vesporcus's legs wobbled. It sank to the ground in a mirror of Connor's suffering. Its fur receded back to its normal brown; the black aura emanating from it faded to nothing. The darkness swirled through and around Connor before dissipating into nothing.

"We'll take it from here," Ninette said.

She and Sheena stepped between him and the vesporcus. Ninette raised her sword, icy crystals swirled around Sheena's fingertips.

"Let's kick its ass," Sheena said, smiling at Ninette.

The vesporcus roared, fear and anger commingled with its bestial drive to survive. Perfectly normal red flames issued from its snout. Ninette brushed them off like they were nothing. It dug in its hooves and talons, gearing up for one final rush. When it charged, it was slower than before but no less deadly. Fire gushed out ahead of it. Sheena constructed wall after wall of ice in front of it to block the fire and slow its progress, but the vesporcus shattered through them all, hellbent on impaling Ninette. It stumbled through the last wall, losing control and speed, into Ninette. She planted her feet, glittering sword held firm in both hands and drove it straight into the gaping maw of the vesporcus.

The monster's momentum drove her back a dozen feet. It gurgled and choked as it tried in vain to clamp down its teeth and tusks, but its strength ebbed, and it only grazed her shoulder. It trembled, the light in its eye faded, and the massive body collapsed on the gym floor.

Ninette tugged on the sword for a moment before giving up and leaving it lodged in the pig's skull. She tried, in vain, to wipe the blood and soot off her dress. Sheena stepped delicately around the vesporcus to help Connor back to his feet. She had somehow managed to avoid getting a single drop of blood on her.

"James dragged Garrett through the shadows," Connor wheezed, recovering from the shock of… whatever he did. "He can't be too far."

"This is it then. Let's tell a teacher. Hard for him to explain kidnapping a kid, right?" Sheena said.

"What teacher? Mr. Masters? Soarra?" Connor answered, waving his arms at the chaos around them.

Groaning and unconscious kids covered the floor, along with a few of the said teachers. The battle had left the gym littered with smashed bricks and splintered wood. The acrid stench of burned clothes and melted laminate flooring wafted through the eerie stillness. The few conscious teachers scrambled to work triage.

"There's no one left but us," Connor said. "Quick, give me your return stones."

The girls produced them, and Connor held out his. With a trickle of Earth Magic, he destroyed the extras, then activated the remaining one. It jolted to life and tugged his arm toward the gaping hole in the gym wall.

"Come on." Connor took off at a run with Sheena right behind him.

Ninette hesitated. She glanced at the bleachers, hoping to see Van emerge from the rubble. *He's okay,* she thought, but her insides clenched in a knot. *He's okay. He's over there passed out.* She gathered herself together and chased after the others.

They burst out into the warm night, Connor in the lead with his hand extended, letting the stone drag him like an excited dog. It took them into the gardens, but unfortunately, it couldn't distinguish path from hedge.

"We don't have time for this crap," Sheena grumbled.

She extended her palm and released another perfect bar of light, expanding to blow a tunnel through the garden walls. In minutes they were on the other side and into the field—back toward the forest.

They stopped at the fringe of the woods where manicured grass gave way to wilder tangles of weed and root. Ninette didn't slow down, but Connor grabbed her wrist.

"Wait. We don't want to get lost again. What are we looking for in there?"

"Garrett," Ninette said firmly.

"Garrett," Sheena agreed, as though there were no other options.

"Garrett. Let's get our friend back." And, as one, they entered the forest.

The woods were wilder than before. The thorn bushes reached out for them, intent on slowing their progress. The forest actively barred their passage with snarls of impenetrable foliage, but Connor knew its tricks. Keeping Garrett singularly in his mind, he pressed ahead, the girls close behind. He ended up losing his tie and tearing his shirt while Ninette ditched her shoes, a sacrifice Sheena was vocally unwilling to make. They found a stream meandering in roughly the same direction they were going and upped the pace as best they could. An unnatural fog snaked in between the leaves. The magical aura of the glade passed over Connor, a ghost of its former self. Through the enhancement of the focus glove, he saw it flicker from one color to the next, even as it faded away.

We have to hurry. Connor urged his feet to move faster. *We're out of time.*

He dashed blindly ahead, ignoring the cries for him to wait. He could feel wrongness in the air, and fear for his friend gripped his heart and dragged him forward. A final burst of speed and he hurdled out into the clearing. What he saw halted him in his tracks long enough for Ninette and Sheena to catch up. Sheena screamed.

Viscous fog unfurled in shadowy, dark tendrils across the ground, slowly creeping outwards. It filled the glade, pouring out of a giant set of circles carved deep into the earth—they didn't have to count to know there were eight—surrounded by raised stones marked with glowing runes that pierced the gloom. The great tree glowed faintly in the night. It stood in weak contrast to the menacing aura of the ritual before it.

James sat cross-legged at the edge of the circle, still in his tuxedo, and levitating a foot off the ground. Sweat dripped from his forehead, and his wet hair clung to his face. His eyes were closed, twitching rapidly as though he was dreaming. His furrowed brow and the firm set of his teeth conveyed the frantic pace of his thoughts. Spread around the circle in similar poses, were five shadowy mannequins, each one translucent enough to see the blood pumping through them in a mockery of human veins and arteries. Garrett occupied the last spot, shackled to the ground by chains of black. His skin was wan, and his eyes struggled to stay open. Shadows clung to him like shrink wrap. The circle hummed with life and the rings spun lazy circles.

Connor gave no warning before he sent a shockwave rumbling through the earth toward James. Right on his heels came a molten ball of flaming stone from Ninette, dripping lava as it rocketed through the air. Both evaporated before connecting with their targets.

"Oh, come on," Connor groaned.

Out of the shadow of the tree stepped the grimmalkin. It hissed at them with its hair on end and teeth bared. Its previous playfulness was nowhere to be seen.

"Just need a few more minutes," James mumbled through gritted teeth.

"No chance," Connor shouted.

He reached into his pocket for the headmistress's stone, but the grimmalkin yowled and fired Ninette's flaming projectile back at him, destroying the stone and searing Connor's hand.

"Fine with me," Ninette yelled. "I'll beat the smug out of you myself."

"I need... more... time," James snarled between sharp breaths.

From the other side of the tree appeared Van, shoulders slumped and a grim line on his face. He dragged himself in between the kids and James, but he could hardly bring himself to look at them. His clothes were rumpled and torn from his brief bout with the vesporcus, adding to his hangdog appearance. Ninette's arms fell to her sides and all traces of attack magic fell to pieces. Tears poured from her eyes, but her lips twisted into a furious grimace.

"No. No, you can't be here," she stammered shaking her head. "You got knocked out protecting me. You protected me. You told me you're not a part of this. YOU. TOLD. ME." She hurled each word at Van.

Van said nothing, his eyes only left the ground in brief twitches to make sure Ninette wasn't about to obliterate him.

"Say something, you bastard," Ninette cried. Her lips trembled. "SAY SOMETHING!"

"No one was supposed to get hurt," Van mumbled, unable to look at her while he said it. "Everyone was going to recover. We'd complete the ritual out here, then finish school like nothing happened. No one would even know we'd done anything."

"What ritual?" Connor said.

James uttered something under his breath. His face scrunched and contorted and beneath his eyelids, his eyes twitched rapidly. Every muscle in his body tensed, about to snap. Van spoke instead.

"He's opening a portal to the shadow world or whatever. He said they would make him stronger if he let them out."

"So that's all it took, huh? A little promise of power to turn you into his pet puppy?" Ninette sneered.

Van tried to protest, but James got in first. "That's not fair, Ninette. Puppy. So diminutive. Van is a valued collaborator. His blood let me summon up these beasties, after all. They've been listening to him, not me."

"There's no way," Sheena said, doing a mental reassessment of Van and coming up short. "If you summoned them, they should leash to you."

"You'd think that," James explained, finally beginning to relax. "I certainly did, but the effects of his blood were surprising. And they listened right away. No taming required. I guess they know who the real monster is."

"He was your patsy if anything went wrong. Anything we caught would lead us to Van, not you," Connor said. His eyes darted to the roiling energy permeating the glade. The shadows grew and spread across the grass. The summoning circles spun faster, and the runes within glowed with blackish purple light. "If things went south, Van was the one going down."

Van looked at his friend, wide eyed and struggling to speak as understanding finally reached him. "No, you told me that… you said you needed my help. You said, you said you'd fix me. But you were never going to. You can't, can you?" Something in Van snapped and he fell to his knees and howled. Even as a human his cry chilled to the bone.

"Oh, Van," James said, rising to his feet. "Of course I needed you. A dog is man's best friend after all."

Van screamed as he changed and the sound of it shook Connor. Van's suit hung off him in loose tatters as the metamorphosis completed, and he wasted no time leaping for James, claws outstretched and lips bared to reveal his jagged teeth. He flew through the air, but as he passed over the summoning circle, its thrum grew to a shrill whine. The circles and runes blurred together to become a bottomless pit of midnight. Van stopped short, suspended motionless in the air.

After a short second, he dropped to the ground. His tongue lolled out of his mouth and his eyes rolled back in his head. Connor watched as darkness from the glade and the portal mingled together, coalescing around the unconscious werewolf. James stepped into the circle and he, too, succumbed to the darkness, shuddering before he fainted, engulfed in shadow.

Sheena cracked her knuckles and tried to take them both out with an ice spell, but the grimmalkin shook its head "No." Sheena grit her teeth and concentrated as hard as she could. Veins burst out of her forehead; the cat watched her, giggling its raspy laugh and taking furtive steps in her direction. Sheena clenched her fists so tight her nails drew blood, and finally a slender dagger of ice swirled into place before her. Her surprise was nothing next to the grimmalkin's, its yellow eyes bulged out of its head. It fired Connor's previous earth spell at the trio, scattering them in all directions to dodge the tremor.

When they recovered, James and Van were standing up. Ghastly gray fur covered Van, but darkness radiated off him in waves. James's skin was pale as a corpse, with black veins racing through his arms and face. Most disconcerting of all were their eyes: they had completely inverted, the whites jet black and the pupils terrifying pinpricks of white. The two looked at each other and then themselves, as if seeing each other for the first time. James removed his glasses, giving them a confused look, then crushed them in his hand and discarded them. He smiled, not his usual smirk or the fake, plastic grin he played for the teachers; a smile of madness unleashed.

He opened his mouth, and the familiar voice that escaped it sent tremors through their minds.

"AT LAST."

Chapter 29

> Magic 101 – Essence (continued)
> The pattern of one's essence is as unique as their DNA. In the dark ages, some attempted to increase their power by grafting one being's essence onto their own. Necromancers sought to bind the deceased's essence, thus increasing their power. Most were destroyed by those they consumed, creating an entirely new, often twisted, personality.

James and Van attacked. A wave of black liquid spurted from James's palm. It splashed off Connor's shield and ate through the ground around his feet. Van dropped to all fours; saliva flew from his mouth, and he lunged for Connor's throat. Ninette intercepted him. She caught Van by the shoulders and hurled him away. The wolf twisted in midair to land on his feet and launched himself again.

"You take James. I'll deal with Van," Ninette called out.

"Right." Connor nodded. Sweat ran down the side of his face.

"You're leaving me with the cat?" Sheena huffed. "Fine. Let's do it, fleabag."

From across the clearing, Garrett's eyes fluttered open, and he pushed himself up onto all fours. "A little... help... here?" He sank back down to the ground, exhausted by the effort.

The summoning circle is still open, Connor observed. *If I can break it, that might free Garrett.* He raised his hands and dredged up huge chunks of ground and lobbed them at the outer ring, hoping to interrupt the summoning, but they shattered in the air before reaching it.

"IT WILL NOT BE THAT EASY," James said.

He approached Connor, one deliberate step at a time, throwing spears of fire, ice, and lightning, all of it corrupted and black. A kaleidoscope of destructive power whorled around the nightmarish team captain as he manipulated several types of essence simultaneously. The ground shook where he stepped; shadowy fissures radiated outward from his feet. Connor retreated until the trees scraped at his back. He had nowhere to go but forward.

A swirl of red around the tree in the center of the glade caught his eye. His gloved hand twitched.

I need to use the essence around me, Connor thought. *I can see it. He can't. It's my only chance.*

"WE WILL NOT LET YOU LEAVE." The voice intoned. It spoke as though still growing used to James's mouth.

"Is James still in there?" Connor shouted.

He surrounded the possessed captain in a wreath of flames that shot up into the night sky. Connor launched a storm of grass—a burst of needle-point blades set ablaze as they passed through the fire—but James knocked them away with a wave of his hand and exhaled a cone of crackling electricity.

"WE ARE JAMES AND WE ARE MORE!"

Hand in paw with Van, Ninette struggled to keep him from ripping her face off, much less letting him loose on her friends. He snarled and snapped; his breath was moist and hot on her face.

He wants to kill me. The thought echoed hollowly in her mind.

Every blow aimed at her vitals. Every punch swung with reckless abandon. She was giving up ground, so she used the momentum and fell over backward and thrust her feet into his stomach to flip him away from her. She somersaulted to a kneeling position and thrust out both hands, blasting him with a concussive spray of water. He tumbled end over end across the glade.

"Van, it's me. It's Ninette." She didn't like the pleading tone in her voice, but it was all she could do. "You don't want to do this."

Van gnashed his teeth and lunged. Ninette hit him with a boulder the size of a car, but he clawed though it and kept coming. She threw three more at him, but he ripped through them like tissues and knocked her to the ground, slavering over her. His throat glowed red hot. She inhaled deeply, trying not to gag on fetid dog breath, then exhaled a sub-zero blast to freeze Van's face. He stumbled off her and clawed at his muzzle. Ninette rolled to the side and hurled two globes of seawater at James, each spinning through the air casting off foam and salt spray, but both fizzled out before connecting. The grimmalkin cartwheeled across the glade, cackling and grinning from ear to ear.

"I'll teach you to ignore me," Sheena growled. The ground erupted in lethal, frozen spires around the grimmalkin's feet. It leaped into the low branches of the tree and hissed, locking down Sheena's magic and casting Ninette's water spells back at her. Sheena avoided one but was caught up in the other. She fought to swim her way out only to fall to the ground and scramble away, dripping wet and considerably angrier.

Connor watched James for signs of the next attack. His aura whirled from one color to the next, all of them dark. No more boasts; faced with Ninette and Connor together, he fell silent. They needed to take advantage before Van recovered or before Connor collapsed. His head pounded, and his eyes burned from the raw information the focus glove drove into his mind. The whole night felt like a magical sprint, and he knew he couldn't go on for much longer.

Ninette detonated an explosion in front of James, but he crumpled it up like trash and discarded it as easily. Blue essence filled the air, and Connor forged titanic ice cubes and slid them across the ground, one at James, the other at the summoning circle. James punched the first, shattering it and redirecting the jagged shards at Ninette. The other bounced off the circle to no effect.

The aura of the glade turned a leafy green; Connor reached out to the grass below James's feet. He only intended to create vines, but instead, thick saplings sprouted from the soft soil. They spiraled around James's knees, trunks solidifying as they climbed. Ninette pummeled James with fire and brimstone bursting from her fingertips. The spells pelted him, but he appeared unharmed.

James cried out in a sonorous, awful voice and sundered the earth underneath Ninette. Connor channeled a gale to pull leaves from the trees and sharpened them to razor points. James closed his eyes and the trees snaring him rotted away. He stepped aside, narrowly avoiding perforation.

Across the clearing, Sheena worked feverishly to produce a drop of offensive magic, but the grimmalkin's yellow eyes filled her vision, filled her mind. She strained the limits of her Will and focus, bringing every bit of brainpower to bear on a single thought. She panted and sweated until she produced another handful of icicles to fling at the grimmalkin. One grazed its leg, and it snarled in pain. Its eyes flashed dangerously.

"You attacked me," Sheena hissed through bared teeth. "You won't live to realize that was a mistake."

The grimmalkin glared in response, its eyes wide as wide as saucers, and its teeth clenched as it did all it could to cut off Sheena's magic. It closed the distance between them to maximize its effects. It got too close.

"You're mine, fleabag!"

Reaching into her hair, she snatched out the jewels decorating her bun. She tossed them in front of her where they hung suspended in midair, flashing bright as they expended the essence Sheena had stored in them over the last few days. She extended her palm, and three rotating circles glowed in the air. A Dire Wolf as big as a horse, its eyes reflecting purple runes, landed in a ready crouch. The grimmalkin screeched to a halt and scampered in the opposite direction.

Ninette found her feet, but a stream of shadowflame toppled her once more. Dark lightning split the sky, striking her chest. She screeched and writhed on the ground; her arms splayed at wild angles. Her limbs refused to respond to her brain's instructions as the shadowy electricity scrambled her body's connections. At that moment, Van freed himself. Fire and lightning radiated in destructive waves off his body. He shook the remainder of the ice from his fur and howled at the sky, every bit a feral beast.

"THIS WORLD WILL BE REMADE IN ETERNAL TWILIGHT," James cackled, raising a wall of obsidian ice to separate Connor and Ninette.

"I don't know what that means," Connor fired back. He called down his own thunder and lightning on James while directing some toward the summoning circle. James shielded himself; the energy sparked and crackled in the air. He pressed forward, and Connor abandoned his attack on the portal, turning all the energy onto James. James dropped his shield, allowing the lightning to strike him. His skin burned and smoked, but he smiled and licked his lips hungrily.

"YOU WILL SUFFER. YOUR WORLD WILL SUFFER."

He slashed his arm diagonally through the air and a crescent of black flame sliced through Connor. His mind screamed, and his body burned. Visions of his friends being consumed by monsters of shadow assaulted him, all his fault. Always his fault. He shook away the painful images and scrabbled away on his elbows as James approached. The essence within him felt thin and stretched.

Faced with a flaming werewolf, Ninette tried the obvious water and ice spells, but Van exuded too much heat. Every spell she produced evaporated before it connected. He raced toward her and performed a diving flip, hitting her in the stomach with both massive feet. She crashed into the tree at the center of the clearing. Nearby, a more mundane but no less terrifying wolf chased the grimmalkin in circles while Sheena tried to hit it with laser-light blasts. Van threw his head back and howled; the keening note hurt Ninette almost as much as the violent collision with an ancient tree.

He's in there somewhere, she told herself. *He has to be. But if I don't stop him...*

Hot anger welled up inside her. Maybe she loved Van. She hadn't had enough time to be sure, but at that moment, she hated him for being so dumb. So weak. For going along with such an obviously evil plan. She hated James for roping him into it only to turn him into... whatever he had become. She hated herself for being so blind. For being so stupid. Her friends had tried to warn her, and she refused to see it. Why? Because she liked a boy? And yet, she hated the thought of hurting Van, especially when it wasn't totally his fault.

Pain and hurt and raw fury burned in her body. It roared and raged within, threatening to destroy her until she could contain it no longer, and everything exploded out of her. The deafening sound shattered the night. All eyes turned to Ninette.

But Ninette was no more.

In her place towered a blazing avatar of flame.

Fire coursed through her blood, seared her muscles, and erupted from her skin. Her eyes were embers, her hair a blazing comet tail. She *was* flame. Her skin glowed bright and lit up the gloomy night with warmth.

And she felt *good*.

She tackled Van with new, primal strength. His flames couldn't burn her, they were mere candles to her inferno. The power felt incredible. No one had told her about magic like this. She could win this fight. She could win *any* fight. Ninette pinned the werewolf to the ground, now the stronger of the two.

"IMPRESSIVE," James noted. He returned his attention to Connor. "BUT SHE WILL NOT SAVE YOU."

He attacked with more shadowflame, but Connor caught it and returned it twofold. The ground quaked and the trees groaned from the sheer volume of magic. Garrett lay prone with his eyes closed, unnaturally still.

This has to end, now, Connor thought desperately. Throwing all caution out the window, Connor dashed headlong at James. The monstrous boy smiled and reached out to grab him with a pale hand shrouded in darkness.

"Sheena, I need a slide!" Connor shouted.

Sheena waved her hand and froze a sheet of ground in front of Connor. He dropped to his butt, sliding between James's legs, then scrambled up and sprinted the last few feet to the portal's edge.

Looking into it gave him vertigo; it was a bottomless well of nothing surrounded by glowing runes. The shadowy mannequins maintained their rigid posture around it, even as their uncannily human forms slowly melted away. The shadows within the portal seemed to call to Connor, beckoning him to fall inside their depths.

No spell has gotten through it, he thought. *But… Van jumped inside no problem.*

Connor tried to touch the shield and his hand went right through. The Atlanteans, clear inspirations of this runic array, relied on magic to the point of their extinction. James, too, placed an irrational value on magical power—why else would he go to all this trouble? Could it really be that he'd ignored a potential, non-magical solution to his scheme? Connor reached down and dug his fingers into the ground under the nearest runestone. It weighed a ton, but he had adrenaline to spare and pried it away, removing it and breaking the circuit.

The portal wobbled, no longer a perfect circle, but an amorphous shape constricting and expanding. The shadowy figures around it dissipated into nothing, and the blackness that clung to Garrett vanished.

"Oh, YOU have GOT to BE kidding ME!" James cried out. His words were spoken with two voices out of sync, his own, and that of the shadow creatures. James's silhouette blurred around the edges. He clutched at his head and doubled over, staggering in Connor's direction.

"Garrett, stay with me, buddy," Connor whispered. "Maybe don't open your eyes for a minute." Connor grabbed Garrett and jumped into the portal. Together they fell into the darkness.

Sheena's dire wolf hounded the grimmalkin, and when it tried to defend itself, she assaulted it with ice and light. The cat's bad leg slowed it. Even when it snatched Sheena's spells, it could only redirect them at the wolf to keep it at bay. Sheena's magic opened again—her wolf chased the grimmalkin up into the tree.

"Get ready to burn," she shouted, gathering what light she could into a glowing sphere of destruction. The brilliant ball expanded in her hands until she couldn't look at it anymore. With a two-handed toss, she lobbed the goliath energy bomb at the tree, prepared to destroy it, the cat, and anything else between her and some peace and quiet.

Ninette and Van traded blows with no regard for their own safety. Her flaming fist struck his canine jaw; his searing claws ripped into her molten stomach. Both of them were slowing down. Out of the corner of her eye, Ninette saw Sheena's spell and got an idea.

"I hope you're as tough as you seem, you bastard," Ninette roared.

She grabbed Van in a tight embrace, ducked her head, and ran. He snarled and growled, savaging her back with his claws and gnashing into her shoulder. Pushing through the pain, Ninette carried both of them into the heart of the light as it struck the tree and exploded. Dazzling, white light engulfed everything and everyone in the glade.

Connor descended into the shadow world, Garrett in tow, but something was different. For the first time, he could see clearly. It reminded him of the filtered sunlight on the sea floor from the field trip that felt like forever ago. Looking up, he found the source of the light so alien to this world—the portal hovered in the air, still shuddering and shapeless, a rippling image of the forest glade. The faint moonlight was more like a noonday sun in the ever-dark shadow world. He had to get back, but something held him down, an overwhelming curiosity to explore the newly revealed realm.

So all this stuff is actually black.

The trees, the sand, the water, all of it inky black. Even the tentacles waving lazily on the shoreline. Connor took a step back from the water and held on tight to Garrett.

He opened his mind and listened, hoping to get out fast and get the jump on James. Nothing came. No voices, no questions. He took a deep breath, closed his eyes, and exhaled slowly. Racing thoughts and worries receded to the background of his mind until he was left with hollow, empty silence.

"Hello? Need to get out?"

"OVER HERE," a voice whispered within his mind.

It sounded similar to the shadow voices he was used to—like the one now bursting from James's mouth—but weaker, less confident, like a shadow Garrett. A slender figure hid behind a tree. It looked human, like the shadow of one anyway, stretched and thin, but its eyes were reflective pools of silver. It would have been tall if it wasn't crouched down, trying to hide behind the ebony trunk of the tree.

Connor approached tentatively; after seeing what happened to James and Van, he didn't want to get too close. As he neared, though, the creature curled in on itself and retreated further behind the tree.

"Are you okay?"

"THE LIGHT," it said. It shielded its eyes with its hand and shot furtive glances up at the portal. "IT DOES NOT BELONG."

"I don't understand. I thought you wanted to leave?"

"WE SEEK KNOWLEDGE. WE CONSUME IT. THE SUBSTANCE OF YOUR WORLD SUSTAINS US. SOME IS ENOUGH. SOME ALWAYS SEEK MORE."

"Like your friends up there with James?"

"THEY WILL CONSUME HIM. THEY WILL CONSUME EVERYTHING. IT IS WHAT WE ARE." It returned its alien gaze to Connor and its shimmering eyes glittered with hunger.

"Okay, well, it's been fun," Connor babbled. He backpedaled. "But I'd like to go, so if you could just ask me a question or…"

More gathered. Dozens, hundreds of shadows, all hiding yet managing to surround them, all staring at him and Garrett.

"WE WANT THE DARKNESS BACK."

"I don't want my world to be eaten," Connor replied, glancing up.

The creature looked into his eyes. It bowed its head. One by one the entire circle of them bowed to Connor.

"WILL YOU HELP US?"

Connor opened his mouth, then closed it again. Realization dawned on him. "Yeah. I will."

The smoke settled low to the ground before dispersing. The great tree was gone; nothing but a jagged stump and scattered splinters remained. Something dull and metallic stuck out of the charred remains. Van's pale, human form lay sprawled on the grass, barely covered by the smoldering remnants of his suit. Ninette pushed herself up from the wreckage with trembling arms. Normal, non-fiery arms. She had returned to normal, and every injury reminded her of that mortal normalness at once. There was no trace of the grimmalkin. Sheena, blown clear by the blast, sat up to inspect the damage.

"Hell yeah!" she cheered triumphantly.

"Not bad, princess," Ninette groaned.

She staggered to her feet and limped toward Sheena. Before she got far, a shadowy claw shot up from the ground, grasped her throat, and hoisted her into the air. Ninette struggled and tore at her neck, gasping for air.

"YOUR TRIUMPH WAS MOMENTARY AND IRRELEVANT," James said from across the meadow. He hobbled toward them with one hand outstretched and another hanging limp at his side. Sheena jumped up and prepared to cast, but bolts of black lightning lanced out from his eyes and threw her into a tree.

"YOU WILL ALL SUFFER."

"Us, too?"

Connor and Garrett emerged from the unstable portal. Connor struck James in the back with crackling, black lightning bolts. James fell to one knee, and the spell holding Ninette faded.

"I mean, it's four versus one," Connor taunted.

James screamed and hurled black flames in a wide arc. Connor pushed Garrett out of the way and dropped into the shadows, narrowly avoiding being scorched. The unstable portal droned louder, building to a dull roar, and the distortions grew more pronounced. The ground shook violently. Ninette and James teetered and almost fell.

"I think those runes were the only thing holding that together," Garrett cried.

Connor rose behind James and grabbed him by the shoulders. Electricity pumped through Connor's arms and flooded into the captain. James shuddered and swore but wouldn't fall.

"I'm taking you back to where you belong," Connor snarled.

Connor gripped James tight and dragged him down into the shadows. James screeched in fear and the shadows solidified, halting both of them. He flailed and thrashed, and spikes of darkness stabbed out of him in all directions, forcing Connor away. Gasping for breath, James scrabbled free of the shadowy opening and heaved himself back onto solid ground. Connor melted into the darkness. Frantically blasting spells, James spun in a circle, desperate to keep Connor away.

Undaunted, Connor popped up again and again, always able to strike James from behind. Fire and ice, lightning and wind, stone and thorns, even shadow spells; Connor worked in tune with the glade's shifting essence while James snarled and lashed back with a flailing defense. Ninette caught her breath and lobbed fireballs at James with the little essence she had left, keeping him on the backfoot while Connor landed blow after blow.

"I WILL END YOU!" James bellowed.

Connor appeared behind James, trying again to drag him back to the shadow world. James roared and exuded a wave of shadowflame in all directions. Connor couldn't dodge in time and Ninette was too exhausted to try. Both took the full force of the spell and flew backward into a tumble on the ground. James huffed and puffed with a wild look in his eyes, searching for another target that didn't exist.

"What's the matter, James?" Connor coughed. "Afraid of the dark?"

"I WILL NOT SUFFER YOUR INSULTS," James said.

He struck Connor and Ninette with dark lightning. They writhed on the ground and howled incoherently. James formed a blade of shadows and lifted it up, poised to impale Connor, when a sound behind him, a light scrabbling—barely audible over the tortured moaning of the portal—caught his attention.

Garrett scratched out a rune in the dirt with his fingernails. When he caught James looking, he slammed both hands into it; blinding light flared up into the night like a beacon.

James wailed in two distinct voices. The shadow creature and James separated for a split second, each mimicking the other. At that moment the essence of the glade twisted, becoming overwhelmingly, blindingly white. Light essence. Confidence and certainty surged inside of Connor. He knew what he needed to do.

Connor reached for all the essence he could find. The fading light from Garrett's rune, the dull twinkle of Sheena's jewelry, the mysterious essence of the glade, even the light of the stars and moon. He pulled it into himself to combine with his own. The Light Magic felt hot and powerful as it roiled and swelled inside him. James restabilized and growled, conjuring a sphere of liquid night. The shadowy figure lay on top of him, almost aligned but not quite. His expression was anything but human. Connor let the energy within him build until he thought he might burst.

Then he did.

A glorious, golden wave burst out from him. It bathed the forest in the crisp light of a new dawn. His friends covered their eyes and gasped. James had a different reaction. He screamed, one scream becoming two—his own and the shadow creature's. He braced against the radiance, fighting to stay on his feet. The shadow creature peeled away, clinging desperately before being torn free of him. James collapsed, breath hoarse and body shaking. Two shadowy figures raced along the moonlit grass and slipped back into the portal, hissing as they departed. James watched them go and pounded the ground with his fists. He began to cry, his voice weak and hollow.

"How could it go so wrong? I did everything right. I planned it all out, but—" but the rest of his words were lost.

The earth rocked; Connor and his friends toppled to the ground. The trees creaked and groaned, lurching and uprooting. The ground around the portal fissured, deep black cracks spider-webbed outward, and a jet-black tentacle, as big around as Connor's waist, reached out, finding purchase on the grassy turf. It was followed by another, then more and more.

"Well, this has been great," James chuckled darkly. "Good luck with all *this*." He gestured vaguely at the erupting chaos, then slipped into a shadow and disappeared.

"Connor, we have to run!" Garrett cried.

He hurried to help Sheena to her feet. Ninette hobbled in their direction, but one of the monstrous tentacles slammed the earth and cut her off. Connor tried to cut it with wind, but his spell never appeared. When he tried to cast, he felt a sharp pang in his chest. He had used the last of his essence in the burst of light. Ninette dug deep to try and set it ablaze, but her hands only hissed and sparked. Another tentacle fell behind her, trapping her, and they began to inch toward her. She punched at them, but she may as well have been punching stone. A third tentacle slithered from the portal and crawled across the grass toward her.

In a burst of gore and blood, the tentacle behind her gave way. Van slashed through it, returned to his normal, gray wolf form.

"Run!" he barked. He raised a white-hot claw and ripped open a path for her.

Ninette froze. The combination of joy and anger and surprise left her unable to process what was happening.

Van growled and pushed her through the opening. "Now!"

He tried to say more, but the remaining tentacle grabbed him around the neck. Ninette could only watch as it lifted Van up in the air. He forced out a howl, scratched and clawed at it, but it held tight. It shook him violently and, with a sickening snap, Van's body hung limp.

Ninette cried out in wordless agony. More tentacles spawned, and they ripped through the ground, and tore the portal into a jagged, gaping hole in reality. Darkness poured out in waves that killed the grass and stripped the trees bare. The four prepared to flee, but a tree fell, barring their path. Strong gusts of wind buffeted them, and a familiar voice overhead called out.

"Make way, children!" The voice, honeyed and smooth despite its deep rumble, was unmistakable.

High above and coming in fast was a mighty silver dragon. The librarian swooped down, exhaling pure white flame over the glade. Shrieking and whining noises came from within the portal and the tentacles writhed and shriveled. The dragon crashed down between the students and the shadow monster, and from his back hopped Headmistress Leorra Mine looking bruised, bloodied, and pissed.

"Get back, all of you," she instructed. Her hands flew in a blur of precise signs. Runic circles filled the air and coalesced as a dome of light. It slammed over the portal, slicing clean through the creature's writhing appendages. Fingers dancing, she shrank the dome inward. It compressed what remained of the monster and forced it back through the portal. The dome shrank down to nothing; the portal was gone. The glade returned to normal.

It felt like a fantastic time for Connor to faint.

Chapter 30

A New Generation – The Magi School System
For centuries, Magi schools have emerged wherever there has been a need. Over time, these schools formed relationships and built a global magical community. Every school has its own specialties and idiosyncrasies, but whichever school a budding young Magi attends, their time there will be well spent.

Connor awoke swaddled in warm, white, linen sheets. A faded burn mark crossed his chest, and assorted bumps and bruises speckled his body, but all looked weeks old instead of fresh from last night. There were no windows in the room, so he couldn't guess the time. In the bed next to him, bandaged from the neck down like a mummy, lay Ninette. Her eyes were open, and she grinned and waved at him.

"I said next time I didn't want to be the one in here, but I suppose company is the next best thing," she said.

"I think I found your problem," Connor said, sitting up. His aches and pains already felt like memories, but the exhaustion left him a little dizzy.

"Oh, do tell."

"You forget that with *magic,* you can hit things from far away. Don't get me wrong. I can see how punching things is enjoyable to you, but that *may* be why you end up here more than me." He gave her his winningest smile.

"I can think of someone else I'd like to punch," she laughed and tossed a pillow at him.

They were still laughing when the headmistress entered the room, bandages wound tight around her head. She set down a small brown satchel and looked them both over while they tried to subdue their giggles and sit still. When they composed themselves, she sighed a responsible adult sigh, and a crooked smile appeared on her face.

"It is good to see you so energetic," she said. "Mr. Naegus and I believe we have pieced together most of what happened last night, but I want to hear it from you." She folded her hands neatly at her waist and waited.

Connor and Ninette looked at each other for a long moment, neither wanting to speak first.

"It was James," Connor said finally. "He kidnapped Garrett from the dance, and he used the blood he stole throughout the year to power an eighth-level summon. He opened a portal to the shadow world, and he…" Connor stopped, but Ninette nodded slowly. "He and Van were possessed by creatures from the shadow world. They attacked us."

The headmistress studied the children's expressions carefully. "Most witnesses saw Mr. Radimus thrown through a wall," she said in a slow, careful tone.

"He was found beneath the rubble during the recovery effort. Master Borodin and Mr. Naegus searched the glade, but found no evidence Mr. Radimus was ever there.

"What we found points to the late Mr. Fredericks. A search of his room revealed paraphernalia that, while circumstantial, does support his involvement. You recall I previously held a discussion with Mr. Radimus and searched his room as well. I have done so again. There is no evidence he committed any wrongdoing."

"James set Van up!" Ninette protested. "Van… he didn't really know, and now he's…" Tears welled up in her eyes and her voice stuck in her throat.

Connor tried to continue for her, but Leorra gestured for silence.

"I have been a fool, but I am not a complete fool," she said. Her voice sounded strained, as if she wanted to be comforting but knew nothing she said would suffice. "The scope of this year's events is beyond Mr. Fredericks' abilities. He did not do this alone. I did not want to believe it of James," she added, more to herself than to the two of them. "But I must accept the truth.

"Unfortunately, I can take no action save to watch Mr. Radimus's every move for his remaining time here at Mattson. As you say, he planned this meticulously. It would not surprise me if he rode out the next year quietly, and awaited a less supervised opportunity for mischief. I would advise you avoid him whenever possible, though I recognize the challenge this may pose for you two in particular," she trailed off.

"So that's it?" Ninette croaked. She gripped her sheets so tightly her hands shook. "He attacks the whole school. He *kills* Van! And he gets to walk away from it? No. No, just… No!"

Leorra let Ninette sob into her pillow for a moment. "If I may change the subject to a more cheerful one, you found something remarkable last night. The glade alone was something special. I looked for it several times after Connor summoned me there, but because I didn't know what it was, I could never find it." She paused to retrieve her satchel. "The power of that place came from this."

She withdrew a heavy-looking iron hammer. Its head was huge compared to the haft, a cinderblock on a stick. Pictograms and runes decorated every inch. Leorra handed it to Connor, and he found it nowhere near as heavy as it should have been.

An awesome power surged through his body. He felt invincible. He felt like he could fly. Essence ripped through his body. Reluctantly, he passed it to Ninette. Her eyes crackled with lightning while she held it and her muscles bulged against their wrappings. After a short time, the headmistress took the weapon back and returned it to its satchel.

"It will require a great deal of study, but our librarian, with his unique qualifications, believes this is Mjölnir, an artifact of legend on par with Excalibur. It has been lost for nearly a millennium."

Connor and Ninette both sat up straight and shared a look of unbridled excitement, then turned in unison to stare hungrily at the satchel. Connor reached for it unconsciously. The headmistress *tsked,* and he snatched his hand back, blushing furiously. While they gawked, Nurse Poole entered the room with a cart of fresh wrappings and healing elixirs. She raised her eyebrow accusingly at the headmistress and busied herself changing bandages and administering the effervescent red medicine.

"Nurse Poole is informing me I should let you rest." She moved to leave but stopped with her hand resting on the door handle. "You should be proud of yourselves. I expect great things from you in the years to come. Hopefully quieter, scholastic things, but great nonetheless."

Connor laid back down and closed his eyes. The enchantment of the recovery room lulled him into a peaceful doze.

"Hey, Connor?" Ninette whispered.

"Yeah?"

"About Van…"

"He saved you last night," Connor interrupted. "That's enough for me."

She sniffled. "Thanks."

Sheena and Garrett came to check on them toward the end of the day. Both incurred fewer injuries in the fight, and Nurse Poole had dismissed them more quickly. Sheena had a few stitches on her forehead and Garrett, at least physically, appeared unharmed. Weariness weighed heavily on them both, but the reunion buoyed the group into a fit of relieved giggles.

"Thanks for coming to save me," Garrett said, blushing.

"Are you kidding?" Ninette laughed. "It's my fault you got taken in the first place. I think saving you is the least we could do."

"Yeah, man," Connor added. He sat up to pull Garrett into an awkward hug. "We wouldn't let anything happen to you. If we did, then Ninette and I might have to crack open a book ourselves. Besides, we couldn't have done it without your runestones. How do you think we found you?"

Garrett's blush turned a deeper crimson, and he looked away to try and hide it.

Sheena leaned against the wall and crossed her arms. "What happens now?"

"We can't let James get away with it," Ninette said forcefully. "*I* can't let him get away with it."

"Ninette's right," Connor said. "But how? There's only so much the teachers can do. We're supposed to do what they couldn't?"

Sheena snorted. "Obviously. We have been all year, haven't we? Still, another year of this nonsense? I have other stuff to do, you know. That guy did a level eight sort of by himself. Clearly, he's a little better than I want to admit." She added the last in a low grumble. "Mostly I'm ready for my life to get back to normal, not stalk someone who tried to kill me for half the year."

"He tried to kill us all year," Ninette said proudly. "You don't hear us complaining."

Garrett started to say something, but Ninette quieted him with a mock glare.

"You're right. You'd probably be dead weight in a fight anyway."

Sheena shot Ninette a dirty look, then shook her head with a smile.

"You and me, any time, any place." Sheena narrowed her eyes at Ninette, but her lips held the slightest smile. "But I suppose if you guys need a hand with something next year, I could be talked into showing up. I add a much-needed dose of class to this group."

They laughed and joked about small things, avoiding talk of the battle, the monsters, or anything else of consequence. They poked, teased, argued, and gradually let out all the tension, glad to be alive and able to do so. Eventually, Sheena gathered up Garrett and said goodbye.

Nurse Poole discharged Connor and Ninette in time for dinner with orders for an early bedtime and no stress for as long as they could manage. When they entered the cafeteria, they were greeted with a roaring welcome from their classmates. Even those who hadn't seen them defeat the vesporcus heard about it from others. The events in the forest were still hazy, but rumors spread fast, and wild rumors spread faster. Connor and Ninette, Sheena, and even Garrett were heroes.

A strange thing happened over the following days. Stories of the Dance Battle—as it came to be called—coalesced as heads cleared and memories resurfaced. James's absence became a sore spot. Surely the best duelist in years would have been more help. Surely, he wouldn't have been caught unawares like that. Slower but equally damaging were the whispers. Van's guilt was the worst kept secret in the school, but some said maybe Van hadn't acted alone. Maybe Van hadn't been the mastermind, or couldn't have been. Maybe he had help. Maybe one of his friends. Perhaps his best friend.

No one knew where it started, but Ninette smiled a toothy grin whenever she heard someone murmuring it. James's celebrity status faded like a ghost in the sun. In a week, he completely disappeared from school life, locked in his room without another word to anyone.

Final exams came and went. Connor managed A's and B's, except for summoning—though with Sheena's help, he eked out a C. Master Borodin did say he could continue to the next level if he were truly interested, but for the moment, Connor decided to turn his studies elsewhere. Summoning wasn't his thing, and it no longer needed to be, so he was glad to bid it goodbye. Garrett got straight A's, as did Sheena, so she made sure to note that she felt her classes were harder than his. Garrett didn't argue. Ninette passed all her classes and refused to divulge more.

The day after exams, Connor was called one final time into Headmistress Mine's office. He could only shrug when his friends asked him why. For what seemed like the first time all year, he hadn't broken any rules—not big ones, anyway. He knocked on the door. and she bade him to enter. Her casual attire, jeans and a loose blouse, surprised him. She stood with her back to him. gazing out the window with her hand resting on the glass. Outside, students strolled the gardens and ate lunch in the shade of the trees or sat along the edges of the fountains, and generally enjoyed the approaching summer.

"Sit," she said without looking.

Connor nervously obeyed. He didn't like how used to the chair he was getting.

"Some year." She laughed. Not a wry chuckle but a full deep laugh. "I'm glad you survived it."

Connor started to laugh as well, then caught himself. "Wait, are you serious?"

"There may have been a pool going." She turned to observe him out of the side of her eye. "Many of the staff remember a time when recklessness such as yours resulted in a messier end. These days we are much improved in the areas of student safety, though you may not believe it." She laughed again, and her voice was relaxed and full of warmth. "Don't worry. I was always betting on you."

"Thank you?"

"Connor, I want to apologize. I should have believed you. Perhaps if I had sooner, things would be different. Perhaps... but no. For better or worse, you reminded me of myself at your age."

"Thank you, ma'am." Connor relaxed a hair.

"It's not a compliment," she stated. "I was stupid, full of myself, and reckless to the point of mortal peril. I was lucky to survive my time here. At the rate you're going, you will be, too." She caught herself tracing the scar on her face and winced. "But because I saw myself in you, I assumed the worst, and I was wrong." She fell casually into her chair and leaned back to look up at the ceiling. "Still, I hope you learned from this year and finally hear me. Stay. Out. Of. Trouble." She waved him away. "Go. Spend some time with your friends. You'll be heading home soon, I expect."

Saying goodbye proved harder than Connor imagined. He'd never lacked friends, but the secret of magic kept a certain distance between them, and he hadn't thought much of them in his first year at Mattson. Now he had the opposite problem—a host of friends he'd grown too close to be without for a whole summer. He would see plenty of Garrett, they lived close enough, but the rest? They promised to stay in touch as best they could. Ninette even agreed to make it ashore for a weekend or two if her dad would allow it. It didn't seem like enough.

Connor lugged his stuff down the front stairs of the school toward his mom's waiting car; luggage teleportation was a one-way service. *I can't wait to tell them about this year. The good parts at least. Some of it. Maybe?*

The headmistress stepped into view from the driver's side of the car. As she passed Connor, she spoke softly.

"I gave them the report on what happened the night of the dance. Extradimensional peril is something we are required to disclose. I hope it doesn't cause you too much trouble." She patted his shoulder and continued up the stairs.

Connor's father had a white-knuckled grip on the steering wheel, his face alarmingly colorless. He stared ahead, mouth working silently. His mother looked only mildly better. Standing on the school's steps, basking in a perfect June afternoon, Connor wondered if he would ever be allowed to come back.

Epilogue

Tangerine light washed the walls of Mattson Academy in a warm glow as the sun began its steady descent. An army of enchanted custodial supplies waged war on the remnants of another school year. Brooms patrolled in search of dirt, feather dusters did fly-bys, mops and cloths brought up the rear to wipe everything to a sparkling sheen. Leorra's footsteps echoed through the empty halls; the other teachers were all busy elsewhere. She wandered up and down each corridor, peered into every classroom, and surveyed the cafeteria and gymnasium. Everything was as it should be.

The headmistress performed a final inspection every year before locking the school down for the summer. Normally she ended her route with a walk through the gardens—early summer evenings being the perfect time for a leisurely stroll—but today, she found herself lingering in the library.

I never spent much time here as a student.

The towering shelves of ancient, dusty tomes intimidated her, and the maze of aisles, nooks, and hiding spots for studying seemed too easy to get lost in. It still held some of that power today, a foreign kingdom in which she didn't belong, its tyrant king only a whisper away.

A new installation occupied the heart of the library. Levitating a few inches over a wooden podium sat Mjölnir, illuminated from beneath and rotating in slow circles. To most, it would look as if it could easily be taken, but Leorra saw the wards around it—she placed them herself. A barrier of light, almost opaque for all the protective runes she etched, would bar any but her from setting a finger on the mighty artifact.

I wonder if this is enough. She placed her hand against the light, felt its reassuring warmth.

"That will only bring you trouble."

Leorra didn't turn. She knew the voice well. "Hello, Lady."

"Leorra," the Lady of the Lake cooed. "How are you?"

"It's been a year, but aren't they all?" She rubbed her neck. "What are the chances that this," she made a half wave to the hammer, "was sitting less than a mile from the school for so long?"

"Not chance," the Lady said. "It was where it was meant to be."

"I suppose you're right."

The ghostly form of the Lady danced across the floor to alight next to Leorra. They gazed a long time at Mjölnir without speaking.

"Was there another reason you came here, other than to be cryptic and foreboding?" Leorra sighed.

"I came with a warning and an offer. One has been delivered."

"You're not taking it," Leorra stated matter-of-factly. "Bad enough we have to have it. I'm not putting two of them together."

"It would be safer with me."

There was no insult in her voice, but Leorra took it as such.

"I dare anyone to try and take it out from under me." She turned to face the Lady, stood up straight and threw her head back. Her eyes were hard and challenging behind the glint of her glasses. "I don't recall any stories about the Lady of the Lake defeating a dragon."

"I have no doubts about your abilities, but my school is older, better protected. We have more resources, and—"

"Enough," Leorra snapped. "I won't have anyone speak ill of my school, especially while they're standing in it."

The lady floated away from the pedestal to placate Leorra. "The others are awakening. Many will seek to take this one from you."

"Let them try." Leorra turned back to the floating hammer. *It couldn't hurt to set a few more traps.*

She knew her school was safe. The only recent threat had come from within. From its hiding place within the woods, Mattson had to be safer than the Merlin Academy. Right? She never visited the old castle anymore, but she recalled it being a rather obvious and decrepit structure atop a cliff. One that drew visitors from far and wide.

"How is Excalibur?"

The ghostly pale Lady bowed her head and clutched her breast. "He wails for his kin. I pity him, and I hate him, and yet, I am afraid. I fear soon he will be gone. That will be worse."

"Yeah, well. You made him," Leorra snorted. She turned around, but the Lady of the Lake had left as silently as she came.

In her place, another figure emerged from the shadows.

Karronus Naegus, smartly dressed in a button-down shirt, a crisp vest, and pressed slacks joined the headmistress in front of the twirling artifact. Its soft light reflected off his golden eyes. He, too, went to place his hand against the invisible barrier, but he stopped an inch short.

"Always a treat to hear the words of the Lady," he said in an oily voice.

"I have a feeling you'll get to more often." Leorra wasn't thrilled at the prospect. "Did you need something?"

"Wanted to see how you were doing," he grinned. "My favorite headmistress had a rough year. As always, I offer my assistance." He extended his palms in a gracious gesture.

"Your help is always half what you offer and twice as costly."

Naegus pantomimed staggering backward. "I'm wounded! You'll recall I let you ride me the other night. None living and few deceased can claim that privilege."

"A privilege I bought and paid for. In full." She glared at him, but the look contained no menace, only age-old frustration.

"How *is* your eye?" Mr. Naegus said with a mischievous glint in his own.

"You would know," Leorra growled, rubbing at her scar. She sighed again, resigned. "I will need your help. And I don't appreciate you getting my kids into trouble without at least warning me."

"Those kids are more than capable" Naegus folded his hands behind his back and smirked. "I look forward to seeing how much trouble they can get into."

"They make me feel old."

"You're only as old as you feel," the dragon said. His rumbling chuckle sounded like a coming storm. "Maybe some childish recklessness would be good for you. Have a good night, Headmistress."

Leorra watched him leave, but she stayed behind. She spent a great deal longer staring at the dangerous weapon she housed within her school. The one she had now chosen to be the protector—or warden—of. She wondered when, and how, she would pay for that decision.

~ The End ~

Acknowledgments

    I am so grateful to have had the opportunity to make Mattson Academy into something that I could share with the rest of the world. It took a long time and a lot of work from so many people to make this pet project into a presentable novel.

    First and foremost, my lovely wife, Kathleen. She has spent many long car rides over the last few years stuck as a captive sounding board for my characters, plot twists, random ideas, and favorite scenes. She gave me the idea for the vesporcus because she likes flying pigs so much. I have yet to fully adopt her advice about writing these ideas down somewhere, but maybe someday.

    Second, and no less important, my son James, who more inspired Connor than he did the character with whom he shares a name. He's a wonderful kid with a big heart and a big brain that he is sometimes too excited to use fully, but he did say that once my book was published, I'd be his favorite author. That'll keep him in my good books for a little while.

    It cannot be overstated that you wouldn't be reading this book without the invaluable support of my publisher and editor, Bre Stephens and Peyton Frederickson. They both took a chance on my little story and have helped me craft it into its final form. Bre has provided wonderful guidance about the publishing process from start to finish, and Peyton has been amazing in making sure I spell "gray" consistently and capitalize the words I had meant to all along. I can tell she cares about this story as much as I do, and that's been an amazing experience. Thank you both.

Last and certainly not least, the friends and family that read early versions of Mattson, some of them more than once. Hearing from them how much they enjoyed my story gave me the confidence to keep at it until I got it just right, and many of them provided feedback that was crucial in fleshing out this magical world and the people in it. Seer Brokk wasn't even in the first draft! Whether it was telling me generally what they liked (or didn't), offering detailed chapter-by-chapter breakdowns of notes, running statistical analyses on different versions to make sure I wasn't repeating words or word clusters too often, or just giving me the support to push on, the story wouldn't be what it is without Sofia, Nikki, Nichole, Tracy, Scott, Casey, Luke, and many others.

Thank you, everyone. This book exists because you all Willed it into the world.

Jay O'Keefe grew up in Maryland, raised primarily on video games, anime, and fantasy novels. Though he had always wanted to work in game design or art, he eventually turned to writing. He decided to bring his childhood to life in his writing by crafting a fantasy novel that read like a video game, all while evoking a manga splash page in the reader's mind. When not writing or drawing, Jay spends time with his wife and son, or is buried within the myriad of pets his wife and son bring home that he (not-so) secretly loves.

Thank you for reading Jay O'Keefe's
MATTSON ACADEMY.

BSC is proud to publish Jay's debut work of YA fantasy fiction and hopes you've enjoyed reading this novel.

To learn more about Jay O'Keefe,
visit his author page:
BSCPublishingGroup.com/jay-okeefe

If you would like to interview or invite Jay
to an author event, email:
BSC@BSCPublishingGroup.com

We appreciate your support!

Check out more books from BSC Publishing Group

HANNAH AND OTHER STORIES
by Rami Ungar

This collection of seven horror short stories examines the thin veneer between the world of the ordinary and the world of the strange. Sometimes, one must search for the entrance of the strange and then walk into a world where the laws of reality and humanity have no meaning. Other times, people find the horrors in this strange world simply by going to a toy store, a sibling's home, or a party in the Paris catacombs. These seven horror short stories aim to take the reader on a twisted journey that will make the reader question their reality – of what's real and what's not.

Available in eBook.
Release Date: Sept 23, 2023
bscpublishinggroup.com/rami-ungar

APOCALYPSE DANCE
by Ethan McGuire

This debut poetry chapbook is a collection of poems that work together to illustrate the crazy world we live in and our engagement in an inevitable apocalyptic dance. The collection is arranged around personal and universal themes in such a way that it begins as easy-to-read bites of consumption that gradually grows in length to become a dense space for cathartic darkness and meditation.

Available in Chapbook
Release date: Winter 2023
bscpublishinggroup.com/ethan-mcguire/

DEAR HEART
by Atlas Booth

This poetry chapbook collection is an LGBTQ+ discussion of love and loss between two beautiful male souls who are tragically separated way too soon. Love at first sight hits hard between the two males, so it is no surprise that they begin a life together. Happiness flourishes quickly and the two find their place in each other's hearts and arms. They share a love for the ages until one of the men becomes ill. Will illness break their bond or do they remain together through thick and thin? Join these men on their adventure of love, passion, and loss.

Available in Chapbook
Release date: Winter 2023
bscpublishinggroup.com/atlas-booth/

BSC Publishing Group
bscpublishinggroup.com

Printed in the USA
CPSIA information can be obtained
at www.ICGtesting.com
LVHW030523280124
770020LV00002B/150